FORBIDDEN

A Gangsterotica Tale

Shaun Sinclair

Copyright © 2013 by Shaun Sinclair
Cover by: Hartdesignz Inc.

Pen 2 Pen Publishing

ISBN-13: 978-0-6158-0160-5
ISBN-10: 0-6158-0160-9

Book Website:
Pen2PenPublishing.com
Email: contact@ Pen2PenPublishing.com
Give feedback on the book at:
Pen2PenPublishing.com

Printed in U.S.A

ACKNOWLEDGMENTS

All praises are due to the Most High, the Most Beneficent, the Most Merciful, the Lord of the Worlds. I am humbly grateful for being blessed with the gift and opportunity to pursue my passion and my purpose. I realize that this is truly a gift to be able to envision images on the landscape of my mind, and then meticulously weave them into vivid stories that entertain, inspire, and educate. I am eternally grateful.

Thanks to my family for supporting me through my journey, and for supporting my writing endeavors. Mom, Sheryl, Roy, Kina and particularly my Big Sis, Mishell. You inspired me from the first time I sent *Street Muzak* home and you typed it up for me. I knew that if *you* took the time to type it up, I must be working with something. Thanks to Gwen, who sent me books on the regular to keep my creative juices flowing. Thanks to my son, Lil Shaun for giving me the motivation to be the best man I can be so I can be an inspiration to you. I want to show you that you can do anything you put your mind to. Aunt Lene (you couldn't find the books I liked, so I had to write my own. Lol.) Thanks to my Pop, Johnny Lee Gore. You really inspired me to write my own books waaay back in the 90's when you showed me the book you wrote, *Black Gangster*. This was before the new Black literary renaissance. I thought it was so cool that a *real* street dude could actually write a book. The seed you planted years ago grew into a tree that sprouted branches of books. Special thanks to my lady, Amanda Smith. You helped me get this thing off the ground by being supportive and assisting me with whatever I needed, from additional typing to preparing those wonderful meals.Much Love. I'd like to give a special thanks to the very talented, classy, bestselling author of *All is Forgiven*, Mrs. Tameeka Williamson. I can't quantify your help, and I cannot put into words my amount of gratitude.

Thank you for everything, from the letters years ago, to the resources you selflessly shared. Much Love. I'd like to thank Lamont Hart at HartDesignz for the wonderful cover, and everything else you assisted me with. You went above and beyond and exceeded my expectations. This is just the beginning.

Thanks to all the brothers in the belly of the beast that inspired me to finally put the pen to the paper. Zahir (Kenny Ray), Wack (Kevin Goodwin), Hanif Adisa, Ali Al-Barr Abdullah, Jaba, Sha Born, Phil, Bone, and my big brother from another, Mr. (Allworld) Eddie Mack. Thanks to all the bothers inside who read my joints when they were handwritten in white binders, from Kershaw to Stevenson to Manning. I would call names, but they're just too many to count. You know who you are! Thanks a million.

Thanks to the block for making me everything that I am, and everything that I'm not. Atlantic Beach stand up!!! Ant Live (R.I.P.), A.B., Halla Hussane ,Tommy Gun, Dee, Omar, Tody, Slim, Snipes, Squirrel, Smoke, Tip Ski, Step, Qima, Tracy, and everybody else who made ABP a force to be reckoned with. Thanks to Fayettenam, my other home. Bunce Road, 71st, hope I do you proud. To my military family. Stay strong! Last but not least, I'd like to thank all of the authors who propelled this movement forward, and made reading interesting again. I am standing on your shoulders and I hope I do you proud!

Contact me at:
Pen 2 Pen Publishing, Attn: Shaun Sinclair
2316 South 17th St., Suite #140, PMB #308
Wilmington N.C. 28401
s_sinclair12@yahoo.com
pen2penpublishing.com

DEDICATION

THIS BOOK IS DEDICATED TO MY BROTHER AND SISTER, ROY AND MISHELL READY.FROM DAY ONE YOU HAD MY BACK AND HELPED ME, EXPECTING NOTHING IN RETURN. YOU TOOK ME IN WITHOUT HESITATION AND HELPED ME REGAIN MY FOOTING AS A MAN. YOU WEREN'T CONDESCENDING, OR TWO-FACED, BUT ALWAYS GENUINE. YOUR ONLY WISH WAS FOR ME TO BE SUCCESSFUL AS A MAN, BROTHER, SON, AND FATHER. I HOPE I DID YOU PROUD. I LOVE YOU!

PROLOGUE

It wasn't supposed to happen like this. He was supposed to penetrate my vagina, not my mind. He was supposed to rock my world, not turn it upside down. We were supposed to leave our thing on the island, along with the other skeletons in our closet, not drag it back to the States, resurrect it, and breathe fervent life into it.

It was insane, this thing of ours, but it could not be denied.

I was crazy about him. Simply gone.

Every time he came inside my mouth, I came between my thighs. Every time he came inside my body, I had an orgasm that reached my soul. His strong presence had insinuated itself inside every aspect of my life. Claimed the number one position. Right above career and God.

I was putting it all on the line for him. Everything I had dreamed of being my whole life was now in jeopardy because of him.

But what was I supposed to do?

I couldn't just let them kill him. I couldn't allow him to be sent up the river and castigated like some animal for something I knew he didn't do.

Or was it love blinding me into naïveté? I was confused.

Some people thought I was crazy for being by his side. Some thought he was some sinister criminal mastermind, deceiving everybody in his path. Thought he had wrapped me around his good penitentiary dick and rugged, model looks.

I tell them they never knew love. Not the good kind that melts your heart and raises wings where you never knew they existed. Not the kind of love that sears a permanent smile on your face and rubs joy on everyone you encounter.

But for every smile, there is a story; for every bond, challenges have to be surmounted. Ours just happened to begin on opposite sides of the law.

1

We're telling our truth so that when the annals of our history are opened up, people will have the facts of our case before they render their judgment against us. They will see this wasn't just two people lost in a fling, disregarding reality.

Or maybe they will see different.

Maybe they will understand the depth of love when it's viewed through the prism of our eyes. We can't choose who we love, no more than we can choose who loves us. Love is love. Love knows no boundaries, limits, or laws. Love just is and can never be *forbidden.*

This is our story...

1

The bulky armored truck tumbled down the highway at an irreversible clip until it came upon the early model Monte Carlo bisecting the highway. The driver of the truck slammed on the brakes, and they squealed in protest.

But it was too late.

The truck skidded to a halt mere inches from the passenger door of the Monte Carlo. I immediately sent one of the armor-piercing rounds from my Desert Eagle through the windshield of the truck. The bullet whizzed through the air, cracked the two-inch window, and shattered the illusion that anyone inside was safe.

The driver dropped down so quick it spooked me. I didn't intend to hit him. Not yet anyway. I was out of the car, flashing my iron, before he even lifted his head. "GET THE FUCK OUTTA MY TRUCK!!!" I screamed, waving the Desert like a lunatic.

To my left, Cadillac was already on top of the passenger with his AK aimed at his face. Dude saw the chopper, and his resolve and knees hit the ground at the same time, without Cadillac having to help him. I collared the driver as he fell from the truck and marched him to the back of the truck in front of me. On the other side, Cadillac was doing the same thing to his vic, just as we had planned earlier.

Cadillac harangued his guard in front of the peephole in back that doubled as a gun port, just in case someone wanted to buck the jack. He yelled, "Come on out 'fore we kill both these motherfuckers!"

Up front I saw Dirty and Lil' Mo anxiously getting ready for phase two of the plan.

"You got three seconds ..." Cadillac warned, and began counting. Before he made it to two, I capped my hostage in the knee. He screamed like the stuck pig he was, but it did the trick.

1

The back door creaked open and two more guards fell out with their hands grabbing some sky. One of them was a brother and I kind of felt bad.

But being broke was a worse feeling.

I gave Dirty and Lil' Mo the signal, and they sprang into action. Lil' Mo whipped the Monte around in the opposite direction while Dirty hopped in the cab of the armored truck, ready to roll. Everything was going according to plan ... until the brother had to open his mouth and whine.

"Why y'all doing this, man?" His whining upset me a little, 'cause it was always the black man trying to protect the white man's shit. But Cadillac? He was livid!

"What the fuck you say, nigga?" Cadillac barked, as if he didn't hear him whimper clearly enough the first time. His neck dropped deeper into his shoulders, and he tightened his grip on the chopper. "Say it again, nigga. G'head. Say it again."

I stole a peek at my watch and tried to keep control of the situation. "Come on, dawg. We gotta move," I advised him, hoping he'd take heed to the warning.

Seconds later, we had the guards hogtied and thrown in the ditch beside the road.

As we headed back to the truck to claim our position — me inside the back with the bags of money, Cadillac in the passenger seat — tragedy struck.

The last thing I remembered seeing before my chest exploded in a burst of solid pressure was a flash of light from the back of the truck. My body armor was fitting tighter than a wetsuit so I wanted to feel secure, but the pain I felt hijacked any security. My back was plastered to the ground, and I was fighting to catch my breath.

I raised my head to see the source of my pain. Apparently we hadn't cleared the truck properly. We'd left a guard lingering inside the back. As soon as I opened the door, he lit my ass up like a stick of dynamite with his shotgun.

Through blurred vision, I watched Cadillac creep around the side of the truck and open fire on the guard. I saw the guard's head burst open like a piñata before everything went dark ...

BEEP ... BEEP ... BEEP ...

"At this time we ask that all passengers buckle their safety belts. We are preparing for landing on the beautiful island of Anguilla ..."

Shaun Sinclair

2

Anthony

"Wake up, nigga! We here." That was Dirty, slapping my arm like he ain't have no goddamn sense.

"I'm up, Negro!" I told him, wondering to myself if I jumped like that every time I had *that* dream. The dream had been my constant companion for the past six years. The incident happened seven years ago when I was nineteen, but the dreams didn't start until my first year in the feds.

That's right; I was just coming home from doing six bullets (we call it a full-round) in the federal pen for armed robbery. I'm not talking 'bout no bullshit home-invasion, or hitting up no peon dope-boy either. We were into the real bread. Good, old-fashioned, bank jacking. Balls-to-the-wall robbery. But instead of actually holding up banks, we hit the armored trucks when they left the banks. Far as we were concerned, they were bringing the money right to us, so we didn't have to go inside the bank. We planned everything down to the minutest detail, too.

For instance, we knew the trucks were supposedly bulletproof, so we armed ourselves with rounds that could slide through the windshields easier than a rich man could a golddigger. You wouldn't believe how those drivers anted up that dough when them bullets blazed through their windshields! On one lick, when I shot through the windshield, the driver got so shook, he got out and *helped* us load the money into our car. Talk about crazy!

Normally we didn't take the whole truck unless it was a real big take and we had to be left alone with the truck to get all the loot.

Normally.

As it turned out, one of the few times we deviated from plan, we got knocked.

Well, I got knocked.

They tried to get me to give up my comrades. Said they'd been on to us for awhile. I told them motherfuckers, if they were onto us for so long, they should already have what they needed. Of course, they flipped out, beat my ass a bit. Promised me they'd deliver all the pain, short of hell itself.

But in the end, I held strong. Didn't snitch. Claimed my pedigree as the last of a dying breed. My loyalty was rewarded with eight years, but that was nothing compared to losing my dignity. I couldn't see myself sacrificing peoples' lives who had always shown me favor. Plus, we were paid. We, meaning, my family.

I was adopted by my aunt and uncle after my parents OD'd together on some of that good Westside dog food when I was younger. Without a second thought, they added me to their decent-sized family, which already included three boys and one girl. All of them were two years apart, and older than me. Their youngest son, Moses, who we all called Lil' Mo, was only a year older than me, so naturally we clicked the hardest.

My uncle was a real estate mogul with commercial and residential properties scattered throughout the city of Charlotte, and up and down the East Coast. My aunt was his personal assistant/accountant. That's what it said on paper anyway. In reality, my uncle was the mastermind behind our capers. Using his intricate web of connections, he would gather and compile valuable information for our licks, supply us with hardware, and offer any other assistance we needed. In return, we would fork over the dough and he would use the stolen money to finance his real estate ventures, then set up business straw accounts for each of us. It was lucrative for everyone involved, and no one expected a thing until Unc bid on an important piece of property related to the Charlotte Bobcats franchise. Then all hell broke loose.

The property was valued in the millions, so city officials (and the authorities too, no doubt) wanted to know where Unc got that type of money from. According to their records, his businesses and investments weren't lucrative enough to provide him with the kind of capital needed to finance the deal. They weren't convinced he could complete the project alone. Long story short, my uncle persisted, causing them to dig a little deeper into his background. They discovered some shady things that suggested he wasn't the upstanding entrepreneur he presented himself to be, and halted the deal. Unc filed a defamation lawsuit against the DA's office, who in retaliation, became committed to bringing him down ... by any means necessary.

That was over seven years ago.

"Ant, Ant, you getting this, nigga?" Dirty was nudging my arm like he didn't just hear me say I was up. "Look at that pretty-ass water. Been awhile since you seen something this pretty, huh? Matter fact, been awhile since you been able to see some water you ain't have to fight over, huh?" Guess Mo thought that was funny, but looking out my window, I had to admit the beaches of Anguilla were beautiful. I had been to a lot of places in my life, but none of them were half as beautiful as this.

As we landed at Wallblake Airport, a euphoric feeling washed over me. Snippets of my life for the past six years slowly clipped through my mind, forcing me to realize the huge disparity that twenty-four hours of living can make. A day ago, I was surrounded by despair and the dregs society had to offer. Now I was basking in the best that nature had to offer.

At the airport, a Chevrolet Suburban awaited us. Black on black with tinted windows. We looked like stars as we descended onto the island. (or at least, I felt like we did.) Out of the four of us, two wore linen short sets with open-toe sandals. Me and Lil' Mo rocked square-cut tank tops along with white-on-white Air Force Ones beaming brighter than the sun nesting in the sky.

Once inside the truck, Dirty lit up a blunt he had stashed away somewhere. We puffed the goodness, while admiring the plush scenery leading us to the hotel. I expected the driver to flip out on us for fogging up his wheels, but he just bobbed his head to the reggae on the radio, as if smelling weed was as common an occurrence as breathing.

We were staying at the Grand Royale Hotel. They had rented one of the open-air bungalows that sat behind the main property, which offered us a certain level of privacy. When we arrived at our bungalow, it was just after four in the afternoon, but that didn't matter to my cousins. They were ready for me to celebrate my freedom.

They made me walk in the door first, and the strong scent of Loud just bombarded me from all directions. Before I could determine the source of the weed, six beautiful women surrounded me, carrying a banner that read: **Welcome Home, A.P.!**

I was speechless.

Please believe it, I was tearing off dymes before I went to jail (in some cases quarters), but the women that stood before me were drop-dead gorgeous! No bullshit. All of them were different complexions, from Somali black to Caucasoid white and everything in between. Though some of them were skinnier than others, all of them were shaped like wasps: tiny waists and wide bottoms. None of them had stretch marks, tattoos, gunshot wounds ... nothing! I knew, because they were standing before me as naked as the day they came into this world.

Cadillac slapped me on my back. "WELCOME HOME, NIGGA!!!"

Dirty whispered in my ear from behind as he openly ogled one of the beauties' jewels. "Look at all that monkey. You ain't ever seen a pussy that pretty."

"Damn, cuz! You see something you like?" Lil Mo joked, as I stared at the shaved V between one of the girls' legs.

All I could get out was, "Uh ..." Everyone burst out laughing. I knew I sounded lame, but I had been surrounded by a bunch of stiff dicks twenty-four hours ago. And now this?

But I did recover.

Immediately, I locked eyes with the chick on the far end of the right side of the banner. She was high yellow, looked like she was mixed. Had hazel eyes, a pointy nose, and porno lips that brought to mind only one thing. I let my eyes wander down the rest of her body and noted firm C-cups and what Dirty said – the prettiest pussy I had ever seen in my life! She saw me looking, and to my surprise (and pleasure) put her hands on her hips, putting herself on full display. I started in her direction, ready to close the deal, but Cadillac pulled me back.

"Chill, dawg, there'll be plenty time for that later," he assured me. "Right now, enjoy the show we got for you."

As if on cue, the music (that I hadn't even noticed) changed to a slower tempo, and Cadillac took over the celebration. He came and slung his arm around my neck.

"Ladies, this is my cousin, A.P. Why don't you introduce yourselves," he suggested.

The women dropped their banner, fully revealing themselves, and the first girl stepped out of the line. "My name is Layla."

She was red, the color of the sun just before it set. Had long wavy hair and a button nose. She shook her big titties from side-to-side violently, and then stepped back in line.

The next girl stepped out. "I'm Peaches."

Peaches was baaad! Light, bright, and damn near white, she was almost my height. I'm 6'3" barefoot, so she had to be, at least, 6'1". Her hair was cut short and dyed reddish-blond, but her most striking feature was her light green eyes. They peered out at everything as if they held secrets only she was privy to. Without compunction, she dipped her index finger inside her pussy then offered it to me. I didn't budge, so she shrugged her shoulders, stuck the finger inside her mouth and sucked the sticky juice off herself.

Next up was Netta. Jet-black with hair hanging down to the top of her basketball-shaped ass. She was the shortest of the group, and to me, the sexiest. There was something primal about Netta. She just oozed sex and sensuality through her ice-gray eyes. Her voice carried an accent, and she spoke with a lisp when she introduced herself. As soon as she slid her tongue through her thick lips, I saw exactly where the lisp came from though. Her tongue touched the bottom of her chin. *The bottom of her chin!* My shit bricked up just imagining the possibilities.

While my mind was stuck on Netta's gift, the next female stepped up. "Hi! My name is Butterfly."

Butterfly was caramel-colored with light brown hair, which she wore in tiny braids. I could tell from her toned physique that she worked out more than me. She turned around to show me her pear-shaped ass, and I saw one-half of a butterfly tattooed on each cheek. She made her cheeks jump in unison, causing the wings to flap as if the butterfly was actually alive. I was impressed, but Butterfly was not done. She faced me, still standing, then raised her right leg up beside her head and held it there with her arm, giving me a bird's eye view of her womanhood. (I noted even her pubic hairs were shaved in the shape of a butterfly.) When she was sure she had m undivided attention, she tightened and relaxed her long pussy lips, making that butterfly flap its wings as well.

Seeing that trick, we all lost it!

"Oh, shit, shawty!" Lil' Mo croaked.

"Daamn," Dirty whispered, with his mouth hanging open. "I got that one first. I got to!!!"

I glanced at Cadillac through my peripheral. He had been observing me the whole time with a crooked smile on his face. He didn't think I'd noticed him gawking, but I did. I was watching him just as he was watching me. Strangely, he appeared unfazed at what he had just witnessed.

I know cuz ain't going sideways, I thought.

I was thoroughly enjoying my little shindig and I hadn't even been introduced to my little sweet thing yet. I couldn't wait to see what she had to offer, what kind of theatrics she would perform. I couldn't wrestle her away from my wicked thoughts! To my surprise (and pleasure), when it was her turn, she didn't wait in line like the others. She walked over to me and whispered in my ear. "My name is Mona ..." she cooed, sucking on my earlobe. She stuck her hand in my pants and cuffed my meat. "And I can't wait to really get to know you."

Just as it was getting good, Cadillac barked on her. "Aiight, Mona. That's enough!" He smiled, then added, "You gon' spoil the rest of the show."

Rest of the show? Is there more? I wondered.

The girls returned to their rooms and reentered the main room minutes later, one by one, each in a fancy costume. For an hour, they performed sexy solo routines, then danced together. After the dancing was done, four of the girls formed a half-circle in the middle of the floor while we formed the other half. Inside the ring was Netta and Peaches.

Netta laid Peaches down and spread honey all over her breasts, then led a trail down to her shaved vagina. Then suddenly, she stood and left the room, leaving Peaches sprawled on the carpeted floor like dessert. All eyes were locked in on Peaches as we waited on Netta to return with more surprises. Peaches kept us entertained with various tricks, from shaking her ass cheeks to doing splits. All kinds of freaky shit ran through my mind as we awaited Netta's return. We stared in awe as the cool breeze caressed Peaches' nipples, and they hardened like coins. Her plump pussy glistened with moisture, drawing me into its hypnotic embrace. My mouth began to water in curious anticipation of what she tasted like down there. I was ready to follow up on my devilish thoughts in front of everyone. Fortunately, Netta returned.

Netta sashayed over to Peaches and paused over her naked body as if she was waiting on something while we all held our breaths, eager to see what was next. Eventually, the sounds of R. Kelly's "Honey Love" filled the room. Netta smiled at us and went to work.

She used that long tongue like a paintbrush, dabbing honey from Peaches's beautiful nipples to her mouth. Peaches sucked the honey off as best she could, but Netta's tongue was so long she could only get half of it inside her mouth. Netta followed the trail down Peaches's belly, then licked all around her center before opening her up, and plunging that monster inside. As my eyes were riveted on the show, I couldn't decide if I was more aroused at the way Peaches was squirming under Netta's pressure, or at the masterful job Netta was doing. Talk about jealous! I glanced at the others to see if I was the only one enthralled, and sure enough, the Netta Show had captivated everyone. Even jaded-ass Cadillac was squirming and readjusting his shorts as he and Layla inched closer to get a better look. I looked at Mona and her eyes were locked on me, no doubt trying to gauge my reaction to the show. I threw her a wink, but returned my attention to the show. I had been dreaming about this type of shit for over half a decade. There was no way I wasn't going to get me an eyeful.

Netta placed her voluptuous ass right on Peaches's face. I saw her little tongue dart in and out of Netta's tightness like a snake tasting the air. Netta squirmed a little bit, but it was clear she was still in control. She waved to me with her long tongue then focused all her attention on Peaches. Honestly, I had never had the privilege of a threesome or seeing two women go at it — in person anyway — though I've thought about it plenty of times, mostly while in prison. Usually I pictured something freaky and kinky, like two women lost in the taste of each other's pussy, like some crazed mutants or something. But what I was witnessing now was two women making love, with no shame or compulsion. This wasn't a freak-fest; this was passion. These women obviously felt something for each other. Realizing this, I began to feel a little uncomfortable about eye-hustling on such a special moment. Cadillac and the others must have sensed my shift in mood because he abruptly ended the show.

Turning to me, he asked, "Which two do you want tonight?" Before I could answer, he selected two for me. "Netta. Butterfly. This you tonight. Take care of my little brother."

Tonight? Shit, I wanted me some now! I hadn't had no pussy in six years. (Well, one year, but the female guard at my last prison didn't count.) What I really wanted was Mona's fine ass. I knew by the way she was eyeing me, the feeling was definitely mutual.

"Nigga, let's roll," Dirty piped up. "Fuck them hoes. They gon' be here. I want some foreign pussy."

He yelled that out as if the women weren't still in the room. But that was typical Dirty. Rude. Brash. Arrogant. And a pussyhound. You wouldn't think he had a wife back in Charlotte so fine she could be on the cover of *BLACK MEN* magazine. Apparently, they had an understanding because, the whole while I was away, he sent me flicks of different chicks he was skinning throughout the Queen City. Never mind the fact he and his wife had been together since middle school. Dirty was twenty-nine, so I'm talking over fifteen years! She had to know about his philandering, but I guess he kept her so laced that it didn't matter. She knew we didn't call his sneaky ass Dirty for nothing!

We changed into our swimwear and hit the beach, wide open. Rode jet skis for an hour. Snorkeled for two hours. I kept pressuring them to parasail, but my family wasn't having it. They threw out more excuses than a guilty man going to court:

"God wanted me to fly, he would've gave me wings, nigga."

"Only time I'm trying to go in the sky is when I die."

I know Cadillac would've been game, but he had to shoot back to the villa for something, so I ended up going solo.

When I arrived at the docks, there was a small line of people waiting to parasail. Only three boats were reserved for sailing, so I had to wait. As I waited impatiently in line, I noticed a beautiful woman a couple of spots up, waiting in line also. She looked like a native with her long, silky, black hair. She had a deep tan, and wore one of those lime-green shorts/bikini mash-ups. The shorts were riding up her plump ass so high it was hard not to notice her. She wasn't thick, but her waist was so small it looked like her ass just exploded from her frame. She was so stunning, just looking at her eased my sour mood. So I chilled and enjoyed the view while I waited in line.

When ole' girl's turn to ride came up, there was only one space available in the carrier. The carriers actually sat two, but the other side of hers was being occupied by a drunk old white man. She was not happy about that at all! I heard the beauty voice her protest in a mixture of Spanish and English before storming off in my direction. Each stomp that brought her closer to me revealed another layer of her beauty. With each step, I became more and more impressed. When I finally saw her up close, all I could say was, *DAMN!* She was finer than anything in the villa. Matter fact, she was damn near finer than anything I had ever seen in my life!

I tried to stop her, offer her a ride. She looked at me thoughtfully for a second, then mumbled something in Spanish. I wanted to kick myself. I knew I should've learned some of that Spanish shit my dudes were learning inside the joint. But noooo, all I wanted to do was read, exercise, and jack off.

I pointed to the departing boat, then to myself, tried my best attempt at Spanish. "El ride ..." She followed my hand from my chest to the boat. Her face scrunched up, and if eyes were swords, I would've been beheaded in that moment. I heard her mumble under her breath, *"Es Stupido!"* Then she brushed past me, leaving me in awe.

Oh, I understood that clearly. The broad had called me stupid.

As she assaulted the ground with her heavy steps, I continued to admire the way she tossed her hips around so liberally. I shook my head just imagining the secrets those curves held. Finally my time arrived to parasail. I ended up strapped in beside Dragonbreath. Rather than let the toxic shit he was spewing spoil my ride, I inhaled it, hoping not to get a contact. I had been waiting on this moment for awhile. I wasn't about to let anything impede my vacation.

Once we got in the air, everything and everyone faded from my senses as I took in the beauty before me. Anguilla was pretty from the ground. From the sky, it was breathtaking! Green mountainsides. Azure waters. Aquatic wildlife just beneath the surface of the water. I retrieved my camera from my pouch and began snapping away. Every beautiful sight my eyes captured, my camera encapsulated the image on film forever. When the ride was over, I bid Dragonbreath farewell and started off in the direction where I'd left my peeps.

That's when I saw her ...

3

SOLDADA

I slid from the comfortable queen-sized bed, naked, and opened my blinds to admire a beautiful sunrise.

Anguilla.

I couldn't believe I was finally here! I had been anticipating this trip for four *loooong* years. Finally, I was here. This vacation was about more than just the destination, more than just fun in the sun. This trip was a gift from my parents for graduating from law school. Yep, after four rigorous years at the University of North Carolina's prestigious school of law, I graduated summa cum laude. That meant that I was the best. Not the top five percent...*The Best*! I was the best at what I did for the better part of four years, and you can bet your ass I was going to toot my horn every chance I got for the next four years because I busted my ass to get here.

While the rest of my classmates were out partying, I was studying. When they were visiting home, I was studying. Eating, drinking, sleeping ... I was studying. When they were fucking? You guessed it. Studying. Now all of my studying had paid off. I was in a position to reap the fruits of my labor. At just twenty-six years old, I had accepted a job offer in the Mecklenburg County District Attorney's office as an assistant district attorney. Most people didn't even sniff at such a position until their early thirties; I was there at twenty-six. I had a right to be proud, and I was going to celebrate by doing Anguilla up real big.

I brushed my teeth, tied my Nike Air Max sneakers tight, and prepared to go for my morning run. Running was a passion of mine that I began in order to keep my heavy Cuban genes in check. Lord knows, the battle of the bugle was real in ethnic communities, so I tried my best to pick up arms in the war; lest my perfect size 7 balloon into a size 17. I was looking forward to inhaling the cool morning air, and it was everything I'd anticipated. I practically ripped up the coast in a record time for myself, completing three miles (one more than usual) in twenty minutes flat. My thighs, ass, and chest burned like I had fallen into a lake of fire, and my feet ached like I had been rolling with the Flintstones all 15,840 feet. Still, somehow, I persevered, conquered my task, and felt marvelous when it was over!

After my morning run, I showered and threw on my lime-green G-string bikini. Standing before the mirror, I posed and admired my bronze-colored curves. My ass was so pretty it should've been featured in the Smithsonian under *voluptuous*. I'd never been thick. My ass just sprouted from my back like an extra appendage, like it deserved its own lane. It had the curve white men craved and the cuff at the bottom that made the brothers go crazy. I turned to face the mirror, and cupped my 38Cs in admiration. To me, they were perfect with large nipples and areolas the size of half-dollars. I wasn't old enough for them to sag yet, although my mother assured me that, if I kept refusing to sleep in bras, they would. As I let them go, they laid comfortably above my six-pack, and my torpedoes hardened instantly. (I called them the torpedoes because they protruded any time the wind blew hard.) All in all, I was very pleased with my body. It was a shame that no man had roamed over my dangerous curves in nearly a decade. No one since Trent, whom I had lost my virginity to.

Trent was beyond fine! Tall and broad, with smooth light skin and wavy hair, I should've known he was no good for me. In his deep voice, he blew promises smoother than a lullaby and rocked me to sleep. By the time I awoke from my naïveté, Trent was gone and had taken my virginity with him. I put the kitty on lock after him, and had been too driven by my own ambition to allow any other man to even sniff at it. *Maybe I could knock some dust off it this weekend,* I thought to myself, jokingly. *After all, wasn't that the point of vacations?* But as soon as the thoughts surfaced, I dismissed them.

As pleased as I was with my body, before leaving, I still slipped on the matching shorts to my bikini. I wasn't ashamed of my body, but that didn't mean I wanted everyone to see it. Besides, an ADA had to exercise a little more discretion, vacation or not, I reminded myself.

When I arrived on the beach this time, more people were out, and all eyes were on me. The fresh air seemed to soothe my mood as I pranced around the beach like a schoolgirl on summer break. Every male I encountered thought I was fair game. They were obviously seeking a fling because they all approached me with the same line in, at least, a half-dozen accents: *"You want to come back to my place?"*

I admired their audacity for even thinking that someone like me would venture off anywhere with someone like them. I mean, it was always the worst looking men with the most courage. Why couldn't the handsome men muster enough guts to ask me out? In perfect Spanish, I politely declined every indecent proposal that came my way, silently cursing myself for wearing the lime-green bikini.

On my way to the beach, I spotted some brothers who were clearly from the States. All loud in their sagging shorts and loud jewelry. *I mean, really, who wears jean shorts to the beach and thinks it's cool?* One of them kept staring at me with a hungry look in his eyes. I shot daggers at him, put an extra twitch in my step to make him want more of what he would never get, then dashed into the warm azure water, headfirst. When I came up for air, I spared a look in his direction. Sure enough, he was still looking with that starving look gleaming in his eyes. He spooked me a little, so I decided to leave the area to do something else I had been dying to do.

Parasail.

I arrived at the docks where the boats were kept. The line was so long and the sun so unrelenting that I started to turn around. Fortunately, they were seating people in twos. I noticed how quickly the line was moving and decided to tough it out. As my bad luck would have it, it appeared I was going to be seated with some old hillbilly-looking drunk. I began looking around frantically for another partner, but came up empty. I tried to wield my feminine charm to voice my displeasure with the operator, but he wasn't falling for my flirtatious overtures. In broken Spanish, he matched my language and tone, scolding me:

"*No quieres vas? No es mi culpa, señorita. Pero, muervete por favor!*" He shrugged his shoulders like it was nothing to him.

That pissed me off!

I unleashed my sharp tongue on him, giving him a piece of my beautiful mind, rolling my Rs in the sweetest lilt. Then I spun off in a cloud of dust, the debris echoing my mood.

As I was departing, I ran into this tall, handsome brother. He was so fine; he looked exquisite. His sculpted arms seemed to bulge from his Prada tank top. His chiseled shoulders rolled from his neck like his skin was stretched over boulders. He just looked *strong*. His wavy hair was thick, dark, and trimmed to perfection. His hairline looked as if an artist had etched it. His eyes were hidden behind dark aviator-style shades, but I imagined them to be as dark and sexy as him. I don't know if it was the sun or my hormones, but I swear he seemed to be glowing! I couldn't help myself; I tossed a quick look below the belt of his jean shorts. Sure enough, he seemed to be tenting around the middle of his thigh. My feminine part thumped in admiration. *Now there is a man that I wouldn't mind hitting on me,* I thought. I could only hope that he hadn't caught me ogling him, but just as I thought I was in the clear, he stopped me and offered to let me ride with him. As bad as I wanted to take him up on the offer, I didn't trust myself being that close to him. I was liable to rape him in the sky. Still, I hesitated a moment and teased him just to bask in his glory.

"*¿Que?*" I asked him in Spanish, just to see where his head was at. He looked at me dumbfounded, all innocent, like a deer caught in headlights. Ironically, instead of making me disinterested, it actually turned me on even more. This big, handsome, powerful man humbled to silence? His humility was like a breath of fresh air compared to all the arrogant men I had been encountering lately. (Or maybe I was just mesmerized by how gorgeous he was.)

He stammered, "El ride ..."

Bless his heart. He didn't know a spit of Spanish, yet was trying to accommodate me. The subtle thump between my legs was rapidly growing into a full-fledged throbbing. I hurried to dismiss him before things got intense and out of control. I sized him up one last time, seared his handsome image into my mind for future reference, then stormed past him. I called him an idiot in Spanish, just because I knew he didn't understand the language, and because I was upset at myself for being so drawn to him.

As soon as I arrived at the beachside café to grab an ice cream to cool my temperature, I ran into the same hoodlums from earlier. They were sitting at a table, ogling the natives, being loud, boisterous, and typical. I tried to slip by discreetly. All I wanted was an ice cream, but nooooo, ole boy had radar or something. I had just made it to the counter when I heard his footsteps creeping up behind me. I tried to ignore him, hoping he'd disappear.

Fat chance.

I heard, "Excuse me, beautiful. Allow me to introduce myself."

I turned to look at him. He was a little taller than my Adonis from earlier. Looking closer, I realized they even slightly resembled each other a bit, except this guy wore designer braids and a bucket of confidence that bordered on arrogance. I mean, the way he stared down at me was like he was daring me to refuse whatever he was offering. His whole demeanor just screamed, *"I AM THE SHIT!!!"*

I had a trick for him though.

"¿Que?" I asked him, looking dumbfounded. *"No hablo Ingles."* It worked earlier, so I deployed the same method again. Besides, a language barrier would prevent further harassment. Or so I thought. Ole boy raised his eyebrows at me, then fired back. *"Perdonneme, Señorita Bonita. Permittame presentarle a mi mismo. Me llamo, Cadillac."*

I was beyond shocked, to say the least. He extended his hand. I shook it. *"¿Cadillac? ¿Como el carro?"*

"Si. Cadillac."

"¿Y hay su nombre?"

"Yeah, that's my name. I mean, *si,*" he corrected.

I giggled, continuing to play the role. *"Lo ciento, pero estoy aqui con el novio mio,"* I informed him. He looked at me as if I shouldn't have had a boyfriend, and if I did, I was in error for bringing him with me.

"¿Donde?" he asked, looking around, calling my bluff. *"¿Donde esta el? Porque ... yo no verlo."*

His demeanor said that, if my boyfriend did show up, he would pummel him to gain my affection. Thinking fast, I peered around, as if searching for my boyfriend. Just then, I spotted my Adonis approaching the cafe. I pointed toward him and lied, *"Alli."*

Cadillac laughed. *"¿Alli?"*

I waved my hands frantically toward Adonis. *"Aqui, mi amor! Soy aqui!"*

When my Adonis started walking toward me, I expected my stalker to disappear, but he just stood there, arms crossed, a smug look on his face.

When my Adonis reached us, he queried me with a weird look in his eye. "Yo, what's up?" Confusion was evident on his face.

I rushed to hug him, whispering quickly in his ear. "Stalker alert. Please follow my lead." He clenched me tighter and peered over my shoulder at my stalker. I concluded that meant he was game.

"What's up, man?" Adonis barked at my stalker.

"This you, brother?" Cadillac asked, pointing at me like I was an invisible piece of meat.

Adonis held his head high, his jaw set. "Yeah."

"All right, bro. My bad, my bad ..." He raised his hands in surrender, then slowly backed away, leaving us alone.

I closed my eyes and inhaled deeply, ready to thank my savior, but before I could utter a word, he tore into me.

"What the hell was that about?!"

"Nothing. This guy was stalking me, so I told him I was here with my boyfriend."

He crossed his arms over his broad chest. More muscles rippled down his thick arms, his tank top raised a few inches.

"Ohhh, so you used me?" he prodded. "And you speak better English than me?" he noted.

I tried to look away from those powerful arms, but a light sigh escaped my lips before I could tear my eyes away. "Well …"

He snapped. "I tried to be cordial to you at the docks! You called me stupid. Guess I'm good enough to help you get rid of your undesirables though, huh?" He jerked his finger in Cadillac's direction.

"No, it's not like that. I …"

"So what is it like then? No one is good enough for you, huh? I guess you're just a regular hell-raiser, a goody-two-shoes …"

Through my peripheral, I saw Cadillac. He was still staring at me with a smirk on his face. I wanted to be rid of him for good and put this whole situation behind me, so while Adonis was still talking, I stole the moment and planted a wet one right on his lips. The kiss caught him off guard, at first, then the next thing I knew, he had slipped his tongue inside my mouth and pulled me into his hard body. His kisses tasted like candy, his body felt harder than I imagined. I allowed myself to get lost in the moment …

Until he cupped my ass with those big hands.

I broke the kiss and hissed, "What are you doing?!"

He raised his eyebrows. "You wanna play? Let's play." He slid his tongue back inside my mouth and grabbed a chunk of my ass like he owned it. I moaned, groaned, and squirmed, but I had to stop him before this whole episode turned pornographic. I was attracted to this man beyond reason! My body was doing things I was unfamiliar with. I quickly realized this could get real dangerous, real fast. And I didn't even know his name.

I detached my lips from his, and pushed him away. "Okay, okay! Thank you for bailing me out back there, but this is a bit much," I mustered, almost out of breath. "I appreciate it, but this is the end of the road. Fair exchange is not robbery."

He reared back. "Fair exchange?"

"Yes. Fair exchange. You helped me out of a bind and I rewarded you with a kiss for your troubles. Quid pro quo."

"Quid pro quo?" He chuckled, raising his thick eyebrows. "Ohhhh, so you're a lawyer now?"

"As a matter of fact, I am. Thank you very much." *I would kill for eyebrows that thick and shiny,* I thought.

"Well, *Counselor* ..." He spit the word out like it was vile. "I didn't agree to any deals. Besides, you enjoyed that kiss far more than I did. Way I see it, you owe me. Twice."

Ooooh! I swear he was working my nerves with his fine self.

"Okay, okay, I didn't come all the way to Anguilla to accumulate debts so —"

"Where? You didn't come where?"

"Anguilla," I repeated with proper pronunciation.

"You mean An-gwee-la?" he sounded the word out as if I was in a *Hooked-on-Phonics* class.

"No. I mean An-gee-la. The word isn't European. This may be a British colony, but last time I checked, the indigenous people are of Indian descent. In their tongue, it's pronounced more closely to the way I said it."

He smiled. "Ohhh, so you're a lawyer, a linguist, and a history professor?"

"No. I am a proud Latina. Simple as that. What are you?"

"A man."

"Don't be facetious. What do you do for a living?"

"Usually whatever I want," he joked, poking his chest out. "I'm an entrepreneur."

I crossed my arms. "Let me guess. You own a record label, right? Or a nightclub? Wait, a barbershop?" That wiped that cute smile off his face. His face seemed to light up more when he was pouting, so I teased him a bit more. "What? Was I that far off?"

Suddenly, he tilted his head, pursed his lips, and clapped his hands loud and slow. "Congratulations, Counselor. You have done your part in perpetuating stereotypes. Your university must be proud of you." He shook his head, scoffed, then turned to walk away.

I grabbed his arm. I don't know why; I just did. "Wait. I apologize. I didn't mean to offend you ..." I waved my arms, searching for a name.

"Anthony."

"Right. Anthony ..." I rolled his name around in my mouth. Liked the way it felt. Imagined how it would sound coming out of my mouth as I cried out in ecstasy ... I flashed back to reality. "My name is Soldada. Soldada Andrews. Do tell, Anthony, what kind of business are you into?"

The smile that flashed across his face sent lightning straight to my center. "My primary business is real estate," he told me. "But I'm in the process of developing a few other things also. So, no, Soldada, I am not an aspiring record mogul."

His whole demeanor changed when he spoke of his aspirations. Assurance leaped from him like sparks from a flame. His confidence was refreshing. I told him so.

"Thank you. Without the right amount of confidence, you're dead before you begin," he mused like a sage. "I learned that a long time ago."

A few awkward seconds of silence slipped by. I took the opportunity to end this encounter before it escalated into something I may regret later. It had been a long time since I'd felt for a man what I was feeling for Anthony at that moment. As each second ticked by, Anthony was beginning to look more and more like Lucky Number Two.

"Anyway, Anthony. Thanks again for everything. If you don't mind, I have some things to attend to," I lied, attempting to regain control of the situation. I extended my hand. "Maybe I'll see you around."

He hesitated a moment with this weird look on his face. Then, finally, he took my hand. "Yeah, maybe I'll see you around, indeed."

I scurried away quickly before my body betrayed my mind. Anthony's aura was too much to absorb at once, and my kitty was still purring from that kiss we shared earlier. I was half-joking about having a fling, but the more I stayed in his presence, the more the possibilities grew.

~

Anthony

"Damn, nigga! Don't take you long, huh?" Mo harassed me as soon as I made it back to the table at the beach café. The fish they were wolfing down tickled my nose like a fairy. I still hadn't eaten any real food since they'd scooped me from prison, and my stomach was cussing me out every time I dared to glance at the table.

"Yeah, A.P. You a real Casanova," Cadillac added with a frown on his face. "Guess I can cancel what I had planned for you tonight, huh?"

"Cancel? Hell naw!" Dirty exploded. "This nigga ain't had no pussy in years. If it was me, I'd be trying to fuck everything wit' a hole that smelled like pussy."

"What you got planned?" I asked Cadillac, curious myself.

"You'll see later," he answered, evasively. He sipped his drink. "What's up with you and ole girl, though? When you meet her?"

"Ain't nothing up. I just met her." I allowed a slight smirk to tug at the corner of my mouth as I sipped from Mo's mai tai. I knew this shit was killing Cadillac! He always seemed to want to compete with me when it came to the ladies.

"Damn! And already lip-locking?" Dirty squealed. "Boy, you ain't lost shit! Nigga still got it." He swigged his mixed drink, then placed it on the small, circular glass table. "Muthafuckin' A.P.! First day out the joint, bagging foreign bitches and shit. That's my nigga." Dirty dapped me up, as did Mo. Only one who didn't was Cadillac. He just gazed at the diamonds in the bezel of his watch, as if he was mesmerized by the shine. Guess he was a little salty 'cause I'd beat him to the punch with Soldada.

I looked around, admiring the landscape, and asked, "How long we staying?"

"Not long. Probably a couple more days," Cadillac answered. "I gotta get back. Got some business to handle," he added with conviction. I wasn't exactly sure what any of them were doing for money these days, but I knew none of them appeared to be hurting, so I asked.

Turned out, Lil' Mo had a counterfeit and fencing racket going. He had hooked up with some white boys who knew how to print money better than the U.S. Treasury. He would sell stacks of counterfeit bills for real money in increments starting from $1,000 all the way up to $100,000. He'd trade $3,000 counterfeit for $1,000 in authentic bills. Depending on who he was dealing with, he would tax some harder than others. In addition to the counterfeiting ring, he also served as a fence for unloading expensive merchandise. He'd take orders for furs, plasma televisions, jewelry, cars ... whatever. Next, he would commission a crew of young Mexicans he dealt with to retrieve the goods for him. Then, he'd sell the stolen merchandise to people who didn't want to pay full price for the items. He seemed to be making good money off his rackets ... hear him tell it.

Now Dirty, he had turned into the seafood king. He owned (and operated, at times) a chain of seafood spots in both Carolinas. Some of them sold raw seafood, others served cooked food. His pride and joy was his restaurant in Uptown Charlotte. It served food from a five-star menu, and often catered to the city's elite. His restaurant had recently been mentioned in the *Charlotte Observer* and highlighted in *Creative Loafing* as one of the best places to eat in the Queen City.

Of course, with Dirty there was always a catch. To maximize his profits, Dirty would recruit dock workers from the ports in Charleston to steal any cases of seafood they could get their *geechee* hands on. If they spotted any shipments slated for his competition in the Charlotte area, they were instructed to divert the shipping orders to his places of business. What they couldn't swipe for Dirty, they threw back into the sea. We're talking crates of fish just floating in the water! I did time with some brothers from the Chuck. If they were involved, I knew Dirty was caking because those brothers from the Chuck was all about that *fetti*.

And lastly, was Cadillac. He had the best racket going. Period. Seems he had become quite the social character while I was away. He owned an escort service-slash-brothel. Well, brothel would be the wrong word. His operation was more sophisticated than that. He would scour the local colleges and universities for potential prospects then swoop down like an eagle when the opportunity arose. As Cadillac explained it, most college girls were desperate for money. Being far away from home for the first time often made them vulnerable and destitute since decent jobs were difficult to come by while juggling a load of classes. Add Charlotte's rapidly growing influx of Latinos to the equation, and jobs were divided in half. This created a reservoir of women to draw from. When Cadillac breezed through with the top dropped on his Cadillac XLR, the ladies flocked to him like birds, begging to be put on and get that bread.

He had his company set up legitimately with a plush office inside a high-rise in Uptown Charlotte where his Panamanian receptionist remained draped in the finest fashions. Cadillac had his stable (for lack of a better word) divided into A, B, and C teams.

The A-team was the finest, most experienced women. Most of them had college degrees, had traveled the world, and spoke, at least. one foreign language. The A-team was the crux of his company, *Ladies of Distinction*. They strictly offered their services to attend events, assist as travel companions, or just keep wealthy men company. Believe me, they had to be wealthy to reserve time with the A-team because they started at $1,000 a night! Per Cadillac's orders, they did not trick. To the best of his knowledge, they adhered to his rules like the Gestapo to Hitler. Disobedience would not only result in dismissal, but the women would be ostracized from Cadillac's entrenched stronghold on the city.

The B-team was next in order of distinction. They pretty much equaled the A-team in accomplishments, education, and beauty, but the similarities screeched to a halt there. The B-team got down for their dollars! For the right price (like a G or better), you could have your wildest dreams fulfilled. Cadillac was slick, too. He had it lined up so all the money was funneled through the company account, never touching his hands directly. According to him, the bill was paid before any B-team girls were even contacted for their dates. The dates would usually consist of outings to expensive restaurants, galas, or games, all followed by a "nightcap." Most of the B-team girls started as C-team girls who decided to stay on board after their graduation from school.

As for the C-team, they were strictly college girls, or chicks that showed a hint of class and a glimmer of promise from the gentlemen's clubs he frequented. Young, nubile, fine, and gullible as hell, they were primarily girls Cadillac had macked with promises of riches. By the time they realized exactly what he was offering, they were already knee-deep in, literally. They held no pretenses. They were sucking and fucking. Straight up. Cadillac's proposals were too sweet to pass up, so they remained loyal, and he kept eating. Ladies of Distinction had this nigga living like he played for the Bobcats or something. In addition to his fleet of Cadillac sedans, trucks, and coupes, he also owned a red Ferrari 458 Italia Spider with the glass back showcasing the engine. When I was in the joint, he sent me pictures of it when he first got it. I totally lost it! I must've showed that car to everybody on the compound, I was so excited. That car just screamed: *"Nigga, I am SHITTING on you!"*

By the time everyone gave me the rundown on their rackets, it was approaching dark. We were all worn out from the day's events, so we decided to retire to the villa. Personally, I was ready to get a ball off, so I rushed back.

Mona was the first to greet me, just as I walked through the door. She wore a purple thong bikini that left little to the imagination. I wasn't mad at her at all. I could tell from the smell permeating the air that the girls were in there getting right. Smelled like that purp. As I focused on Layla, I peeped Mona looking at Cadillac as if asking for permission to be with me. I had already put two-and-two together and realized these bad-ass broads were from Ladies of Distinction, probably B-team, from what I was told. I prayed none of them were A-team 'cause I wanted to have my way with all of them before we left. Unfortunately, I wouldn't be fucking Mona. Cadillac killed my plans with a quick shake of his head. I instantly knew something was up with them. I made a note to watch them a bit closer in the future.

"Where is Netta and Butterfly?" Cadillac asked.

"In back, waiting on him," Mona answered.

"Good, good." He turned to me. "Well, cousin, the night is yours. Don't hurt yourself."

With those words, Cadillac sent me into the Garden of Eden. When I entered the room, Netta and Butterfly were laying seductively on the bed like two felines. Both of them were naked, their smooth skin and perfect bodies glowing beneath low lights. Netta beckoned me, her voice raspy with seduction. My dick went brick just thinking about what was about to go down. Before I could remove my clothes, Netta slithered across the bed and whipped my meat out. She stroked it gently while I continued to grow inside of her hands. When I was fully erect, Netta commented on my size, then took my whole nine inches into her mouth in one whop.

My knees buckled.

Butterfly leaned back on the bed, watching us, playing with herself while Netta wrapped her lips around me. As Netta let it do what it do, I became mesmerized watching Butterfly's juices ooze onto the bed from her tight opening. Netta took my dick out and rubbed it all over her face. Then she started J-ing me off, flute-style, sucking it from the side like she playing a flute. I'd had that done before, but never like this. Netta was literally wrapping her whole tongue around my wood.

And that shit felt good!!!

Granted, I hadn't fucked anything in years, but I could've just rolled off a piece, and my mind still would've been blown with that shit.

Netta must have sucked me off for close to an hour, pulling tricks out of her bag I'd only read or heard about. She sucked me slow, fast, and deep. She swallowed my balls. She did it all. But for some reason, my nut eluded me. Guess I needed the real thing.

Like a madman, I bent Netta over, slipped my hardness inside of her gushy pussy, and pounded that ass like a jackhammer. Still unable to get right after a few minutes, I threw Netta aside and grabbed Butterfly.

Instantly, I felt a difference. Butterfly was extra tight, like cobwebs lined her walls. As if that wasn't enough, when I finally managed to get inside her, she started clenching her muscles like she was milking a cow. She kept whispering in my ear, begging me to cum, while winding her wide hips like a snake. Still, as bad as I wanted to oblige her, I couldn't for some reason. Behind me, I faintly heard Netta joke about me taking Viagra. Then she tried to stick that long tongue of hers far enough up my ass to make me question my manhood. The initial sensation was good, but I couldn't get into the way she was trying to dagger my ass. Felt *too* much like she was trying to fuck me. I gently, but firmly, pushed her away from my exit, then continued my quest to cum.

I fucked them hard.

Soft.

Slow.

Fast.

I fucked them so hard, my dick started to hurt. I put Butterfly in the double-lock-butt-hole-roll, where I cradled the backs of her knees into the hollows of my elbows and rolled her legs over beside her head. Nothing was in the way now, granting me full access to her long, tight pussy. I closed my eyes, slow-stroking to savor every inch of what I was stuffing inside of her, ensuring she felt every thrust.

Imagine my surprise when a picture of ole girl from the beach popped into my head.

Soldada.

Rather than try to shake the vision, I embraced it. Imagined Soldada was beneath me. Imagined that she was trying to milk my juices. Imagined this was her pussy I was trying to knock the bottom out of. I pumped maybe six more times before six years of pent-up frustration exploded all over Butterfly's stomach. She rubbed my essence all over her belly while I stood on my knees desperately trying to capture my breath as it raced away from me.

"'Bout time!" Both women chimed in unison. They laughed to themselves, then began rubbing me all over. Netta disappeared, then returned seconds later with a hot, soapy wet rag and washed any remnants of sex off me. Meanwhile, Butterfly rubbed my chest like I was a king.

Me?

I was tripping over the fact that I was with two of the baddest chicks I'd ever had, and was still fantasizing about the one I didn't have.

4

SOLDADA

I was admiring Adonis's strong, firm, body as he performed a striptease for my viewing pleasure. As I focused on the promising package threatening to burst from his designer briefs, I applied pressure to the throbbing between my legs in hopes of dousing the fire that burned there. My center was roasting as juices ran from my opening like a river. I used two of my fingers like a dam, plugged them in, then rode the waves to ecstasy. Just as I was about to climax, someone banged on my door.

And woke me from my dream.

I unclasped my fingers from between my legs, shocked that I had actually began masturbating in my sleep! I threw on my complimentary white terry cloth robe and rushed to see who had interrupted my pleasure. As I passed the nightstand, I took a glimpse at the time. It read 8:45 a.m.

"Who is it?" I mumbled, groggily. The person kept banging. "This better be good!" I groaned. I snatched open the door and was standing face-to face with my Adonis. "Anthony?!"

I slammed the door in his face.

What the hell? How did he get my room number? Better yet, why was he here at eight a.m.? All these questions flashed through my head in about point-three-seconds. I rushed to the bathroom, combing my fingers through my unruly hair.

He banged on the door. "Soldada? Open the door! I'm still out here."

"Just a sec!" I yelled. Quickly, I washed my face, and gurgled mouthwash simultaneously. Running through the room, slipping on my tank and damp sweats, I stumped my toe on a table.

"Shit!" I muttered.

"What was that?" Anthony called from the other side of the door.

"Nothing," I mumbled. I unlocked the door and cracked it open to peep at him. "What do you want, Anthony?" I hissed through the slit in the door. In that split second, my eyes took all of him in. He looked simply scrumptious standing there in cream linen shorts, matching tank top, and cloth Gucci slip-ons. His smile beamed so bright, he could've endorsed Colgate.

"I came to collect my debt," he claimed, boring into my eyes with those irresistible peepers of his.

"Your debt?" I huffed, with more attitude than I wanted to show. "What debt?"

He waved his hand. "Totally irrelevant. Get dressed. You owe me a day."

"A day? A day of what?"

"Yeah, a day. That's my price," he stated, calmly glimpsing the silver chronogram with the white band on his arm. "So quit wasting the day away with your questions and come on. And just relax, I'm not gonna bite."

There was that smile again. My knees buckled a bit, but I recovered. Hell! I didn't know him! He was just some dude I kissed on the beach. For all I knew, going with him could make me end up like that girl on TV a few years back, who vacationed in the islands and never returned. I told him exactly that.

"Girl, please, don't nobody want you. If I wanted to do something to you, it'd been done already. Quit flattering yourself!"

It was obvious he wasn't going to let me be, so I invited him inside. Told him to sit on the loveseat while I got ready. Twenty minutes later, I was following him down the beach.

"Where are we going?" I pouted.

"You'll see," he said, not bothering to look at me. The more we walked, the more familiar the scenery became. We were headed toward the docks.

"You looked so disappointed yesterday when you couldn't ride, I decided to make sure you experienced this," he told me.

"Aww, man! It's so beautiful up there! You'll love it."

We arrived at the docks before the rush came. In fact, we were the only people there. This time we were quickly strapped into the harness, and the boat took off, lifting us up into the air gradually. We caught a little altitude, and I began to freak out a little. Anthony reached for me just as my body began to jerk.

"Don't be scared. I got you," he assured me. "You're safe with me."

"Really?" I wondered aloud, afraid to open my eyes.

"Really." He patted my hand with sincerity, and it did the trick. I felt safe.

As we rode the wind over Anguilla, Anthony made sure to point out beautiful spots he had noticed the previous day. The gorgeous azure water below contrasting with the lush greenery sprinkled atop the hillsides created a euphoric feeling. I was instantly humbled by so much beauty. Felt so mortal in the presence of God's creation. I snapped picture after picture, capturing these moments in time forever. Meanwhile, Anthony shared his knowledge of various buildings as we flew past. I, in turn, schooled him on the history of the island. During my freshman year in college, I scaled my family tree and learned my maternal ancestors had roots in Anguilla. Ever since then, I had studied the history of the island in my spare time. Anthony seemed all too eager to learn about everything I mentioned. He turned out to be a very good listener as I called out structures I'd only read about for years.

When we returned to earth, Anthony led us to some horse stables. After receiving brief instructions, we climbed aboard two shiny, black thoroughbreds and followed a tour guide through trails that could only be reached by horseback. In his thick accent, he explained that the true treasures of the small island were hidden inside the cracks and crevices. He led us to a crystal lake surrounded by cliffs on all sides.

That was when Anthony started acting like a fool.

He dismounted his horse before I could draw mine to a halt and scooped me right off into his powerful arms.

"NO! Anthony, stoooooop!" I begged for him to put me down, but my pleas must have gotten muffled in the wind. He ran straight to the water's edge and pitched me in. I feigned like I couldn't swim, splashing around like a fish out of water to teach him a lesson. To my surprise, he dived in to save me. In seconds, he had me wrapped up in his cocoon of safety.

"Chill ... chill, I got you," he cooed into my ear, as he enveloped me from behind in his chiseled arms. We were standing chest-deep in the middle of the lake, and the cool water couldn't calm the fire raging through my body when we touched. "Relax, Counselor. I'm not going to let anything happen to you. I told you that," he reminded me, getting all serious on me. His voice had dropped an octave, and I felt his penis growing to poke my lower back.

I kicked away from him and swam off smoother than Michael Phelps. I turned over backwards and gave him two fingers as I drifted farther away from him. I don't know why, but I was really feeling myself. I just felt so ... carefree in his presence.

"Oh, I know you didn't ..."

He came after me. I ducked under and swam to the floor. Unfortunately, the water was clear, so I couldn't hide from him. When I broke the surface, I was looking right in his face. I ducked back under but suddenly felt myself being hoisted into the air.

"Put me down!" I screamed, kicking like a dying cockroach.

"Oh, you want me to put you down?"

"Wait! No, wait!"

Next thing I tasted was warm water rushing through my nose. Anthony thought I was joking again, so he dunked me a few more times until I broke out in a spasm of coughs. He pulled me up and hit my back hard enough to make me spit water.

"Damn, Counselor! My bad."

I gave him the meanest look I could muster, then punched him in the chest. "Brute!"

"What?"

"You heard me." I punched him again, then ran out of the water, tossing a flirtatious smile his way. He chased me, following me onto one of the cliffs above another body of water. Just before he reached me, I cannon-balled off the cliff into the water below. He dived in behind me, but I evaded capture.

We continued this routine until we had jumped from all four cliffs surrounding the bigger lake. I eventually grew tired of running, so I allowed him to catch me. He playfully roughed me up some more, each touch licking my insides like flames.

A couple of hours later, we walked back to the stables hand-in-hand. He carried the reins of both our horses inside his free hand, while we chatted away. We had agreed earlier not to get into too many particulars, like where we were from, family matters, et cetera, et cetera. Neither of us held any expectations beyond this moment, so the stipulations were convenient. This allowed us the freedom to speak freely without fear of being judged.

He questioned my decision to become a lawyer. I relayed my story of how watching so many brothers get railroaded made me want to pick up arms in the struggle, contribute to the cause of freedom, make a difference. (I conveniently left out the part about my father catching a life sentence in his native Cuba because he was a big-time revolutionary.) He laughed at me when I told him I wanted to be a judge someday. Made some comment about men catching charges just to get sentenced by me.

However, he frowned when I told him I'd have to spend time in the prosecutor's office to satisfy that end.

He told me he had been celibate for six years. Said he was jaded with women; they all were the same. Said it all grew mundane after awhile. He wanted something special. I told him I could relate to that. Shared with him how long it had been for me, blamed it on my education.

He grunted like he was ready to show me what I was missing right then and there.

I held my breath because I wanted him to show me.

As the conversation flowed, I found myself attempting to break our agreement, delve deeper into his life, find out who he was, what made him tick. He, however, always managed to shift the conversation back to me, encouraging me to share my thoughts. I thought nothing sinister of it. It was refreshing to have a man focus on me for a change, make me feel comfortable. So it was no surprise I fell right into his charm.

I shared a portion of my family history. Told him about my absent Cuban father, and my Cuban-and-black mother who raised me by herself. He learned that my childhood was filled with love, despite the longing for material possessions. He learned that my mother left my father for dead in a Cuban prison. I never told anyone that story. There was just something about Anthony. I couldn't put my finger on it, but he made me feel safe. Secure. He was a welcome contrast to the men I'd known most of my life. He was smart, articulate, and worldly with just a hint of street lurking beneath the surface. Plus, he was humble yet confident. In other words, the perfect balance that I desired.

By the time we reached the resort, it was nearing dark. We agreed to freshen up, then meet back at my room for dinner. Seemed neither of us wanted this night to end.

We had dinner at a beachside eatery with tables that sat right on the shoreline. Each round table was decorated with a simple white tablecloth, basic silverware, and a single candle burning in the center of the table, crafting a soft glow. On stage, a live band jammed calypso and reggae riddims while we dined on lobster, oysters, and scallops, and cheered on the couples that grooved to the beat.

Halfway through the meal, Anthony grabbed my hand and pulled me to the dance floor, which was actually just dirt packed in from the numerous people who had danced there over the years. We two-stepped to a rendition of Bob Marley's "Jammin'." Anthony grabbed my hand, and I allowed myself to be putty in his hands as he twirled me around like a ballerina. I had to admit, the brother had moves.

The band switched it up to R. Kelly's "Jamaican Girl," and the atmosphere changed. It became charged. He pulled me closer, and I unleashed my moves, started windin' and grindin' all over him like a high-priced stripper, inviting him to my curves. I felt his nature rise. I grinded on him even harder, tried to merge our bodies together. I don't know where my mind was at. Maybe it was the alcohol. Maybe it was the island atmosphere. Maybe it was the way he lightly palmed my hips as I wound my waist. Maybe it was all of that and more that had my G-string so drenched I could have wrung it out like a dish rag!

Anthony gradually slid his finger down my bare back all the way down to the V at the top of my skirt, just above my ass crack, then ran it back up to the top of my neck and tickled my earlobe. I grabbed my hair coiled atop my head in Nubian knots, exhaled his name in a whisper of hot lust.

"Anthony..."

He must have thought that was an invitation. I felt his tongue graze my neck ever so slightly. I craned my neck up to meet his kiss. Right there in front of everyone, we shared a passionate lip-lock. A long, deep, sensual kiss that took my breath away and sent me sailing like the boats in the distance. His kiss was electric, as if it was his first time ever. So much passion.

"Ant, we can't do this. Not like this. Not right here," I whispered.

With heat brimming from his eyes, he told me, "You're right."

He scooped me into his brawny arms, and I became oblivious to everything except us, locked into our own pocket of paradise.

I don't remember when or how we made it to my room. I felt like I was drifting on a cloud. The wine we sipped at dinner had my body moving like lava, hot and lethargic. Resistance was nil as Anthony gently placed me on my bed and showered me with kisses. Trying to regain control of the situation, I maneuvered from his grasp and slipped out onto the balcony. Overlooking the sea twenty stories below, I struggled to catch my breath.

I felt Anthony come up behind me. "Don't fight me," he pleaded. "Feel how bad I want you." He placed my hand on his penis. As soon as I felt that thick muscle, it was a wrap!

He kissed my back, shoulders, neck. Spun me around. Slid the spaghetti straps off my shoulders. The cool breeze massaged my hard nipples like an extra lover. He cupped my heavy breasts in his hands and kissed them softly back and forth. He sucked my left nipple, fondled my right, and slipped his free hand under my skirt to play in my kitty.

Talk about multitasking! Ole boy was playing my body like a fiddle.

I leaned back against the railing and lifted my left leg to grant him easier access. Just as I did, a wave rushed over me as the first feeling of an orgasm gripped me. He removed his mouth from my breast and gave his hand some company below my waist. The moment his mouth touched my center, I came.

Hard.

But Anthony was undaunted. He drank from me like a fountain and slid two fingers inside of me.

"Ooh, Anthony ... ohhh ... st...don't stop. Stop!!" I moaned.

My mind could not keep up with my body. The more my mind said, *"no, no, no,"* my body was saying *"yes, yes, yes, dammit yes!"*

Anthony pulled my skirt and panties down and off smoother than a cat burglar, leaving me naked on the balcony in the pale moonlight. I popped the buttons off his linen shirt with force. Sucked his nipple. Then I tossed the shirt over the balcony. I didn't think it was possible, but upon seeing Anthony's statuesque physique, I became even more aroused!

I kissed my way down the ripples in his eight-pack stomach, licked around his navel, and sank to my knees, continuing south. I slid his linen trousers down, and his dick popped out stiff and slightly wavering like a diving board. I wrapped both hands around it and stroked it slowly, amazed at how thick and long it had grown inside my hands. Even with both of my hands on his manhood, one in front of the other, the head of his penis still protruded stubbornly, as if it refused to be doused. He had to be carrying at least nine to ten inches!

While I stroked and admired his blessing, I contemplated my next move. *Should I or shouldn't I?* Without too much thought, I figured, *What the hell?*

I put it in my mouth.

I tried to stuff all of him into my mouth, gobble him up, but he was much too big for my amateur jaws to handle. I gagged as soon as he hit the back of my throat. I spit him out. Licked and sucked the head. Stared into his eyes as I laid down my hypnotism. His eyes rolled into the back of his head. His moans propelled my desire into the stratosphere. I pulled harder until his pre-cum peppered my mouth. I never would've thought my first time giving head I'd enjoy it so much, but here I was sucking him like a pacifier.

What can I say? I'm a fast learner.

Anthony slid his penis from my mouth, lifted me on the railing, and entered me slowly. The initial sensation was heavenly. Hard, hot, and thick, he pushed deeper inside of me, expanding my narrow walls until I felt as if I was being torn in two. He opened my legs wider and buried himself so deep inside that I felt him in my stomach. I cried out in a mixture of pleasure and pain as he slid in and out of me with slow, powerful strokes.

I clasped my legs around his waist, trying to control the depth of penetration, but he would not have it. He wrapped his arms around my waist, planted his hands on the railing, and pounded my pussy like he owned it. Despite the pain, I took it like a big girl. I rocked back with him a few times, but he hit a spot, and I lost it.

I threw my head back and wailed like a cat in heat.

I was numb to anyone who may be watching or listening. We were on the twentieth floor. I seriously doubted anyone could see my ass hanging over the railing. It was already being palmed by Anthony's huge hands.

I felt him growing, pulsating inside of me, signaling his arrival. I squeezed him three times, and felt his strong eruption splatter the back of my canal. Seconds later, I unleashed my river on him as I came in an orchestra of moans, whimpers, quivers, and shakes.

I cradled his head into my naked chest. "Ohmigod ... Anthony ... what are you doing to me?!" I wailed. He stirred inside me, just a little, and I came again ... and again. He squeezed me tighter, ensuring our connection didn't break.

I came again.

Anthony was still inside of me, slowly hardening again like concrete. I was not prepared for this. He was like Superman!

He withdrew from my warmth, briefly. I thought he was giving me a break, but before I could catch my breath, he spun me around and bent me over the railing. I begged him to wait. Let me catch my breath. Give my kitty a break.

He wasn't hearing it.

He crammed his dick inside of me and lowered the boom on my ass! With each stroke, he went deeper, harder. He spread my cheeks really wide, stood on his toes, and went to work. He was hurting me soooo good! I braced myself on the railing. Looked back at him. Threw my heavy ass back at him. He grunted like a madman. I started talking shit, "You love this pussy, don't cha? Huh? Harder! *Dame mas!! Mas fuerte!!!*"

Felt so good, I reverted to my native tongue. He didn't understand Spanish, but what I was giving was universal. He loved it.

"I'm ... gon' ... make you...love...this dick!" he growled, clutching my small waist inside his big hands. I thought he was going to tear me apart.

Little did he know, I was already loving it. The way he was putting it down, I gained the years I'd lost back with every stroke. For the first time in my life, I was really being fucked. And I loved every stroke of it!

5

Anthony

I slowly opened my eyes, trying to recall where I was and whose bed I was in. At first, I thought I was still inside and just had another one of my countless wet dreams, but the smooth, bronzed thigh draped across my midsection helped me recollect my thoughts.

I'd had butt-naked sex on the balcony, to the floor, to the bed, with the woman of my dreams, who was really a stranger to me. A mystery. Oh, I knew her in the biblical sense. My sore tool that was stuck to my thigh with her dried wetness confirmed that. The more my mind peeked through the fog in my head, the more I realized I actually knew this woman really well. True, the particulars were kept to a minimum — on my part anyway — but what we shared was more intimate than any words that could've been whispered. After a day of stimulating conversation, we fucked, made love, and screwed up an undeniable bond. Granted, I was prone to having a tender dick because I'd just gotten it off the shelf, but I still felt like what me and Soldada shared was something I never felt before.

As I was trying to make sense of my sexcapade, Soldada moved her leg, snatching me out of my thoughts.

"Ow! That hurts," she whined, repositioning her leg over my thighs. She craned her neck to the nightstand and croaked, "What time is it?"

I planted a kiss on her forehead. "A little after ten."

She rubbed her soft hands over my six-pack. "Maybe you should go," she suggested.

"Why? What's wrong? Expecting company? I'm saying, we got room."

She nudged me. "No, crazy." She paused. "I-I don't like how I'm feeling. Don't want to make these feelings disregard our rules."

She was speaking in her lawyer voice. I noticed she did that every time she wanted to disconnect from her emotions.

I traced circles on her neck. "What are you feeling?"

"Oh, my gosh! You don't want to know. Besides this pain right here..." — she patted her shaved mound and smiled — "... you don't want to know."

"Sure I do." I rolled her over, onto her back, kissed her deeply. "What's on your mind?"

"This," she moaned. "I don't ever recall feeling like this. You make me feel so good, and I-I-I don't want to get attached to this feeling. Remember the rules ..."

I was ready to say "fuck the rules!" I was really feeling Soldada. She was everything I was looking for in a woman. Confident. Intelligent. Driven. Professional. Down-to-earth with a wonderful sense of humor. She was actually more than I wanted in a woman, and that was good. She would keep me on my toes. I hadn't even breathed the Carolina air yet, seen the suga dymes of the Queen City, scoped my prospects ... but I knew what I wanted, and I knew what I was feeling was real.

But I wasn't ready to be tied down. Didn't want to leave one prison and jump into another. So I let her statement linger, crushed her ambition.

"It's okay, Anthony. This is just a fling. No need to get sentimental. We're both consenting adults," she whispered, her voice cracking. "I enjoyed last night, but you really must go." She pushed me away from her, shoved me from the bed. If I didn't know any better, I would've thought shorty was catching feelings, hard feelings.

"Wait, Soldada."

"What, Anthony? There's nothing more to be said."

"I'm leaving tonight," I informed her. Her face dropped. "I wanna spend more time with you before I leave," I admitted.

"You mean you want to fuck me again."

I grinned like a hyena. "Not just that," I snickered. "You know, I dig your company. I wanna kick it with you." I nudged her arm playfully.

She shook her head slowly. "Unt-unh, no need to put strings on a no-strings-attached affair," she said softly. "Good-bye, Anthony." She turned her back on me. I'd never played the Keith Sweat role, so I slowly lifted myself from the bed and got dressed in silence.

On my way to the door, she called out to me. I stopped in my tracks. "Yo?"

"Can I know just one thing about your real life? I mean, I'm not a stalker or anything ... I just need to know more about ... about ... the man of my dreams." Her eyes were closed as if she was praying.

I granted her wish. "Shoot."

"Where are you from? I mean, what state, county ..." She flailed her hands, fumbling for words. "*Something.*"

There was a long pause, pregnant with anticipation. I hesitated because, based on what she told me, I knew I was about to rock her world.

"Mecklenburg County. Queen City. Charlotte, North Carolina."

As I shut the door behind me, I heard her moan, "Aww, damn!"

Shaun Sinclair

6

Anthony

It felt good to be back in the good, ole Queen City.

Immediately after we hopped off the plane, we snatched up a rental, and shot to Mo's spot. He couldn't wait to show off his new pride and joy, a tricked-out purple '71 Caprice. As I rode down Independence in the back of Mo's heavy Chevy, I noticed how much the city had changed. Tall buildings had replaced old warehouses. Parking lots were now where tree lines used to be.

But the most drastic change were the Latinos.

They were everywhere! Mexicans, El Salvadorians, Guatemalans. I'd read that Latinos were the new majority-minority in the U.S., but there was nothing like actually seeing the difference. Hell, it looked like they were all in Charlotte. I said as much to Dirty.

"Don't knock they hustle. Them little muthafuckas work, cuz!" He laughed. "Plus you can pay them for the low 'cause a lot of 'em here illegal. And because they on that gang shit real hard, the police be sweating 'em hard. Hell! Between them and them Arabs, shit, a black man can finally live in peace."

I really didn't agree with the blanket prejudice, but the brother did have a point. Mo turned the music up, and T.I. drowned out our conversation as we merged onto the 485 Loop. We were headed to my uncle's house in Ballantyne, where a gathering was being held in my honor.

As soon as we turned onto the road leading to my uncle's home, I saw the circular driveway congested with luxury cars, most of them belonging to my uncle. We parked and entered the marble foyer of the big house. My uncle's part-time housekeeper, Maria, greeted us.

"Ah, Mr. Anthony, es good to see you again," Maria chimed in her thick accent. She squeezed my cheeks. "So beeg. You are so beeg now. Everyone is in back. Come. I show you."

We followed Maria out back where everyone was gathered around the Olympic-sized pool. My cousin, Rosalynn, was sunbathing in a leopard-print bikini, trying to darken her high-yellow skin.

Rosalynn was my aunt and uncle's eldest child, and only girl. A C.P.A. by trade, she owned and operated a P.R. firm that handled a lot of the big corporate accounts in Charlotte. Rose (as we called her) was thirty-three, but looked twenty-years-old in her bikini. Growing up, she was the cousin I wished wasn't my cousin, so I could make her my girl. She always protected me and made sure I was straight. Even when I was locked down, Rose kept my books loaded. I guess you could say we were more like sister and brother than cousins.

Rose jumped from her lounge chair to meet me halfway, her 38 Ds bouncing bountifully. "Anthony! Come 'ere and give me a hug."

"Wassup, big cuz!" I grabbed her in a bear hug.

"Damn, boy. You done got big!" She groped my biceps through my tight T-shirt. "Don't go too far. I got somebody I want you to meet." Turning from me, she punched Mo in the chest. "Wassup, nucca, you ain't gon' show your big sis no love?"

That was the thing I loved about Rose. In her work-related capacity as *Rosalynn*, she was the consummate professional. Conservative skirt suits, perfect enunciation — the works. With us, she was just Rose. A slang-spitting B-girl with guts. She was my uncle's first child, so she was brought up when he was still building his empire, and was rough around the edges. His ruggedness was passed down to her through osmosis. She was still single with no kids because most dudes couldn't handle her. Either they were too soft, or they were intimidated by her money and fortitude. Nonetheless, Rose was still happily living the single life with a rack of girlfriends just as fine as her.

I asked Rose, "Where's Uncle Roland?"

"He just stepped inside for a second. He's expecting you. He said to send you in when you got here."

A few minutes later, I slid through the heavy oak door into the back of the house, skated down the wide hallway with blond wood floors and expensive paintings hanging from the walls to the first door on the left. I knocked. The door sprang open and there stood my Uncle Roland in all his formidable glory.

Uncle Roland was six-feet-five-inches of pure pride nestled inside a compact 260-plus frame. His barrel chest and thick truck-driver arms proclaimed days of hard work. The slight paunch spilling over his belt testified to days of good living as well. His close-cropped wavy gray hair and precisely trimmed full bread complimented his smooth copper skin to perfection. Even the dark chest hair sprouting from underneath the V of his T-shirt like thick blades of grass didn't look out of place. Unc looked like money.

"Come here, boy!" Unc snatched me in his office, then slammed me into his hard body. Guess that was his idea of a hug. "I'm so glad you're home! You look good, son," he commented, placing his hands on both my shoulders and giving me an inspection. "How was Anguilla?"

Memories careened through my head like a locomotive. In my mind I corrected his pronunciation. "It was straight," I replied simply.

"Just straight? Hell, I wanted you to have a blast!" He took a seat behind his massive desk, motioned for me to sit on the sofa. "Did you, at least, get some pussy?"

"Of course."

"Ha! Ha! That's my boy. Foreign pussy is always the best. Tell me about it. What she look like? Or what they look like? Ha! Ha!"

I relayed my encounter with Soldada in limited detail, hinting that she was Latina, but omitting that she was from the good ole U.S. of A. As I told my story, Unc fidgeted in his seat and looked to the ceiling as if he was reliving what I was telling him. When I was done, he couldn't contain himself.

"That's what I'm talking about, A.P.! I remember I went to Greece one time. Sexiest women you'd ever want to see – and *love* a black man! Tell ya, I did so much fucking that week. Hell! Think I had Athena," he snickered.

We both laughed at Unc's humor. It was refreshing to see that things had not changed between us. Our relationship had always been tight. From day one, he treated me like I was his own son, his flesh and blood. Plus, he always kept it real.

After shooting the shit for awhile, Uncle Roland got down to business.

"Look, Anthony ..." He looked me dead in my eyes. "I want to thank you for what you did. You didn't have to do it."

"Aww, Unc, it was nothing —"

He raised his hand to silence me. "It *was* something! You kept your mouth shut. Stayed true to the code, unlike a lot of these so-called players out here fucking up the game." He reached into his drawer. "Now ... it's time for your reward."

He pulled out a ledger, slid it across the desk to me. "Open it. It's yours."

Perusing the contents, I was shocked to learn my real estate portfolio had multiplied exponentially. According to the ledger, I now owned a 4-unit apartment complex in North Charlotte, a lot that housed a strip mall in South Charlotte, just around the corner from South Park Mall; a duplex in West Charlotte, and another on the Eastside. My most prized possession was a condo on the fourteenth floor of a high-rise in Uptown Charlotte. The condo was where I would be laying my head, and I couldn't be happier. This was how I had envisioned coming home night after night.

Rich.

Something in the ledger caught my eye that I didn't quite understand. There was a $100,000 withdrawal from my account for a purchase, but I didn't see any records of what I'd bought. No pictures. Descriptions. Nothing. I asked Unc about it.

He lowered his head and rubbed his temple like the answer was a thorn in his crown. "Let's take a ride," he suggested. "I'll show you."

I rode shotgun as we sliced and diced through afternoon traffic in his Carolina-blue Jaguar XKR convertible, the late August sun beaming on our heads as we made small talk.

"What you think about Carlo's new business?" Uncle Roland asked over the whine of the supercharged engine. Carlo was Cadillac's birth name.

"It's aiight, I guess." I shrugged my shoulders, nonchalantly.

"All right? That boy is making a shitload of money! Running around here looking like one of them ballplayers. You don't plan on getting involved with that, do you?"

I toyed with the deep waves in my head in the rearview mirror. "Nah. I got my own lane. He had a few of them broads down there with us, though. I hit a couple of 'em," I admitted.

I could tell Uncle Roland wasn't too pleased with my admission. His whole demeanor changed. He glanced at me with words on his tongue, but they never floated to the surface. He was clearly struggling with himself. Finally, the dam broke down as we turned onto Tryon Street.

"A.P., listen to me carefully because I'm only going to say it once." He took his eyes off the road so long I wanted to grab the wheel. "What Carlo got going on is good. It helps woo a lot of clientele in our direction, you know. Nothing has changed. Everything made is still for the family. Pennies for one, is dollars for all. All of our businesses are correlated in some way — from the fish to the fish, if you know what I mean." Uncle Roland chuckled at his own joke, then got serious. "But what happened in Anguilla stays in Anguilla. Under no circumstances are you to fuck with any of Carlo's girls. They're poison. I've seen them wreck homes, destroy lives, families, careers. You — we — don't need that. I need your head in the game. We're about to make some major money. We do not fuck the help. Got it?"

I nodded slowly, the whole time wondering if Unc had ever sampled Cadillac's delights. The way he spoke, seemed like he knew firsthand. I could definitely picture Netta twisting a square dude's head with her bag of tricks and blazing pussy. But not the kid. I was all about my paper like Malcolm, you know, by any means necessary.

We pulled into a construction site off the business section of Trade Street. The ground was cleared for yards as far as the eyes could see. Uncle Roland exited the Jag and walked to a six-foot tall sign, planted in the ground. I followed him. The sign contained computer-generated photos of what was planned for the site. A sixty-story tower tentatively named the Queen's Quarter.

The Queen's Quarter was to consist of luxury condos, a full-scale gym, upscale business suites, a small shopping center, a state-of-the-art ballroom, all capped off with a revolving restaurant on the top floor encased in glass, enabling patrons to view the expansive Charlotte skyline as they dined on their meals or partied in the adjacent V.I.P.

Uncle Roland tapped the sign like a man possessed. "This, my son, is the prize."

He explained to me how I.T.Bs (Intents To Bid) were being entertained to build the project. So far, Unc had submitted the lowest bid and the contract was all but his until recently. Someone had come out of the woodwork, undercutting Uncle Roland so much that it would be impossible to bid lower and still turn a profit.

But Unc had to have this job. It was just too sweet.

Under the deal proposed, not only would he build a huge portion of the Queen's Quarter, but he would also own a controlling stake of the towers, extending his personal fortune up into the upper hundreds of millions. That was simply too much money to pass up. He informed me that he had invested 100K from my account to give me a 3 percent share when the job was completed.

Now his passion became my passion.

When he was done explaining things, I had only one question. "What's the hold up?"

"This fucking guy just won't let up!" Uncle Roland exploded, shaking his fist. "I go low, he goes lower. No way can he build the project with those numbers and still turn a profit. No way!" Unc wiped spittle from the corners of his mouth with a silk hankie. "So that means one thing: someone is fucking with me. Someone is trying to sabotage me." He shook his head slowly. "There is no way I'm gonna let what happened to me with that stadium happen here. No way."

That stadium was the Bobcats arena, aka Uncle Roland's Achilles' heel, the deal that fell through the cracks when the authorities started sniffing around his pot of gold. When Bob

Johnson brought his billions to Charlotte to fund a new basketball team, the city didn't want to support him. They wouldn't up the money for a new arena like all the other cities with an NBA franchise. It was almost as if they wanted him to fail. Mr. Johnson, in turn, began accepting offers from independent investors to cushion the bill. Uncle Roland was one of the leading suitors until his sky began to fall. Mr. Johnson didn't want the perceived spectacle of impropriety clouding his power move, so the deal went awry. Uncle Roland never allowed himself to live that moment down.

"I will do whatever needs to be done to see this project to fruition," Uncle Roland vowed.

"What have you done so far?" I asked. "Have you spoke to this guy? I mean, maybe you two can reach an agreement where you both win."

Uncle Roland shook his head. "Apparently, he's backed by some conglomerate of investors. He's mainly the mouthpiece for his group. We have a meeting coming up in a couple days. I plan to show him how it would be better for everybody if we humble ourselves and work together."

I couldn't stifle my laugh as we walked back to the Jag. The thought of my uncle humbling himself to anyone was a joke. I was cracking up as I settled into the cream leather passenger seat, wondering why Uncle Roland was waiting on my side of the car.

"Here," he said, passing me the key. "This is your car."

"My car?"

"Yeah. Your car. You think I'd really ride around in something this gaudy? White seats? Come on!"

We both laughed. Me, because I was ecstatic with my gift, and happy to be free.

I stroked the Jag and made it purr every chance I got as I drove back to Ballantyne. Pandora radio was pumping the latest Scarface cuts as I reveled in my freedom, and noted all the new changes in my city. Suddenly, Uncle Roland leaned up and killed the music.

"You're the only one of my sons in on this deal," he confided. "Know why?" I shook my head, eager to hear the answer. "Because out of everyone, you seem to be the most

stable ... up here." He pointed to his temple. "Carlo is too gone
in his own world to give something like this the attention it will
need. Leroy's foresight is limited. He does well with his
seafood racket, but he can't appreciate and grasp the magnitude
of something like this. Plus, he has a family to take care of
now, and this could get really dirty. And Moses, he is too hot.
He keeps fucking with those wetbacks, and he's gonna get
jammed up. You watch ..."

As Uncle Roland rattled off his suspect reasoning, I kept
wondering why he really included me in on this. Surely he
didn't need my little hundred stacks to move this mountain.
Meanwhile, he kept stroking me.

"You, Anthony, are the prime candidate for partnership.
You're young, super-ambitious, focused, and a master planner.
When I used to come and visit you, I could tell you were
determined to be successful. I knew that all you needed was a
chance and you wouldn't look back. I know, because I've been
where you were, years ago. Who better to give the Padmore
legacy to? You have nothing to lose, everything to gain, and
you will do whatever it takes to get the job done. Am I right?"

I dipped in behind a black Benz, peeked out, then blasted
past the coupe with my mind on millions.

"Absolutely."

7

SOLDADA

"Ladies and gentlemen of the jury, you may remember me from the opening statements of this trial. To refresh your memory, my name is Soldada Andrews, and I am an assistant district attorney for Mecklenburg County. But who I am is not important. What is important is what I'm here for today. Today, I am here to bring to justice a robber, a rapist, and an abuser.

"I'm sure the media has bombarded you with terms like 'alleged rapist' and 'suspected armed robber' and 'alleged molester,' but the facts are as plain and clear as this air we are breathing. So today, ladies and gentlemen, I ask you ... to snatch those terms away! Snatch 'alleged' and 'suspected' away because they insult your god-given intelligence ..."

I drove each syllable home, beating the palm of my manicured hand, while looking every juror in the eye with a steely glare. Then I abruptly spun on my red stiletto heel to allow the seven male jurors a glimpse of my tight buns indenting my blue pencil skirt as I strutted back to the prosecutor's table. All I had to do was sway the majority. They would sway the rest. I feigned at the table like I was consulting my notes. In actuality, I was letting my words sink in to the jury, just as I had been taught. The silence in the courtroom was deafening. In my mind, this was the equivalent of a standing ovation. Any attorney worth his or her bar card dreamed for a rapt audience and an engrossed jury, in particular. I had both.

My boss, Constantine Annapolis, district attorney for Mecklenburg County, shot me a reassuring wink. I continued.

"Ladies and gentlemen of the jury, Mr. Roberts was arrested with a .357 Magnum, the same weapon used in the crime. His skin was scraped from underneath the victim's fingernails, according to irrefutable DNA evidence. Samples of his semen was extracted from the victim's rectum." I saw a couple of jurors wince at the image I painted, and I knew I was winning. "Sure, my respected colleague, Mr. Bivins, would tell you his client was in the wrong place at the wrong time ... surprisingly ... I agree." I paused, put the bait out there, then reeled it in. "He was still around when the cops showed up!"

My remark drew chuckles and grimaces from the gallery and bench alike. The defense was livid, but they couldn't object. This was my time to shine. I hurried to close before my welcome wore out.

"He wants the good people of this jury to believe that after two — *two* — convictions for sexual assault *and* two convictions for armed robbery, this leopard has somehow managed to change his spots?" I scoffed. "He is a two-time loser that doesn't realize the game is over. Well, today I want you to go into that room and emerge with three words: GUILTY! GUILTY! GUILTY! Send this loser to the bench. Thank you, ladies and gentlemen."

Because the idiot defendant opted to take the stand during trial and bury himself deeper, I closed last, which meant it would be my words ringing in the ears of the jurors when they retired to deliberate.

The judge charged the jury on the application of law while I sat at the table beside Constantine Annapolis.

"Not bad for a week's worth of preparation," Constantine whispered to me.

That's right; I'd only had the case a week. Same day I arrived in Charlotte from Anguilla, I received my assignment via messenger. My instructions were to report to the office ASAP. Mind you, this was at six in the evening on a Tuesday, but as requested, I dropped everything and dashed to the office. Since the city kept the D.A.'s office separate from everything else, our office was located in a high-rise in Uptown Charlotte. This wasn't exactly normal, but since Constantine had more pull than the mayor, certain concessions were made. We even had our own security detail, in addition to sheriff's deputies posted in the basement. Rumor had it that a Mexican gang leader had it in for Constantine because Constantine fed him a life sentence. It was said an attempt had already been made on his life the previous year.

When I arrived, I expected to be introduced to the great Constantine, whom I had heard so much about. Instead, I was given a thick file by one of the underlings with orders to familiarize myself with the case because I had co-chair. I objected, but was sternly reminded that the best way to learn something was to jump in feet-first.

For the next week, I spent every waking hour learning the case, scrutinizing the details, researching applicable case law and statutes to validate my points. When Monday rolled around, I was wired and ready.

I thought I would be working with another A.D.A., but when I strutted into the courtroom, Michael Kors briefcase in hand, the first person to greet me was the legendary Constantine Annapolis. *Talk about nervous!* We briefly conferred at our table about the case. He told me that he planned to open up, then throw me to the sharks. It was sink or swim time. I did the best I could, but only the jury would determine if my best was good enough.

I polled Constantine as we awaited the verdict at our table. "How do you think I did?"

"Great."

"You think so?" My face lit up with his praise.

"Absolutely," he assured me. "Although you may have left a lot of room for appeal. You spread the closing on a little thick. 'Still around when the cops showed up'? Damn! That was cold!" The Great Constantine smiled. "I liked it, though."

I must say, Constantine was too fine! Tall, with an olive complexion and thick, black hair slicked to the back, he was known as much for his good looks as he was for his legal prowess. Some say his good looks were one of the reasons why he was so successful in the courtroom. They say it made it easier for him to win over jurors. Although married with two children, he had a reputation as a notorious womanizer. This was my first day meeting him, and, all day, he had been shooting sparks of charisma my way.

We must have sat in silence for a half hour, getting more worried by the second. The longer the jury remained in deliberation, the lesser my chances grew. I turned to gauge the temperature of the gallery and spotted a familiar face slipping out of the courtroom. He was practically out the door by the time I realized it was him, so I didn't stop him. Besides, I wasn't sure I wanted to. Just seeing his face conjured up memories I was desperately trying to forget.

Thankfully, the word came that the jury had reached a verdict.

We all gathered ourselves and prepared for the rendering. The defendant was ushered back into the courtroom in shackles with his state-appointed handlers prodding him along. He sat uncomfortably at the defense table, scanning every face in the room, as if he sensed this was his last dose of freedom. His eyes locked on me and never wavered until the jury was led back into the room. (I could have sworn he was looking at my ass.)

Minutes later, the old, graying foreperson stood to announce the verdict. Felt like eagles were rumbling inside my belly as I awaited those words. Outwardly, I appeared stoic. Inside, my nerves were a ball of fire.

Judge Cooper's voice boomed throughout the room. "Will the defendant rise!" Constantine grabbed my hand beneath the table. "Madam Foreperson, have you reached a verdict?"

"Yes, Your Honor."

"What say you?"

I held my breath so long it was a wonder I didn't die in there. Inwardly, I felt good about the case I'd presented but you just never know with a jury. Just never know. Hard enough to get two people to come to an agreement on one subject; getting twelve is like committing a murder.

"As to count one, Armed Robbery, we find the defendant ... guilty."

I exhaled. Just a little.

"As to count two, Criminal Sexual Misconduct in the first degree ... we find the defendant ... guilty."

Under the rumble of the crowd, I exhaled a little more until all of the verdicts were announced.

Guilty on all charges.

While the bailiffs took the defendant into custody, Constantine turned to me, shook my hand, and smiled. "Congratulations, Counselor," he said. I could tell he was just as surprised as I was. I returned his smile, but my knees were still trembling from the verdict. I couldn't believe I had actually won my first case — three convictions.

As we gathered our things to leave the courtroom, the victim's family came to our table to thank me. It was as if I had saved the world. Maybe in their eyes, I *had* saved the world — their world. Each thank you they offered and each story they recounted about their son's life warmed my heart and confirmed that I was on the right track. This is what I had in mind when I elected to go into this field.

Outside, we were bombarded by the press flashing pictures and jousting microphones into our faces for comment. It was impossible for us to pass without giving in to their demands, so right there on the courthouse steps, Constantine posted up and gave a statement with me clinging to his side.

"I'd like to take this time to give my condolences to the family of Mr. Jerrod Jenkins and anyone else Mr. Roberts has victimized. Let us not lose sight of what's important here. A man perpetrated his lust on an innocent young boy! Now that little boy can rest in peace, assured that this bastard won't ever do anything like that to anyone again, thanks to Ms. Andrews here and myself ..."

While he paused to poise his thoughts, I gave the camera a straight no-nonsense glare. Inside I was reeling. I couldn't believe he had acknowledged me like that!

"Let me put all of the criminals in this great city of Charlotte on notice: No longer will we tolerate you terrorizing the innocent citizens of this great county. At this time, I am personally implementing a zero-tolerance policy. No more plea bargaining, no more deals. Game over. If you commit a crime in Mecklenburg County, you will do every second of time that the law allows."

I was vaguely listening to Constantine threaten the city while I basked in my fifteen seconds of fame, wondering how my silky chignon would look on the evening news when I heard, "Ms. Andrews?"

Ms. Andrews?!

Constantine had passed me the mic. All eyes were on me. Earlier, in the courtroom, I'd had bundles to say. Now I couldn't locate my tongue. I eventually recovered and spoke into the mic.

"I support District Attorney Annapolis 100 percent. If you commit a crime under our watch, we will bury you!"

Constantine closed with a few more remarks before we were rushed to our idling SUVs that were being driven by sheriff's deputies, then whisked over to a local diner for a bite to eat. Within minutes, we were seated and given our menus. There was myself, along with Constantine, and two other male A.D.A.s at a small rectangular table. Constantine's personal protectors stood guard at the entry and exit points of the quaint establishment like sentries while we ate. Constantine suggested I try the wings. "Best in the city," he claimed.

"I apologize for putting you on Front Street back there, Soldada," Constantine told me as we waited for our food. "I just have a lot of confidence in your ability. You proved your skills in there today, and you deserve to be acknowledged for it." He sipped his coffee while I sipped his praise. The way he sipped his coffee was even cool and classy, I noted. He placed his mug on the table and looked at me. "I've been thinking," he said. "I think I really want you to be the new face of my administration." He left those words lingering in the air, as if he'd just said he was going to the bathroom, rather than about to change my life. What was I supposed to say? He'd already beamed me into the homes of a million people with his decision to let me speak on the courthouse steps. What more could I say? Bestowing any more on me so soon would be like I was robbing someone. Refusing would be robbing myself.

I must not have given Constantine the reaction he was expecting because, as I sat in silence, he ran down his pedigree.

Constantine Annapolis was born in Greece a little over forty years ago to an Italian mother and a Greek father. His family migrated to the states when he was just seven years old. Already versed in Italian and Greek, he picked up English with no problem. Constantine never fit in in any city his parents moved to because of his swarthy looks (though he never had a problem befriending the ladies, if you hear him tell it.) His father was a sailor, so his family moved from California to Florida, eventually settling in Virginia. In Virginia, Constantine found a home. Because of the huge military presence in Virginia Beach, there was a plethora of mixed children residing there. Constantine fell in with a group of misfit mulattoes and began dabbling in petty crimes. He was eventually arrested and sent to the Job Corps. The Job Corps proved to be a life-changing experience for Constantine. He learned order and discipline, as well as discovered his penchant for debate. While at Job Corps, Constantine's father was brutally murdered on his way home from the docks. Constantine found out the news and went crazy! He tried to escape and wreak havoc on anybody he felt was responsible, but was captured before he even left his living area. Turned out he sucked as a criminal, and being captured before he could escape possibly saved his life. His counselor, Mr. Parkins planted a seed in his head that grew to be his life's ambition. He suggested that, rather than fighting crime with crime, why not fight the good fight as a prosecutor? This would allow him to honor his father's memory by preventing some other child from experiencing what he felt *and* make money. To him, it made perfect sense.

After high school, he attended Virginia's most prestigious university where he graduated at the top of his class with a degree in criminal justice. For that honor, he was awarded with a full-ride to Harvard School of Law. After graduation, he dabbled in criminal and corporate law, but found his desire in putting people away. In his mind, every time he prosecuted someone, it was his father's killer at the defense table; each time he won a conviction, he was avenging his father's murder. His tenacity quickly propelled him through the ranks, where he eventually landed a spot in Mecklenburg County as an A.D.A. It didn't take long for him to ascend to the top spot. Along the way, he amassed countless accolades, and even more enemies.

Yet, ten years into his tenure, he was still as invigorated as ever.

When Constantine concluded his story, I was amazed. We had so much in common, yet had taken such different routes to reach our destination. While he was temporarily derailed in his youth, I was the apple in my parents' eye. I told him so.

"Really? I never would've guessed." He laughed. "You're so rough around the edges," he flirted, then prodded me to reveal more of myself. To my surprise, each time I began telling him about myself, he finished my sentences for me with the correct information. I didn't know whether to be impressed or spooked that my boss knew so much about me. Of course it was common for superiors to know a lot about their subordinates, especially in the field of law. It was also common for colleagues to go out to eat and get acquainted with each other. However, this was feeling more and more like a date, especially with the looks Constantine was tossing my way. I'm a professional, but I am a woman first.

I know when a man is coming on to me.

I overlooked Constantine's intel about me and deflected his subtle advances, until he asked me about Anguilla.

I froze.

Constantine immediately honed in on my mood shift.

"Relax, Soldada." He laughed. "No need to be alarmed. A man in my position has to be able to find out everything about anyone, especially someone who is going to be so close to me."

I relaxed, just a little. "Oh, I see."

"As for your trip," he said, "I was just curious as to why you needed time off before you reported for work. Didn't think I'd be that bad, did you?"

I laughed off his comment, and sipped my drink.

He polished off his coffee, paid the bill, then we left.

A half-hour later, Constantine dropped me off at my building, a temporary hostel. I had yet to find a vehicle, so he promised to send a car for me the following morning. He bid me good night with a hug that felt a little too tight, then watched me walk into my building with that look gleaming in his eye.

I don't know why I did it. I knew he was married. Knew I had to keep certain lines clear to gain and maintain respect. Yet, I couldn't resist putting a little extra twist in my hips as I sashayed to the door.

As I slipped my key into the lock, I glanced over my shoulder. He was watching me.

Hard.

Shaun Sinclair

8

Anthony

I had been in my condo for a week, and I was loving it. Beautiful views of the city at every angle. Hardwood floors. Cathedral ceiling. Private laundry service and my own doorman who wouldn't dream of letting me burden myself with so much as a Ziploc bag.

I was definitely loving life!

I had furnished my spot with the latest in entertainment technology, and filled my closet with everything from Jordans to Gators and a whole lot in between. Needless to say, I had no worries.

I was channel-surfing on my 66-inch flat screen, looking for the game, when something on a local channel caught my eye. I turned back to the station and, instantly, my heart skipped a beat.

Soldada's face was on the screen.

I thought my mind was playing tricks on me, at first. I had been thinking about her like crazy since I'd left her that morning ... remembering how soft her skin was, how sweet she smelled, and how fresh she tasted. And the conversations we'd had were etched into my mind forever, it seemed. For a week, I fought to rid her from my psyche, but it was a losing battle.

Now here she was in my living room.

She appeared even more vibrant than I recalled (or maybe it was the pixels in my LCD television) rocking a dark blue skirt with a white satin blouse. A multicolored scarf was wrapped around her slender neck, probably to cover the multiple passion marks I'd left there. Her long silky hair was snatched back into a tight bun. Much as I hated to admit it, the transformation accentuated her beauty.

My eyes locked onto her strawberry-coated lips as she spoke, and I recalled how sensually she had sucked my dick with so much passion. Despite myself, just that fast, I was gone. Started reliving the encounter in my head. Remembered how good her pussy was, how tight the walls were. Felt the scratch marks on my back, still yet to heal.

My dick started swelling ...

Then the camera panned to the left and spoiled my day.

Soldada was standing on the courthouse steps with the district attorney, Constantine Annapolis. I despised that wetback motherfucker! Annapolis had it in for my family in the worst way. He repeatedly launched bogus inquiries on my uncle at will. In fact, rumor had it he was the reason the Bobcats deal fell through. And when I caught my robbery beef, he tried to pin the murder charge on me for that guard, even though the gun they pried from my hand was of a different caliber than the bullet the guard was killed with. When I was going to court, he kept mouthing off in the press about how I was a menace to society — never mind the fact that I didn't have a record. Funny thing about him was that everybody knew he was as crooked as a rattlesnake. (And could be just as deadly.) He was rumored to have his hands in more rackets than John Gotti in his prime.

But in Charlotte, Constantine was Teflon. Mr. Untouchable.

I could only stomach looking at the greasy bastard for so long, so I turned off my television before it became infested with germs just from his presence. If Soldada was down with him, it was best that I left what we shared down in the islands. Besides, I had to get dressed anyway.

Cadillac was taking me out for a night on the town. This was our first time out since I had come home. He had been avoiding me for some reason. Oh, he came by to check out my new spot and drop off a few items, but other than that, he was pulling a magic trick.

I had no idea where we were going, so I opted to wear a neutral outfit. A suede brown Hugo Boss two-piece suit, with soft leather Ferragamo loafers. The leather was so soft it felt like I was wearing socks. The suede on the suit was so rich, the material flapped loosely when I walked, as if the wind was blowing directly on me. I removed the satin scarf from my head and rubbed my hand over my waves. Lastly, I draped a thin platinum necklace over my head and flinched as the heavy diamond-filled lion head slapped the middle of my thick peach-colored V-neck T-shirt. Just as I was done, my buzzer sounded. Cadillac was in the lobby waiting on me.

I almost didn't recognize Cadillac when I walked into the lobby. He was dressed real sharp in a deep black Brioni suit with a cream mock-neck, complemented by two-tone gators. I knew it was Brioni because I had almost picked one up myself until I glimpsed the price tag. I was straight, but I wasn't *that* straight. His jewelry was tasteful, but I knew it was expensive. He just looked like he was getting money. As we walked outside to his black Cadillac Escalade, I thought about Uncle Roland's comment. He did look like a ballplayer.

A beautiful redbone slipped from behind the wheel to open the door for me and Cadillac. I slid in first, right behind Mona in the passenger seat.

"Hey, A.P.," Mona said as I got comfy inside the peanut butter leather seat. Soon as she flashed the pearly whites, my shit went brick. I wanted this chick *sooo* bad! But I was trying to respect Uncle Roland's wishes. This was my first time seeing Mona since Anguilla, when I saw her beautiful naked body. She looked totally different dolled up. Nothing like the dirty stripper I expected her to be because of how she presented herself to me in the islands. Looking at her now, I could see how these broads could catch niggas out there. Hell, she had me quietly fiending for a slice of that pie, and I knew she'd probably had more meat slung inside her than a deep freezer. Still, the more I admired her light skin and pretty eyes, the more I felt my sport coat turning into a cape.

Good thing Cadillac snapped me back to attention.

"So, cuz, how is everything since you been back?" he asked, as he settled in the backseat beside me and we took off.

"It's good. Can't complain," I answered evasively, still thinking about Mona.

"Hell yeah! Anything's better than being in that box, huh?"
He shuddered as if he knew what it was like to have someone
control your movements twenty-four hours a day.

"No doubt," I agreed.

"Uh-huh. Say, I saw ole girl from down the way today," he
informed me. I already knew who he was referring to.

"Yeah, I saw her, too. Big shot lawyer and shit," I
commented, my voice fading.

"I didn't know that though, cuz." Cadillac paused. He was
fishing for something; I could tell. Finally he spit it out. "Did
you hit that or what? I remember your slick ass got missing."

I was never the kiss-and-tell type, so I left his question
open, opting to change the subject.

"What's up with Dirty?" I asked. "I haven't seen him since
I've been back."

"Dirty is Dirty. On lockdown wit' the fam right now. But
check it." He leaned closer to whisper in my ear. "I want you to
go in with me on this. I need a partner to go down with me on
something."

"Something like what?" I countered, aware that Cadillac
was slicker than diarrhea.

Could you believe this nigga shushed me?

"Later," he said, and just stared out the window as if he was
dismissing a peon.

We arrived at the dinner theater, were seated directly in
front of the stage, and given a complimentary bottle of Ace of
Spades before being left alone to peruse the menu. The title of
the play for the month was *First Fruit.* From the program on
the table I learned it was about the original sin of Eve
misleading Adam in the garden. Only, this was a modern
adaptation. The play was expected to last two hours.
Throughout the play, waiters would bring different courses of
our meal for us to dine on while being entertained. Dinner
theater was somewhat new to Charlotte. Before I went away, I
used to frequent the dinner theaters in Atlanta, and this one was
on par with those, if not better.

Shortly after we selected the French course, the play began
with one man on stage, a fig leaf covering his genitals. A few

light tricks later, a woman joined him. She wore pasties over her nipples and a g-string made out of leaves.

"This dinner theater caters to adults," Cadillac informed me when he saw me scanning the room uncomfortably. I thought we were in an upscale strip club. "Don't trip when Eve gets naked. Her titties so pretty look like God himself made 'em. I should know because I picked her out myself." Cadillac took a long swig from his glass, then proudly announced to me, "I'm part-owner of this joint."

"Word?" I was shocked. Cadillac was really doing it BIG. The place was packed!

"Yeah. That's what I was talking 'bout earlier. I need your help."

Cadillac explained to me how this restaurant was demanding more of his time, and because of it, he needed help running his escort service. Initially, I wanted to decline; after all, I didn't know shit about running no hoes. Then, Cadillac told me he only needed a male presence to keep the clients in check. Supposedly, a lot of male clients exhibited their best behavior, until they had the women alone. Then they would try to force themselves on the women, make them perform acts against their will, and sometimes get physical. On a few occasions, Cadillac had to be called in to administer some "act right" on a few clients.

This was what he needed me to be available for.

"What do you mean, *be available*?" I asked, to be sure of just what he expected.

"You know, be on call for the girls, sometimes take them to their appointments, wait nearby when necessary. And if necessary …" He squeezed my biceps. " … use them big-ass guns you toting under that shirt."

I started to protest, but Cadillac shut me up when he told me how much he'd pay me.

"Five grand a week salary, *and* you don't have to work every day. I just need someone I can trust to be in my position. You've always been a stand-up dude. I don't have to worry about you mixing business with pleasure, you know? Don't have to worry about you trying to fuck all the employees." Cadillac smiled.

He must have read my thoughts. Lord knows I was thinking about laying dick to Mona that very second!

I stammered, "N-no doubt."

"So, what you say? Deal?"

"Shit! For $5,000 a week, how can I say no?"

"Cool."

It was official. I was now in the sex industry. Never was this part of my plans, but hey, life has a course of its own. Besides, the amount of money he was offering would allow me to further my real estate endeavors and line my pockets until the Queen's Quarter deal went through.

We enjoyed the play in silence until Cadillac's phone rang. He mumbled a few words into the receiver, then excused himself. He came back right around the time Eve exposed her perfect breasts.

"Yo! I gotta go handle something," Cadillac announced suddenly. He snatched the redbone, Lisa, by the arm then tossed the keys to the Escalade to Mona. "I'll get it later."

Just like that, Cadillac vanished, leaving me and Mona alone, watching a highly sexually charged play from two feet away. *Don't mix business with pleasure?* Yeah, right!

"So, Mona, where are you from?" I asked. It took every ounce of self-control I had not to look at her pretty breasts spilling from her top.

"I'm from a little bit of everywhere," she answered. "Cali. Miami. New York. My mother was a stage performer. She took me on the road with her when she performed. I attended college at UNC-Chapel Hill. I have a B.A. in mass comm. I used to slip into Charlotte to dance in the nudie bars on the weekends for money, and I fell in love with the city. I was introduced to your cousin by a mutual friend. He offered me a chance to make more money in one night than I would make in a month with my degree. Long story short, I've been a part of the team since."

Damn. So much for the small talk.

Mona eyed me in silence with an accomplished look on her face, gauging my reaction, like she was ready to shoot down anything I could spit out. Before I could speak, she rushed me again.

"A.P., let's cut the bullshit. You don't want to know where I'm from and all that. You want to fuck me, as I do you. Am I right?"

I didn't expect her to be this forward. Had to laugh off my embarrassment. "Chill, Mona, you don't even know me like that." Although she was right, I really was not trying to go there.

"Oh? I don't?" she challenged. "Let's see. Born Anthony Padmore. Parents killed when you were a baby. OD'd on heroin, if I recall correctly. Adopted by your aunt and uncle. Went to high school at West Meck. Double-sport athlete, basketball and football. Had lots of potential, but chose to *get it* in the streets. Went to prison at nineteen for robbing an armored truck ..."

Mona recounted highlights of my life like she was reading a book; meanwhile I looked on in silence. She knew too much to be just a casual acquaintance. It was almost like she was obsessed with me.

She continued, "Favorite color: purple, because it's royal. Must I go on?"

"Nah, you straight. How —"

"I know because I've been onto you for a while. I told you in Anguilla; I've heard a lot about you, and I couldn't wait to meet you. I'm a woman who knows what she wants and goes after it."

"Mona, I'm flattered, really. But I can't be with you. I don't mix business with pleasure."

She sucked her teeth. "I hope you don't believe Cadillac's whorish ass doesn't sample his goods?"

"I'm not Cadillac."

She sipped her drink. "I'm not his goods."

We engaged in an intense stare-off, neither of us bending. Then, she softened her eyes a bit and ran down her pedigree.

"I'm Cadillac's liaison; I broker deals for him. I'm basically a face for Ladies of Distinction." I couldn't see Cadillac giving such a lofty position to a former prostitute. I told her just that.

"Don't get it twisted," Mona rebuked, getting all Bomquisha on me. "I was never B or C team. I was always A team. The best. I never cracked my legs. This body is fine art. You can look all you want, but don't touch."

I titled my head. "And yet, you gonna let me fuck for free? Just like that?"

"Don't flatter yourself, A.P. It's not about you. It's about *me,* getting what I want."

Ouch. That pierced my ego.

"You ready to go?" Mona swigged the remainder of her drink, slammed it on the table, then stood to leave. "I'm tired of seeing these raggedy-ass bodies prance around. Hell, they should've hired me," she complained, arrogantly.

Our thoughts under arrest, we remained silent the entire ride to my place. Every time we passed a streetlamp, I stole a peek at Mona's smooth yellow thigh that kept escaping from her dress, as if it was too thick to be confined. Thousands of scenarios played out behind my eyes of how to get her into my bed. Just as quickly as they arrived, I banished them. I knew indulging inside her pleasure would be bad for my business.

She slid the Escalade to a halt in front of my building, left the engine idling. "Can I come up?" she asked. As much as I wanted her to, as much as I wanted to ring her bell, I had to decline.

"I don't think that'll be a good idea," I whispered, amazed that the words were coming from my mouth.

"Okay." She shrugged. "Suit yourself."

I opened the door to leave. One foot was on the pavement, the other inside the truck when she called my name. "Last chance, Anthony. I've never chased a man in my life. I'm not going to start now. I'm offering you a gift."

I fully exited the truck and walked to my building without looking back. Behind me, I heard the Escalade slowly pulled off.

As I stepped on the elevator, I couldn't help but realize how much things had changed. Here I was, a few weeks removed from beating off to airbrushed models in magazines. Now I had a real quarter throwing pussy at me like a pitcher. And I declined?

Damn.

9

SOLDADA

"Soldada, could you come in here for a second, please?" Constantine was beckoning me into his sacred space. I had been working in the D.A.'s office for a month now and had never even glimpsed past the heavy oak door leading to his office. Oh, he had entered my personal space, which amounted to little more than a modest-sized desk mimicking the four others in the office, plenty of times. Sometimes to advise, others to congratulate me on yet another job well done. Mostly, he just dropped by to shamelessly ogle me ... licking his lips, slyly rubbing his crotch every time I turned my back, taunting my senses with his expensive cologne. Please believe it, the rumors were true; Constantine was definitely a skirt-chaser! I only hoped this summons was not another of his attempts to get under mine.

I placed my foot on the threshold of his door, not ready to enter the lion's den. "Yes, sir?"

"Come in. Close the door."

I did as instructed, my eyes immediately taking in his immaculate decor. As expected, his space was laid. I was standing on hunter-green carpet, freckled with specks of gold. The massive desk stretching before me was blond-hued, the wood intricately carved into a swirl pattern. Small, gold picture frames were posted on each corner of the desk. Stacks of papers littered the desk, but somehow, it all managed to look organized. The paintings dangling from the walls were impressive, looked expensive. But the most impressive feature of the whole office was the back wall. Constantine's entire back wall, directly behind where he sat, was a floor-to-ceiling, wall-to-wall glass window offering a view of Charlotte from twenty-floors up. The sun glistened from the steel and glass skyscrapers surrounding Constantine's office. (Did I forget to mention Constantine's status allotted him — and four aides of his choosing — office space in one of the most expensive buildings in Uptown Charlotte?)

Constantine turned from gazing at the five o'clock traffic below to look at me. "Sit down."

I sat in the high-backed chair he offered. An uncomfortable silence settled between us while Constantine shifted, appearing to be weighing his words. Finally, he spoke.

"How do you like the job so far?"

I smiled cheerfully. "It's great."

"Is it everything you expected? An adventure?" I nodded. "Tell me, Soldada, do you like a challenge?"

I assumed he was referring to the job, but the way he narrowed his eyes into slits and pursed his lips effeminately while looking me over, I wouldn't have been wrong to surmise something else.

"On the job? Yes," I answered carefully.

He massaged his chiseled chin. "Um-hmm, I thought as much. That's why I moved you over here with me." Constantine loosened his turquoise-tie and rolled up the sleeves on his crisp white dress shirt. His silver Patek Phillipe watch gleamed in the light of the fading sun. He refilled his coffee mug, offered me a taste.

"No, thank you. I'd be up all night," I replied, eager to get to the point.

"Sounds fun," he quipped with a devilish smirk. I didn't bite, so he continued. "Anyway, I called you in here to discuss your future."

My ears perked up.

"Soldada, I've had my eyes on you for a long time, long before I interviewed you for this position. You're driven, focused, and not to mention, beautiful. You can go a long way in this field. Truthfully speaking, you have the potential to take my job someday, but you must be put in the right position to succeed, given the right opportunities. You understand me? That's what I'm here for." He plopped down in his green leather chair, leaned forward with his elbows on his desk, and steepled his hands underneath his chin.

He asked, "How far are you willing to go?"

"I don't understand what you mean?" *Was this the casting couch?*

"I mean, what are you willing to do to get where you want to be?"

I leaned forward in my chair, locked eyes with him. "With all due respect, Mr. Annapolis, I think my record speaks for itself. Now, I've busted my ass to achieve my goals! I sacrificed every part of my existence to ... to ... get where I am, and I would prefer to let my merit and strong work ethic get me any further."

I almost blanked out on him, took it back to the block, took it back to when I was a little girl scrounging for respect. I stopped just short of rolling my neck, but I was sure he got the point. I was nobody's whore.

Much to my chagrin, Constantine appeared unaffected by my spiel. I thought I saw a smile tug the corners of his lips as he leaned back in his chair.

"Soldada, I respect you as a woman, and I surely respect your work; otherwise, you wouldn't be here, regardless of how cute your ass is. If you are intimating that I want to get in your panties — you're right." His smile told me that I had busted him. I relaxed just a little, comfortable that my point had been made. "But that's secondary." He cocked his head to the side, raised his eyebrows, and clasped his hands together. "What is *primary* is your head in the game — no pun intended. I need you to be able to go hard or go home. What we are about to undertake may go against your personal politics, principles, and values. This isn't some college debate team or rally. This is the real world ..."

He had obviously read my files extensively. I was captain of my debate team in high school and college, and coordinator of numerous rallies for racial equality.

"In the real world, there are real situations. People really commit crimes. People really lie. And yes, people go to jail. Black people, Soldada. So if you have any qualms about putting black people in jail, I need to know now."

"No, sir."

"Soldada, I'm serious. I don't need trouble later," he warned.

"No, sir."

After he analyzed me long and hard, he said, "If you help me complete this assignment, I can promise you rapid advancement. I need objectivity. I've been on this thing for so long that I've become obsessed and biased," he explained. "However, I've just received some information pertinent to the case, info I believe will finally bring this nightmare to a close. Are you with me?"

"Absolutely, sir," I assured him, eager to learn of my new assignment.

"Good. Consider your previous assignments now terminated. I want you to familiarize yourself with this case. Research all applicable statutes, titles, case law. Look up past convictions and acquittals, cross-reference them with new decisions. I'm missing something. I know it. Maybe you can find it." He removed two folders from his desk. One about an inch thick; the other, half its size. "Get copies of everything inside these folders and return them to me ASAP. Now, you're dismissed."

I took possession of the folders and dashed from Constantine's office to the copier. I glimpsed the names on the folders and my heart galloped in my chest. Surely, my eyes were deceiving me.

The first name was foreign to me, but I knew the second name really well.

The second folder belonged to Anthony Padmore.

10

Anthony

Someone was downstairs for me.

Not many people knew where I lived, or that I was even out, so it had to be someone close. I pressed the button to let them in. Minutes later, I opened the door for Uncle Roland. He had a somber expression on his face, and his vibe was unsettling. I took his sport coat and hung it on a rack.

"Like what you did with the place here," he remarked, looking at my paintings. "Less is always more," he added, walking from room to room. I sensed he was searching for more than my decorations. He confirmed my suspicions when he asked, "You alone?"

"Yeah."

"Good. Get an old man a stiff drink and sit down," he grunted, taking a seat on my bone-white velvet sofa. "We gotta talk."

I poured a snifter of raw Hennessy and sat on the sofa next to him. "What's on your brain, Unc?"

"I met with that guy today," he said, gaining my full attention.

I muted the television. "And?"

"And things didn't go as expected. This fucking guy refuses to budge. I bent over backwards to accommodate him, and he still gave me his ass to kiss," Uncle Roland informed me. He lowered his voice, spoke as if thinking aloud. "But I realized something today. He's just a mouthpiece for someone else. Someone else with a lot of money and influence."

"How you figure?"

"Well, I had Theron check some things out. He was with me today, by the way ..."

Theron was the family lawyer. Young, sharp, and ruthless.

"Says this guy isn't holding cash like that, and his credit is shot to shit. Everything is backed by a silent partner, which means he really can't deviate from form."

"You don't know who the silent partner is?" I had to ask because Unc could get anything on anybody.

"Nope. That's why I think — no, I know — his silent partner is dirty." Unc's eyes turned obsidian as he looked at me. I could see the pain etched inside his pupils. "Anthony, I refuse to be denied on this," he vowed.

"So, what you wanna do, Unc?"

He chortled, "There's only one thing that can be done, son." I knew what that meant. As a notorious overachiever, his idea of hunting flies was with a shotgun. "I've had someone following his every move for the past week. I know where he lives, work, everything. Now, all we have to do is find someone to take the contract, and then pass the info along."

"Uh-uh." I shook my head vigorously.

"Uh-uh, what? This is the best way, A.P.! Eliminate the head and the body will fall."

"I'm not talking about that. If he gotta go, he gotta go," I shrugged my shoulders. "I'm saying, I don't feel comfortable letting someone else handle this." What I really meant was I'm not putting my freedom in no one else's hands. If I was going to expose myself to another bid, I was going to control as many options as possible.

"So what do you propose, A.P.?" Uncle Roland challenged.

I thought long and hard, but could only come up with one solution. "I'll do it," I decided.

"You'll do what?"

"I'll take care of him. Just give me the details."

Uncle Roland shook his head. "I don't know, A.P. I mean, you just came home. You don't have to get involved directly. That's the purpose of having money — to pay minions for shit like this," he reasoned.

Despite his reasoning, I knew he was really testing me, seeing if I was down for his cause. Our cause. Somehow, I felt he knew what my answer would be before he ever walked through the door. He knew I wouldn't trust my freedom to anyone else, just as he knew I wouldn't let millions slip through my thirsty palms.

"I have no choice, Unc. It has to be done and I don't trust anyone to do it right but me," I said. "Case closed."

Uncle Roland rose from the sofa, grabbing his gray sport coat. "Then it's settled."

He retrieved some papers from the inside pocket of his jacket. Tossed them to me. "Everything you need is in there. Let me know when."

And just like that, he vanished, with me contemplating the best way to pull off a murder without being caught.

~

I had been wracking my brain, pouring over the papers Uncle Roland had given me for awhile when there was another buzz from downstairs. I figured Uncle Roland had forgot something in the details, and had come back to pull my coat. I buzzed him through. Moments later, I opened my door to a surprise.

Soldada was standing there in baggy, light blue sweats with a Tarheel hat pulled low over her thin eyebrows and smoldering eyes.

"How could you not tell me, Anthony?" she spat, and stormed inside my home. Even with the hat partially obscuring her face, I could see she was upset. Hell, I could feel the heat oozing from her pores when she brushed past me!

"Well, hello to you, too. Why don't you come on in?" I joked, trying to offset her vicious mood. I was also trying to offset the fact my heart skipped a beat as soon as I saw her on my doorstep.

How did she find me anyway?

"How could you lie to me, Anthony?" She spun to face me like I was one of her witnesses on the witness stand.

I closed the door. "Whoa! Whoa! Lie to you about what?"

She placed her hands on her wide hips, rolled her neck like Bomquisha. "How come you didn't tell me you were some common criminal?"

"Ohhh! Is that what your boyfriend, Constantine, said?"

"No," she spat indignantly. "I looked it up in your file."

I shook my head. "Just couldn't leave well enough alone, huh? Brother gives you the experience of your life, no strings attached. But you gotta be a woman. Just gotta be a damn woman."

She recoiled like I'd hit her. "And what is that supposed to mean?"

"Means you came home and stalked me."

"*Stalked* you?" More recoil.

"You're standing in my home, and I don't recall giving you directions or an invitation," I pointed out. "All because you got some good dick on vacation? Just like a woman."

SMACK!

She fried my face so hard I was looking for the gun. Tried to smack me again, but I caught her wrist before it reached my face. She flung her other hand. Caught that, too. Spun her around and pulled her to me in a lax chokehold.

"Let me go!" she pleaded, her chest heaving. I smelled peppermint on her breath each time she exhaled on my hand.

"Calm down," I pleaded, loosening my reins a little. She fought me, so I tightened my grip again. We were at a stalemate. "This is not what I had in mind when I thought about seeing you again," I whispered through clenched teeth. "Now, calm down."

"Don't tell me to calm down! And what did you have in mind, huh? Didn't think I'd find out about you?" she scoffed. "Exactly what did you have in mind?"

"This." I spun her around before she realized what was happening and planted a juicy one on her lips, just as I had fantasized about doing so many nights since I'd left her in Anguilla, pining. She resisted, so I raised the intensity. She became putty in my hands, returning my kiss with more passion than I was giving.

My manhood rose through my sweats.

She finally wrested away from me and pushed away. "This ... is ... not what I came here for." She wiped saliva from her bottom lip and attempted to turn away, but I cupped her chin between my thumb and forefinger.

"I missed you, Soldada," I told her with urgency in my eyes. "I can't get you out of my head. It's killing me ..." I pulled her closer. Our ritual resumed. We kissed hard and deep. Like long-lost lovers, trapped in an inferno.

"I missed you, too ..." she admitted, between kisses. "I can still feel you ... inside ... me ... filling me up." She moaned through kisses. "Please ... please ... make love to me, Anthony ... right here ... right now," she pleaded, tugging at my sweatpants.

In seconds, our clothes lay bunched up in a pile at our feet.

We kissed and fondled each other incessantly, re-familiarizing ourselves with each other's crooks and curves. Soldada gripped my stiffness. Guided me toward her wet opening. Rubbed the head at the tip of her opening. Shared heat. Shared passion. Scratched her itch with my hard desire. Doused me with her feminine flares.

I spun her around. Laid a trail of kisses down the back of her neck. Tasted strawberries. She begged me to enter. Begged me to fill her up. Begged me to fuck her.

"*Damelo, Papi. ¡Ahora mismo! Damelo. Por favor ...*"

Soldada kept repeating that Spanish shit over and over. I had no idea what the fuck she was saying, but the melody chimed in my ear and reverberated, inciting me to more action. I bent her over and gripped the soft curves of her ass, kneaded them like pizza dough a few times, then spread them wide. Her womanly scent seeped out and massaged my nostrils, strong yet sweet, as her juices flowed freely onto my hardwood floor. My mouth watered. Slowly, I entered her. Plowed through the tight objections of her body. Reversed my stroke.

"Ooooooh ... Anthony ... *dame mas,*" she purred.

I plowed through her tight tunnel again, all the way to the hilt. Soldada shrieked. Soldada shivered.

But she did not stop me.

I stroked slow and hard. She bucked back into me, growling like an animal.

"*Si ... hay! Dame ... damelo,*" she growled in Spanish again, taking me there.

So I took her there. Gripped her small waist between my hands, pounded harder. She spread her legs wider for more balance. I rode her harder and harder until we almost slipped on the clothes we had cast aside. This disturbed our groove. I slipped out of her, cursing like a motherfucker!

"Lay down! Hurry! Lay down," I urged her.

Soldada laid on her back on the waxed floor. The initial chill made her jerk. I placed our clothes beneath her, then turned her on her side. Placed one leg on my shoulder, the other extended between my legs.

I entered her again.

Looked into her beautiful face as I pushed deep inside of her. Revealed my fuck faces to her. Allowed her to see my face contort each time she squeezed my dick with her vaginal muscles. I was as vulnerable as a newborn baby. Lost inside wetness. Pumping furiously.

I thumbed her clit and pulled her into me with my right hand planted on the small of her back. My mission was to turn Soldada out. Make her feel for me more than I felt for her. Make her heart skip a beat when she saw me. Drown her in lust.

She reined me in deeper, her center already cosmic. What she was doing with her muscles was plain unfair.

I attempted to even the odds. Rolled her over on her back. The double-lock-butthole-roll. Hammered her pussy like I was John Henry. Lightning in my eye. She took it like a goddess, spitting that Spanish shit in my ear. Neither of us climaxing. Both trying to outlast the other.

Then, she wanted to get on top.

I laid on my back, my dick sticking up like a lighthouse guiding the way. She mounted me, slowly controlling the depth of penetration. "You want this, Anthony?" she whispered, slowly rolling her hips like a snake. Her feet were planted on opposite sides of my body, her legs, wide open, offering me a microscopic view of her pretty pussy. Shawty didn't have that lunch-meat-looking shit. Her lips were perfectly symmetrical and intact. Above her navel, her six-pack glistened with slivers of sweat, flexing hard each time she gyrated. Above her six-pack sat perfect breasts. Large areolas and deep brown nipples that looked hard enough to cut diamonds. Looked harder than what she was riding. I tried to look away before I got caught up, but Soldada was relentless. She sank all that wet-wet down on me like a blanket, then eased her way back up slowly, pausing with just my tip inside, then squeezed like a python. I was trying to let her get off first, being the unselfish lover and all, but after she pulled that move one time too many, I left my babies swimming inside her womb. Seconds later, she unleashed a river upon me, then collapsed onto my chest, exhausted.

I hadn't been home but a few months, and already, I was falling in love.

Soldada

I woke up with my mouth parched and my head befuddled.

Where was I?

I moved around a bit, and felt my answer. Anthony's naked body was behind me, connected to me, actually. We were spooning in our sleep. He was still asleep. Each time he exhaled, he blew into the top of my damp hair, causing me to shudder like fallen leaves in a light wind. I had no idea how we came to be in this position. I definitely recalled us having sex. Hell, the dull ache between my legs wouldn't allow me to forget that tidbit. What I didn't remember was how we ended up in his massive, soft, four-poster bed.

I glimpsed the clock and panic began to set in. Six-fifteen. I didn't have much time. I was expected at the office at eight a.m. to start research on my new assignment.

Oh, shit! My new assignment.

It came flooding back like a tsunami. Anthony and his uncle *were* my new assignment.

I had rushed over here to confront him about all the nasty things I'd found inside his file: The dead bank guard with his brains blown out, the $1.5 million in loot, his crooked family … I'd come to let him know I despised everything he stood for.

Instead … I just came. Literally.

81

I eased my way from under his warm body and out of bed. The glass door leading to the balcony was open, permitting the cool October breeze to permeate the room. I followed the welcoming breeze onto the balcony, letting it caress my naked body. As I looked fourteen floors down at the light dawn traffic, I attempted to make sense of my situation. No matter how I sliced it, the apple still came up sour.

The biggest assignment of my young career predicated its success on the demise of a man I had fallen for. I realized I was being given a golden opportunity that often didn't come twice in life. If I turned it down, I was a fool. More importantly, if I reneged on the job, I would open myself to scrutiny. I could always warn Anthony about the investigation surrounding him, but that would be highly unethical — if not illegal. It would also sink any advancement opportunities I envisioned for myself. My mind said, *"Fuck Anthony. Burn him."*

But my heart was singing a different tune. I couldn't deny the fact I felt something for this man.

"Beautiful view, huh?" I hadn't heard Anthony walk up behind me. He wrapped his heavy arms around me. "Like déjà vu, huh?" he whispered in my ear, his semi-flaccid penis poking me in my back. His comment brought flashes of Anguilla speeding through my head. I'd never had as much fun in my life as I'd had in Anguilla.

But Anguilla was another time. Another place.

He asked, "Cold? You're shaking." He hugged me tighter. Kissed the back of my ear.

"Stop, Anthony. We need to talk." I turned to face him.

"Uh-oh, those are the four most dreaded words in a woman's vocabulary," he chimed. "But before you speak, let me say what I gotta say." He gripped my waist. Pulled me so close I inhaled his morning breath. Smelled like liquor and shrimp.

"Whatever you are going to say isn't going to change anything, Anthony, so please just let me get —"

"I'm falling in love with you."

"— This out. Wait. Now what now? What did you say?"

He took a deep breath, found my eyes. "I said, I'm falling in love with you," he repeated. His sincerity chilled my bones so quickly I had to turn away. "Soldada, did you hear me?"

"Yes, Anthony, I heard you," I snapped. "And this is bullshit! I mean, let's be real, okay? We have great sex. But that does not equate to love. So let's not do this."

I had scarred him. I could tell. I had cheapened his admission. Left him feeling vulnerable and deflated. His silence was deafening. Wisps of wind wafted up, brought the scent of bacon and eggs from somewhere below.

Visibly frustrated, he asked, "Why are you doing this, Soldada? I know you feel this chemistry between us. It's undeniable. Why try to deny it?"

"Because I can't love you back!" I screamed, bursting into tears like a big ole baby. I clasped my hands to my face, trying to catch the tears before they hit the ground. But I'm not an octopus. Didn't have enough hands.

"Come 'ere." Anthony buried my face into his hard chest while I bawled like a newborn. "Talk to me, baby. Fuck what you heard. We can make this work. Fuck Constantine and his bitch-ass! He ain't nobody. Fuck is he? Fuck kind of name is Constantine anyway? And why did you tell him about us?"

I shook my head, still buried deep into his chest. "I didn't," I mumbled, barely decipherable.

"Well, why was he talking about me? Why did he show you my file? Why did ..." He paused mid-sentence, like he was coming upon an epiphany. "Aww, fuck!" he hissed, as the picture came into focus. "Tell me it's not so, baby ... naw ... it can't be ..." He fished my head out, looked in my face. His eyes held a thousand questions. The one of primary importance was already inferred. He didn't even have to ask.

I nodded my head slowly while blood from my soul streamed down my face. My strong affection for him prompted me to betray my covenant without a second thought.

He pushed me away from him and turned his back to me. "You would stoop that low? To sleep with me again to further your investigation?" He floated the question lightly, but its weight was a ton.

"Of course not! I'm nobody's whore!" I snapped indignantly. "I just received the assignment a few hours ago."

"And what's your assignment? To put me back in a cage? For what?"

"Did you kill that bank guard?" I retorted, eager to know the answer to what had been gnawing at me since I cracked open that file. "Did you blow that poor man's brains out? For money? He had two little kids, Anthony! Please tell me you didn't do that?" I was searching for a sign, something to let me know he wasn't as evil as his file suggested. Something to tell me I hadn't fallen for an animal.

"You read the file," he replied with nonchalance, not exactly admitting it, nor denying it.

"Well, Constantine is convinced you killed that guard. Said if the feds hadn't intervened, you'd be in prison for life. Said the guard was a friend of his. That's why he wants you so bad."

"Fuck Constantine!" he raged. The tremors from his words reverberated through my body like an earthquake. "That racist fuckin' wetback!"

"Greek."

"What?"

"I said, he's Greek."

"I don't give a fuck what boat the muthafucka rode in on! He's not an American!" Anthony barked. "And so what? You riding with him now? What about me? My family? It's just fuck us now, huh?"

"I honestly don't know," I admitted.

"And you believe everything Constantine says?"

His tone was detached. Mechanical. Felt like he was lawyering me. He obviously was analyzing every syllable I uttered.

"Of course not, Anthony." I sighed, clutching my forehead. I felt a migraine coming on. "It's just that my career is all I have. I sacrificed everything to get where I am, and as much as I would love to be with you ... I know I can't. Our respective stations in life would never permit it."

I felt *so* stupid baring that truth. Here he was, the man of my dreams, discovered in paradise, rediscovered in reality. Only, fate wouldn't allow us to be together.

Only fate could be so cruel.

"For God's sake, Anthony, I work for the man sworn to bring you down!" I exploded, my inner thoughts coming to the surface. "What do you want me to do?"

He faced me with his eyes watering. Stroked my chin with his hot thumb. I caught the faint scent of my nectar lingering on his fingertips.

"Do what you must, Soldada," he selflessly suggested. "You worked your whole life for a chance like this. I can't ask you to defer your dreams for me. I know what it's like to have your dreams deferred." His voice cracked through the brave façade he was trying to project. "It was fun while it lasted," he told me. "But like you said, it can't go on."

"Anthony, wait ..." My pleas hit his back as he left me in the brisk morning air, my body shivering. It wasn't because of the weather either.

Sometime later, I joined Anthony in the shower. As candles burned from their multiple nests surrounding the cylindered glass enclosure, Adele crooned through the speakers built inside the shower walls, punctuating our moment like only she could. No words needed to be spoken. We both knew this was good-bye. There would be no more turning tables; this was the end. Work be damned, I took my time caressing, stroking, sucking, and receiving Anthony, as the four powerful shower-heads washed away all our transgressions.

When we were done, he dried me off lovingly with a warm towel, taking time to admire every inch of my nakedness that dripped with water. He patted my forehead with the thick towel, then suddenly cupped my chin. His gaze burrowing into my damp eyes, he calmly told me, "Soldada, I hate to spoil your career, but ... I'll die before I go back to prison. And I'll murder anyone and anything trying to take my uncle away from our family. So, there you have it ... you've been warned."

Yep. I'd been warned. If only it were up to me.

Shaun Sinclair

11

Anthony

It had been two weeks since Soldada dropped her bomb on me. Needless to say, that stalled my plans to handle that little piece of work I'd planned with my uncle. Of course, my uncle was alerted about the investigation immediately. I relayed everything I knew, neglecting to tell him the source. Predictably, he already knew about the investigation. In fact, he'd known about it for quite some time. However, he hadn't known of my inclusion, although he didn't appear to be too shocked about that either. As he had explained it, the guard that was killed during the heist that sent me to the slammer was a friend of the D.A.'s. No one paid for the murder. I was the only one convicted in connection with the robbery. That meant, as long as the D.A. had breath, he would be a threat to me. Uncle Roland advised me not to worry. To keep doing what I was doing, and things would be okay, but I wasn't too convinced.

As for the other thing I was supposed to do, it was officially terminated. There was no way I could pull off something of that magnitude knowing there was a chance I was being watched at all times. No matter how much I insisted, Unc wouldn't turn me loose. We were forced to outsource the job to some of the crazy-ass Mexicans that Mo fucked with. We weren't too pleased about it, but we had no other choice. Mo would be our intermediary. All orders would go through him. They wouldn't know who was paying. We wouldn't know who we were paying. Mo was our only degree of separation.

In the meantime, I continued to work for Ladies of Distinction. I really didn't have a position, though I was labeled as vice president. My duties consisted of monitoring everything

— from the firm's accounts (and accountants) to the clients and employees themselves. I didn't think I'd like the job, but it turned out to be straight. After my first week there, I could see why Cadillac didn't have a problem paying me so much money. He made the funky little 5K he was paying me a week in one date. If one of the A-team broads were dating, he'd make double that!

I later learned his secret to why he was caking off so much after having lunch with Mona one day. As she explained it, Cadillac had all of his "employees" on salary (except the C-team because they fluctuated so much.) The ten girls from the A-team received $7,000 a month. The ten B-team girls received $5,000 a month. The C-team paid 50 percent of everything to the agency.

It didn't seem fair to me that the girls, who did the most, received the least. I inquired about why it was this way.

"People always want what they can't have," Mona explained, sounding like a pimp herself. "Make them *think* they can have it, and they'll keep coming back for more. Give it to them and they'll have no need to return. The more money a man has, the greater the challenges he desires. The wealthier clients are willing to pay more for what's unattainable, in hopes that they can be the one to crack the barriers. It's all about the challenge," she concluded, then shrugged as if it was nothing.

"You seem to know the game pretty well. Is that how you do it?" I asked her.

"Excuse me?" She sounded offended.

"I said, are you A-team, B-team, or —"

"How many dates have you seen me go on, A.P.?" she snapped.

I gave it some thought. "None. Come to think of it."

"Exactly."

After seeing her reaction, I didn't make the mistake of mentioning her and the teams in the same sentence again.

Mona and I continued to work side by side in the office, as well as on dates. Some of our clients had been known to get a little heavy-handed with our women in the past, so when those same clients solicited our services again, rather than turn the money away, we provided protection for the girls. Because we didn't want to involve outsiders in our business, I became the enforcer by default.

Mona and I would shadow dates, out of sight and sound, to allow privacy. We posed as a couple ourselves, venturing to the same spots as the customers and our girls. I kept a clear line-of-sight to the tables, just in case the dates wanted to act up. I only had to administer some discipline once on a drunk, old dude. I felt kinda bad tossing pops through the air into that dumpster behind the restaurant, but he had to learn. He must have spread the word around quickly because I didn't have to scuff up my wingtips anymore after that.

Working at Ladies of Distinction was a real eye-opening experience for me. I was surprised at how sick some of these rich muthafukas could be! They didn't want sex in regular places. They wanted the kinky shit. Broads sucking them off during plays. Eating the women out under the table at fancy restaurants and shit. But hey, I couldn't knock it though. You wanted a little fish with your salad? Cool. Just pay extra for the side dish. As long as they were paying the price, I couldn't give a fuck about the vice. As long as they weren't harming the girls, I wasn't harming them. Those were my rules. Simple as that.

As could be expected, the more time Mona and I spent together, the more our undeniable attraction for each other simmered. At first I tried to curb my attraction, but seeing Mona in so many different ways bludgeoned my self-restraint with the quickness.

I tried everything to numb my attraction, make her less appealing to my eyes. Crushing on Mona was bad for business. I knew this, so I tried to substitute my attraction by other means.

I became a regular at the strip joints.

The Gold Club. Uptown Cabaret. Diamonds. Pleasure. Me and Mo made it rain in all them muthafuckas. We even shot down I-85 to Atlanta on a few occasions. Took home the baddest broads from those joints and fucked their brains out. Did all the shit I heard cats in the joint talk about. Two and three chicks at a time.

But none of it worked. I still desired Mona.

More to my dismay, when I finally decided to make my move, Mona shot me down like CPD. Hit me with my own line: *I don't mix business with pleasure.*

Ooooh, I was heated! To make matters worse, she was really fucking with me. Started wearing more and more provocative clothes into the office, rubbing that soft ass against me every time she needed to get to the copier. And I swear, it looked like her skirts were losing inches by the day! As we went over paperwork, she'd lean over the desk with them pretty titties spilling out of her top, showing just a hint of her red nipples, looking at me, batting her eyes like a mermaid. I wanted to bend her over my desk and fuck fire out of her!

One night we attended a black-tie banquet, shadowing one of the A-team girls, Sabrina, on her date. When the limo I rented pulled up to Mona's place, she stepped out looking like Aphrodite in a black satin Prada dress that stopped just above her knees. The dress hugged her body like a second-skin. The gem-encrusted, thin spaghetti straps gleamed like stars when the streetlamps hit it. On her pedicured feet were black satin pumps with four-inch ice pick heels, studded with crystals also. As I helped her enter the limo, I noticed she didn't have panties on. Not even a G-string. The satin hugged her curves unimpeded, like she came out of her mother's womb with it on.

Inside the limo, Mona was up to her tricks again. She didn't sit beside me; she sat across from me, using every opportunity to get her Sharon Stone on. When she reached over to the mini-bar to pour herself a drink, she left her shiny legs open, granting me an eagle-eyed view of her neatly trimmed cat. When she was sure I'd had an eyeful, she gently closed her legs with a smile, leaned back into the plush leather, and stared me down with lust in her eyes while sipping her drink.

At the banquet, poor Sabrina could've been getting gang-raped by every swinging dick in the place, and we wouldn't have been none the wiser. Mona and I sat teasing each other during the whole meal while some anal-retentive speaker droned on and on about county spending. Midway through the banquet, we excused ourselves. We ended up at the end of a dark hallway fawning all over each other. I was able to dip my finger inside her hot wetness for a millisecond before she snatched my hand out and put that same finger in my mouth.

Tasted so sweet, I moaned like I was eating pie.

"Come on. Let's go," I told her.

Throwing Sabrina to the wolves, I led Mona back to the limo. Gave the driver directions, then dived on her in the backseat. She ripped my tuxedo jacket off, and begged me to finish what I started, begged me to taste her pussy. She rested her head on the door, gaped her legs open for me, and smiled. I slid her dress up her wide hips and opened her up with my fingers.

Her scent perfumed the car.

The soft lights running the length of the car's roof illuminated the path like a runway. I paused briefly to admire heaven in the form of a woman.

Heaven was wet. Waiting ...

I licked a path from the inside of her thigh and followed the drip. Flicked my tongue like a snake. Saturated my tongue inside her tightness. Swirled figure-eights on her button. Buried my face in her thick cum. Smiled when some of her juices got stuck in my nose. Savored it. Did everything I wanted to do to her since that first day in Anguilla.

When I was certain Mona was good and ready, I didn't bother to remove my pants. I pulled my wood through my fly and tried to penetrate her raw dog. Mona grabbed my wood in a vice grip.

"What're you doing?" she gasped. "We can't do this."

"What? Why?" I pleaded, determined to seal the deal.

The limo skid to a halt beneath us, just as Mona slid from beneath me.

"Because ..." she panted, pulling her dress down. I could see the sexual tension bleeding through her face. "I don't mix business with pleasure. Remember?"

Mona bolted from the limo into her building before I could stuff my dick back inside my pants and give chase. Left me salivating on the taste of her femininity.

Damn.

Later, as the limo crept through the late-night Charlotte traffic en route to my condo, I couldn't hide my smile. The girl had game. However, unknown to her, Mona's shenanigans were a welcome distraction from my torturous thoughts of Soldada. I hadn't heard from her since the morning she'd left my spot in tears, and every second, I longed for her more and more. I thought about her every free moment I had.

Except when I was with Mona.

As I enjoyed the comfy ride back to my plush home, Mona's words reverberated inside my head. *"Make them think they can have it, and they'll keep coming back for more. Give it to them, and they'll have no need to return."*

I still tasted her pussy in my mouth.

Guess that meant I would be coming back for more.

12

Soldada

This case was making me sick! Not only was it preventing me from tossing thoughts of Anthony out of my head, it was also wracking my brain. I started out with Anthony's file because it was the smallest. Yet, it consumed more of my time than I'd ever anticipated.

Enclosed inside the file was a copy of the court proceedings that sent him to federal prison. The more I read (and reread) the proceedings, it became clear he was protecting someone.

The only questions were who and why.

The only thing more sickening to me than the time the case occupied was the case itself. The case was bundled at every step of the way, from the second they peeled Anthony's stiff, bloody body from the pavement. They never even gave him medical attention — not even a Band-Aid — for his wounds. (Luckily for him, he was wearing illegal body armor.) From the scene of the crime, they stuffed him into a jail cell, unattended, for sixteen hours straight. The only time he was acknowledged was when department photographers ventured to his cell to take pictures. He never received a phone call, never was Mirandized, and never given a chance to contact his attorney. After three days, the family attorney finally managed to bust through the barricade, and stormed MCDC with a barrage of questions.

It was apparent that, throughout the three days Anthony was in custody, he was tortured for information, coerced into statements, and threatened repeatedly. One strange thing I noticed was that Constantine himself was directly involved throughout the entire debacle. Constantine spearheaded the orders to the detectives prior to Anthony's arraignment, but after the arraignment, it seemed he mysteriously disappeared (from the record anyway). When the feds intervened, usurping jurisdiction from Constantine, he went ballistic! He desperately tried to gain special consideration from the courts to retain jurisdiction, arguing that the charge of Murder outweighed the Robbery. He was denied at every juncture. The courts ruled that, since Anthony had pled guilty in federal court to Robbery, Possession of a Firearm during the Commission of a Felony, and Illegal Possession of Body Armor (during the act of a violent crime), the federal government retained jurisdiction of the case, and by extension, Anthony.

Not to mention, there was insufficient evidence to support a murder charge.

Constantine pitched a fit, but in the end, there was nothing he could do. An accessory charge was moot also since the story Anthony was selling amounted to "he was robbing the truck alone when someone shot him." According to him, the next thing he recalled was waking up in a cell. There was no one to refute his story, so it stuck like Velcro.

My job was not to catch Anthony in a lie back then. My job was to find statutes or cases that would allow us to charge him with something, anything, now. The only thing he was ever charged with in the State was murder; therefore we could charge him with anything, including murder, free of double-jeopardy concerns, since a jury was never convened to decide the murder charge.

A part of me was hoping I wouldn't find anything amid all my research, but my instincts told me, where there was smoke, there was fire. As tenacious as I could be, my resolve was weakened every time I glimpsed the cubicles of my wall. Photos of Anthony were posted everywhere. Most were pre-prison. He was considerably smaller, but still very handsome. Some were as recent as a few days ago. Those were the ones that sent my heart aflutter. To my colleagues, it seemed like the pictures were posted for motivation.

In truth, I liked to look at his handsome face and amazing body, and reminisce about the stolen moments we'd shared.

His smile was medicine, his eyes a disease. Even as a youth, his steely gaze was already intact. Every time I looked at his pictures, my heart skipped a beat, and my vagina thumped in memory. When I was sure no one was looking, I caressed the photos, all the while wondering to myself ...

What if?

What if I made the wrong decision? What if I sacrificed my happiness for a job? What if Anthony Padmore was really the man for me?

After combing over so many cases, I was seeing numbers and names in my head. I was eager for a break. Luckily, Constantine came to my rescue. He peeked his head around my cubicle and barked, "Freeze!"

"You startled me!" I shrieked my hand on my chest.

"Good." He smiled, all of his big, white teeth glowing. "No more work for today. That's an order. Tidy up. We're going out."

I weakly tried to protest, although there was nothing I needed more than a break.

Thankfully, he would hear none of it.

"For-get it, Soldada. This is not a negotiation," he said sternly, pulling me from my chair. "We pull out in twenty minutes."

"Twenty minutes? Where are we going?"

"To the game. Kobe is in town tonight."

~

We had seats on the second row of the arena, damn near on the floor, across the court from the Bobcats players' benches. Looking at all the people in their jeans, sweat suits, and fancy jackets, I almost felt overdressed in my linen slacks, cowl-neck cashmere sweater, and camel-colored heels. Fortunately, my colleagues were dressed up as well. Constantine, in his ubiquitous tailored pinstripe suit, the other two ADAs in their dress pants and expensive shirts and shoes. I didn't regard security as part of our entourage. They deftly disappeared into the crowd, framing a circumference with us in the middle, as soon as we reached our seats.

We sat down just as the second quarter was beginning. Kobe had already scorched the Bobcats for eighteen points in the first quarter. It looked to be a long night for the home team.

"Soldada, hope you don't mind being the single wheel on our boys' night out," Constantine apologized, signaling for popcorn.

"No, actually, this is a treat. I'm a huge basketball fan."

"Really? Well, anytime you want to come to a game, let me know. I got carte blanche with the team."

"That's good to know. I'll be sure to hit you up when Lebron comes to town."

"Lebron?" Constantine scoffed. "You mean the dumb cock who set a whole franchise back?"

"The one and the same." This guy never quit! He may have been charismatic in the courtroom, but he was a pure brute outside of it.

"Well, I'll tell ya, he's one talented stud on the court, but off it, he's just a common thug. Guess it's true what they say ..."

"What's that?"

"You can take the nigger out the ghetto, but you can't take the ghetto out the nigger."

"Phew!" I spit my drink out. *No, he didn't!* I'd heard people say that about Iverson before, but they were black. This was so ... different ... so incendiary coming from his white mouth.

"Oh, I'm sorry. Did I offend you?" he asked innocently, as if he hadn't just docked two centuries off the night.

"Of course not," I retorted. "Why would I be?"

"Good. I mean, don't get me wrong. I'm glad blacks have a way out the ghetto and all, I just think it stinks that they squander it away by trying to 'keep it real.'" He formed quotation marks with his fingers. "And I say this as unbiased as possible because I'm not a racist. Of course, I don't have to explain this to you. You know I'm no racist."

Of course not. After all, you've been trying to get my sweet black pussy since the first day we met. Before I could say anything, the Bobcats' center blocked Kobe's dunk, setting up a fast break. When the starting guard for the Bobcats threw down his dunk, the crowd erupted, prompting a timeout by the Lakers.

Simultaneously, my phone chirped. It was my new friend Carlo, beckoning my attention. Carlo was also known as Cadillac, the bugger I'd met while on vacation in Anguilla. He had tracked me down in the States, and began calling my office. Through a few phone conversations, he had, indeed, redeemed the blunder we shared in Anguilla. However, now was not a good time to talk, so I sent the call to my voice mail, and redirected my attention to the court.

Actually, my attention was suddenly diverted past the basketball court toward the Bobcats bench, for sitting directly behind the bench was Anthony. A dark blue snap-back hat was pulled low over his eyes and a gold hued mink bomber was swallowing his nice frame. And yes, the globes dangling from his earlobes were blinding me from a distance; however I could definitely tell it was him, sitting there cheesing it up with some high-yellow heifer.

Wow! Weeks of steely resolve sank like the Titanic.

~

Anthony

My beloved Bobcats were getting punished by the Lakers, but they were starting to show some promise. The momentum quickly shifted as our All-Star point guard threw down a monstrous dunk. Truthfully, I was just happy to have my face in the place. I'd always been a huge basketball fan, and was plain sick when my Hornets relocated to New Orleans. Fortunately, the Bobcats came to town, and I immediately adopted them as my new team. Because I was in the clinker all those years, I'd never had a chance to see them play live until now. Apparently, one of the Bobcats players had used our services before, and had fallen in love with Mona. Seems when she told him she didn't date clients that bolstered his confidence. He pursued her with flowers and season tickets to all the home games, hoping she would come around. I guess he finally got his wish. She finally showed up at one of his games.

Too bad she came with me.

We weren't out on a *date* per se, but we weren't exactly *just friends* anymore either. We stopped being that when she left her flavor lingering in my mouth. I still hadn't hit yet, but I knew it was just a matter of time. I had been acting disinterested for the past few days, but shit was starting to get old. I had quarters throwing panties at me daily, and I had to chase Mona?

But there was also another reason I was at the game.

Tonight was the night Mo and his Mexicans were supposed to handle that piece of work. Just in case the authorities were following us, we were spending our evening in a very public place. Uncle Roland was at the game also, more than likely seated inside the skybox. We figured if we split up, the authorities would have to work that much harder. Meanwhile, we would be busy enjoying our lives.

"Get him, Kobe!" Mona screamed out, next to me. She was really having a ball.

I looked at her with my mouth twisted, "You better get away from me rooting for that soft-ass nigga."

"Ah-ha, don't hate." Mona waved her hands all in my face, her smile brighter than the arena lights. Her brown hair was pulled up into a ponytail, putting her high cheekbones on display. Large, gold hoop earrings hung from her ears, and her pouty lips were glazed with a light coat of lip gloss. Her ponytail was twisted into a long braid that extended past her bare shoulders to the middle of her black Baby Phat vest. Skintight Baby Phat jeans were stuffed inside of black, knee-high crocodile-skinned boots that cost about ten racks. Mona looked like a supermodel, and I felt a tinge of pride just being with her. Felt like a star myself.

The dude she gleaned the tickets from was staring at us so hard, he couldn't even focus on his game. His teammates were staring at us also, envy apparent in their eyes. They weren't even focusing on the clipboard with the Xs and Os drawn up. They were too preoccupied with Mona. I raised my jaw in a silent salute, forcing them to pay homage to me while I put on for them with Mona.

"I ain't hating," I coolly responded to Mona, my eyes still beamed on the players. "I just think dude is a bitch. That's all."

"Why, because he's rich?"

I sucked my teeth. "Please. I would never hate on the next man's chips, especially when I got my own. I been had bread," I reminded her.

"Yeah, I know, Jesse James."

"Ohhh, you went there!" I grabbed her in a headlock, laughing along with her. She tried to push me away, but I stuck my face down by her ear and taunted her. Then suddenly, her face popped out and met mine. Before I could move, our lips met. It was awkward at first, but we both loosened up and went with the flow. The kiss only lasted a few seconds, but it felt like a lifetime. I heard the crowd erupt in applause, so I thought the game had resumed. When I broke our kiss and looked around, all eyes were on the Jumbotron. I looked up and saw that we were on it.

Mona's eyes followed mine. She giggled, "Let's give them something to really look at." She kissed me again, more passionately this time. More applause rained on us, and for a brief moment, we had usurped the attention of the crowd.

For the remainder of the game, we held hands and exchanged pecks periodically. I couldn't wait for the game to end, so I could see what was really good. My dick was ready to bust through my $400 jeans.

With two minutes left in the game, and the Bobcats leading, my cell started buzzing incessantly. It was Uncle Roland.

"'Sup, Unc?" I chirped into the phone, my tone riding the winds of happiness.

"Meet me at the B parking section. Something's come up," he ordered. Just by his tone, I could tell something serious had occurred.

"Aiight. I'll be there in about ten minutes."

"Now, A.P.! Fuck this game. We leaving *now*." Click.

I grabbed Mona's hand. "We gotta go," I told her, pulling her up.

"What? It's only a minute and a half left!"

"Don't matter. We leaving now." She must have sensed the urgency in my voice because she stood to follow me with no more questions asked.

We were almost to the exit at the end of the hall leaving the arena when I felt a hand grab my shoulder. I spun around, ready for action, but before I could make any moves, I was thrust back into the wall and pinned there by some burly white dude that couldn't have been anything other than a cop.

"Yo! What the fuck?" I bellowed. To my right, Mona tried to intervene, but big-man held her off with a stiff arm long enough for another big dude to stand in front of her, creating a wall between Mona and myself. Recognizing I was outmanned and overpowered, I repeated my question with more authority, then barked a mean threat that went unnoticed. My heart raced as I attempted to make sense of the situation. I knew these two white dudes weren't about to beat me, not in front of all these people. Dude had me pinned good, though. I couldn't budge!

A million scenarios sprinted through the tracks of my mind, none of them making sense. A crowd began to gather around us. A few brothers slowed like they were ready to spring to my aid. The second burly dude whipped around and snatched his black jacket open.

They sped past, and didn't look back.

I didn't have to see what was inside to know what was there. That was a universal conversation.

Dude was packing heat.

"Calm down," the first burly dude suggested with more pressure on my throat. "My employer wants to speak with you."

Before I could gather the words to tell him to go fuck his employer, bitch-ass Constantine strolled up with his hands clasped behind his back, looking like he was big shit. Two flunkies were trailing him, and someone else hid in the shadows behind them.

"What's up, Anthony? Or should I say A.P.?" Constantine smirked, looking around the chunks of muscle I now deduced were cops. "How's freedom treating you?"

"Fuck you!" I spat with venom.

"Oh, you are going that route now? Knew it wouldn't take long in there to make you switch teams, but I'll pass. Men still screw women out here in the free world," he retorted. "Course, you've been away so long you probably forgot how good a woman feels." He jerked his thumb in Mona's direction and winked at me. "I see you're trying to play catch-up though."

That pissed me off for some reason. "Greasy bastard!" I barked. "You real tough with your goons around. Catch you by yourself and I'll —"

My words got caught in my throat as the flunkies moved closer and revealed the other person who stood in the shadows. Constantine thought he had intimidated me, but it was his other companion that had numbed me to silence.

He came closer and gripped my chin. "You'll do what? Huh? Say it. You'll do what?" he taunted, trying his best to provoke me to crack his jaw. "Do me like you did that guard?"

I remained silent, my eyes riveted on who had emerged from the shadows. Her face was poker, but her eyes could not belie the hurt she refused to express. The same hurt had surfaced when she left my place that morning, the morning she chose her career over me.

The morning she told me her job was to put me back in a cage.

"I didn't do anything to that guard!" I hissed, more for her benefit than his. "Now let me go."

"Let you go? I should —"

"No, Constantine! Not like this." Soldada piped up, coming to my rescue. *Or so I thought.* "We'll get him in due time."

What? What the fuck was that about?

Constantine continued to hold my chin in a vice grip. I was contemplating my next move when someone roared from behind Constantine.

"CONSTANTINE!!!"

The word echoed off the wide walls of the arena tunnel like a trumpet, snatching everyone's attention. I knew that voice from anywhere. The crowd parted to reveal Uncle Roland.

"Get-your-damn-hands-off-my-son!" Uncle Roland ordered, his voice brimming with bad intentions.

Constantine and his goon released me immediately, then turned their attention to Uncle Roland and Big Drew, his driver/sometime bodyman. Two other foreign-looking dudes that appeared to be monied-up were trailing them.

"Are you crazy?" Uncle Roland asked Constantine. Meanwhile, I readjusted my mink and stood my guard, just in case we had to thump.

Constantine shrugged his shoulders innocently. "Roland, I was just welcoming my friend home. Nothing wrong with that, is it?"

Uncle Roland stepped closer to Constantine and spoke so low I struggled to make out the words. "I'm only going to tell you this once: Leave my family alone! You go on another witch hunt and I'll sue. I promise you! My son served his time. Now leave him be."

"Hardly, Roland. I'm going to burn his black ass for that murder," Constantine swore. "Incidentally, he's not who I really want though."

"Really?"

"No." Constantine paused. "*You* are!"

"Well, everyone wants to go to heaven ..."

"Um-hmm."

"But they must *die* first!"

"We'll see who has the last word," Constantine guaranteed. He beckoned his crew to leave, but left me a parting shot over his shoulder. "Don't get too comfortable with your freedom, Anthony. I don't plan on letting you keep it long."

I watched him walk away with pure malice burning in my eyes. Soldada, in back of the entourage, turned to look at me. She wore a frown on her face, and her steps were heavy, but I offered her no solace. I kept my head up, jaw set, and rolled my eyes at her like a bitch. As far as I was concerned, she had made her decision. The battle lines were drawn, and she was rolling with the opposition.

I owed her nothing.

"You okay, son?" Uncle Roland asked. I nodded my head. "Good. Let's go."

"Unc ..." I gestured toward Mona.

"Look, Anthony, take care of it dammit! Some shit's come up. We gotta go. *Now!*"

Something was seriously wrong. It wasn't like my uncle to be rude in front of company or a woman. He was a Southern gentleman to the core. I pulled him to the side.

"What's up, Unc?" I whispered. "What's going on?"

Uncle Roland scanned the passersby for signs of danger. I'd never seen him so on-edge, so ... wary.

"Moses has been shot," he whispered.

"What? Where? How bad is he?"

"Later," he stated dismissively, his eyes still scanning the crowd. "The sooner we get out of here, the better."

No more words needed to be spoken. I rushed over to Mona, passed her the keys to my Jag. "Here, take my car to your place," I told her. "Sorry I can't walk you out, but something's come up."

"Wait, Anthony!" Mona grabbed my arm. "Is everything okay?"

"I can't talk right now. Just go home. I'll get the car later."

"No!" she yelled. I looked at her like she was crazy. She changed her tone. "I mean, call me when you're finished with your business. I'll come pick you up."

"I don't know how long it's going to be," I replied honestly.

"Don't matter. I'll wait on you, all right? All right?"

I nodded. "We'll see."

Mona kissed me. A long, deep kiss. "Please call me, A.P.," she begged.

"We'll see."

Outside in the parking garage, Uncle Roland bid farewell to his companions while I climbed into the backseat of the Bentley Mulsanne. Minutes later, Uncle Roland joined me and proceeded to relay what he knew as Big Drew piloted the Bentley through traffic.

"I don't know what's wrong with you kids," he began, speaking indirectly. "You all have to stick to the script. Don't get involved with bullshit ..."

I let Uncle Roland ramble until he'd had enough time to calm down. I knew he would get to his point eventually. Everything he was rambling about had meaning, I knew. Just had to let his thoughts boil down to it. Finally, he came out with it.

"Fucking Moses decided to get the job done himself," he informed me. "Went out with some wetbacks to handle things. Next thing I know, he's calling me, crying and bleeding, running through the streets like a runaway slave. The fuckin' Mexicans disappeared. Now, I gotta interrupt my business meeting to go all the way to the Southside and save his dumb, hardheaded ass! And you ..."

"Me? What I do?" I complained, defensively.

Uncle Roland thumped me on my head. "What I tell you about fuckin' with Carlo and his bitches?"

"Unc, that's just a little something to keep money in my pocket."

"I'm not talking about that!" He snapped. "I understand you gotta do what you gotta do to keep money in your pocket, and I know he is paying you well. I don't like it, but I understand," he reasoned. "But wasn't that one of Carlo's girls you were plastered on that damn Jumbotron screen with?"

I smiled. "That's different, Unc? She's not one of the hoes. She doesn't work."

"You don't think I know Mona? Hell, I probably know Mona better than you," he scoffed. "Anthony, I tell you shit for a reason. I know you think you have it sweet, but know what you're getting into. I hope you're not stupid enough to jeopardize what we're building for a piece of pussy."

"Unc, it's not that serious."

"It *is* that serious!" he barked. "Tell you what: ask yourself why Carlo is willing to pay you near a quarter-million a year for something he could do himself, huh? Ask yourself that! Now I'm done with it. Take a right up here, Drew. Cut the lights," he instructed. "Pull up to the last house on the left."

We eased into the driveway of a dilapidated house. All the lights were out. No signs of life anywhere. Uncle Roland dug into the wood-grained center console, extracted two pistols, and passed me one.

"Come on," he ordered. "I go in on the right, you take the left. We clear every room until we find what we're looking for. Got it?"

I nodded yes, even though I was confused. I thought we were in South Charlotte to pick up someone, not something.

We climbed the few steps to the front door. Uncle Roland used a key to unlock the door, then suddenly thrust the door open and charged inside, his weapon was aimed at the right side of the house. I followed behind him, my weapon trained to the left of the room, ensuring not to go beyond a 40-degree arc. I couldn't see further than the red dot beaming from the end of my gun, so I just followed that beacon of light. Told myself, if anything darkened that neon sliver of guidance, I was squeezing.

We cleared the front room, then moved on to the next room, off to the right of the room we were in. My adrenaline was pumping like a piston, my mouth was dry. Sweat drenched my body. But I pushed on. Followed Uncle Roland's silhouette through the darkness as he thrust the door open, and we repeated the same routine as we did in the first room. This time my beam fell on a figure lying prone.

A deep breath clutched my chest. I gripped my gun tighter. The red beam shone brighter, illuminated the figure. I put the dot on what I estimated was the figure's back, raised it to the head. Just as I was about to squeeze the trigger, the figure turned its head.

My red beam blinded my cousin.

"Ahhh, don't shoot!" Mo shrieked, shielding his face with his forearm.

"Nigga, it's me," I grunted.

"A.P.?"

"And me," Uncle Roland snarled. "Get your ass up, so we can go."

"I-I can't move," he stammered. "I'm hit."

We lowered our weapons and rushed to his side.

"Where you hit at?" Uncle Roland asked.

"My stomach and my side," he grunted.

"Hold tight. We gonna get you out of here," I promised. We grabbed him on opposite sides, carrying him through the door out into the cool night air. He grunted and grabbed his side as we stumbled down the stairs to the awaiting car, our eyes scanning the night for signs of danger. We stuffed him in back, then climbed in behind him.

"Go to Dr. Simmons's house!" Uncle Roland directed Big Drew.

Big Drew maneuvered the big Bentley through backstreets like an Indy driver, while me and Unc tended to Mo's wounds under the bright interior lights illuminating the cabin.

"Damn, nigga! You leaking everywhere!" I swore as I noticed his blood wetting my coat. Looked like my mink was bleeding. The rich wood console bisecting the rear of the car was soaked with blood, too.

"What you think, nigga ... I've been shot!" he whined, writhing in pain as blood gathered in the corners of his mouth. Uncle Roland saw the blood and panicked a bit.

"Don't talk, and be still," Uncle Roland advised. He used his silk hankie to apply pressure to the wounds.

We entered the gates of the esteemed Ballentyne, but instead of making the left to go to our house, we took a hard right, barreling down the quiet street at breakneck speed.

We pulled up to a three-story beige stucco home, and Big Drew doused the lights. A gray-breaded man in pajamas was on the lawn, waving us inside. We scooped Moses and followed the man inside, where he directed us to a room on the first level. The room resembled an OR, all the way down to the stainless steel table lined with disposable paper, and mountains of machinery.

"Set him on the table," the man (who I assumed was Dr. Simmons) ordered. He slapped on gloves and a mask. "Give me a sit-rep."

"He's been shot twice," Uncle Roland relayed. "Once in the stomach, once in the side. The bullet in the side looks like it went straight on through. I don't know about the other one."

We watched in silence as Dr. Simmons went to work, mending Mo's wounds. When the pain became unbearable, he issued Mo a sedative. Once he drifted into a light sleep, Dr. Simmons was able to extract the bullet from his stomach.

"Oooh! That's a nasty one," Dr. Simmons commented, scrutinizing the bullet under the bright light as he held it clasped between the tip of his bloody pincers. "Someone was trying to take him out, Roland."

Uncle Roland offered no comment. He just stroked his hairy chin in deep thought as Dr. Simmons finished his surgery, then patched Moses up with a ton of gauze to soak up the excess blood.

"That should take care of him." the doctor announced after a moment. "Of course, he'll need about a week's worth of rest so as not to impede the healing process. Other than that, he should be fine." Dr. Simmons walked to a cabinet, removed two bottles of meds, and passed them to Uncle Roland. "Make sure he takes these. These are for pain. The others are antibiotics. Careful with the first ones, though. They're like Oxycontin. If you have any problems, notify me immediately."

"Thank you, Doctor." Uncle Roland peeled a roll of money from his pocket, pressed a knot into the good doctor's hand. He noticed us looking and ordered us to take Moses to the car.

Outside, I was surprised to see the Mulsanne had been replaced with the Yukon XL. Guess Big Drew must have went to the house and traded the Bentley for the truck to accommodate Mo. We tucked Moses inside and waited. Minutes later, Uncle Roland joined us, all business.

"Drew, after you drop me and Moses off, take Anthony wherever he needs to go and come back. I got some things for you to do."

Drew grunted compliance as he whipped the big truck around. Uncle Roland was still in deep thought, but something wasn't right. I could tell.

"Unc, what are we going to do about Mo?" I pried.

"Nothing we can do, but wait. When he starts talking, we'll know what to do," he answered, stroking Mo's head in his lap while he slept.

"Meanwhile?"

"Meanwhile, fix that situation with you and that yellow girl."

I tried to explain that it wasn't like that. Me and Mona weren't fucking, at least not yet. But he wasn't hearing it.

"Keep your eye on the prize, son. You just got back out here, so I'll grant you that. But trust me, this shit is more trouble than it's worth. Find out a little more about your lady friend before you fuck things up and jeopardize millions," he advised.

"All due respect, Unc, but I can't see how this female has anything to do with our business."

He laughed. "Anthony, when you're on the level we're about to be on, when this thing goes through, your personal life and business life are inextricably entwined. A perceived small thing could end up being the biggest mistake of your life, huh, Drew?"

Drew cosigned like a parent on a delinquent loan.

"Besides, this thing is a lot more than you're giving credit to. I don't expect you to know that, you just coming home and all, but I do expect you to trust my judgment. You'll thank me later."

Uncle Roland made it seem like I was cavorting with Jezebel herself. In fact, I never remembered him giving so much attention to who I was laying the pipe to. This is the same man who took me to get my first piece of pussy!

Something was afoul, and Drew was going to drop me off at Mona's, so I could find out.

13

SOLDADA

Just seeing Anthony again caused my blood to boil. When I first spotted him across that arena, my heart skipped a beat. I was even amazed that I was able to recognize him from so far away, and in fact, I was a bit skeptical that it was him, until I saw his face flash on that Jumbotron, kissing all up on that high-yellow heifer.

I wanted to hurt somebody!

Apparently, Constantine felt the same way. Only, his violent ambition was fueled by hate. Mine was fueled by ... love?

When Constantine saw Anthony's face pop up on that screen, I thought the vein bulging in his neck was about to burst. I heard Constantine mumble through clenched teeth, "Enjoy it now, you prick." He tapped me on the shoulder and pointed Anthony out, then he dispatched his security detail to get closer to him and keep a closer eye on him. They radioed back when Anthony left his seat. Next thing I knew, the junior aides and I where chasing Constantine and his security through the crowded tunnel. By the time we caught up to them, Constantine was already taunting Anthony.

I must admit, my heart wept when I saw my Adonis being humiliated. It took every bit of strength I could muster to keep my face poker, to not intervene. When Constantine put his hands on Anthony, I'd had enough. I intervened before I even realized what I'd done. Hoping to avoid suspicion, I added extra sauce to my words when I suggested to Constantine to be patient. The bewildered look on Anthony's face bore witness to a job well done.

We engaged in a tense stare-off until I heard a loud voice boom from behind me. I turned and saw Anthony's uncle. I was surprised at the sheer size of the man. Large and powerfully built, the way he carried himself made him seem even bigger. He wore a beautiful black leather coat trimmed in ample amounts of light brown fur at the sleeve and collar, hugging his large frame. The black leather bowler hat tucked over his large dome matched the coat. Three other men were with him, one of them I surmised was his personal lackey. However, they were non-factors.

The true star of their entourage was Roland Padmore.

Nothing I had studied in his files could compare to meeting him in person. Nothing in his current persona spoke of a humble, grimy upbringing on the streets of South Charlotte. He didn't carry the look of a man who had to scrap and scrape for everything, except his juvenile record, which was littered with numerous felonious assaults. His juvenile record alone should've shattered his prestigious façade like cheap glass. But it didn't. I was in awe of him. Just looking at Roland Padmore evoked a mixture of emotions from fear to security and everything in between. Just thinking about the encounter gave me chills. And when he barked at Constantine, I had never seen him move so fast. Constantine may have put on airs like he was unaffected by Roland Padmore, but I'd been around him long enough to know.

He was terrified of Roland Padmore.

I saw his dark olive skin blush red undertones when Roland demanded he release Anthony. I heard his voice crackle like a broken radio when he tried to talk slick. And when Roland insinuated that he would die before he allowed Constantine a victory, I saw my boss scowl slightly. Even my skin crawled when Roland Padmore made that declaration. He spoke with so much passion, so much fury, I questioned if I was, indeed, over my head.

The ride back to the office was a quiet one. The only sounds heard were Constantine mumbling to himself. They dropped me off at my apartment on the plaza with little more than a cursory nod from Constantine. The tinted SUV peeled out, leaving me on the curb alone with my thoughts.

That was over an hour ago.

Now all I wanted was a nice hot bath to soak my bones, a glass of cold wine to tickle my throat, and some Jill Scott to soothe my soul.

I lit a few candles, set the music low, and leaned back in the scented bubble bath I drew. Totally relaxed, I let Jill croon to me about how *he loved her.*

Just as I got comfortable, I was bombarded with thoughts of my sexcapades with Anthony, or A.P. (as I realized he was really called.) I don't know if it was due to me seeing him again, or if Jill was just fucking with my head. Maybe it was both, causing the pleasant memories to flash through my mind's eye more vividly than a peacock's tail. Slowly, I began to get that familiar tingling between my legs again. Inwardly, I cursed myself for feeling this way, but it would not go away. What I felt for this man could not be denied. Go figure. The one time I dropped my guard, let someone inside me, I get knocked out.

Then it hit me.

The best way to forget a man is with a man, my mother used to say. If only for carnal purposes, I reasoned with myself, throwing caution and rationale to the wind.

I slid from the tub. Foam clinging to my body like I wished a man would, I grabbed the phone. Dialed the number.

Someone picked up on the second ring. Despite the time, I heard loud hip-hop music blaring in the background.

"Soldada?" The voice said. "*¡Que suprendido! ¿Estas ocupado?*"

"No."

"*Bueno. Quiero verte. Ahora mismo.*"

I smiled at the invitation, but I had to decline. "*No posible este noche, Carlo,*" I told him. I heard the air leave his sails as soon as the words left my mouth. "*Pero, manana es todo libre,*" I negotiated, putting hope back into his life, as well as mine. I could tell he was smiling through the phone, satisfied that he had finally worn me down.

I smiled, too.

The future was looking brighter already.

~

Anthony

"Come in, Anthony."

Mona invited me inside her humble abode wearing a satin robe the color of her skin that stopped about mid-thigh. She threw her arms around me as soon as I crossed the threshold. "I'm glad everything is okay. I was so worried! Are you hungry? I have some baked chicken and steamed vegetables still warm in the oven."

I'd smelled the food the second I stepped through the door. My stomach was doing somersaults, but food was the last thing on my mind. "I'm good," I told her.

"You staying awhile or do you want me to get your keys for you?" Mona asked with a sexy look that dared me to think about leaving. She still had her arms wrapped around my neck, hypnotizing me with those hazel eyes. I gripped her small waist, and my hands sank into her soft flesh. She leaned into me, her eyes pleading with me to stay.

"I-I'm not sure," I stammered.

"Oh? You're not sure?" She cocked her head to the side. "Come on, Anthony. It's been a long night. I know just the thing you need," she claimed, pulling on my arm.

I reluctantly followed behind her toward the bedroom. "Look, Mona, I'm not up for the little games tonight," I advised her, my frustrations creeping to the surface. The episode from the limo was still fresh in my mind.

"I'm not playing, Anthony. I'm on the up and up tonight. I got chu'," she claimed. The bedroom lights were low. A single candle burned on the nightstand beside a four-poster bed. Beside the candle was a bowl of thick liquid. A strong hint of potpourri lingered in the air. A female was wailing a folk song through the Bose speakers, sounding so smooth I wanted to crawl inside the notes and go to sleep.

She had been waiting on me. She knew I was coming back for more.

"Take this off." She tugged at the black mock neck sweater I had changed into. (I had discarded my bloody mink in the truck on the way over for Drew to get cleaned.)

"Hold up, Mona." I moved her hands. "I gotta talk to you about a few things."

"Well, talk. I can walk and chew bubblegum at the same time." She went right back to removing my clothes. Seconds later, I was standing in my damp boxers. "Lay on the bed on your stomach," she instructed me.

"Mona. Serious. We gotta talk," I insisted, getting on the bed, lying on my stomach.

She climbed on me and reached for the liquid in the bowl on the nightstand. With her legs splayed on opposite sides of me, and her soft ass resting on my butt, she massaged me with the warm oil.

"Talk."

"First of all, I want to know what's up with you and my uncle."

She chuckled. "Your uncle? What about him?"

"He thinks you're poison. Why?"

"Is that what he said?"

"Oww! Oww ..."

"Sorry ..." She lightened up. "Is that what he said?"

"Nah, but he acts like it."

She got her technique in groove. Kneaded the oil deeper into my back. Her hands were strong, but still soft. Shit felt good. My eyes started to get heavy.

"Oh," she replied vaguely. That got my senses riled up.

"Oh? Hell that supposed to mean?"

"Ask your question, A.P. Say what you want to know."

"Did he ever fuck you?"

She laughed, a little too hard for my taste. "Boy, bye. Hell no."

"No?"

"No." She confirmed.

"So why does he act like that?"

"Your uncle just doesn't understand a lot of things. That's all."

This was a newsflash to me. Far as I knew, my uncle understood everything.

"Well, how do you know each other so well?" I asked.

"Me and your uncle — be still — we go way back. But it's not like you're thinking."

She eased off my butt and slid onto my back. I thought I was tripping at first, but then I realized exactly what I felt. My mind wasn't playing tricks on me. Mona's bald, moist pussy was sitting directly on my back.

My dick stretched out like a wide receiver diving for a ball.

I became too uncomfortable laying on my stomach. Started fidgeting. "Why is Cadillac paying me so much for so little?" I asked, striving hard to divert my attention from the velvety softness leaking onto my back.

"Who knows?" I felt her shrug. "You never know what that one is thinking." Mona's hands slowed down. Stopped kneading and started rubbing my neck. I could feel her getting wetter. "Anthony, I really dig you. You know that?" She leaned down closer to the back of my head. Readjusted herself on my back. Straddled me, then leaned over to lick on my neck. "I always have liked you," she whispered.

"Yo, Mona, what are you doing ..."

"Shh ... don't talk. Just feel ..."

And so it began. The long, slow dance to consummate her seduction.

Mona kissed a trail down my back, causing me to shudder. She licked and kissed both of my ass checks before turning me over and laying kisses down my hairy legs. She got to my feet ... paused a second ... then licked my toes slowly. Then she sucked them. I must admit. That was a first for me. I had never had a woman suck my toes before. I'd sucked a few in my day, but never had it done to me. Experiencing it for the first time, I could see why chicks went crazy over it. It was a pleasurable feeling like no other I'd ever experienced.

After sucking my toes, Mona moved back up my body, exploring her way with kisses. As she reached my torso, she shed her satin robe and pulled my boxers off, greeting my saluting dick with her warm mouth. I knew I was sweaty down there from running earlier that night, but it didn't seem to faze

Mona. She tenderly licked my shaft up and down, before engulfing me into her mouth again and again. Each time she inhaled my dick into her mouth, she drew me deeper down her throat. Eventually she was deep-throating me with a nice rhythm, staring up at me with those pretty hazel eyes. Mona definitely had the O-game on lock.

After she deep-throated me for a while, she started tea-bagging my balls. First one, followed by the other. Then she dropped both of my balls in her mouth at the same damn time, simultaneously jacking me off. The shit felt so good I thought I was going to break my toes in two I kept cracking them so hard.

Mona felt me about to erupt and started jerking me off harder, while pulling my balls deeper into her mouth. I was gone, loving it, lost in the bowels of her good mouth. Ready to bust off something strong.

Then Mona stopped.

I crunched up into a modified fetal position. Mona held onto my midsection for dear life as I writhed and tensed up like I was mutating into some creature from another world. I tried to reach down and finish myself off before I burst a vein, but Mona grabbed my hands.

"What chu doing?" I cried out.

She teased me, restraining my hands. "That's what I'm here for," she reminded me.

She withdrew a condom from the granite nightstand and wrapped me up. I was so aroused, just the feeling of her hands touching my dick had me about to explode. After she rolled the condom on, she ran one of her long nails down the underside of my dick. I shuddered like it was below 30 degrees in the room.

She chuckled, "Mmm, that's what I like to see."

Mona held my stiff rod steady and mounted me slowly, moaning as she sat down on the whole thing. I raised my head, tucked my chin to my chest and enjoyed the view of Mona's beautiful body as she rocked her way to ecstasy. Her beautiful titties smiled down on me. Her light-colored nipples seemed to wink at me. She leaned over for me to suck them. I took them into my mouth and admired them with my tongue, while gripping her small waist, moving with her rhythm.

In concert, we moved to our own vibe, doing all the freaky things we had imagined doing with each other from the first time our eyes locked in Anguilla. It wasn't long before I filled the condom up with enough fluids to put out a forest fire. Mona came right behind me in a melodious symphony of oohs and ahhhs, then collapsed on my chest, chanting how good it felt.

A few minutes later, her light snoring ripped through the air. A few minutes later, she wasn't the only one asleep.

We both surrendered to the dream master, snapshots of our beautiful night hinged upon the fringes of our dreams.

I awoke the following morning to my phone vibrating incessantly. I snatched the phone and looked at the caller ID.

"What's up, Unc?" I croaked into the receiver.

"Moses is up. Get your ass over here. We got work to do." Click.

Just like that Uncle Roland ended the call with his raspy voice ringing in my head louder than the visions of my beautiful night. I could sense that it was shaping up to be a long day.

I slid from under Mona's arm quietly. Went to the shower. Quickly, I washed the sex from my body. Minutes later, I exited the shower, wiped steam from the mirror, and took a long look at myself, reflecting on my new life. All things considered, I was living any man's dream. I had mad money, goals, possessions, and I was fucking more than a porn star. Yet I still felt a tiny twinge of something deep inside. Doubt? Regret? Unhappiness?

I shook it off and collected my clothes from the floor. When I emerged from the bathroom, Mona was sitting up on the bed naked.

"Who was that? Your wifey?" she probed.

I didn't even grant her an answer. I collected my particulars from the nightstand and gave Mona a deep, lingering kiss. "Listen, I may not be in the office today, but I'll call you later," I informed her.

She caught on to my curt mood. "Is this about last night?" she asked, appearing to be worried all over again.

"Something like that," I answered cryptically. "Anyway, I really appreciate you helping me forget my troubles last night, even if it was temporary," I added with a smile.

"It's the least I could do." She smiled back, trying to play it cool, but I saw it coming a mile away. "Was that all last night was? Temporary refuge?" she asked.

"Listen, Mona, I dig you. You know that," I began, hating to have to lay the law down. "But right now is not the time for this conversation."

"I understand, Anthony," she claimed, saving me from really having to take it there. "I know you have a lot on your plate. I apologize for going there." Mona kissed me, tried to pretend she was unfazed, but I could see hurt dancing behind her eyes.

That was her problem though. "All right. See you later then," I told her, then took my cue and exited stage right while I still had the chance.

Thirty minutes later, I pulled around Uncle Roland's circular driveway and parked my Jag behind Cadillac's new XTS sedan. I noted Dirty's Infiniti coupe in the driveway as well. Inwardly, I braced myself. Just like old times, the gang was all here. This was serious business.

Maria ushered me into the conference room where the gang was already seated. Uncle Roland at the head, Cadillac and Dirty at the two sides. Mo was sitting at the table in a wheelchair. The empty chair belonged to me. I knew the seating order well, for this was the same room we'd used over the years to plan heists that took off millions.

"How you feeling?" I asked Mo, as I settled into my chair.

Dirty answered for his little brother. "Aww, that lil' nigga all right. Sitting there looking like Tupac when he went to court that time. Lucky, Julio and them tried to kill his dumb ass," Dirty laughed. Then he got serious and pointed at Mo. "I told this nigga to stop fucking with them damn wetbacks!"

Cadillac blanched at Dirty's use of profane language in front of Uncle Roland, but he always cussed in front of adults. When we were younger, the only reason he ever got kicked out of school was because he cursed out the school principal. In third grade.

"Tell us exactly what happened with the Mexicans," Uncle Roland demanded. Mo dropped his head. He knew he had fucked up.

"I don't know exactly. All —"

"Speak up!"

"ALL I know is they flipped on me. One minute, we was closing in on dude at the light to pop him; the next minute, Cruz was shooting at me! I ducked, tucked, and ran. Cruz jumped in the truck with the cracker and they peeled off!" Mo explained disbelievingly. "That's the last I saw of 'em."

"Did they get the money?" Uncle Roland inquired.

"Every dime."

"You see this *bullshit*?!" Uncle Roland cried, addressing each and every one of us. "See what happens when you try to be slick?"

Cadillac and Dirty looked confused.

"Dad, I don't mean no harm, but what the hell is going on here? You had something to do with this fool getting popped?" Dirty asked, jerking his finger at Mo.

"Nah, son, it was all this fool's fault," Uncle Roland answered, icily. He punked me and Mo down with a harsh stare that told us to keep your mouths shut, keep Dirty and Cadillac in the dark. They were here to see about their wounded brother, nothing more. They were not a part of this business, our business.

"I told him a thousand times about dealing with his *compadres*," Uncle Roland continued. "They're only loyal to themselves. We're the only ones loyal to this family. Am I right? We are loyal to this family, aren't we?"

This was more of a request for a declaration of allegiance than a question. The implications cut the air like a sickle. And like dominoes, we all fell in line, bowing our heads to the unsung beat.

Uncle Roland nodded with a far off look. "Good. In the very near future, I'll need all of you in one way or another to contribute to setting things right with this family. Is there a problem with that?"

Again, like dominoes, we fell in line.

After he was sure his point was made, Uncle Roland excused Dirty to go tend to his family, but held Cadillac back to sit in on the rest of our meeting against his wishes. Cadillac clearly had something more important to do because he kept checking his Rolex with the diamond-encrusted face every few seconds.

But Uncle Roland didn't seem to care much. "Carlo, you have something for me?" he asked Cadillac, all but daring him to say no.

"I'll have your money day after tomorrow," Cadillac slid through gritted teeth.

"Tomorrow," Uncle Roland corrected.

"Dad, I have a full day tomorrow," Cadillac whined.

"Carlo, you're my son, and I love you, but business is business," he reminded him.

"All right, Dad. Tomorrow." Cadillac huffed, slid his chair out, and stormed from the room, leaving Uncle Roland staring at the door long after he disappeared through it.

If looks could kill, we would've buried Cadillac that day.

Uncle Roland regained his composure and turned his attention back to me and Mo. "Moses, you know where these Mexicans hang out, right?"

"Sure, Dad, but it's a whole tribe of them over there," Mo warned.

He turned to me. "Anthony, you still have that number?"

"Which number?" I asked, unsure of what he was referring to. Didn't he know how many numbers I had?

"*That* number," he stressed. I immediately knew which number he was referring to then. *That* number.

"Of course," I answered.

"Okay. This is what we're going to do ..."

Shaun Sinclair

14

SOLDADA

I adjusted my bustline and gave myself the final onceover in the full-length mirror.

Had to say, I looked damn good.

I was wearing a black satin dress that dropped to my knees, and black strappy sandals that stretched up to my calves. My cream-colored satin bodice was strapless. My hair was curled tight, then pulled up into a coil. Yeah, I was doing it. Hell, I was beginning to think I looked too damn good for my date.

After weeks of hounding, Carlo had finally cornered me into a date. Oddly enough, I was actually looking forward to it.

Carlo had become my rainbow after the storm. After countless nights at the office, pouring over endless paperwork, Carlo began leaving me something special to come home to every night, be it a dozen long-stemmed roses waiting at the door or a simple phone call to let me know I was on his mind. The kind gestures eventually melted the ice around my heart. It felt good to come home to something special for a change. As of late, my life had become my job. I found myself going through the same monotonous routine I'd gone through in college, and that wasn't good for the soul, especially after my fling with Anthony Padmore.

The scary thing was Carlo reminded me so much of Anthony! Each time I spoke with him, he reminded me of my Anguilla excursion since that was where Carlo and I initially met. Every fiber of my being was telling me to bolt. Don't get involved with Carlo Barnes. Screw his magnetic personality. Screw the kind gestures I was beginning to get accustomed to. Screw his wealthy, fine ass, then bolt.

But another part of me propelled me forward in pursuit of happiness. Told me to suppress the memories of Anguilla. Swallow the fear rearing its ugly head, trying to spear my chance at happiness.

Yet still, undeniably, Carlo reminded me of Anthony.

Maybe because I couldn't have Anthony, in some twisted way, I was substituting Carlo for the person I really desired. Either way, Carlo appeared to be a good alternative.

I agreed to let Carlo pick me up from my place. I would've never done that before, but working in the D.A.'s office gave me an extra sense of security. Like, *I wish somebody would fuck with me!* Plus, I had started carrying a gun at all times. At the behest of Constantine, all ADAs carried a sidearm. I understood his logic since we were responsible for denying a lot of unscrupulous, dangerous people their freedom. Tonight, I carried my Glock in my clutch.

At about a quarter after six, my buzzer rang. I tidied up a bit, donned my mink stole around my bare shoulders, and went to meet Carlo in the lobby.

One look at Carlo, and any doubts I previously had evaporated quicker than a water puddle on the sun. There he stood in my lobby, tall and regal, wearing a tan cashmere overcoat with a V-neck that opened all the way down to his waist where it was tied with a belt. The beautiful coat flowed completely down to his ankles. Tan-and-cocoa colored alligator shoes jutted from his long feet. The cocoa flecks corresponded perfectly with the brown two-piece suit peeking from beneath the overcoat. His long, silky hair looked smoother than mine. He wore it snatched back into a ponytail, extending past the collar of his coat, held in place by a diamond-encrusted barrette. The barrette matched the huge stones gleaming in his ear. I estimated them to be, at least, three carats each. His wide, full beard was tapered sharper than my bikini wax, accenting his handsome, chocolate face.

Carlo turned to me and smiled when he saw me enter the lobby. "Hello, Soldada. These are for you." He handed me a beautiful bouquet of yellow roses.

I returned his wide smile. "Aren't you the charmer?" I said, genuinely pleased.

"No, not at all. I just wanted to put a smile on the face of the woman who has kept me smiling all day."

"Ooooh, and smooth, too," I joked, passing the flowers to the man behind the desk. "Put these up for me please."

I was still living in the hostel I had settled in upon arriving in Charlotte. The rate was astronomical, but the service was impeccable. There was no way a commoner could afford to live here. Fortunately for me, Mecklenburg County was footing my bill. However, management were the only ones privy to that small detail, so all the employees treated me like royalty. A young, black female *living* here meant I was either very important or some VIP's mistress. I'd probably had the benefit of the doubt at one point, but after the way Carlo's expensive presence came through, I'd probably be regarded as a mistress now. The way the normally-friendly desk clerk snatched my bouquet confirmed my suspected demotion.

"You ready?" Carlo cradled my elbow in his hand and led us outside to where the valet stood guarding a red Ferrari. I watched in astonishment as the valet passed Carlo the keys and Carlo slipped the valet a bill.

"Yo, this is a nice-ass car!" the valet gushed, obviously in awe.

"Thanks," Carlo offered nonchalantly, as if there wasn't over a quarter-million dollars of machinery crouched on the pavement before us. He slipped the young man a business card. "Call me. Maybe we can discuss a few things, see if I can't help you get one of these for yourself." The man moved on to the next customer, while Carlo led me around to the passenger door of the Ferrari, but not before I was able to look at the shiny, red, and chrome engine showcased under transparent glass in the rear of the car. I also noted that the rims were chrome also. This was a really nice car. I told him so as he opened the door for me.

"Thank you," he returned, rather bashfully.

Carlo slid underneath the wheel, started the car, then gunned the engine, snapping my head back into the monogrammed headrest as we zipped into traffic. As we sliced and diced through cars and trucks, the gears changed effortlessly, but I never saw a gear level.

"Is this an automatic transmission?" I inquired, surprise evident in my voice. "I don't see any gears."

"They're right here." Carlo motioned at the wheel. Paddles were on both sides. "See?" He flicked the paddle on the left side. The car squatted lower while the engine note raised an octave. Then he flicked the right paddle and the car sprang forward as if we were launched from a cannon.

"That's neat," I replied, amused with his demonstration. "I can't imagine how much this must have cost ..." I wondered aloud.

"Not too much," he replied modestly.

Everything was so blasé with him; he seemed so cool. "I bet you have to beat the women off with a stick, huh?" I joked. He just smiled and didn't answer, so I prodded further. "I know the women chase you like a bloodhound."

I saw the wheels turning in his head as he drummed up a suitable answer. Finally, he said, "I'm kinda jaded, ya know. I don't really dig females like that," he claimed. "In my business, I've seen the worst side of women."

"Really? What exactly is your business?" I asked. Carlo shot me his killer smile then bumped the Alpine up a level. For the remainder of the ride, the exotic whine of the Italian engine coupled with Mary J. Blige was our expensive soundbed.

Carlo never answered my question about his occupation.

We arrived at the restaurant at a little after seven p.m. The exterior of the restaurant was all white. In fact, it resembled the White House. I couldn't tell what type of food they served because a mélange of smells drifted from inside. A red-jacketed valet rushed the Ferrari before Carlo could stop. He whisked the car off and we went inside.

My first impression of the restaurant was that it was definitely high-class. Gold-plated cathedral ceilings and silk-lined walls with gold flecks interspersed inside a predominately cream pattern surrounded us. We were escorted to a table near the back. Our table sat maybe ten-feet away from a wood-burning fireplace, on line with only four other tables. We weren't secluded, but we weren't crowded either. The low lights gave the room an intimate feel. Set atop the table, directly in the center of the circle, seated inside a fancy glass container, was a bottle of Dom Perignon being chilled by a metal wire connected to a block of ice. Framing the champagne were two candles set inside a glass container matching the champagne holder.

Before we could take our seats, a host appeared from nowhere and pulled out our seats. He greeted Carlo in deep Spanish using, *usted,* which connoted respect. In fact, his whole demeanor exuded deference to Carlo. The man kept ducking his head like a chicken chomping on feed. Poor fella, I was thankful he didn't break his neck. Before he left, I heard him compliment Carlo on his *mujer linda* while stealing glances at me. I felt my cheeks color. I was thoroughly enjoying myself. The whole night just felt exciting.

Carlo pulled out my chair then sat across from me. A menu in Spanish was placed before us. I opened it and perused the items briefly. Much to my merriment, most of the menu consisted of Cuban dishes. My poker face must have been trash. I looked up to see Carlo grinning at me triumphantly.

"I never told you I was *Cubana.* How did you know?" I inquired, narrowing my eyes suspiciously.

"Aside from your Cuban features?"

"What Cuban features?" I challenged.

He looked at me sideways, as if I had escaped the loony house, then rattled off, "Your high cheekbones, full lips, the texture of your hair. Not to mention your *culo grande bonita.*" He drew a heart with his hands. I blushed so hard. "I thought you might like this place. It has the best Cuban food outside of Miami," he declared confidently. He just knew I was impressed with his arrogant ass! However, all I kept wondering was how he knew the menu and staff so well. In my usual outspoken way, I confronted him.

"Did your last date like the menu?" My frown clearly let him know this was not a complimentary question.

"What do you mean?" he asked innocently.

"I mean, obviously you've been here before. You know the menu so well."

He chuckled and dropped his head. His light chuckle broke out into a full-fledged laugh. Guess I was cracking him the hell up. He placed his hand over his chest and held up his palm toward me, still laughing. He was starting to piss me off.

"What's so funny, Carlo?" I crossed my arms, awaiting his answer, ready to walk out the second he spit some bullshit.

"You. It's just ..." He laughed some more, but clammed it up when he saw me shooting daggers at him. "Hold up a sec," he said, suddenly serious again.

Carlo motioned for the waiter. He came running like his ass was on fire, but this was a different waiter. This man had to be, at least, mid-sixties.

"Oui, Monsieur Carlo. Commente la vous?" The old man eagerly reached out for Carlo's hand. Carlo clasped the man's thin olive hand in his palm, and responded in French. Then the both of them fired off a brief conversation in rapid French, cackling like old friends. Finally, Carlo returned his attention back to me.

"Léfonte," Carlo said to the old man. I surmised that was his name. "I've been coming here for what? Couple years?"

"Oui." The old man nodded obediently.

"And how many women have you seen me come in here with?" Carlo asked, his eyes zeroed in on mine. Guess he wanted to assure me he wasn't telling the old man how to answer.

"None," the old man replied in accented English. How predictable.

Carlo's eyes never wavered from my gaze. "Satisfied?"

Apparently, he didn't know who he was dealing with. I graduated from law school. I was skilled in the technique of cross-examination. My witness.

"Mr. Léfonte, is it?" I asked. The old man nodded. "How long have you been waiting tables here?"

He shook his head. "I, no waiter. I am head chef," he corrected me, pride about to burst from his chest.

"O-kay. I stand corrected. How long have you been the head chef here?"

"I here two years now. Since open."

"Um-hmm. And you see Mr. Carlo each time he comes in?" I inquired, skepticism bleeding from my voice.

"Of course," he answered like I was the dumbest broad in the world for questioning him. "Monsieur Carlo only eat my cooking." He smiled then added, "This is first time he request Cuban menu. But I am happy to oblige Monsieur Carlo any time. He very generous."

The old man grinned sheepishly, showing off white teeth so pretty, at his age, they had to be fake. Meanwhile, Carlo seemed embarrassed at the mention of money. The lawyer in me couldn't resist. I had to ask.

"You seem very fond of Mr. Carlo."

"*Oui*. Monsieur Carlo give me new life in America when he give me my own restaurant." He glanced at Carlo, wondering if he had gone too far, I'm sure. "Well, not my own, but I am manager here. Of course, Monsieur Carlo is boss."

I didn't get it at first. I understood his broken English fine, but what he was saying with it, I couldn't grasp. Then I realized exactly what he was implying.

"Carlo, you own this restaurant?" I blurted out.

Carlo, the embodiment of cool, calmly dismissed Léfonte, then answered. "Yes."

"I thought you told me you were —"

"A business manager? Yes, I'm in the business of managing people," he clarified. "Now let's order."

I ordered *Arroz con frijoles negro y pollo fritos*, which was basically Black beans and rice with fried chicken, done up in a special Cuban sauce. Carlo mimicked my order. While we waited, he clarified some things.

"I own a number of businesses. Some profitable, some not so much. My main source of income is the Ladies of Distinction, an escort service. And before you go on a legal tirade, let me assure you, my business is legit." He took a sip of Dom, then waved the glass in the air. "And I don't owe anyone any apologizes. This is America, land of free enterprise ..." Carlo's voice trailed off. He looked away, as if contemplating just how much to divulge. I knew that, where there was smoke, there was fire. Carlo was entirely too defensive about his business dealings, which meant something was amiss.

So I dug deeper.

I didn't know what I was looking for. Something. Maybe I was forever doomed to pick fights when I discovered chinks in someone's armor. Maybe I was naturally combative. Whatever the reason, I dug deeper.

"Carlo, no one said anything derogatory about your business," I replied, attempting to set him at ease before I hit him with the kicker. "But I do see how someone could have something derogatory to say about poorly-disguised prostitution."

I purposely tried to hit a nerve. Make him angry. Expose the truth through the defensive lies he would launch.

But Carlo was too smooth for that. He was a thinker. Plus, I'm sure I wasn't the first person to come at him sideways about his business.

He leaned back in his chair. Sized me up like he was deciding which angle to take. Wheels burning rubber in his head.

He asked, "Prostitution huh?"

I nodded.

"I don't prostitute anyone, nor do I advocate it. I'm simply helping young women help themselves."

"Would you want your daughter receiving your kind of help?" I retorted.

"Absolutely."

"Really?"

"Yes," he insisted, then expounded on his reasoning. "I would rather have my daughter spend time with someone who can help her situation, than some knucklehead who can't do shit for her, but chase behind her begging for her ass. Hell, it's hard out here for a woman. Doubly so, if she's in college. At least, if she's hooked up with me, she doesn't have to starve or compromise her integrity while completing school. She gets a lot of money to have successful, intelligent men show her a good time, and if she's lucky, teach her a thing or two. I wish I could do it. Hmm, matter fact … there's an idea."

I picked up on something from his diatribe. "Are all your employees in college?" I asked.

"For the most part."

I sighed deeply. "Let's cut the bullshit, Carlo. It's not like you would tell me if you were running a prostitution ring. I do work for the court, after all."

Carlo sipped more Dom, then swirled the remnants around, holding the flute by the stem. He placed the glass on the table. Looked me square in the eye.

"Let me assure you of one thing, Counselor," he said. "If I were —and this is a strong if — but *if* I was running a prostitution ring, there would be a lot of people with more to lose than little old me. Therefore, you would be the least of my worries."

Maybe it was the alcohol, but the more Carlo talked, the more he reminded me of Anthony. And when he called me counselor, I almost spit my drink out! As if those substitutes weren't enough though, the arrogance oozing from his pores definitely conjured up memories of Anthony. I just couldn't shake my Adonis. I decided I didn't like the tone of the conversation, so I switched it up.

"Fair enough," I conceded. "Do you have any siblings?"

He told me he had one sister and two brothers. Said they all owned businesses in Charlotte. His sister was a CPA by trade. His brothers' trade was real estate. Carlo intimated to me that he and his father had a rocky relationship based on his decision to forego college sports for a business degree. His father wanted him to pursue, at least, one of the three sports he excelled in — basketball, football, or track. However, Carlo had goals of owning things, and he didn't want to wait until he was thirty to achieve them. Minus a few bumps in the road, he had reached his goal in spades.

"What about you, Soldada?" he asked when he was done bearing his history. We had polished off our main course, and were both nursing dessert entrees of fried ice cream. "What made you decide to become a lawyer. Too many Cosby reruns? I don't remember Claire working for the State."

I laughed at his attempt at humor, then shared a brief of my history, touching on my mother's plight as a single mother. Told him about her dependence on her brother until he was forced into prison forever on a trumped-up, bogus, narco-trafficking case. After that, we fled Miami to the Carolinas for bluer skies and better (cheaper) living. Unfortunately, my experience in the Carolinas, especially South Carolina, mirrored what we had fled from in Miami. Not directly, but indirectly through the countless young, black males I'd witnessed become enslaved to the criminal justice system because of bogus cases. This list included a few of my would-be stepfathers. I'm not so naïve as to believe all of them were innocent. But were all of them guilty? All of them?

Their gross injustices were the catalyst to my law degree. That and the money. A win-win in my book.

"That's admirable, Soldada," Carlo commented when I was done recounting my history. "But ahh ... tell me something ... you work for the State, don't you? That's a little backwards, wouldn't you say?"

Again, predictable. I battle with it every day.

"I would," I agreed.

"So?" He shrugged his shoulders, palms upward, begging clarification.

"I want to be a judge someday," I shared, bashfully. Expressing my ambitions always made me feel vulnerable. "The only way to do that is spend some time toiling for the State."

He dipped into his fried ice cream, mulling over my words. He looked so innocent sucking on his spoon, I wanted to throw him over my shoulder and burp him like a baby. A tall, strong, handsome baby.

But I knew I was dealing with a slick one, this one. Definitely a hyena. Grin while gobbling you up.

"A judge ..." Carlo whispered thoughtfully. "That's a new one. We do need more black judges."

I nodded with glee. "Um-hmm."

"But that still doesn't negate the fact that you're locking brothers up now," he argued. "Ever thought some of them could be innocent, just like all those faces you saw growing up?"

I sighed deeply. He hit a nerve with that one because the more I worked my current assignment, the more his words rang true. Roland Padmore may have been guilty of a lot of things, but I couldn't find one. I felt low for even continuing my phantom pursuit, but my advancement was predicated on his demise. In my mind, I rationalized that if I railroaded him, I could always just release him when I became a judge.

As if it were so simple.

"Yeah, I've thought about it ..." I paused. Contemplated a moment on whether I should tell him. Then, "In fact, I'm working a case right now that has me in a dilemma."

He put everything down and delivered me his undivided attention. "Really? How so?"

I explained my precarious situation in limited detail. Of course, I left out names. Definitely, left out my fling with Anthony. I just shared the gist of it.

"So why continue?" Carlo proposed, like it was easy to just walk away from my job.

"Excuse me?"

"I'm saying, why violate your principles for profit? You say the guy isn't guilty of anything, so why force it? Why try to force something to fit? We have it bad enough as is. Remember O.J.?"

O.J.? Surely he was jesting. "O.J. was guilty! He bought his freedom through the race card. Never mind the fact he loves white women."

He smiled like he had checkmated me. "Don't we all pay for our freedom?" he posed philosophically. "Don't the rich flourish in freedom, while the poor perish in servitude?"

"It's not supposed to be that way," I offered weakly, knowing only a fool could deny the facts.

"And yet, there's a thick line between idealism and reality, just as there is a fine line between who people are and who they appear to be."

Carlo scolded me with precision. Didn't allow me to retort. Guess he thought his remark was beyond reproach.

"All I'm saying is, today it could be the dude in your caseload. Tomorrow ..." He dipped into his ice cream, sucked the spoon. "Tomorrow ... it could be me ..."

Carlo dropped me off at my place around two in the morning. I slipped into bed naked, thoughts of our great conversation reverberating inside my head like timpani drums. He was kind. Intelligent. Articulate. Charismatic.

He was sexy as hell.

Try as I might, I couldn't deny the attraction. The quivering between my thighs wouldn't allow me to. For the first time since my vacation, I allowed my fingers to travel the familiar path to my center and strummed myself into a frenzy with thoughts of Carlo ravaging my body.

Just before I climaxed, Carlo received company ...

Anthony was there also.

15

SOLDADA

For the next month or so, Carlo and I saw a lot of each other. Convinced there was nothing to find on Roland Padmore, and not wanting to find anything on Anthony, I began shirking my duties in the name of fun. Time I was supposed to be dedicating to my assignment was actually spent with Carlo.

On one date, Carlo and I visited a shooting range, where he showed off and put three rounds inside a circle the size of a dime from fifty feet away with a .45, .357, and a .40 caliber. He nailed it on the first try with each weapon. Seeing as how I faltered to even pierce the target from twenty-five feet away with my Glock 40, I was extremely impressed.

On another date, we went white-water rafting in the mountains. The water damn near turned me into black ice, I almost drowned twice, but all in all, it was fun. Different. I learned something new while thoroughly enjoying myself.

On another outing, Carlo took me to the new dinner theater I had been hearing so much about since arriving in Charlotte. I was beyond shocked to learn that he owned that place as well. Carlo seemed to be a budding mogul. An octopus, he had his hands in more pots than a five-star chef. Just being in his presence was a welcome contrast to my boring life of *Shephardizing* cases and rummaging through lawyers' digests. With Carlo, it was as if the city was laid at my feet — even more than when I traveled with Constantine. Both men had the city at their beck and call, but there was a major difference in the manner in which both men were received. Constantine's reverence was based upon fear. (After all, he had the whole law enforcement community in the city as his personal arsenal.) Carlo's adoration seemed to be rooted in respect. People genuinely *liked* him. I could tell.

Constantine may have been Charlotte's district attorney, but Carlo was the city's unofficial mayor.

By the time Carlo and I consummated our affair, I had already been seduced by him for weeks. I dripped with anticipation each time we were together, wondering when the time would come that he would lay me down and stroke me like I knew he was capable of. I was the one ripping off his clothes, kissing him all over like a lovestruck teenager. Meanwhile Carlo remained cooler than Alaska. Like a predator toying with his prey, he ensured I knew that he was in control.

Until the night he got revved up and released his freaky side.

On more than one occasion he had relayed to me he was freakier than the average, but the first time we were intimate, he spooked me out. First, he demanded I sit on his face, so he could eat me out. Of course, I had no problem with that. I enjoyed oral just as much as the next girl. The problem came as we got more into it. He started rubbing his damp fingers around my ass. Not my humps. My *ass!* As in anus!!! It threw me for a loop initially. This was all new territory for me. But I eventually warmed up to the idea of exploration, and before long, it started feeling good. Different. But good.

Just as I began enjoying it, he plugged his finger in my ass. Deep.

I shrieked and tried to raise up, but he held me in place with his free hand, gripping my waist tighter than an anaconda, while continuing to whirl his tongue around inside of me. He got the hint that I wasn't feeling the finger action, so he removed it then slid me down, guiding me toward his hardness.

I gripped his long dick in my hand like a joystick, inspecting and comparing it at the same. He wasn't as thick as Anthony, but he had him by a few inches. Carlo's dick looked like a cobra ready to strike. Wide mushroom head, crooking off to the left. I placed the head at my opening and slowly slid down on it, enjoying the sensation of him opening me up. I glided down his hot, hard flesh about halfway of his full length, then reversed back up, squeezing the head as I flexed my inner muscles. I expected him to squirm, moan, or something, but he just eyed me with that same cool look on his face. I did the same thing a few more times, and was met with the same response. Moderate interest. I decided to turn the heat up.

I straddled him in the reverse-cowgirl, moving real slow so I could prepare to take him all in. I sat all the way on his dick, and I swear I felt it in my stomach. I rocked back and forth on him, grinding my hips with passion, leaning forward to give him a perfect view of my wetness. I looked over my shoulder, just knew he was enjoying the view I was giving him. His bottom lip was clasped between his teeth deep enough to draw blood.

He reached out with his big hands, cuffed my ass. Spread my cheeks apart, so he could see himself glide in and out. Started talking that shit I like.

"Yeah ... that's it ... take this dick," he whispered, as he thrust harder. "Take it!"

I looked back at him, dropping my ass like it was hot. Felt like my insides were being seared by a hot needle. A long hot needle. *"Es mio?"* I moaned. "Is it mine? *Digame! Quiero esgucharlo ... Es mio."*

"Es tuya," he groaned, surrendering to my feminine dominance. Guess it was feeling just as good to him. He started rising up on the bed. Next thing I knew, my face was planted in the pillow, my ass was raised high in the air like a Luke dancer, and Carlo was pounding me with long, powerful, strokes, trying to bury every inch of himself into my tightness.

I felt myself about to climax. Carlo started playing around my ass again, but this time it felt different. Heavenly. The sensation seemed to be heightened by his plunges this time. He rubbed his wet finger all up and through my damp crevice. I threw my head back in ecstasy. Carlo wrapped my hair in his hand, and pulled me toward him with every stroke, growling like a dog ...

"Ahh ... Carlo ... I'm about to ... ahh ... cum!!!"

At the exact moment, my orgasm gripped me, Carlo plunged his whole finger in my ass to the first knuckle.

Lightning flashed. Flowers bloomed. Thunder rolled. Convulsions wracked my body as I experienced THE most powerful orgasm ever in life. My mouth gaped open, but words escaped me. I was powerless, enslaved to the tremors of passion rippling through my body. Prisoner to the shattering, rhythmic vibrations claiming my nature.

Carlo lodged his hardness into the depths of my core and held it there, continuing to twirl his finger round and round inside my backdoor, granting me orgasm after sweet, torturous orgasm.

In my eyes, at that moment, he had turned into God.

16

SOLDADA

About a week later, we were at the Sheraton. Carlo had rented a suite. He was hosting a party in the hotel ballroom for some of his high-profile clients, while hoping to attract a few new ones. I was supposed to be his date for the evening, but due to my hectic work schedule, I dashed in toward the end of the night. I hadn't had time to change clothes, so I rushed straight from the office in my understated pantsuit — a great contrast from the rest of the black-tie crowd. Still, Carlo escorted me around like I was Selita Ebanks. On more than a few occasions, I noticed the older men ogling me like I was a walking fountain of youth. One of the old freaks even flicked his tongue out at me. I frowned at him as if he was spoiled milk. Another one of the older men had the gall to approach Carlo and inquire about me. I couldn't hear everything he said, or Carlo's response, but I knew it wasn't favorable. Carlo scowled some harsh words at him, pointed at me, then thumbed his chest forcefully. The old man scurried away in a cloud of fear.

Carlo settled me down at a table cordoned off from everyone, raised on a platform like a queen. I was feeling very regal, like the center of every man's universe.

Until they strutted through.

A bevy of beautiful women paraded through the ballroom, garnering the attention of everyone with a heartbeat. They shined like actresses, but appeared classier. The ensembles they wore were tasteful and expensive. Every extremity was bejeweled. I tapped Carlo, and inquired about these women, though I already had my suspicions. With pride bursting from his voice, he told me those were his Ladies of Distinction.

Instantly, I became more interested in his business. I was curious as to how he was able to secure the loyalties of women this beautiful for such dubious employment. As Carlo worked the room with me on his arm, we interacted with a few of the women. They were obviously comfortable with him, joking and patting him on the arm. I felt a burst of jealously swirling in my stomach. *Surely, Carlo could have his way with any of these beauties, couldn't he? Or was it all about me? What did we share anyway, he and I?*

Questions overwhelmed me, and all of a sudden I started feeling sick. I told Carlo I was "rued to go," attempting to use humor to mask my jealously. He laughed then asked me to wait a second while he handled something. When he returned, we left the party.

I expected him to walk me to my car and bid me farewell. Much to my surprise, when we got inside the elevator, instead of pushing P for parking, he selected PH, as in Penthouse. He extracted a key from his tuxedo jacket and slipped it into the key bank on the wall.

"Where are we going?" I inquired.

"You're staying, right?" His question was really more of a confirmation. His mind was already made up for the both of us. "I got something for you," he promised with a smirk.

As expected, the suite was immaculately plush. (I'd come to expect nothing but the best from Carlo.) No sooner than we crossed the threshold, he stripped naked and bolted to the Jacuzzi, leaving a trail of expensive clothing on the floor behind him. I tell you, the man held no shame, walking around the suite with his long dick swinging between his legs like a tail. He adjusted the water temperature then looked back at me.

"You coming or what?"

I quickly stripped down to my thong and bra and put one foot in the water. He stopped me.

"Whoa, whoa, what's wrong, Sol? You bashful?"

"Not at all."

He motioned to my panties. "Can't tell."

I tossed my Vicky's Secret over my shoulder and climbed in his arms, my back to his chest.

Carlo rubbed my back tenderly for awhile then played in my hair. "So what do you think?" he asked.

"About?"

"About the party, my business. Convinced it's legal, Counselor?"

I had to admit, I could see why wealthy men would pay top dollar to spend time with women so beautiful. Still, I wasn't totally convinced everything was on the up-and-up. I wasn't totally convinced nothing illegal occurred when they were alone. I told him so.

"Shit, me neither." He laughed. "But I do my part to discourage it as much as possible."

He sounded so sincere I left it alone and moved on to my next concern.

"Do you sleep with any of your ladies?" I said *ladies* with so much grease, the word tasted foul in my mouth. I don't know why I even bothered to broach the subject. Not like I expected him to tell me the truth. Yet, I did want to hear his answer.

"The only lady I want to sleep with is right here between my legs," he professed, as if it was gospel. He kissed my neck and I melted, but the fact he deflected my question was not lost on me.

"Carlo … Carlo …" I raised up and turned to face him. "I'm serious."

"I'm serious, too," he insisted. "I'm really feeling you, Soldada. You're fine as hell, intelligent, driven. Plus, you have that X-Factor."

"X-Factor?"

"Yeah. That thing I just can't put my finger on, but has me wanting to stay around until I do."

He pulled me onto his lap and smothered me with kisses. This time I didn't resist. I reveled in his affection. Felt his hardness probing at my entrance.

"Could this be the X-Factor?" I wondered, rubbing my wet slit on his rock.

"Please," he breathed between kisses. "I've had pussy since pussy had me."

"Oooh, you so nasty," I purred seductively.

"You don't know the half ..."

Carlo kissed a trail from my lips down to my breasts. Deftly, he slipped two fingers inside of me from behind, using one hand to spread my round mounds while he dipped the fingers from his free hand inside my bowl. Then he slid me on his dick, gently entering me like a knife into a sheath. He gripped my waist to control the depth of penetration, but I wasn't satisfied. I wanted to sail this ship.

I gripped Carlo's shoulders and rode him like a wave. Rode him deeper into the bubbly water. Rode him until only his head was above water. Rode him until he nearly capsized. Funny thing, I noticed he kept scooting closer toward the jets on the bottom of the jacuzzi. At first, I thought he was just caught up in the moment, trying to escape his climax, but the more he slid toward the jets, the harder I rode him. I wanted to make him feel as good as I was feeling. Wanted him to lose his ubiquitous cool.

Soon, I felt him expanding inside my walls. Proof that I was doing something right. But he still kept sliding toward those jets. I felt him expanding wider, each time he slid by those jets.

Then, he blatantly sat his ass right on one of the jets, and immediately exploded inside of me.

I screamed, and jumped off his lap in a hurry. Feigned as if I was concerned about getting pregnant. In truth, birth control had coursed through my veins since my days as a teenager. I'd stopped him because he threw me for a loop when he purposely sat his black ass on that jet.

What was that all about? I wondered.

I stalled as long as I could, but Carlo was worked up, and he wanted more. He carried me to the bed and drank from my juices. No matter what was said about Carlo, one thing was certain: the man could eat some pussy! He did that shit so good, he could've taught a class on it, maybe even written some books. Hell, he should've been given a medal! After a few minutes of his tongue-lashing, any reservations I had were booked.

But that damn Carlo insisted on interrupting our flow. I don't know how he got it, but suddenly I felt something buzzing my legs. I looked down and saw this blue thingy, shaped like an arc, strapped to two of his fingers.

I spazzed out. Clamped his hand in a vice grip. "What the hell is that?"

"Calm down, Sol," he urged. "It's a Dolphin."

"A what?"

"A Dolphin." Now how the hell did I know what a dolphin was? Last I checked, dolphins swam in the sea. "Just chill and lay down before you spoil the mood."

Me? Spoil the mood? All kinds of slick shit was on my tongue, but Carlo's confidence stilled me. He had a calming effect over me, like everything was always under his control. I only had to sit back, and enjoy the ride.

Carlo turned that Dolphin loose on me and had my center spitting like a blowhole. He sucked on my clit while sticking that vibrating arc inside of me and watched me squirm and shake like I was being electrocuted. I came so hard I nearly blacked out. When I surfaced, Carlo had the Dolphin thingy strapped to the underside of his long dick, just waiting to run up in me. I spread my legs wide and welcomed him in.

He made me feel things I'd never known were possible. It felt weird at first, the vibrations coupled with his hot, hard flesh, but the pleasure was so intense I was rewarded with orgasm after orgasm each time he stirred inside me. He made me feel sooo good I felt compelled to reciprocate, and bless him with a little head.

That's where the problem came in.

I must've sucked him off for, at least, thirty minutes. And he gave me nothing. Admittedly, I'm no pro. But DAMN!!!! Nothing?! Not even a little jizm? Pre-cum? Nothing?

I gave up, collapsed onto his chest in a huff. "What is wrong with you? Damn! You can't be human. My jaws are tired, and you're not even partially satisfied!" I tapped his semi-flaccid penis and complained, massaging my jaws. "Look at you. You're not even hard."

Carlo lightly pushed me away. "You all right, Soldada. It's not you though, it's me. I just can't bust off from a blow job like that. Not just off head," he whispered.

"Really? Well what does it take?" I inquired, ready and willing to please.

"Seriously ..." His voice trailed off like he was debating whether or not to share the secrets of Solomon's temple with me. "Don't trip, but ..."

"What? What is it? You can tell me, Carlo. What is it?"

He paused and appeared to be scanning me for signs of distrust. Then, "I like a finger in my ass when I'm getting head. No homo."

No homo? Was he serious?

"Wait. Now what now?" I raised my head from his chest to make sure I'd heard him correctly. "What do you mean, a finger in the ass?"

"Yeah." His face was as straight as an arrow. "Double-stimulation is the shit. Didn't you enjoy it?" he quipped, sarcastically.

"Yeah, but I'm a woman!"

"Exactly."

Exactly? I was waiting on him to elaborate, but he never did. So I said, "Exactly?"

"Yeah. You women don't have a monopoly on double-stimulation," he claimed. "People seem to think a man liking a finger in his ass makes him gay. Nothing could be further from the truth! Shit, if a man has sex with another man, he is gay. Period. Personally, I've never had any sexual contact with another man. I'm just a little freaky, ya know. I like different shit when it comes to sex, but not no fuckin' man. Hell naw! Fuck that shit!"

"I don't know. It just seems a little weird to me. That's all," I admitted.

In reality, I was having a hard time buying it because, to me, there wasn't much difference between a finger and a penis. If a man will take a finger in the ass, then he's just a few drinks away from a penis following it, in my book. I told him just that.

He laughed. "Look, I'm not about to sit here and debate about my sexuality. I'm secure in my manhood. More importantly, I'm secure in my humanity. If I was gay, I would say it and be it. I told you before, I don't owe anyone any apologies for me. Shit, I'm me! If you can't play in my league, sit on the bench, but don't ever accuse, or even insinuate, me being gay."

I didn't respond right away. My mind was busy processing what he said. I was analyzing words, tone, inflection, and history. Especially history. All things considered, I deduced I was dealing with a man's man, a free thinker. More so, because he wasn't afraid to march to the beat of his own drum.

"Okay," I whispered. "I apologize for questioning your sexuality. It's just a little … different. That's all."

"You're right, it is different," he admitted. "But that's my job. To make you experience different things. You make me feel different things because I'm open to the possibilities of what this can become. Just be open with me, and we can experience different things together."

He pulled me closer and sealed our pact with a kiss. No, all of my fears were not allayed. No, I was not certain he was hetero, but until he showed me otherwise, I was comfortable with him.

We resumed our tryst. I slid down Carlo's body to complete what I'd started, and yeah, maybe even get on his level. Unfortunately, my phone shrilled with a special ring tone. Only one person had that designation, and he never called past midnight, unless it was important.

"Hello," I answered, gasping for breath.

"Soldada? It's me," Constantine sniped. "Meet me outside your hotel in fifteen minutes. We finally have a break in your case."

Damn. Just when things were getting good, duty called.

Shaun Sinclair

17

Anthony

Damn! Damn! Damn!

I must've sworn a thousand times as I escaped through the woods to my car. I don't know how I let that muthafuka escape my wrath! I knew I had clipped him with, at least, one shot, but he kept running. It was either chase him down and chance letting his *compadre* crawl to freedom, or finish the job and address the collateral damage later. Dude ran too fast to get an accurate description of me, so I opted to let him hear — loud and clear — the shots that ended his man's life.

Once I settled in my car, and regained my composure, I made the call. Uncle Roland's gruff voice greeted me, curt and short.

"It's done," I said, and ended the call. I pulled my mask off, and sank down in my seat.

How did it come to this?

After the Mexican double-crossed Mo, my uncle sent his hounds out to gather information. Who. What. When. Where. Why. Of course, they came back with the bones. After poring over the details repeatedly, we decided loose ends needed to be tied. By any means necessary. If the right information leaked to the wrong people, our mutli-million dollar deal was toast. Mo left too much information floating around in the Mexican's head, so we had to air it out.

With the info gleaned from Uncle Roland's hounds, I broke everything down and plotted the best plan of action. During our bank jacking days, I was the designated planner, so this was natural to me.

I staked those fools out better than the feds.

Cruz was the main concern. Not just because he double-crossed the family. It was bigger than that. This was business. Cruz held the most potentially damaging information, so he was the target.

Unfortunately, Cruz kept a *compadre* with him at all times. I noted that during my stakeout. Didn't matter to me, his *compadre* would just be collateral damage. No problem. I blamed it on Cruz.

Cruz lived in an apartment complex off Albemarle Road, just past Eastland Mall. The complex was surrounded by woods. Next to the woods was another complex, then another. I parked my hooptie in the second complex, trekked through the woods, and waited on Cruz.

I couldn't tally how long I waited in the woods before I saw Cruz's Dodge truck behind the corner, but as soon as I saw it, I sprang into action.

Keeping low, I emerged from the tree line gripping both .357 revolvers so tight it's a wonder I didn't crush them. I slithered through the darkness, back planted on car after car, until I was in range. Cruz never saw me coming until I popped up on the other side of the car, dumping.

The first shot split his chest open like an autopsy. A crimson burst of blood puffed into the air, as the impact threw him off his feet, and the back of his head smacked against the pavement, breaking his fall. In the split second I took to inhale the pungent smell of gunpowder clouding the air, his partner took off like Usain Bolt in the Olympics. I licked two shots from my other burner and watched as they slammed into his back.

He howled like a werewolf, but he kept running.

I lined my aim up and fired three more deep, thunderous rounds that sent tremors through my body. The lone street lamp illuminated the gun smoke like a ghost. He buckled a little, but kept running. I heard dogs barking in the distance. People clamoring.

My window was closing.

I returned to Cruz. Put him out of his misery with two to the face, and bolted to my car.

Mona was unknowingly playing a big part in my alibi, should it come to that, so after disposing of my dirty clothing, I dashed to her spot.

It was well past midnight when I arrived. Mona opened the door for me wearing lace boy shorts and a half bra. Her hair framed her face as it dropped to her shoulders, giving her an angelic glow.

Pressure left my body like an exorcism.

One thing I loved about Mona, she preserved the sexy at all times. No matter what mood I was in, I could always count on Mona to wield her femininity to slay my dragons. Ever since the night she finally let me smash, the night Mo got popped, we had grown kind of close. We weren't in a relationship, per se; we just had an understanding. Translation: I was the only one knocking the bottom out that pretty ass, and I was still free to do me. Strangely enough, I wasn't exercising that freedom because Mona kept me satisfied in the sex department. Her sex game was the exact opposite of her looks. Straight-up beast mode! Her head game was heroin, and she had so much control over her pussy muscles she could probably crack walnuts with the shit. Word!

Mona pulled me inside, straight to the bedroom. She knew me so well. I was still tight from my earlier business, and getting a ball off was just what I needed.

I dipped in the bathroom, took a shower in record time, and stepped out in my birthday suit, dripping water on the floor. Mona's crazy ass was right there waiting for me ... with a video camera rolling.

I barked on her. "Yo, Mona, what the hell you doing?"

She cheesed at me, steady shooting footage of my upper body. "Smile for the camera." I turned away from the camera, shielding my wood. "Let me find out you bashful," she remarked.

I ducked and dodged the lens, trying to hide, then suddenly, an idea hit me. I thought about the convenience of the camera, in relation to the night's events. The camera recorded date and time.

Perfect.

I started posing. "Get your shoot on," I told Mona. "But you might need more film to record all this," I joked, cuffing my dick in my hand and shaking it at her. Her retarded-ass kept right on shooting, leading me to the bed.

Without warning, I snatched the camera. "Give me that! Now, you dance."

"What?"

"You heard me. Dance! Hold up a sec though ..." I turned up the stereo. Sade trickled through the Bose speakers. "Aiight. Go 'head."

I readjusted the focus on the camera and Mona started doing her thing, rolling her lithe body like a belly dancer while I captured the whole thing on camera. After a few minutes of her dancing seductively, I switched the music up. I didn't select anything in particular. Just let it do what it do. Next thing I knew "No Ordinary Love" came creeping through the speakers ... beating, too.

"Oooh, that's my shit!" Mona gushed.

"Aiight, show me then. Take that shit off," I suggested.

The first thing she lost was her bra. She cupped both of her heavy Ds in her hands and licked the nipples like ice cream cones. I zoomed in with the camera just as they hardened. Her brown nipples definitely deserved to be remembered forever. Mona seemed more aroused by the camera. She dropped her titties, spun around, and started shaking that ass even harder. She spread her legs and pulled her boy shorts down over her wide hips. The shorts hit the ground just seconds before her hands. She bent over and spread her cheeks like mayonnaise. I zoomed in on, still, the prettiest pussy I had ever seen, glistening and damp, begging for me.

I adjusted the camera and slid right up in her, camera in one hand, her slim waist in the other. I kept the camera trained on the in-and-out of my strokes as I dug deep inside of her. My joint looked big as hell on camera gliding in and out, looked like I'd gained a few inches, felt like King Dong up in that muthafucka! I pumped a few times then slid out.

"Mona, I want you to taste it. I want you to suck this dick," I told her, panting, trying to race down my breath. I sat on the edge of the bed and leaned back to give her easy access.

Mona dropped to her knees between my legs and gulped me inside her mouth. I kept the camera on her the whole time. When she swabbed the bottom of my meat, the camera was right there. When she sucked the head, it was there. When she licked my balls, although it was a struggle holding it, the camera was there. And when she —

What the fuck! Was that a finger?!

I dropped the camera and kicked Mona dead in her chest, away from me.

"FUCK YOU DOING?!!!" I roared.

"What?"

"You know the fuck what! Don't play with me," I raged.

She grinned. "Oh. that? I was just trying to please you. Damn, A.P.! Lighten up."

"Lighten up, my ass! I don't play that shit. That's an exit only. Aiight? Aiight?"

She frowned, gave me puppy-dog eyes, and nodded. I felt bad. Here she was just trying to make me feel better, and I had spazzed. I know some cats in the joint who liked the type of shit she was trying, but I wasn't one. I just had to let her know.

"Come 'ere." I pulled Mona onto my lap, whispered in her ear. "Yo, I ain't mean no harm. I just don't get down like that, feel me?" She nodded bashfully. "Now if you really want to please me, you can do what you do best."

"And what's that?"

"Ride this dick."

I retrieved the camera from the floor, and recorded Mona as she did her thing, silently in awe of her beauty. After a few minutes, she stopped moving, and shot me a questioning look. I nodded, and Mona slid me inside her hot, sticky third-input. It was maaaad tight back there! But she handled it well. Meanwhile I had the camera locked in position, documenting all the freaky fuck faces she made. Pain turned to pleasure then reversed. Her eyes rolled into the back of her head. She howled and clenched my dick tighter. Felt like I was trapped inside a fiery vice grip.

I gained my composure and redirected the lens down low to capture what was happening down there. On the screen sticking out from the side of the camera, I could see me inside her other hole, at the back — only if I peered past the obvious. Mona's masterpiece of a jewel was front and center, dripping all that sweet juice onto my midsection. I tell you, shit was such a sight to behold, had me wishing I had two dicks!

Mona must have picked up on how good I was feeling, because she took the camera and started filming me.

"You ... like this ... A.P.? Huh? Show ... show ... me. Cum ... for ... me ..."

I made exaggerated fuck faces because I knew I was on candid camera. Then, shit started feeling so good I didn't have to exaggerate. I played with Mona's swollen clit for all of twenty seconds before she rewarded me with a gut-wrenching orgasm so powerful I felt the concussions vibrating through the hole I was in. She squeezed my joint so hard I thought she was going to break it in two!

I erupted inside of her ass like a fire hydrant exploding, blowing Mona clean off of me where she collapsed onto my chest. Exhausted.

"Damn! I should've had the camera!" I joked breathlessly.

Those were my last words for the night.

Later, I lay in bed awake with Mona on my chest asleep. Thoughts of my dirty deeds assaulted my mind. It baffled me how I could perpetrate such evil without a second thought, how I could extinguish a life absent remorse. Yet, the facts were what they were. If Cruz's partner had not escaped my wrath, I would have been congratulating myself on a job well done, as opposed to nursing a dilemma. I'd never considered myself extra tough. Definitely, didn't consider myself a cold-blooded killer; I was just efficient. I had been taught at an early age to do whatever needed to be done to acquire what I needed in this world. Laws be damned. The law in my land was survival! In life, you get what you can make happen for you, or what you can't prevent. Period.

Now, I found myself in a precarious situation. A witness to murder was still roaming the streets, wounded, but roaming the streets, nonetheless. He couldn't identify me, but that was irrelevant. I had seen too many loose ends grow into the fuse to light the bomb to obliterate someone's life. I was not trying to have that happen to me.

"Penny for your thoughts?" I hadn't noticed that Mona was awake.

"Hmm? Oh, nah ... I'm cool."

"It's ..." She craned her neck to see the clock. "... three forty-five in the morning, and you're awake staring at the ceiling? No, things are definitely not cool."

"Yeah, you right," I admitted. "Just business, though."

"Business? The money is rolling in good, to my knowledge. I didn't know we had a problem with money," Mona snickered. She sat up. "Wait! Does this have anything to do with that lady from the D.A.'s office?"

"What?" I raised up, my heart galloping in my chest. "What lady from the D.A.'s office?" Surely Mona wasn't referring to Soldada. Hell, I hadn't seen her in weeks. Not since the night at the basketball game.

"The young Puerto Rican chick that was at the game that night with the district attorney. She was at the party tonight," Mona informed me.

"What party?"

"You know, the meet and greet at the Sheraton I told you about. She was there tonight."

"She was there? Doing what?" I asked.

"I think she was with Cadillac."

"You think? What you mean, *'you think'*? Was she?"

"Is something wrong?" Mona asked, concern cracking her voice.

"Mona, answer the damn question! Was she with Cadillac or not?"

"I-I'm not sure, but I know she was at the party because I remember one of the clients mentioning something about her. Said she thinks she's hot shit because she's fucking the D.A."

For some reason, that rubbed me the wrong way. Yeah, I had just finished knocking the bottom out of Mona's pussy, but I still felt funny about the *thought* of someone else running up in Soldada's goodness. And Constantine?! Definitely not that greasy motherfucka. No way was he laying up inside that good pussy!

"And when did Cadillac leave?" I asked.

"I don't know, but I did notice after he left, I didn't see her any more. Why? Is something wrong?"

"Nah. Everything straight." I couldn't hardly keep a straight face I was lying so hard. A million scenarios stampeded through my mind. None of them positive. "Get some rest."

I played in Mona's hair to put her at ease, but inside I was a ball of unbridled fire and confusion. I couldn't begin to imagine what Cadillac and Soldada would have in common, other than the investigation. Even that was farfetched because Cadillac was not directly tied to the family. Not on paper anyway. Cadillac did not have our last name because he was not Uncle Roland's biological son. Uncle Roland had raised him since he was two years old, ever since he stole my aunt from Cadillac's daddy. Out of respect for his daddy's memory, he never changed Cadillac's name.

A million questions invaded my mind, and at the crack of dawn, I planned to answer all of them.

Right after I slayed Mona again.

18

SOLDADA

We stormed into the Carolina Medical Center like paratroopers. Constantine and his security detachment at the point, Thomas (one of the aides) and I trailing. We followed a deputy deep into the bowels of the hospital, into a reserved room. The room was absent any of the gadgetry that normally littered hospital rooms. The only equipment, besides the bed, was a metal stand holding an IV bag. I followed the trail of wire and saw a man lying in bed with saline solution dripping into his arm. We stood by the door while Constantine approached the bed and shook the man awake.

He awoke, sputtering gibberish, shaking his head vigorously. He must have thought Constantine was coming to finish the job. Come to think of it, Constantine did kind of resemble an outlaw in his dark blue dungaree jeans and black crew-neck sweater.

Constantine leaned over the bed. "I'm here. Talk." The man began mumbling in Spanish. Constantine stopped him mid-sentence and turned to me. "Soldada, come here please. This fuckin' wetback doesn't even speak English."

I rushed over to the bed and got a real good look at the man for the first time. He was clearly Mexican and surely troubled. Sweat drenched his brow, his pupils were dilated, and the entire right side of his body was wrapped in bloody bandages. Constantine wanted answers ASAP, so I rattled off the basics of interrogation. Who? What? When? Where? Who did it and why? I fired the questions off in rapid Spanish. He answered just as fast.

He told me his name was Jorge Rivera Luis Cruz-Rivera de Juarez, or just Jorge for short, thank God. Said he and a friend were ambushed at his friend's place. He was shot attempting to save his friend's life after his friend was attacked in the parking lot. He never got a good look at the assailant, but on a previous occasion, his friend had told him about some work he was doing for the Padmore family. Said his friend felt uncomfortable. Scared. His friend told him that, if something were to happen to him, it would probably be at the hands of the Padmores. Courtesy of that same friend, he was now in possession of some powerful information that could bring the Padmore family to its knees. If anything ever happened to his friend, he was ordered to contact the D.A.'s office and only speak to Constantine Annapolis.

I relayed the story to Constantine.

"What?" Constantine scoffed. "You gotta be fuckin' kidding me. I was dragged out of my bed for this bullshit? You tell that motherfucker I'm pissed! Unless he can come up with something and spit it out faster than a goddamn cobra, I'll make him wish he never heard the name Constantine Annapolis."

I communicated Constantine's threat to Jorge, though it was moot. Rage was a universal language.

Jorge elaborated on his story without hesitation. Seemed his late friend had contracted a murder through the Padmore family. He had hard evidence to prove it in the form of a recording and phone call. When I told Constantine this, I could've sworn he had an orgasm. His face scrunched up and he started giggling like a villain in a scary movie.

Constantine yanked Jorge up from the bed, oblivious to his screams. "Where? Where is the evidence, you slimy bastard?"

"Constantine! Wait! I got it. Get off him!" I exclaimed, ripping Constantine off the victim. He retreated to the shadows with the rest of the team, and let me work my magic. A few minutes later, I joined them with the information firmly ensconced inside my brain. But Constantine wasn't pleased with the time frame.

"When he gets out the hospital?" he exploded. "Hell no! We need that evidence *now*, so I can see the judge in the morning and get the warrants for Roland and that fuckin' Anthony."

Constantine was foaming at the mouth like a rabid dog. I hated to break the news to him, but I had to.

"Uh, Constantine," I interrupted while he was barking orders at Thomas. "I'm afraid we won't be able to get the warrants for those two. He didn't mention either of their names."

"What?" He waved me away. "Look, it doesn't matter. You get the evidence, and I'll get the warrants, okay?" I nodded meekly. "Good. Now you all unlock those tubes, find his clothes, and cuff him. I'll be downstairs waiting in the truck."

Constantine turned and left us there; Thomas unhooking Jorge, and me desperately trying to explain to him the change in plans.

19

Anthony

After leaving Mona's place the morning after she dropped the bomb on me, I headed to Uncle Roland's for brunch. He had summoned me earlier as I was burying more of my frustrations between Mona's thighs. He didn't go into detail. He never did over the phone. Just beckoned me with the same curtness I was accustomed to.

I arrived in Ballentyne a little after noon. Maria ushered me inside Uncle Roland's office where I sat and waited on the green suede love seat, while watching *SportsCenter* highlights. A few minutes later. Uncle Roland showed up pushing Moses in a wheelchair, looking all the part of the doting father. We exchanged pounds and nods, then got down to business.

"How'd it go?" Uncle Roland asked. I assumed he wanted details because I already told him over the phone shit was gravy.

"According to plan," I answered vaguely.

There was no need to go into detail about the dude that went rabbit. Way I figured it, he was never part of the job anyway. He was a ghost in this equation. No alarms needed to be sounded. Dude had no idea who clipped him. Surely, they'd crossed more people than Mo in their reign of crime, so it was impossible to narrow it down to me. I knew this: there were too many Latinos in Charlotte to track that one down without putting fire on myself. I decided to pursue that situation if, and only if, the situation pursued me.

"Saw it on the news this morning," Uncle Roland informed me. "Said there were no witnesses, but they are following some leads."

No witnesses? Music to my ears. Unfortunately, the beat didn't play long.

"Turns out this Cruz fella was a snitch, an informant," Uncle Roland relayed, frowning at Mo.

"What?!" I nearly jumped out of my seat. "How you figure?"

"Said so on the news. *'A high-level police informant was found shot to death outside his apartment building.'* You know anything about this?" He thumped Moses on the noggin.

"N-ah, Pop. 'Course not."

"Of course not." Uncle Roland sighed heavily. "Don't matter now. Dead men don't tell tales, right?" He chuckled triumphantly. "Let's go eat. Maria hooked us up some steak, eggs, and Lord knows what else."

We left his office and passed the large dining room that offered magnificent views of the outdoor pool. As we approached the kitchen, we heard commotion at the front door. Maria was yelling, firing off in rapid Spanish as she blocked the door to prevent someone from entering.

Uncle Roland left Mo coasting down the hall as he bolted to the door to investigate, with me hot on his heels.

First thing I saw were snippets of black jackets trying to muscle Maria out the way. Uncle Roland snatched the door open to confront whoever it was. That was when I saw a rack of police vehicles in the yard, all on the grass and shit. My aunt was going to flip out; she didn't play about her grass! Uncle Roland pushed Maria aside and barked at the lead officer.

"What the hell is going on here?" he demanded.

"Sir, we have a warrant —" the officer began, but Uncle Roland wouldn't let him finish.

"A warrant, my ass! Hey, hey, get those goddamn trucks off my fuckin' grass!!!" Uncle Roland yelled over the cop's head to the black Suburban that had just pulled up and slid to a halt, leaving a long tire trail through the grass. The officers attempted to address Uncle Roland again, but they were overshadowed as the man of the hour popped out the back seat of the truck.

Constantine Annapolis.

Before it could register in my head, Uncle Roland had pushed the cop aside and was storming toward Constantine, full-throttle. Of course, a few burly deputies hemmed him up from behind in a chokehold before he reached him, but his intentions were undisputed.

"You don't ... know ... who ... you're ... fuckin'... with!" Uncle Roland wheezed between breaths, as Constantine walked right up in his face while his sycophants held Uncle Roland back.

"Of course, I do. It says so right here on this search warrant," Constantine quipped, flashing a piece of paper. He turned to the deputies. "Gentlemen, we are looking for a large caliber handgun, size-twelve boots, and soiled and bloodied clothing! If you find anything, do NOT touch it. Notify me immediately!"

Given their orders, the officers tore through the house like a tornado. Uncle Roland was released from the torture rack and allowed to console my aunt, who had appeared in the doorway, and went into a tizzy.

Me? I was shaking in my size-12 Jordans, wondering how in the hell they had managed to link me to the killing. In my mind, all I heard was the judge sentencing me to life. Heard the metal door slamming, never to be opened again for me. Smelled the awful stench of prison. Bile rose in my throat as I tasted the terrible food. I shook my head, blinked away the visions.

Then I saw her slide from the back of the tinted Suburban.

Even in my anguish, I immediately noted how beautiful she was. For a brief second, time stopped as I admired her fling her pretty hair into the air and storm toward the house. The beige slacks she wore clung to her ample curves like an infant on a mother's tit. Her white silk blouse was smothered by the chunk of blue body armor she sported with the police insignia emblazoned in the corner. Her face looked tired and haggard, but still radiated with beauty. My mind relapsed back to the wonderful nights we shared, first in Anguilla, then at my place.

Then I snapped out of it. This wasn't a personal visit. She was here to do me harm. To do my family harm.

I slapped a scowl on my face, and positioned myself, so I'd be the first face she saw when she opened the door. Either my scowl worked or she had cramps, because when she followed a deputy into the house and saw me, her face dropped as if she was riding a roller coaster.

"Anthony!" she gasped quietly. I stole a glance to make sure no one was looking, then snatched her inside the foyer closet just behind the front door.

"What are you doing?" she squealed.

"That's what I want to know about you," I retorted, blocking the door.

She peeked over her shoulder, then whispered, "Anthony, are you crazy? Do you want to go to jail?"

"No place I haven't been before," I snapped. "Now answer the question. What are you doing here?"

"My job, Anthony. Now open the door!" she hissed.

"Why do you have to be involved?" I screeched. "Don't you get it? This guy wants me dead! Doesn't that mean anything to you?"

Above us, footsteps thudded. Soldada looked away in silence. Thought I glimpsed a tear or two struggling not to drip from her eyes. I hoped my words were penetrating that iron will of hers. As I watched her gnaw on her bottom lip, my heart raced, cognizant of the reality of all that was going on around us. Somehow, somewhere, I had fucked up, and I needed someone's mercy to save me.

"Anthony, it's not you he's after! I've seen the warrants; your name isn't on any of them," she shared, then narrowed her eyes. "Why? Should it be?"

I shrugged my shoulders. "I don't know what you're here for, so I couldn't tell you." *Who did she think she was dealing with? A rookie?* "Only thing I'm guilty of is caring for your selfish ass!"

"Whatever, Anthony," she scoffed, crossing her arms. She looked so sexy when she was upset. I wanted to take her right there and wear her out while her cronies stormed our home. "You better let me out of here before people start missing me," she advised, crossing her arms.

I placed my hand on the door, pump-faked like I was about to let her out. Then, I turned back to her. "Whose name is on the warrants?" I asked.

"Open the door, Anthony!"

"Whose name is on the warrants?"

She looked away, bit her bottom lip, mumbled, "Unbelievable ..."

I prodded further. "Well?"

She hesitated, then answered. "Your cousin, Moses Padmore."

I dashed from the closet down the hall to where I'd last seen Mo, but I was too late. Moses was already on the ground in handcuffs with a deputy's knee jammed into his back. Another deputy was pulling his arms back like a slot machine. A speed knot was slowly rising on his forehead.

I broke through the fracas and pushed a deputy aside. "Get the fuck off him!" I yelled, then pointed at the toppled wheelchair. "Can't you see he's injured?"

One of the deputies, a blond crew-cut motherfucker, sneered back at me. "I don't give a fuck if he's dead; we got a warrant for him and we taking his black ass in!"

I stepped aside while they hoisted Mo to his feet. I didn't want to further escalate the situation, so I fell back. I figured it best to let the (il)legal process run its course, then take it from there. Or as I learned in the feds: live to fight another day. Our money was deep enough to fight any case they could pin on us. That was for sure.

A couple of hours later, the authorities had gone, leaving the house twisted. Their search failed to turn up anything of substance besides some registered pistols, but their hunt had left an indelible impression on the whole house. My aunt had retired to her bed after being issued a sleep aid to deal with her discomfort. (Lately, it seemed as if she had been reduced to a pill-popping caricature of her former self.) Meanwhile Uncle Roland barked orders over the phone to Theron. Apparently, Theron had been unavailable to personally spring Mo from jail. He had sent one of his minions instead. Uncle Roland was taking this seemingly-slight affront personal. With all the money he was paying Theron, I couldn't blame him. Then, to make matters worse, Cadillac still had not shown up. Dirty had arrived within an hour of receiving the call, but Cadillac was pulling a Houdini. We were planning to go to the precinct to retrieve Mo in full force, right after Cadillac arrived, but apparently that wasn't going to happen. Tired of waiting, Uncle Roland instructed Theron to meet us at the precinct, then ended the call.

We arrived at the precinct looking like we meant business. Big Drew in his ubiquitous black, Dirty in an expensive black sweater and black slacks, and Uncle Roland in a plush black floor-length mink coat, alligator-skinned briefcase clutched tightly in his left hand.

Theron's minion was waiting for us on the steps of the courthouse, but Uncle Roland brushed past him as if he was shoe soil. "Let me know the second Theron arrives," Uncle Roland called over his shoulder to the minion.

"Sir, I don't think he'll be able to make it," the minion protested.

"The second he arrives," Uncle Roland repeated, using his right hand to keep his fedora in place.

Once inside, we were immediately accosted by Constantine. He walked right up in Unc's face and released a tirade on him.

But Uncle Roland wasn't up for it this time. "Constantine, I'll deal with you later. I just came for my son," he declared. Constantine smirked but left us alone. He went to the back somewhere, undoubtedly watching our every move on one of the cameras. A few minutes later, we watched Mo emerge from one of the back rooms and reclaim his belongings. As he started in our direction, a smile tugged at his lips. I knew that feeling well. Nothing like your family having your back when the system was trying to tear you asunder. I smiled back at him, ready to tease him about popping his cherry, his first night in jail.

Unfortunately, his night was not done.

Two white men, whom I assumed were detectives, appeared from a small room in the hallway and snatched Mo inside with them. Uncle Roland immediately hopped on the phone, desperately trying to reach Theron. Fortunately, he walked up behind us before the call went through. Uncle Roland whispered a few harsh words to Theron, then unleashed him toward the room where Mo and the detectives had disappeared.

We waited and waited. Waited until my mind started playing tricks on me. I started imagining Mo spilling the beans and implicating us all. I could see the bars closing in on me forever. Could see Constantine cackling because he finally had his day.

I reeled my thoughts back in just in time to hear Uncle Roland mumble something. "What was that, Unc?"

"That little bitch think she all that," he repeated, jerking his head toward the conference room. "Bet her pretty little hand is all up in this." I followed his gaze and saw Soldada slinking from the room with a folder clutched tightly to her breast. She saw me, cut her eyes at me, and kept right on rolling. I decided right then and there, I was really done with her. This chick was really trying to bury my family!

After about another hour of waiting, Theron emerged from the room with Mo in tow. Big Drew rushed to push his wheelchair, and we peeled out without a second glance.

Inside the truck, Drew slid the partition bisecting the vehicle up and allowed us privacy, so Theron and Mo could school us to what happened in there.

"They ain't got nothing, Dad," Mo stated, proudly. "They threatened me a couple times, kept asking how I got shot. I told 'em, 'Hey, it's a dangerous world we live in —"

"That was my idea," Theron interjected, eager to regain Unc's favor.

"Yeah. So then, they asked me where I was at such and such time. I started to tell 'em since I was nowhere near the scene, but Theron advised me against it."

Uncle Roland turned his attention to Theron. "What they got, Theron? From a legal standpoint?"

Theron cleared his throat. "Basically, nothing. They have him charged with murder, but no evidence. It's just a stall tactic, prosecutors do it all the time. Charge high to get him to plead low, or better yet, get him to roll," he explained. "They know he isn't the shooter, but for some reason, they have their sights locked on him. I didn't want to ask in there, but is there anything I need to know, Moses?"

Mo glanced around the cabin, swallowed the lump in his throat, then answered, "Nope."

Theron twisted his mouth. "So you don't know anything about this Mexican getting popped? Not that I care one way or the other, but I just need to cross my Ts and dot my Is for this preliminary hearing."

"Whoa ... preliminary hearing?" Uncle Roland said.

"Yeah, Mr. Padmore. This thing is serious. They claim to have some kind of evidence linking him to the crime," Theron informed us. "They have to. Otherwise, it would be career suicide to go after him this hard. My guess is they have some kind of informant feeding them info."

My breath caught in my throat. Surely I hadn't fucked up that bad? There was no way the guy I popped could have tied his misfortune to us! By my estimate, he should've been slumped over in the forest somewhere or laid up in a hospital someplace, not snitching.

"We should have more info by the time the prelim rolls around," Theron guessed. "If they don't have anything concrete by then, we should be able to put this behind us."

Uncle Roland seemed pleased. "Good. That shouldn't be a problem then," he said, eyeing me as if our lives were held inside my palms. "I know, for a fact. my son was home convalescing with me last night," he assured Theron.

"Good enough then," Theron figured. "By the way, I have some new info on that piece of property. I tracked down a friend who deals with locating things. Within the week, I should be able to tell you exactly who the other person is on this bid, especially the silent partner." Like I said, Theron was sharp.

Uncle Roland patted him on the back, beaming. "Good job, son," he told Theron, then bid him farewell. I watched Theron practically skip to his Lexus LS with pride bursting from my chest. As long as he was on the case, Mo would be fine.

I, on the other hand, had a lot to be concerned about. If that informant was the man I left alive, all hell could break loose. I had one option. Find him, and eradicate him.

20

SOLDADA

I couldn't believe what my life had become. I was slowly spiraling out of control. My emotions were conflicted, and my morals were being tested at every turn. Just seeing Anthony the other day had thrown me for a loop. I desperately tried to make myself not feel anything for him, lobotomize my brain, but I was an invalid. I couldn't even win the battle against self. Anthony was in my psyche deep, permeating throughout my pores so much it was impossible to ignore.

As if that wasn't taxing enough, Carlo was demanding more and more of my time. Granted, he had become my pot of gold, but I just couldn't find time to indulge! Since I had been tasked with the preparation of Moses Padmore's preliminary hearing, I had only spoken to Carlo a few times on the phone. Now he was requesting — no, demanding — that I make myself available tonight. Said he had something special planned for me. I hated to disappoint, but there was a strong chance I wouldn't be able to make it. I only had four days remaining to perfect my case and my ass was riding on this. The more I analyzed things, the lousier I felt. It was painfully obvious that Moses Padmore was not the shooter in this case. I couldn't speak for the Cruz murder, but he definitely did not shoot Jorge, unless he was Wolverine, or had borrowed his adamantium skeleton. There was no way Moses Padmore could have done anything to anyone with those fresh gunshot wounds. However, his gunshot wounds did tell another story.

We checked hospital records, and Moses Padmore's name was nowhere to be found, not in the last few weeks. Not in the last few years. In fact, the only place his name showed up in the hospital was birth records. This definitely suggested something was amiss. But murder?

Unfortunately for Moses, it wasn't up to me. My orders were to build a case for murder against him, and despite my misgivings, I was going to do just that.

Like I said, my moral compass was spinning in reverse, and I had no desire to readjust it.

I had reviewed the case so much that I had it memorized by late afternoon. Nightfall found me mixing and matching applicable Rules of Court and citings to correspond with what I had before me. Soon, I had patched together a pretty strong body of work.

I was leaning back in my chair, massaging my temples with my eyes closed when I sensed someone enter the room. I opened my eyes and was greeted with a forest of roses headed straight toward my desk. I was alone in the office, so I braced myself, fingered my Glock-19 just beneath my desk in a holster attached to the underside of the metal.

"Ms. Andrews?" a voice called out from behind the roses. He sounded muffled.

"Yes?" I sang, my interest piqued.

"These are for you, ma'am ... and so is this." A card appeared on my desk. Still unable to see the deliveryman, I read the card aloud:

> "You have my permission to stop working for the day and enjoy your birthday.
> P.S. Even a mule gets a day off."

The card was signed *"C."* Only one person had the gall to pull something like this.

"Excuse me, sir. Do you have the sender's address?" I tried to peer around the roses to see who I was talking to. Suddenly they parted and revealed his handsome face. "Carlo?!"

"That's right!" He placed the arrangement on my desk, pulled me to him, and planted a wet one on my lips. I noticed he was carrying his disguise to the limit. He even had on a workman's hat, glasses, and a jumpsuit.

"What are you doing?" I asked through kisses.

"Obviously, saving you. You didn't even realize it was your birthday."

He was right. I had totally forgotten. "This case ..." I sighed heavily. "It has me stressed out."

"Well, stress no more. You are officially relieved for the night, as of right now."

"Carlo, I can't —"

"Shh ... get your things. I have something for you. I want to take you to a special place."

Downstairs in the parking garage, Carlo had a long, black, shiny Cadillac limo waiting. After he ushered me inside, the car lurched forward. As he changed out of the jumpsuit, I noticed he had acquired a new tattoo on his chest. I couldn't resist asking the question I always wondered.

"Why do they call you Cadillac?" He seemed surprised that I remembered. "In Anguilla, when we first met, you introduced yourself as Cadillac," I reminded him.

"Oh, I remember," he said, sliding into a pair of black slacks, taking his time to show off the bulge inside his silk briefs. "When I was younger, they called me Cadillac because I was big and smooth."

I could imagine his young-ass being big and smooth. Bet he had all the ladies. I told him that, and he laughed, brushing my comment off.

"So you want to talk about this case?" he offered, fixing himself a drink from the mini-bar in the limo. "It seems to be weighing you down, and whatever affects my baby, affects me."

His gesture was sweet, but I declined. It was my birthday (even if I did just remember), and I was going to salvage what was left of the evening. I took the drink Carlo offered and swigged it.

"Where are we going?" I quizzed, as the car whizzed down a country road.

"My place."

A few minutes later, the limo eased through tall, black wrought-iron gates, and stopped in front of a spectacular home. The thing that stuck out most was it looked like the White House. Literally. The home appeared to contain two or three levels, and huge pillars framed the entranceway, towering above us as we exited the limo. We climbed the few steps, and the large oak door opened before us.

Carlo led the way inside, where a huge self-portrait greeted us in the dimly-lit hallway. We pressed on into the great room, and words escaped me. The place was breathtaking! Cream-and-gold marble floors stretched before me as far as the eyes could see. I followed Carlo up marble-tiled stairs, down a long, wide hallway. He opened a door, and before me was spread the most plush bedroom I had ever seen. It was more elegant than a Trump suite. The bedroom was divided into two sections. One side was a mini-sitting room, complete with a leather sofa, flat-screen TV, two glass tables, and a fireplace. One of the tables held a heart-shaped birthday cake with twenty-seven lit candles.

I felt giddy, like a little kid.

Carlo sat me before the cake. I made a wish, then blew out the candles. Carlo fed me some of the chocolate cake. Then we danced for a long time to a medley of R&B tracks before he took my hand and beckoned me further inside the bedroom.

One look at the huge bed on the raised platform, and the juices began percolating between my thighs. I imagined sexing on that bed was like fucking on a big cloud. But we didn't stop there. He led me past the bed into a large bathroom.

"You know the drill," he stated.

I stripped while he adjusted the multiple showerheads. When he was satisfied with the temps, he stripped and joined me.

Carlo washed me down so tenderly. By the second time he lathered me up, I was floating.

"How you feel, Sol? You like that?" he cooed into my ear. "I want to take you to a place you've never been before." He said this while slipping his soapy hand all through my inner crevices. Felt so good I had to brace myself on his hard chest.

"What's taking you so long?" I purred softly. My head was in a fog. The hot water pounding my back and the steam surrounding us had the champagne I'd consumed in the limo pulling an encore. I felt loose. So loose I could do anything. Felt free as a bird. I always felt free around Carlo, he always alleviated my stress.

"Before I take you there, you have to trust me ..." Carlo blew in my ear. "Do you trust me, Sol?"

"Hmm-mmm." I nodded obediently.

"Yeah? Let's see."

We exited the shower. Carlo supplied me with a purple silk mask to cover my eyes. Sat me on the bed. I was beginning to get anxious. I wasn't too sure about the blindfold, but I thought the least I could do was oblige him. After all, he had gone through all this trouble to make my birthday special.

"Yeah," I whispered. "I trust you."

"Okay. We're gonna play a game. I want you to taste a few things, then tell me what they are. Ready?"

This was interesting. Different. I was game.

The first thing he fed me was a chocolate candy bar. Maybe a Snickers. Was so easy to figure out, I guessed it right away.

He rewarded me with a deep kiss, lots of tongue.

Then came the banana. I smelled it before he even placed it in my mouth. I licked it a few times to tease him, tried to assert some feminine control into this game of his.

He rewarded me with another kiss.

Then, he slipped his finger into my mouth. I sucked it seductively, and I swear it tasted just like ... pussy. Maybe I was tripping, paranoid even. Surely, any of my juices that previously coated his finger were washed off in the shower. Still, I swear his finger tasted just like pussy!

He removed his finger. Seconds later, I felt something warm probing around my mouth. I opened up to retrieve what he was offering, and this fool pushed his hard penis right inside my mouth. *Deep!* He nearly cracked a tooth and I gagged at first, but I caught my rhythm and sucked on his wonderful offering for a few minutes. My impeded sense of sight heightened my sense of taste. I could faintly taste alcohol and a lot of salt from the pre-cum coating the tip of his penis. I was beginning to enjoy it when, suddenly, he pulled back.

I snatched the mask up. "What's wrong, Carlo?"

"Nothing. This is your night. I want to please you like never before," he claimed, directing me further onto his huge bed. My insides thumped in anticipation of his championship oral skills. Instead, Carlo had more tricks up his sleeve.

"What are you doing with those?" I asked, skeptically eyeing the shiny silver handcuffs he had produced.

"Oh, these? These are trust," he remarked with a smirk.

"Trust?"

"Yeah. You said you trust me, right? Well, trust me to give you a birthday experience like never before."

How could I refuse? He had made good on all his promises thus far, so I laid back and allowed him to cuff my hands, then latch them to the headboard over my head.

"All right, Sol? No peeking."

The room went dark as he placed the mask over my eyes again. I felt him leave the bed. Moments later, smooth jazz filtered through my ears. I thought he had just left to adjust the music, but seconds morphed into minutes, and the cool breeze blowing on my naked ass dampened my warm mood. Anxiety started taking hold of me.

"Carlo?" I called out, suddenly not so sure this was a good idea. "Carlo?"

The light breeze grazed my naked body, building on to feelings of vulnerability. My nipples hardened like cement. A slight chill of fear coursed through my veins, shivers wracked my body. I began to panic until I felt Carlo's warm mouth engulf my big toe.

He sucked each toe like they were the sweetest things he'd ever tasted, leaving thick trails of saliva oozing between them. Then he slid his long tongue up my inner thigh, pausing to nibble on each knee. My body quivered in anticipation of what was to come. I squirmed a little, but my restraints kept me in place. He kissed all around my center, knowing exactly what I wanted, but refusing to accommodate me.

My juices flowed like Niagara Falls.

I thrust my hips forward, silently begging him to eat me out soooo good, begged him to slurp my essence draining on the purple sheets. I spread my legs wider than the Grand Canyon, allowing him full access, my only regret was not being able to see him wield his expert tongue. Even with the mask on, I still saw flashes of joy as pleasure wracked my body. I thrashed around violently, loving the caged freedom. It was a different feeling, submitting to someone. Surprisingly, I liked it. Maybe because I was in such good hands.

Carlo massaged my breasts, while continuing his relentless onslaught on my center, lapping up my liquids to no end. When he grew tired of my kitty, he headed further south, spread me open, and began tossing my salad. He wasn't bashful about it at all. He attacked my ass like he was searching for a new universe back there. *I'd never felt so good in my life!!!* I squirmed and squealed my way to another orgasm, flooding the satin sheets with my happy juice. Thankfully, Carlo didn't pause.

Not for a second.

He slid his hot, wet tongue through every nook and cranny of my rear, then slipped two fingers inside of my kitty. Dual-stimulation, with my senses on alert, sent me into overdrive! I was yearning for him to fill me up, complete this cycle with a hardcore fuck. I wanted him to take me like he owned me.

"*Damelo, Carlo ... damelo, Carlo ...*" I begged, reaching for him blindly.

"*Quiereme?*" His breath was hot and heavy.

"*¡Sí! ¡Sí!*" I panted.

I felt Carlo move around, place his body on my chest. He jammed his hardness into my mouth just as I begged for more. I eagerly greeted his long dick with hardcore sucks, making a loud, popping sound each time I released it from my clutches. He snaked his head down my body, spread open my folds, and reciprocated. We were in a sixty-nine, with him on top.

Everything was going blissful until I felt something strange down there. Felt like Carlo had company. Seemed as if two tongues were down there. Unless he was a mutant, a copilot was assisting Carlo in helping me blast-off.

I freaked out. Clamped my legs shut. Raised my body to buck Carlo's heavy ass off of me. I tried to spit him out, but he refused to let me. Kept choking me with it.

"Sol, calm down," he urged, restraining my legs with his powerful arms. "You trust me, remember?"

Those few words jolted my memory back to our agreement. *I trusted him ... I trusted him ...*

I trusted him.

I slowly eased my legs back open and allowed him to get back to doing what he did best. I relaxed, enjoying every stroke of his tongue that graced my center.

Then, I felt it again! Two tongues. No mistaking it this time. There were definitely two mouths down there now. One mouth sucked on my clit, ever so gently, the other penetrated me with a long tongue. The tongue slid inside of me deep and did a wave.

Any objections I had were drowned out by the long wailing sound I made as I came instantly from both mouths stimulating my kitty. Dual-stimulation. The feeling was foreign to this world. Words were too weak to define it.

Carlo stripped his penis from my mouth and joined the woman down between my legs. I knew it was a woman, because a man couldn't do what she was doing as well as she was doing it. Not even Carlo. Her tongue had to be, at least, six inches long! At least, three inches were inside of me, moving up and down, waving at my uterus, prompting me into fits of convulsions.

A part of me was thankful for the blindfold. No way could I enjoy this encounter without it. The only way I would have allowed a woman to have her way with me was if I wasn't privy to it. The blindfold was a necessity.

However, another part of me told a different truth, a truth I was ashamed to admit. In truth, as good as I was feeling, as good as she was making me feel, even if I would've been able to see her, I wouldn't have stopped a thing.

Carlo whispered in my ear. "Get on my level, Sol ... I'm here to please you ... cum for me, Sol ... get on my level ... cum for me."

Carlo kissed me passionately while *she* tortured me below. Millions of thoughts vied for my attention. Millions of questions stampeded through my mind. I settled on none. Only pleasure won out, only pleasure left a stain on my mind's window.

I came so hard I cracked all ten of my toes in unison. My mouth slacked open, but I was beyond words. I exhaled, then inhaled deeply. Smelled her scent permeating the room. Sweet pungency. I opened my mouth, exhaled again, the pleasure too intense to retain. Carlo slipped his hardness into my mouth. I tasted her now, all over him. Her taste was so strong, so womanly, so … exciting. I sucked him harder, savoring the smell, taste, and feel of his sex — her sex — in my mouth. Suddenly, a wave of testosterone flooded my nostrils, overpowered my sense of smell.

Carlo was about to erupt.

She stopped whirling her hurricane tongue around inside of me, abruptly ended her sweet torture campaign. I sensed her hovering above my stomach, felt whisps of her long hair graze my midsection. Suddenly, an explosion slammed the back of my throat with the force of a fire hose. I tried to swallow all of his essence, but it was too much fluid to consume in one gulp. Then …

Carlo raised my mask.

I saw her. For the first time, I saw her … licking his ass while I choked on his girth. I glared at Carlo. His eyes were pinned in the back of his head. Clearly, he was not in this room. Physically he was here, but mentally, he was on another level. He had transcended to a place of utopia. A place where nothing existed but him and his passions. I almost felt jealous. Almost.

I stole a closer look at the woman. She was simply beautiful. Smooth, onyx skin stretched tightly over taut muscles. Jet-black hair, streaming down her face like a banner, shimmering. Her naked body was flawless. Slightly athletic and extremely curvy.

Looking at her, I couldn't deny I felt slightly jealous. Jealous and privileged. Jealous of her beauty. Privileged to have a woman this beautiful slurping from my center as if my fruit was discovered in the Garden of Eden. *Imagine that!*

Carlo descended back down to earth and attempted to introduce us as if nothing was wrong, as if *I* commissioned this sexcapade.

"Netta, this is Soldada," he said, vying to chase down his breath, still winded from his climax. Drips of his release crowned the rim of my mouth, as it gaped open in horror. "Soldada, this is —"

"I don't want to know!" I screamed, writhing in my restraints. "Untie me. Now!"

"Calm down," he urged.

"Calm my ass, Carlo!!! Untie me. *NOW!*"

My head was cloudy, floating in utopia. Tremors slithered through my body, spreading sexual euphoria like a potent drug. I was feeling better than I'd ever felt in my entire life.

Still, I felt violated.

This man had manipulated me into letting a woman lick my sweet spot. Last I checked, I was NOT gay. *But did this mean I was gay now?*

Carlo loosened my reins, and I bolted to the bathroom. Of course, he followed me, beating on the door like a madman, but I wasn't hearing it. I was too busy trying to regain control of my body. My legs were jelly. My heart raced. Every time I moved, my body convulsed, and fluid drained down my inner thighs. I tried to dismiss the feelings as anxiety, but there was no denying it. I was still aroused. My body was still responding to the intense pleasure I'd just received. And so was my mind, as flashes of the stunning, chocolate beauty invaded my thoughts. My kitty thumped in remembrance of how good she'd made me feel with her monstrous tongue.

"P-please ... go away, Carlo," I pleaded, breaking down into tears. *What was happening to me?*

"Sol? Sol?" He must have heard me weeping like a willow. I heard his heavy steps plod away, then return. "Sol?"

I didn't answer. Seconds later, I heard the doorknob jiggling, then Carlo rushed in clutching a butter knife. He saw me in shambles and rushed to my aid. I collapsed into his arms, sobbing uncontrollably.

"What's wrong, Sol? Huh? Talk to me." He clasped my chin between his thumb and forefinger, forcing me to look up at him. His fingers still smelled like feminine sex. Couldn't tell where her scent stopped and mine began. "Why are you shaking?" he asked.

I shook my head from side to side. "I can't take it, Carlo. It's too much." I wrung my hands, searching for words. "You're ... too much for me. What was that in there?"

Can you believe this fool just smiled like I wasn't traumatized by what had transpired, like it was every day I let a strange woman eat me out.

That did it for me. I brushed past him, and out of the bathroom, snatching a terry cloth robe from the door. I ran downstairs, across the cold marble floors, all the way out of the house.

I ran as far away from him as possible.

Shaun Sinclair

21

Anthony

Today was the day of reckoning. The day I would know if the fuse would be lit that would ignite the explosion to blow up my life.

Today was the day of Moses's preliminary hearing. Today they would either free him, or have him stand trial for murder.

The whole family came out in full support. We resembled a platoon trooping out for war. Even Cadillac's shifty-ass was present, although he didn't sit with the family. It spoke volumes that he showed up, because, being that it was only a preliminary hearing, Moses didn't even have to be present. This was basically a forum for lawyers and the judge to bicker over a bunch of bullshit to determine if they were either going to put a nigga's head on the chopping block, or set him free. We were there in full force to let them know we weren't going for the okey-doke. They were not going to stick a banana in a Padmore tailpipe.

We exited the elevator on the fifth floor of the courthouse, ready to do battle. We settled in the gallery just as they brought Moses out in chains. He managed to take a seat at the table with Theron and a paralegal, then looked back at us. He offered us a slight smile, but I could tell that, underneath, he was nervous. It was like déjà vu for me. I recalled when I was sitting at that same table with my heart in my nuts. Sure, it was a different courtroom, but anybody who has ever sat at one knows all defense tables are the same. Your life could change in the blink of an eye, with one wrong verdict, in the little amount of time it takes for a judge to bang his gavel.

I shook off the case of shudders that had descended upon me and watched in disgust as punk-ass Constantine walked into the courtroom from a side door. Everyone perked up, sweating him like he was God or some shit. Ole girl walked in behind him, wheeling a cart full of folders and a snazzy laptop, sniffing up his ass like a trained bitch. Even though she disgusted me at this point, I still paid special attention to the way her dark peach skirt suit hugged her curves. I peeped her scoping me out of her peripheral, but she didn't dare acknowledge me. I stared her down with a twisted smirk, like I could just smell the bullshit steaming from her. Meanwhile, she continued to survey the room with her dark eyes and stoic expression, as if it was all about her. I tried my best to draw her in with my thoughts, make her notice me, force those sultry peepers of hers to dawn on me, if only for a second. She wouldn't look my way for all the money in the world.

I saw her look toward the back of the courtroom, and her face dropped. It was only for a split second, but I caught it. I followed her line of sight, and sure enough, she was looking at Cadillac. Nigga saw me looking and gritted on me. He knew I was still pissed at him for not playing his position with the family. He was the oldest; he was supposed to lead by example. Instead, he was shirking his duties big-time, putting my aunt and uncle through the bullshit. I had been meaning to ask him about Soldada, also, but I never got to catch him one-on-one yet. We didn't have much contact outside of Ladies of Distinction, and when I did see him at the office, he'd breeze in and out. He even lacked the common decency to drop by the day Mo was arrested. Maybe it was best we had limited contact. He was coming real foul. I felt like baptizing him, laying hands on him.

The judge finally entered the courtroom to much pomp. Some (dis)Honorable Fuck-a-Brotha or whatever his name was. Everyone rose, giving him his just due, and court was called into session. The court reporter read off a whole bunch of bullshit case numbers and what not, but the only thing that stood out to me was the charge. *Murder in the First Degree.*

The judge opened the floor, and Soldada spoke first.

"Your Honor, we have concrete evidence and a witness to corroborate the fact that on the night of December 18, the defendant, Moses Malone Padmore killed, one, uh ..." She consulted some papers on the table. "Antonio Cruz, by shooting him in the head twice with a large caliber pistol."

As soon as the words left her mouth, my mind flashed back to the night I popped Cruz. I saw his head explode in a burst of crimson. Heard the two shoots echoing in my ear, loud and clear, as if someone in the courtroom was firing them. My body chilled over for a second.

When I reeled my thoughts back in, the judge was asking Theron for his rebuttal. Theron stood, cleared his throat, and made me proud.

"Your Honor, my good friend, the district attorney insists on harassing my client about this very unfortunate incident when there is insurmountable proof that shows my client was convalescing at his parents' home on the night in question. As a result of this very glaring fact, the defense moves the Court for a motion to dismiss all charges immediately."

As always Theron was smooth, sharp, and to the point, not to mention he looked good while doing it, in a pin-striped three-piece suit. I was more than impressed. Fuck Obama! Theron made me proud to be a black man.

The judge looked at Soldada for her response, but something was wrong. She appeared flustered and confused. I saw Constantine reprimanding her quietly, but forcefully. Though he was whispering, it was evident he was chewing her out. I threw a smile in her direction and winked.

"Is everything all right, Mr. Annapolis?" The judge looked down over his half-moon spectacles.

"Yes, Your Honor. We just need a second, please."

The judge huffed. "Very well. We'll take a brief recess. If you haven't offered anything of substance by then, I'll make my ruling."

~

SOLDADA

I fled from the table into the conference room, my face in my hands, my heart in my toes. I attempted to put on a brave face, but inside, I was torn to pieces.

I had been through too much over the last few days. I hadn't had a decent night's sleep since the night I walked home from Carlo's place with my head twisted, emotions fried, and body trembling. My only consolation was a strong bottle of booze. Not some fancy champagne either. Straight Jack D from the mini-bar in my hostel. That night I drowned my sorrows in so much liquor, Constantine had to peel me from the floor the following morning. He scolded me in looks only, and kept reiterating how he trusted my professionalism. At work, I tried to block everything out and focus on my task, but the night's events kept invading my serenity.

So much pleasure yet so much confusion.

To make matters worse, Carlo would not leave me alone. He called all day on my cell and office line. Of course, I wasn't taking his calls. Why should I? He had taken my trust and betrayed it. Tremendously.

But Carlo was persistent. I give him that.

When I came home each night, he was waiting on me in the lobby. He wasn't being forceful, just persistent. Eventually, he relented, left me be. I thought I had rid myself of him for good until I spotted him in back of the courtroom. Just being in his presence had muddled my thoughts.

As if that wasn't enough, Anthony was there also. He looked so handsome in his tailored suit. I just wanted to reach out and rub my hands all over his smooth skin, tug at the lapels of his fancy suit. But I could tell he was disgusted with me. I could see the hurt in his eyes. Truthfully, I was affected as well. My stomach felt like a marching band was drilling inside of it. I tried to suck it up and present my case, but my facade crumbled like the Berlin Wall. Felt like I was in a quadruple crossfire with Carlo, Anthony, my case, and my emotions all sniping at me, trying to rip a chunk from my ass.

Constantine entered the room and gently pulled the door closed behind him. "Soldada, you okay?" he asked.

"Um-hmm," I feigned, holding my stomach. "Must be something I ate."

"Something you ate, huh?" I knew he wasn't buying it. Silence drifted between us for what felt like an eternity, but was only minutes. "Soldada, look, you're a smart woman. Focused. Driven ... I selected you for those reasons. I know no one can do a better job on this than you. Not even me." He picked my head up with his forefinger. "You know what this case means to me. In the short amount of time I've known you, I've seen you take on way tougher cases than this with your eyes closed. This is a shoo-in! Granted, we may not be able to get an indictment for Murder in the First, but we can definitely get the case before the grand jury with the evidence we have. Even if we can't get a conviction, the idea is to strike the bushes, so the birds will scatter. Got me?" Constantine slicked his hair back, and stuffed his hands in his pockets, waiting on my compliance. Eventually, I nodded.

"Good. Now let's go out there and kick some Padmore ass."

~

Anthony

I was damn near giddy with excitement. Ole girl was botching the case! Moses was going to go free! More importantly, if Moses was exonerated, they would have to leave the rest of us alone. If they didn't, we could file all types of harassment suits against their asses. *Shit, shorty botched the case up any worse, and I'd be obligated to give her some more of the dick as a token of my appreciation.*

That's what I was thinking, until I saw her emerge from the conference room with that look on her face, and an audio player in her arms. Court resumed and the joke was on me.

"Your Honor, the State would like to submit into evidence an audio tape of the defendant collaborating with the victim to commit murder ..."

Theron made all kinds of objections, but the judge shot them down quicker than the CPD on a black man. Next thing we heard was Mo's voice crackling through the courtroom's JVC speakers, conspiring with Cruz about killing Maynard Jackson. Names, locations, and figures were discussed in vivid detail. Moses even offered to supply Cruz with the hardware if Cruz promised to shoot dude in the head. Twice. The stickler was when Moses promised Cruz that if he didn't carry out the job properly, he would shoot him in the head. Twice. The threat echoed through the courtroom speakers clearer than the Macintosh system in my Jag, the words so cold, my blood cooled over.

Fuck!

"Your Honor, we don't even know if that's the victim on the tape!" Theron screamed.

"Your Honor, we have an eyewitness who was present when the tape was made! He is willing to corroborate it." Soldada interjected. "He can identify the defendant as being the person on the tape. This witness was also present on the night the defendant and the victim attempted to carry out this murder, and has agreed to testify in exchange for immunity."

I couldn't believe this shit! The luck!!! I knew exactly who the witness was, and if I had known he would come back like this, I would've murdered his ass first. Now look.

Ole girl was pouring it on thick, too.

"Your Honor, where is this witness?" Theron asked, looking around the courtroom absently to illustrate his point. "We don't have anything in the record about this witness."

"You do now," Soldada quipped.

"Your Honor?" Theron was looking for help. Anything.

"Mr. Shields, calm down," the judge advised.

"But, Your Honor, the tape is inadmissible." Theron insisted. "Hell, it could be you on the tape for all I know!"

"Mr. Shields." The judge gave Theron a stern look.

"Your Honor, we have an eyewitness to corroborate the tape. This more than meets the requirements for the case to go before the grand jury," Soldada persisted, grating on my last nerve.

"Ms. Andrews, I know how to do my job, thank you very much." The judge turned to Theron and Moses. Mo looked so defeated, my heart wept for him. "In light of the evidence, I'm going to bind the case over for the grand jury to deliberate on."

"Your Honor?!" Theron shot to his feet.

"That is my ruling, Mr. Shields."

Soldada smiled at Theron. "Your Honor, the State asks that, due to the severity of the charges, Mr. Padmore's bond be revoked, and he be held in custody until trial ... or he plead guilty." She winked at Mo when she took that last dig, then cut her eyes at me.

While Theron struggled for a rebuttal, I turned my attention to Constantine. Sucka was sitting at the table looking like he owned the world. Legs crossed, fingers interlaced and steepled at the knees, showing off his gold Rolex. I swear you couldn't tell that bastard he wasn't the shit. So many times, so many times, I wanted to put two in *his* head!

Finally, Theron gained his wits. "Your Honor, Mr. Padmore has given no reason to revoke his bond. He has complied with all the court's wishes, thus far," he argued.

But Soldada was on him like a piranha. "Sir, Mr. Padmore *is* a threat to society, and most importantly, the witness —"

"Your Honor, my client doesn't even know about this phantom witness."

"He has the means to flee from justice, and I believe this tape definitely speaks of his propensity for violence."

"The tape may not even be admissible!"

"THAT'S ENOUGH!!!" the judge roared. "Now, I'm calling the shots here. As for now, the tape is admissible; provided the State can produce this eyewitness to corroborate its contents."

"Your Honor, sir?" Theron threw his hands up in exasperation. *"Come on."*

"Mr. Shields, you'll have your chance to further address the admissibility of the tape, but for now, it's in. As to the bond ... it is hereby revoked."

"What?!" Uncle Roland was on his feet like a rod. "Revoked? I put up $100,000 for your campaign! What, my money ain't good no more now that you a judge?"

"ORDER! Order in my courtroom!" The judge banged his gavel, repeatedly.

My aunt pulled Uncle Roland back down in his seat. He sat, but he was so pissed, I saw steam shooting from his ears.

"Bailiff, take the defendant into custody."

22

SOLDADA

Relieved that this part of my caseload was over for, at least, the next few weeks, I gathered my things to make my exit, prepared to slay another dragon.

Carlo had been harassing me because he wanted to talk. Okay, we'd talk. Still high off my partial victory, I was ready for Carlo. Unfortunately, when I looked into the gallery for him, he was gone.

But Anthony was still there. And if looks could kill, I'd have been annihilated. Nine lives couldn't have spared me. Pure malice lived in his eyes. I tried to return his stare with ice of my own, but I was no match. I felt as if he was burning holes through me. He backed out of the courtroom, his steely gaze following me all the way until he joined his family in the hallway.

I got on the elevator alone. Constantine and his ubiquitous entourage had disappeared as soon as the judge banged his gavel for the final time. I made it to the parking lot to retrieve my rental, and saw that I had company.

Carlo's shiny, black Escalade was blocking my rented Chrysler.

I braced myself for the confrontation, and dived straight in. "What, Carlo? What do you want? You've been stalking me for days now. What?"

He was alone in his truck, the tinted window parted halfway. I could see that he had shed his sport coat, opting to show off the pinstriped vest of his three-piece suit. Up close, I noted his long hair was braided in a neat design straight to the back, and his beard was trimmed to perfection. A boulder gleamed from his ear, flashing its brilliance at me like paparazzi. As usual, he looked like a million bucks.

Until I examined his face closer.

His face wore a sad expression, and if I wasn't mistaken, his eyes were damp. He looked like a broken man. I wasn't sure if I should leave or stay.

"Carlo? Here I am. You said you wanted to talk. Here I am."

He said nothing. I had never seen this side of him. Normally, he was the embodiment of control, the personification of cool. Now he was just ... there. "Carlo, what do you want?" I needed to get some type of reaction from him. Surely, he hadn't been hounding me for this? Surely, he hadn't followed me into court to reward me with this crazy-ass, far-off look. I repeated my question with homegirl attitude.

Carlo started the truck. Let it idle for a few seconds. Looked away from me, said, "Nothing."

Then he drove away.

Nothing? Hell did he mean nothing? He called for days on end for nothing? I was at a loss for words.

As I tossed my material into the backseat of the rental, a cranberry-colored Bentley Mulsanne slowly crept up behind me. With all the things twisting through my mind, I didn't even see the car, initially. Luckily, the W12 engine idled as loud as a plane. I reached for my pocketbook, gripped my Glock, prepared to put holes in anyone before they could put them in me.

The car drew to a halt right behind my bumper. The back window slowly glided down and revealed the face of Roland Padmore.

My heart thumped a new beat inside my chest. The vibes coming from the luxury auto were all wrong. I looked around the parking lot for possible assistance, if it came to that. I was alone. People were milling about, but no one paid me any attention. I was, in effect, alone.

Mr. Padmore fixed his dead eyes on me. His presence was so strong, I buckled under the pressure. Even sitting in the backseat of a $300,000 car, he still looked menacing. I palmed my pistol, ready to send a barrage into the car the moment he made his move.

He sat up abruptly. I jumped back, almost out of my skin, the Glock now at my side.

He looked at the small pistol shaking in my hand. Smiled.

Then the Bentley drove away slowly.

Later, when I made it back to my hotel, I called Constantine. Told him I was ready to leave the hostel. Ready to find my own place. Felt too vulnerable here. I needed a place where strangers weren't free to roam about. A place I could feel secure. He empathized and agreed to take me home-hunting the next morning.

I laid down that night with my thoughts running one hundred miles an hour, all in different directions. Couldn't sleep. Looked in the corner. Saw my medicine.

Thirty minutes later, I was sleeping harder than a corpse.

Shaun Sinclair

23

Anthony

What it boiled down to was this: if that witness made it to court, Moses was through dealing. Theron drove that point home like a spike. 'Course, he didn't know who the witness was because he didn't have the complete case file from the D.A.'s office. No one knew who the witness was. No one, but me.

Uncle Roland knew I knew something. I could tell. He couldn't wait to dismiss Theron, so we could talk. Didn't take much convincing for me to tell him the whole truth. As expected, he blasted me out, ferociously.

Then came the planning.

The ultimate decision was a no-brainer. The only question was how to carry it out, now that we were so hot.

The man that Moses was accused of plotting was none other than Maynard Jackson IV, also known as THE paragon of high-society. Maynard was one of the most popular (and richest) people in Charlotte. An astute and shrewd real estate tycoon, Maynard donated money to shelters, churches, political campaigns, and anything else he could throw his millions at, all in attempts to clean up his soiled rep. See, everyone knew Maynard had obtained his wealth through fraud and racketeering in the early nineties. He'd served two years in Club Fed for money laundering in the late nineties, paid his restitution, and bounced back from the federal pen stronger than ever, snatching up properties all over the southeast. Unfortunately for him, his past clung to him like a cheap suit until he started playing Phil the Philanthropist. Then, he became accepted overnight. His money was now good, which was why he was the perfect front man for the Queen's Quarter. He was the perfect mouthpiece because, although not everyone liked him, they had to respect his millions.

Around these parts, plotting to assassinate Maynard Jackson IV was akin to plotting to murder the president of the U.S. So, of course, this was front page news now.

For the past few nights, Mo was being paraded on the news as some sinister criminal. Every chance they got, the reporters made sure to stress the fact that the would-be victim was Maynard Jackson IV. They even interviewed him one night, looking dapper in his bespoke tailored suit and tapered S-Curl. If I didn't know better, I would have thought he was white, that is, until he spoke. He carried his words like a southern Baptist preacher, all pregnant pauses and sorrow, as he vowed to continue to be a man of the people. Most importantly for us, he promised not to coop himself up like some scared animal. He stressed that he would not hire any additional security to protect him from the threats of *ruffians*. He was banking on his acts of goodwill and God to protect him.

Little did he know, he was dirty dancing with the devil.

Uncle Roland was ballistic! He wanted to murk *everybody*. The judge, the witness, Constantine, and Soldada. Much to my dismay, he *really* wanted to dead Soldada! He was taking it personal that she had insisted on revoking Mo's bond. He felt she went extra hard to punish the family. For that, he wanted her to pay with her life. I tried to calm him down, you know, keep him focused on the real business at hand, the witness. But he accused me of being sweet on the broad.

"You just like the little bitch, with her smart ass," he announced.

Little did he know how right he was. I was smitten with Soldada, but it just could not be. She wouldn't behave, couldn't separate her profession from her personal life enough to give us a fair chance. For that reason, I rationalized that we could not be.

Yet, she was like a drug. I knew she was bad for business, but I still wanted more. Fact, the only thing I wanted more than Soldada was money. Lots and lots of money. Unfortunately for her, for us, she was in direct opposition to my riches. The fact that she was heading the calvary attempting to dismantle my family put extra sauce on things. Bottom line: Soldada was Padmore Enemy #1.

If only I could shake her from my thoughts ...

Shaun Sinclair

24

SOLDADA

Things were looking up for me. Work was going as well as could be expected, and I'd moved into my own place, just off South Boulevard. It was a nice, quiet condominium complex with a pool, tennis court, on-site gym, and other amenities. I lived in the third building on the third floor, which was perfect, because if the elevator ever went out, I wouldn't have long to row. (I felt sorry for the people on the sixteenth floor.) My unit boasted hardwood floors throughout, a glass door leading to the balcony, and two bedrooms. Constantine had shown me this place first. There was no need to go elsewhere. The price was in the low 100s, but on my new salary, I could easily afford it. I signed the paperwork and moved in the next day.

Constantine was tired of chauffeuring me around, so while the moving company was setting up my furniture, we turned in my rental and went searching for a car.

I saw an Audi A5, and fell in love with it! An hour later, I was driving it off the lot. Black with silver accents and nineteen-inch factory alloys, the car fit me to a T. Compact, wide, dependable, and fast! I drove by to show it off to my best friend, Shana, and she loved it also.

Shana had been mad at me because I'd failed to keep in touch with her. I blamed it on my hectic work schedule, but in reality, I was avoiding Shana because she stayed on some self-righteous bullshit. I told her as little as possible about my life, especially my personal life. Knowing Shana, she would eat the Carlo fiasco up, so I definitely didn't mention a word about him to her. Knowing Shana's propensity for getting around, and Carlo's stronghold on the city, it wouldn't be a surprise if they'd crossed paths before. I kept it light with Shana, shared a little gossip, then beat a hasty retreat.

After leaving Shana's place, I rushed home to get prepared for the banquet I was attending later that night. It was a black-tie affair hosted by some VIP with important ties to the city's legal community, so Constantine was making me go. I had no desire to spend my night hobnobbing with some stuffy crowd. Rather be home listening to Mary J., trying out some of the new toys I'd purchased to ease some pressure from my lonely nights. But Constantine insisted. Said it would be good for my career. Some influential people with the ability to propel me further in my career would be in attendance. He reminded me, with a smirk, that cases were often decided long before the first gavel was banged, and if I wanted to dance in his shoes one day, I had to go "pay the band" now. Whatever that meant.

Turned out, the gala was being given by Maynard Jackson IV. Mr. Jackson was the same guy Moses Padmore was accused of conspiring to kill, along with his victim. I had heard of Maynard Jackson IV before, spoke of in hallowed tones, but was never allowed the privilege to rub elbows with him. I imagined it would be fun to finally meet the man behind the myth.

At six p.m., Constantine texted me. He was downstairs waiting on me. I was Constantine's date for the night, and we were traveling by limo. I did a final onceover in the mirror, then joined him downstairs.

"Damn! You look good," Constantine remarked, as he helped me into the Benz. I was wearing a velvet, midnight-colored dress flowing down to my ankles where silver-strapped four-inch stilettos encased my pedicured feet. The top of the dress was cut into a V, stopping just above my bustline, and a diamond encrusted (okay, cubic zirconium) brooch was pinned just above my navel to keep the dress together. My firm breasts were held in place by double-sided tape. The back of the dress was wide open, showcasing my well-toned back.

"You don't look too bad yourself," I returned.

Constantine was sporting a black tux with a red bowtie. It was traditional, but the way he wore it made it appear as if it left the seamstress table that afternoon. His thick hair was slicked straight back, highlighting his olive skin. A small diamond ring shone from his right pinkie. On his left hand, his wedding band glowed like a forbidden reminder.

As we cruised around town, he complimented me on my case.

"You had me worried for awhile," Constantine chuckled. "I thought you were going to let me down." He paused for a moment, then added thoughtfully, "I got a lot riding on you ... a whole lot."

"Don't worry, Connie, I won't let you down," I assured him. He bristled at the use of the pet name I'd given him. Leaning over to fix me a drink from the bar, he queried me. "You ever wonder why I never pursued you?"

"'Cause you're married?" I retorted.

He passed me the drink. "Cute. But seriously."

"Okay. I don't know. Why don't you tell me?"

He leaned further back into the plush leather seat and wrapped his arm around me. "Because I can see that you're special," he claimed. "Now don't get me wrong, I'd love to tap that pretty ass, believe me ..." Must have been the liquor, but as soon as he said it, I pictured him on top of me, grinding and sweating his way to a climax. "But I believe you deserve better than being a mistress. Deserve better than what I can give you." He swigged his drink and chuckled. "Bet it'd be an experience though."

Constantine and I continued to subtly flirt until the limo slid to a stop in front of an expensive townhouse.

"Why are we stopping?" I asked.

"Gotta pick up Michael and his date," Constantine explained.

Michael was the newest addition to our special task force. Born and raised in Los Angeles, California, Michael was mixed (black/white). Like me, he had graduated at the top of his class, but his alma mater was the University of South Carolina's School of Law. I didn't know much more about him; I'd only met him once.

"This is his introduction to the city, Soldada, so be nice."

I sucked my teeth as Constantine left the limo. He returned to the car, minutes later, with Michael and his date in tow. I was eager to see Michael's taste in women. He was a real pretty-boy and seemed to have a touch of class to himself. I couldn't wait to see his date. Constantine climbed in beside me while Michael's date climbed into the seat across from us. I looked at her and my heart stopped.

His date looked ravishing. Her dress was similar to mine, but hers had a long split down one side, showcasing thick, toned, chocolate legs. Chandelier earrings hung from her large ears, the diamonds flickering a shiny blue, almost the color of her eyes. Her silky hair was pulled back into a chignon allowing me to clearly see her face.

Netta smiled at me.

As Michael climbed in, he introduced everyone. "Mr. Annapolis —"

"Constantine." Constantine held up his hands. "It's Constantine."

"Very well. Constantine, this is Netta. Soldada? Netta. Netta, this is my boss, Constantine, and my colleague, Soldada."

I was wondering how she was going to play it. Bust me out? Ignore me? What? From her mischievous smile, I could tell she was replaying that night in her head. I was damn sure replaying it in mine. I felt myself moisten the second I laid eyes on her.

Netta shook Constantine's hand. "Pleased to meet you, Constantine and ... how do you say your name?"

"Soldada. Sol-da-da," I enunciated with much attitude, letting her know I wasn't the least bit amused.

"Yes, yes, Soldada," she said, nodding her head. I detected a light accent, possibly West Indian, maybe Spanish. "That's a pretty name. Spanish, right?"

I smiled, then looked away. I did *not* want to engage in small talk with her. "So, Michael, where did you meet Netta?" I asked. "You two look so good together."

Constantine nudged my arm like I had said something wrong.

"We really just met," Netta cut in, saving Michael the embarrassment. "As soon as I laid eyes on him, I knew he was someone I wanted to get to know a little better." She placed her hand on his lap, smiled. His skin blushed darker, discomfort evident.

"Really?" I asked, not believing a word she uttered. "So are you from here?" I queried. She wanted to play games? I was going to expose her for the fraud she was. Carpetmuncher.

"No. Yo soy de Panama," she answered, in flawless Spanish. She looked at me as if to say, take that!

"You speak Spanish?" Constantine perked up, impressed by this wench.

"Sí," she beamed. "Of course." She was making me sick, sitting all prim and ladylike, like she wouldn't attack a wet pussy like a dog on a bone.

"Really impressive," Constantine praised, glancing at Michael. "What do you do for a living?"

"I have a degree in business administration from Florida A&M. I'm working in the service industry right now, but I'm in the process of opening a full-service spa. Here's my card." She extracted a gold, black-embossed card and passed it to Constantin. She winked at him. Then she stole a glance at me. "You may find it useful in the future."

"Michael, I'm impressed," Constantine said. "Not in town a good two weeks and already found a winner."

"Thanks, sir. I always have had good taste in women," Michael responded coolly, leaning over to kiss Netta on her cheek. Instead, she turned and kissed him on the lips, slipping that long, thick tongue in his mouth for a quick second.

My lower lips quivered. My body shuddered in rememberance.

I was so glad when we finally made it to the ballroom.

As soon as we found our table and got settled, I threw down two glasses of champagne to calm my nerves. Just being in Netta's presence had me rattled. Constantine saw my discomfort and slipped me a quick mood check.

"I'm okay," I assured him. "Just a little parched."

I wanted to add that I'd be splendid if this freak wasn't sitting beside me, but that comment would have been out of place. Michael sat directly to her left, while Constantine sat to my right. A fresh bottle of champagne sat chilled on the table, and like magic, our glasses were topped off each time we sat them down.

A waiter replaced our old bottle of champagne with a new bottle of something I couldn't pronounce. "This bottle is from Mr. Maynard, sir," the waiter informed us. Constantine thanked him and he disappeared.

Constantine made small talk about how Maynard was such a good person, and how he'd known him for years. He talked about how bad he wanted those "hooligans" punished for trying to destroy such a great man. I was all ears until I felt a hand on my leg.

I shifted my leg and shot Netta a murderous look. The heifer just smiled.

I slid my chair from the table. "I'm going to the ladies' room," I announced, giving Netta an obvious look of contempt as I left the table.

I was in the restroom, crouching in the last stall when I heard people enter. The women began talking about Constantine, of all people.

"Oh, he is so handsome!" one of them purred.

"Yeah. He looks better in person," another one observed.

"I wonder who that woman is with him. I thought he was married?"

I flushed the toilet and exited the stall. The two women jumped like I was transparent and glowing. They were both white. Both in their mid- to late-twenties. Both dressed in simple LBDs. As I washed my hands, the shorter of the two said, "You look familiar." Her finger was beside her mouth as she tried to recall where she knew me from.

"Probably recognize me as the woman with Constantine Annapolis," I retorted with a tight smile. The taller woman blushed.

The shorter woman snapped her fingers. "Now I know! You're a district attorney, right? I saw you … on television. You were with … *Constantine*. Riiiight, you're not his date. You're his colleague!"

Her revelation seemed to lighten the mood. Like suddenly, Constantine was up for grabs. I had been promoted (or demoted) from mistress to woman-in-arms.

She stuck her hand out. "I'm Melanie. You're Sol ... Sol ..."

"Soldada Andrews." I shook her hand. I hadn't noticed Netta walk in, neither had Melanie and her friend.

"Mr. Annapolis is waiting on you, ma'am," Netta announced, innocently.

The women took that as their cue to leave. "Well, nice meeting you, Ms. Andrews. Keep up the good fight." She gave me a woman-in-arms fist pump, then Melanie and her friend left, leaving me alone in the ladies' room with Netta.

Netta quickly closed the distance between us. Walked up behind me at the sink, a little too close for comfort. As I checked my makeup in the mirror, her beautiful face appeared over my right shoulder.

"I take it you enjoyed the other night?" She was looking in my eyes through the mirror. I didn't say a thing. "Of course, you did. I can still taste your sweet pussy on my tongue."

"Look, you dyke bitch!" I whirled around to face her.

"Dikes are used to stop water," she replied sarcastically. "I made your water *floooow*."

She tried to caress my breast. I moved her hand. She replaced it. I tried to smack her. She caught my hand. I tried to smack her with my other hand. She caught that too, then pinned me to the sink.

"Stop fighting it, Sol," she whispered, nudging closer and closer to my ear. "Most people would thank someone for giving them multiple orgasms."

Just the mention of that night caused my body to lose control. *Or was it because she was blowing in my ear?* Whatever the reason, my slit was leaking like a faulty dam.

She kept whispering in my ear. "You can fight it, but don't deny it — you loved when I had that sweet pussy in my mouth, didn't you?"

She palmed my breast lightly. This time I didn't move her hand, my body having a mind of its own. I felt my head tilt back and revel in her caress, heard a moan escape my lips. She wrapped her long tongue lightly around my neck. I moaned even louder.

"One more time," she pleaded, sliding her tongue inside my ear. "Just let me taste you one more time ..."

"Nooo," I moaned weakly, my body betraying my words.

She slipped her fingers between the split in my dress in one deft motion, felt my wetness, fingered my lies. Then she brought her fingers to her mouth and sucked them.

"Hmm ... like candy. I know you want me. Tastes so good down there."

I didn't know what was happening to me. Her touch was zapping my power to resist. I'd never even considered the possibility of being with a woman, never allowed the thought to strike a shadow on my mind. But Netta really knew how to handle her business. Her touch was gentle; her skin was so soft. It was almost like touching a feather. And she was so beautiful! Her funny-colored eyes magnetized me every time I dared stare into them.

But women weren't my hype.

I pushed her away from me. "Stop! I'm not gay," I announced, more to myself than her.

She laughed and shrugged. "Me either. I just like a little spice in my life every now and then."

Every now and then? Who was she kidding? She ate pussy like it was her occupation.

"Look, stay away from me, okay?" I insisted, adjusting my dress. "I'm not down with that other shit that Carlo imposed that night on me without my knowledge. Please, just accept that and respect my wishes. Please?" I turned to the mirror to fix my makeup. My face was blood-red from embarrassment.

"Whatever you say, sweetie," she sang. "Hurry up before people start getting worried."

As soon as Netta walked out, leaving me alone with my thoughts, my stomach lurched. I vomited in the sink. Couldn't stop shaking. I splashed a little water on my face, careful not to smudge my makeup. I was just getting myself together when I heard my phone shriek to life, scaring the hell out of me.

An unlisted number.

I answered reluctantly, unsure of the caller. "Hello?"

"We gotta talk."

"Anthony?" *What was my life becoming?* "Why are you calling me?"

"Like I said, we gotta talk. I'll be in touch."

Just like that he hung up, adding a whole new dimension to my twisted night.

I returned to the ballroom just in time to see Constantine receive a plaque from Maynard Jackson. As I took my seat, the crowded room began chanting.

"SPEECH! SPEECH! SPEECH!"

I took my seat, and pulled it as far away from Netta as possible while Constantine spoke. I wasn't paying attention to a word he was saying. All I could think about was Netta.

I watched her interact with Michael and a wave of emotions washed over me. With me, she was hyper-aggressive. With him, she turned into a purring kitten. Demure and sensual, but not slutty. Beautiful and accessible, yet still regal and distant. Tilted her head like a seductress when she spoke. Caressed his hand when he spoke. Laughed genuinely at his feeble attempts at humor, and clung to his every word. No one in the room — male or female — could tear their eyes from her. Some tossed subtle glances her way, others were more overt. Netta had captured the whole room in her clutches. If only they knew!

I tossed back flute after flute of champagne in an effort to mask my discomfort. Seemed like Constantine would never shut up! He droned on ... and on ... and on.

When he finally returned to our table, I was good and tipsy. Sure enough, he noticed right away.

"Whoa! Someone's had a bit to drink," he noted, scolding Michael with cutting eyes.

"I'm ready to go." I slurred, wavering at the table like a weak tree in a strong wind.

Constantine frowned. "As you should be."

Inside the limo, I was forced to sit beside Netta because Constantine had to discuss something with Michael. While they sat across from us, giggling like teenagers, the things Netta whispered in my ear began sounding better and better in my inebriated state. I almost wanted to take her up on her offer to *stick the whole tongue inside*. But I managed to decline.

Constantine instructed the driver to drop Michael and Netta off at Michael's townhouse. Then he drew closer to me as the Benz coasted through the late night Charlotte traffic to my condo.

"Soldada, I'm getting a little worried, doll," he admitted quietly.

I slurred my words. "About what?"

"About this!" He snatched the drink from my hand, threw it out the cracked window of the limo.

"You've been hitting the sauce pretty hard lately. Think I didn't know you were drunk at that hearing?"

I groaned.

"If the job is too stressful, let me know," he pleaded. "I can get you some help. Just between me and you, of course."

"It's not that," I lied.

"Well, what is it then? Because this is not the girl I selected!" He lowered his voice. "Trouble in your personal life?"

I sniffed. "Sorta."

He smiled, then mumbled, "Men." Then he took my hand into his, garnered my full attention. "Let me give you some advice. Men? We're all dogs. Every last one of us, so, get what you can out of us before we crush you."

I laughed a bit. "Wow. That's encouraging."

"Seriously, Soldada, we destroy all that we love, or all that love us," he lamented.

Sounded like more than just advice for my problem. I asked, "Trouble in paradise?"

He exhaled a chuckle. "Just a little bit." Then he smiled that wonderful bright, white smile. "You know, all the years I've been married, my wife put up with my philandering — even participated in a few threesomes to curb my desire for that type of thing, truth be told. Never once threatened me, you know. Now, when I start to change my ways, she starts hassling me more than ever. Funny, huh?"

I nodded.

He downed his drink slowly. "Like I said, we destroy what we love."

The limo let me out in front of my building. I stumbled onto the elevator, and into my place, ready to crash.

But my night was not over.

I saw the silhouette of his knee jutting out from the corner of my loveseat. My living room was bathed in darkness, save for the small light peeking from the bathroom in the hallway. Nonetheless, I could make out his tall frame as if a spotlight illuminated the room. I flicked on the light and his handsome face came to life.

"How did you get in here?"

"Irrelevant," he replied. "I came to warn you." He paused, took a deep breath. "You're barking up the wrong tree."

"What are you talking about?"

He looked past me, still in deep thought. "Your case ... you don't want to go there." He shook his head. "You are being a patsy for something bigger than you understand. And you deserve better than that."

"Oh? Let me get this right. You stalk me in court for one day. Now you're an expert on my case?"

"Would you stop flattering yourself for a moment? I'm telling you something for your own damn good," he insisted.

"Your smooth talking ass can't tell me shit for my own good because your word ain't shit!" I exploded, getting a whiff of the alcohol reeking from my breath.

He stood, tried to get closer to me. I backed up. "Sol, leave this alone. I'm begging you. You have no idea what you're up against — from either side."

"Did the Padmores send you here?" I don't know why the thought didn't cross my mind sooner. Surely, Roland Padmore's tentacles reached far. Maybe he had reached out to him. Maybe he had intertwined yet another one of my would-be lovers into his web of conspiracy.

"Listen, I'm sorry I misled you that night. You trusted me, and I ... I ... guess I betrayed that —"

"Guess?!"

"Look, you weren't complaining too damn much when we were eating your pussy!"

I tried to smack skin from his face.

"Get out!"

"Sol, I'm serious about this ..." His protests fell on deaf ears. I wasn't trying to hear any more of his faux-righteous crusade.

Eventually, he got the point and left. I slammed the door behind him. Locked the chain on the door. Put my back to it, shaking my head to suppress the bile threatening to erupt from my stomach. I felt sick, and it wasn't because of the alcohol.

I was sick of what my life was becoming.

I slid down the door onto my butt, dropped my face in my hands, and wailed like a lamb.

~

Anthony

It was simple. All I had to do was make Soldada accept my proposal and this would all go away. I replayed my spiel over and over in my head while Mona bent my ear about *something*. I couldn't concentrate with her yakking, so I abruptly ended the call, and focused on the task at hand.

I was outside of Soldada's new spot, staking the joint out. I figured I would wait until she was settled, then we would talk. I'd already witnessed a limo drop her off a little while ago, then peel out. Of course, she stepped out looking like a million bucks, breasts and ass hanging all out of her dress. But I refused to let her beauty deter me. I was here for one reason only.

I peeped at my silver Patek Phillipe and decided two a.m. was late enough.

Just as I stepped one foot out of my Jag, I saw a familiar gait slide out of Soldada's building.

What the fuck? Cadillac? Thought I was supposed to make the proposal?

No sooner than the thoughts crossed my mind, it hit me: *The young Puerto Rican chick that was on the news ... she was at the party tonight.*

I never believed in coincidences. Something was up. I had never gotten a chance to speak with Cadillac about her before, but there was no time like the present. He was walking right in front of my ride and didn't even realize it.

I popped out of the car in a flash. "Damn, cousin, you creeping kind of late, ain't 'cha?" I asked, blocking his path. Startled, he jumped back, reached for his piece, until he saw it was me. "Damn, nigga, you scared the shit out of me, dawg."

"Yo' scary ass," I joked with a chuckle, attempting to lighten the mood, set him off guard. "So what up? You got one over here, too?" I asked, narrowing my eyes suspiciously.

"Uh ... yeah, yeah," he stammered. "You know, got a potential prospect for the team."

"Oh, yeah? Shit ... don't look like she doing too bad now." I motioned to the nice condos behind him. I was pitching, trying to get him to bite. I'd already noticed that he wasn't his usual confident self when he first walked out, which meant he was hiding something.

"Well, you know how it is," he said. "So what you doing over here?"

Slick-ass was trying to switch shit up. Thought he had all the sense. "Same thing you doing," I answered. "So who's the broad? Wouldn't want to bump heads wit' 'cha."

He saw how I was looking at him. Knew I wasn't buying his story.

He narrowed his eyes, challenging me. "Something on your mind, cuz?"

"Matter fact, it is."

"Well, you need to get it off your chest then, 'cause I'm not digging that little funky-ass look you throwing me."

"Who you over here seeing, cuz?" I slid the question through gritted teeth.

"Nigga, don't question me! I'm grown. I already let you have my leftovers. Be happy with that."

"Your leftovers?"

"Yeah, my leftovers!"

I didn't know what kind of shit he was on. Flexing on me, throwing accusations around about some leftovers. All he had to do was tell me who he was seeing, and we could end the charade of hostility. But Cadillac had always been too arrogant for his own good.

I asked, "Sureyou ain't buzzing over my leftovers?"

He sucked his teeth. "Nigga, please! You been in a box for the last six calendars, while I been out here ... *getting it.* Anything you can think about fucking, I pro'ly done slutted out already. Don't believe me? Ask Mona."

So that was his ace in the hole. Mona was *his* girl. Now it made sense.

Before I could respond, he walked off with his usual swagger. He knew he had stunned me. He must have regained his swagger at my expense 'cause he strutted to his Ferrari like he was the shit again. Fired up the engine, reversed all the way back to me in a cloud of smoke. When the smoke cleared, he was staring at me through the open window, screw-faced.

I stared back just as hard.

He smiled, then floored the Italian rocket. The engine lit the cool night up with its banshee-like wail. I followed the circular taillights all the way out of the parking lot. For a few seconds, I could still hear the car's note echoing through the trees lining the road to the complex, as he continued to gun the engine. Then, the only thing I heard were my reservations, bouncing around in my head like a ping pong ball.

I wasn't convinced he and Soldada didn't have something going on. Since he wasn't going to tell me, I was going to have to go another route.

To the source.

~

"Who is it?" Soldada whimpered through the door. "Go away."

I don't know what kind of shit she was on, but I wasn't leaving until I did what I came to do. "Counselor, open up. It's me."

"A.P.?" I heard her whisper. After some scurrying around, the door finally cracked open with the chain still attached. "What do you want?" She breathed in my face, and I nearly got drunk off the fumes.

"Whoa!" I dodged the toxic fumes from her hot mouth.
"Open the door, Counselor. I told you, we gotta talk."
"Go away, A.P."
"Soldada, I'm not going anywhere. You might as well open
the door."
A brief pause. The door slammed in my face. A couple
clicks later, the door opened up to reveal Soldada in a terribly
drunken state. Tear lines streaked her frowning face. Her damp,
curly hair was disheveled. A red satin robe clung to her curves.
I noticed all of this in one glance.
She was distraught. I was distracted.
"What? You came to kill me now? Well, here I am, Mr. Bad
Man. Do it." She spread her arms like Jesus on the cross.
"What? Sol — "
"Do it!"
Her eyes were shut tight, her arms still spread outward. Her
breasts heaved with every breath she took. I didn't come for all
this drama. I came for business.
But seeing her so frail and vulnerable moved me.
I took a step forward and ... kissed her ... long and deep.
She faltered for a hot second, then met me halfway in our
ignition of intensity. I wrapped my arms around her fragile
waist, and pulled her into me.
"Oh, Anthony, I missed you so much," she moaned. "Please
make love to me."
Music to my ears. Those few words let me know I wasn't a
fool to feel how I had been feeling, or, at least, not the only
fool. Those words let me know she was thinking of me as well,
just as hard as I'd been thinking of her. I tasted the alcohol on
her tongue as she lathered my mouth over and over again,
whispering erotic things in Spanish. I parted her robe and tasted
the sweat on her chest, thumbed her nipples, so hard yet so soft
to the touch. She cradled my head in her arms as I sucked her
breasts, moaning her appreciation to the heavens. I dipped two
fingers inside of her pussy, then tried to pull them out, but she
held my hand in place, started fucking it, slow and steady. Felt
like her insides were on fire, oozing hot lava onto my fingers. I
let her get off for a hot minute, then flipped the script.

I hoisted her into my arms, and she used her feet to slide my sweatpants down. My dick popped out, strong and long.

"*Damelo*," she whispered, gripping my throbbing meat inside her tiny hands. "Give it to me."

I thought my dick was going to explode it was so hard! I pinned her back to the front door, palmed and pulled her soft ass apart, and went up in her.

Felt like Heaven. Really, felt like Heaven.

I pinned her back to the door again and again, like I was tattooing her to that motherfucker. She held my head to her chest, moaning louder with each thrust. Begging me to go deeper, she draped her legs over my forearms. I planted my palms on the door and drove deeper than hell's furnace. She shrieked my name and shook violently. Gripped me with her inner muscles. I lost a stroke as my nut came closer to the surface.

She pleaded with me not to erupt yet. Save my seeds. Go harder. Longer. Faster. Harder. Longer. Faster. I wanted to oblige her, but she had that fire. Shit was blazing, good, too good. Felt like the deeper I went, another hole opened up, and enveloped me there. I didn't want to stop. But I needed to release this pressure. Either that or bust a vein.

I pinned her back to the wall, pushed every last millimeter of myself inside her gushiness, and splattered my rage inside of her canal. My nut was explosive. Firecrackers and lightning lit up my dome.

Soldada wrapped my head in a vice grip and shuddered like rafters in a thunderstorm as her orgasm wracked her small frame.

After the convulsions ceased, I carried her to her bedroom, and we repeated our routine again until we had no energy to repeat it again.

I fell asleep, feeling happier than I'd ever felt in my life.

25

SOLDADA

A phone was vibrating. Incessantly, it kept shaking my bed. I reached out through my sleepy haze and felt ... a hairy leg. Initially, I thought I had given in to Netta's invitations, but the hair killed that thought. I opened my eyelids and realized I had done much worse.

Anthony lay beside me in my bed, naked, with a satisfied grin plastered across his face while he snored lightly.

"Oh, noooo," I groaned.

Anthony stirred, reached out for me in his sleep. "Hmm? C'mere, babe."

"No, this can't be happening, this can't be happening ..." I whispered to myself, shaking my head, as if doing so could erase reality. But his sperm, leaking out of me each time I moved, confirmed our consummation. Proof of our lust. Our unprotected lust. My stupidity.

What have I done?

Anthony's phone continued to buzz. Finally, I picked it up. Saw the high-yellow heifer that was kee-keeing in his face at the Bobcats game that night. Just as I began to answer it, Anthony stopped me.

"Leave it," he croaked. "She's not important right now." Anthony was fully awake, and eyeing my legs like he wanted more of what was between them. "C'mere." He pulled me onto his chest.

"N-no, Anthony, we can't do this."

"What you mean, *'we can't'*? We just did! All night long, too."

"I know and ... and ... it was a mistake." I planted my face inside my hands. "I-I was lonely ... the alcohol ... stress. I ... it never should've happened."

"Look," he fished my face from my hands, clasped my chin in his fingers, forcing me to look at him. "We did what we both wanted to do. It's time we stop frontin', Soldada. It's bigger than the both of us."

"No, this situation is bigger than the both of us," I corrected.

"Only if we let it be."

His determination was hard to resist. Sincerity brimmed in his eyes when he spoke. I could feel it in my bones, how serious he was, and his overtures were getting harder to dismiss. At every turn, it seemed as if our lives were inextricably entwined. Our paths seemed to dance to a duet of their own choosing.

But it just could not be.

"Sounds real good, Anthony," I whispered softly. "But just because we deny reality, doesn't make it any less real." I slowly pulled away.

But he was adamant. "Our reality is what we make it!"

"So what do you propose?" I challenged. "Huh? What?"

He looked deep into my eyes, drawing me in. "We could leave this place. Just you and me. No more law shit, no more family business. Just you and me, on some Anguilla shit, living it up. I got enough bread to take care of us, forever. Never have any worries."

I was speechless. His words were music to my ears, music to any woman's ears. Any woman worth her vagina dreamed for a man to whisk her away to some exotic location to live happily ever after. But what happened when the calypso *riddims* stopped chiming? When reality reared its ugly head? What happened when *ever after* morphed into *today*? Then what? More importantly, was he serious or was he just misleading me for a bigger purpose?

I was so tempted to take him up on his offer. So tempted to just leave. My heart said yes, but my mind was wailing like a tea kettle.

"Anthony, we can't be seriously thinking about this. This is insane!" I told him, trying to convince myself that this was too good to be true.

"Soldada, this is not insane," he assured me. "I know you care for me, and I l—"

My buzzer rang, interrupting his sentence. Anthony released my hand, so I could answer the door. As I left the room, I paused to admire his naked body lumbering into my bathroom.

~

Anthony

I splashed water on my face to wake the hell up. *Fuck was I thinking?!* I'd come over here to offer this broad some money to throw the case, and here I was about to betray everything I loved and believed in for a piece of pussy. *I should have never fucked her last night,* I kept thinking to myself. I had successfully extricated myself from the situation, and now here I was, right back in it. Dick deep.

I wrapped a towel around my waist and crept out to see who was ringing her bell at ten in the morning. I peeked out the bedroom door, and saw punk-ass Constantine strutting around the living room like a fuckin' peacock. Even at ten in the morning, this motherfucker still looked made up, with his slick hair packed with gel, and a tailored suit hugging his slim frame. I heard him ask Soldada if she was okay about a thousand times. Every time she nodded yes, he asked her again. (Fuck was he, deaf?) I wondered if he could smell the sex on her, could he smell my babies on her breath every time she spoke?

I saw her fix this nigga some orange juice. As he sat at the small bar drinking it, I toyed with the idea of walking out there, right in his face. Fuck it! Walk out there and drop the towel so he could smell the scent of his little protégé's pussy all on my dick. Bet he'd love that! Bet that'd help his case. Fuckin' grease-ball!

Suddenly, my phone buzzed to life on the nightstand, and everybody froze.

Constantine looked toward the bedroom door and reached for his pistol. Soldada ignored the sound, as if the buzzing was just inside Constantine's head. I had the door cracked just a peep, so I doubted if they could see me. But I could see them clearly. I tried to burrow my hate into Constantine through my stare, induce him to just drop dead, but it didn't work.

After a few seconds, everything returned to normal. A few minutes later, Constantine stood to leave. Only then, did I look at my phone.

Mona. Again.

~

Soldada

I let Constantine out, and rushed back to my bedroom. Anthony was slipping on his sweatpants with a scowl on his face. The abrupt mood swing startled me. I mean, I knew he didn't care for Constantine and all, but he looked like he was ready to murder somebody. I saw him tuck a large, black handgun into his back. That's when I really lost it.

"Anthony, are you out of your mind?! What are you doing with that? You're a convicted felon! Do you want to go back to jail forever?" *How wasted was I that I didn't realize he had smuggled a gun into my home?*

"Don't matter. I told you, I'm never going back ... not for a day. Not for nothing." He directed his attention to his phone buzzing in his hand, looked at it like it was infested with the plague. He answered it with a bark. "Look, Mona, I don't have time for this bullshit ... I'm handling business ... What? ... Yo, fuck that nigga, straight up! I'ma deal wit' 'im ... whateva."

He clicked off his phone, reached into his pocket. Pulled out a stack of money and tossed it onto the bed.

"Look, what happened last night? Forget about it. Aiight? It was never supposed to happen. You were right; I was wrong. Okay?" He wrung his hands, looking from the floor to the hunk of cash on the bed, never looking at me. He appeared so fragile, a part of me wanted to comfort him.

But another part of me wanted to strangle him for invoking this epiphany in me. See, for the first time in a long time, I no longer felt confused about what I had been feeling. I now knew what I had been suppressing, what I had been denying.

I wanted to be with Anthony.

As I tuned back in to his babbling, I heard him mention timing, direction, and something about it not working.

"What did you say?" I asked, not sure I heard him correctly.

"I said, it won't work because ... I love you. Aiight? There, I said it."

My heart skipped a beat. Wasn't sure if he was gaming or not. After all, there was a bundle of money on my bed. What was he saying?

"Love?" I scoffed. "You don't even know me enough to love me."

"How well do I have to know you, huh?" I didn't answer. All I could do is look away. Too intense. "Besides, I don't have to know you to know I love you. All I have to know is me. And knowing me, I know ... I love you." The three words oozed so much conviction this time, it scared me. Suddenly, he punched the air. "It's just this fuckin' bullshit, man!"

I could see the misery of his indecision, the bane of his dilemma. I wanted to do something to comfort him, something to ease his pain. Something to let him know he wasn't swimming in that lake alone. I dug deep and came up with my truth.

"I love you, too, Anthony," I whispered. But he was so lost in his own thoughts that he didn't hear me. So I repeated myself. "I said, I love you, too."

He stopped rambling, looked at me. "What?"

"I do," I admitted. I wanted to add, *but I love my career more*.

He mulled my words over in silence for a moment, as if I had said nothing. Then, I noted remembrance register in his eyes as he abruptly switched gears. He swiped the stack of money from the bed and addressed me.

"Counselor, listen. You know what's going on in my life, my family's life. You know I know what's going on. You know that I know you know my cousin didn't kill anyone. He's a lot of things, but he's no murderer."

"Wait." I raised my palms toward him. "Not now, A.P. I cannot and will not discuss this. This is not the time or place…" I attempted to school him on the ethics and protocol of the Law, but he wasn't concerned with any of it. I shouldn't have been surprised; after all, his chosen profession had made him an outlaw for most of his life.

"Soldada, shut up and listen for a change," he scolded me. "This shit is bigger than you or me. Aiight? Now what I'm about to tell you is real. It's more of a warning than anything, and I'm *only* telling you because I love you and don't want to see you get hurt," he claimed.

Seemed every man in my life had advice about my fucking case, like I couldn't handle my load. I listened, seething, as Anthony put his cards on the table. The whole time he spoke, I wondered if sleeping with me was a ploy to gain the advantage.

"I am extending to you a one-time offer," he said. "There's ten-thousand dollars here; a show of good faith."

"For?"

He looked at me like I was stupid. Inside, my heart wept, for I knew what was coming next. "You know what this is," he told me, averting my gaze. I did know, but I wanted to be sure. I wanted to hear him say it. "We are offering you one-hundred thousand dollars to throw the case. Cash. Separate from the act of good faith."

Wow. $100,000! Cash! For one case?! Was he serious? Was my integrity for sale?

"Trust me. You need to take this money," he insisted.

"Or?"

He dropped his head, whispered, "You need to take this money, Soldada."

"Or? Are you threatening me?"

"No one is threatening you!" he snarled. "I'm offering you the consolation package to gracefully bow out. Just botch the case. Otherwise, I can't protect you. So just botch the case, early."

"You don't have to protect me, Anthony. I can fend for myself just fine. And I will not botch my case."

He mumbled under his breath, "You won't win."

"Excuse me? Are you saying I won't win my case?"

"Absolutely not. I'm guaranteeing you won't win, and it's no disrespect to your ability. It's just that things can and probably will get nasty." He looked at me with a smirk on his face, like he was hiding a dirty little secret. "Don't know if your boyfriend told you or not, but in court, cases aren't won by what you learned in law school. Cases are decided out of court, long before a trial ever starts. It's all about who can manipulate a situation first." He chuckled, then offered a prediction. "Not only will Moses walk, but your other little case you're trying to build against me and my uncle? It'll be the worst mistake of your life, if you don't drop it."

"Oh? And do I get another hundred-thousand to throw that one, too?" I was being smug, but he thought I was serious.

"If need be. And we can find you a job in another state if any heat comes behind it."

He was seriously incorrigible. I'd had enough. I walked to my bedroom door and opened it wide. "Get out."

He looked surprised that I turned his offer down. "I'm not going to beg you, Counselor," he replied, indignantly. "Either take this money, or I'm washing my hands of you. Only reason why you're getting this offer is because I care for you, purely on the strength of that! Defy me, and I can't protect you. Now, what's it gonna be?"

I repeated myself. "Get out!"

He gathered the remainder of his things. His face hardened as he sauntered by me. At my front door, he looked back at me. "Don't come begging for help later. You had your chance."

Before he could walk out, I broke down in tears. "Get out!"

He laughed in my face, then slammed the door.

Shaun Sinclair

26

Anthony

From Soldada's place, I rushed over to Mona's to deal with another situation. Normally, Mona was my place of refuge when the world was crumbling on my head. Mona was the silver lining in the cloud when I was in a storm.

Now, Mona was my storm.

She greeted me at the door in gym shorts, a tank top, and *Spring* Nikes. Her hair was pulled back into a ponytail. A thin layer a sweat coated her whole body. A slight frown laced her face.

"Oh, so you finally got time for me?" she complained as I walked past her into the living room.

"Shit, I'm surprised you have time for me, with all the shit you been up to," I remarked, as I plopped down on her red velvet sofa. "Why didn't you just tell me, Mona?"

"It wasn't important A.P."

"Wasn't important?! Got me looking like a fuckin' fool!"

"I'm sorry, A.P. It's just … just …"

"Just what?" I turned my back on her.

"You just don't understand," she sniffed softly. Guess I was supposed to fall for the crocodile tears. Wrong!

"You damned right I don't! All this time I thought I could confide in you, at least, a little. All the while I been confiding in my cousin's leftovers. Ain't this a bitch!" I punched my hand in my fist, wishing it was her face I was drilling.

"A.P., it's deeper than that!" she swore.

I scoffed. "I should've listened to my uncle. He told me you wasn't shit!"

"WHAT?!" Guess I hit a nerve. "Your uncle?! Oh, I ain't shit?"

"Yeah, you ain't shit! How could you be when you let Cadillac fuck last night? Last night! Goddamn, we were just together a couple days ago, Mona. What the fuck?"

She walked past me, took a seat at her glass kitchen table, and placed her forehead in her palms. Her strength leaked out inside of her tears as she bared her truth.

"Cadillac was going to be my husband," she said softly. "We were engaged to be married during my sophomore year of college. I gave him the idea to start Ladies of Distinction, even sent a few of my friends in his direction to help him start it. That's when things went wrong. Seemed Cadillac couldn't keep his dick in his pants." She sniffed hard at the memories. "I was going to leave him, but I got pregnant. Around that same time, your uncle found out I was dancing when he came in the club and tried to buy a night with me. I turned him down and he grew vindictive. Told Cadillac *I* tried to give *him* some. One thing led to another; Cadillac kicked my ass ..."

"And you lost the baby," I finished for her, feeling a little sorry for her. Just a little.

"No. Ladies of Distinction took off," she corrected. "I threatened to sue for half of everything. Didn't work. I threatened to put him on child support for eighteen years when the baby was born. Didn't work. In the end, we put our son up for adoption and he made me a silent partner in Ladies of Distinction. I keep the books, so he can't cheat me. He keeps up with our son, so I can't cheat him. The only way I have contact is through him."

Damn. I had jumped right into what I had been trying to avoid: a clusterfuck of drama. Seemed everywhere I shot my seed was damaged land. A nigga couldn't get a break. First, the situation with Soldada, then this!

I listened to her story and each sentence raised more questions. "Why did you allow him to have his way with you at will?"

"Because I loved him."

That was all I needed to hear. Mona and I were officially done. There were too many queens in the Queen City for me to

her, too. But I pushed her too hard, too fast. She would've come around eventually, but when I saw her trying to box my little brother in, I lost everything I felt for her. Just like that." He snapped his fingers. "I immediately thought about how I could use her to get him off. Thought long and hard. Then, I realized I already had the answer..."

I was sweating in my pants, waiting for him to reveal his master plan, unveil an unknown layer of Soldada to me. But he moved on to another subject.

"Lil Cuz, don't ever think you can trust a bitch. Never put a bitch before family. And never think a bitch can get over on me. I'm a muthafuckin' don! I mastered this shit. Aiight?" I nodded my head. *Whateva.*

He stood, dusted off his slacks. "I'm going to wash this smell off me, but while I'm gone, take a look at this." He tossed me the remote.

"What the hell is this?"

"The answer."

He left before the tape started. Good thing he did. Otherwise he would've saw my eyes mist up.

On the large screen was Soldada, naked, except for a purple mask over her eyes.

I watched in agony as she pumped her hips urgently toward Cadillac's darting tongue. Then, I saw another tongue enter the picture. I knew who this tongue belonged to. I'd had that same monster molesting my nether regions in Anguilla. Netta slid her taster inside Soldada's sweetness, and she did something I was all too familiar with.

She came again and again.

Shaun Sinclair

27

SOLDADA

When Carlo and Anthony both insinuated I wouldn't win my case, I took it as a challenge, and acted accordingly.

First, after Anthony left my place that morning, I made it my business not to contact either of them again. Since I was still pissed with Carlo for tricking me, it wasn't too hard to put him out of my mind. Plus, I'd realized he was just the consolation prize for my life. For all of his sexual prowess, there was still something lacking in our chemistry department. We just didn't mesh. It seemed there would always be something missing.

Anthony was a different situation altogether.

See, I *wanted* Anthony, in a big way. I wanted him to be mine; I lusted for him like a virgin did a stripper. He was like gas to my fire, lust to my desire. Try to deny as I may, I couldn't set aside the fact I wanted him to be the crown jewel in my life. We were good together. He knew it, and I knew it. We both knew we knew it.

Yet we had both made a conscious decision against each other. How ironic. How cruel.

Not one to cry over spilled milk, I poured myself into my work. It was a cruel irony that for me to succeed, Anthony, and those he loved, had to fail. This was not lost on me as I frantically searched for the information to bury his cousin's chance for freedom at the upcoming grand jury hearing. We couldn't rely on the court to just rubber stamp True Bill on the indictment as we'd done to so many others in the past, because the Padmores were fighting every step of the way. I wasn't totally convinced we could indict Moses Padmore for murder, but, at the very least, we could get a variance of the charge, and later amend the indictment to Conspiracy to Commit Murder, a charge that would box him in for a quarter century. Faced with this, we were banking on him to fold like a cheap lawn chair, and give up the goods on his family. It was a long shot, but it was worth a try.

Unfortunately, everything was predicated upon our confidential informant corroborating the contents of that tape. I say, unfortunately, because C.I.s were notoriously not dependable. They sold their souls to the highest bidder in exchange for freedom. For that reason, I despised dealing with the snake, Jorge.

Fortunately, I had Michael.

Michael had proved to be an invaluable asset to the team. Since day one, he had worked indispensably to fit in. Whatever the job called for, he did it in spades. I was initially skeptical of him due to his involvement with Netta. I didn't know her exact connection to Carlo, nor did I know how deep their relationship was. I suspected Netta was one of Carlo's concubines from the mobile brothel he masqueraded as an escort service, but I was not sure. And although each time I ear-hustled on Michael's conversations with Netta, my body flamed up, I didn't wish to see her again. At times I wanted to alert Michael that his new girl was a DL carpet-muncher, but he seemed so happy. Who was I to disrupt that? Besides, I definitely couldn't stand a shakedown of my own life. I was being extra cautious because of Cadillac Carlo's warning that I was playing out of my league. It wasn't farfetched for Carlo to use Netta to extract info from Michael. As skilled as Netta was, and as green as Michael appeared to be, he was sure to be putty in her hands. So I kept a close eye on him.

Constantine had appointed Michael to be the liaison between the witness and our office. Because Michael's Spanish was shaky, at best, I was pegged to tag along when he visited and interacted with the witness.

Because of the powerful reach of the Padmores, and their propensity for retaliation, our witness was being holed up in a safe house in West Charlotte. The neighborhood was seedy, but this served a greater purpose, in that, two blacks constantly venturing in and out wouldn't arouse suspicion in the neighbors. Each day, Michael and I would visit Jorge to gather information, and prep him for his grand jury testimony. Of course, Jorge, being the slimeball he was, knew he was in the care of the government, and consequently milked us for everything he could get. He ate like a dying man. Pizza, Greek, Japanese, Indian, Chinese, the leech ate everything, but Latin food. Go figure.

Then there were the other requests — DVDs, a Playstation console and games, and alcohol were the demands we could account for on the record. As for the other requests, Michael would clear the house of everyone, but himself and Jorge. Judging by the smell seasoning the air when the security detail and I would return, I'd say Jorge's requests were definitely conjugal. Unfortunately, he couldn't remember much because his brain cells were toasted after each episode. I didn't condone any of the activity one bit, but Jorge could light his brain up like the Fourth of July as long as when it came time to produce, he produced. I learned to think like Constantine: the ends justified the means.

As for Constantine, he had left the entire team to fend for self, as he hobnobbed with Maynard Jackson IV all over town like he was running for president of the Maynard Jackson fan club. Every time I turned on the TV, I saw Maynard donating money to this cause, or that one, the requisite flashbulbs setting his face aglow. Each time he posed for the cameras, just over his left shoulder was Constantine, smiling like a proud parent.

It seemed Mr. Jackson had become even more popular since the assassination plot had been revealed. The media played him up as the mint of a courageous man, staring danger down in its fiery eye, and backing it on its ass. However, I knew better. I was there when Constantine informed him an attempt had been made on his life. I watched him turn more bitch than me. I witnessed the great, powerful Maynard Jackson IV whittle down and weep like a spoiled child. I was the only person (besides Constantine, of course) privy to the fact that he was providing the top-notch security that guarded the safe-house Jorge was camped out in. These guys were rumored to be the best of the best. Personally, I thought it was a waste of money and resources to have four highly trained, able-bodied men guarding the scum of the earth. I thought it a travesty... until Constantine phoned me with disastrous news.

That call had me question for the first time: Was I out of my league?

28

Anthony

It went down like this.

Uncle Roland decided we couldn't leave things to chance. Not only was his baby boy about to be crucified, but the smear a conviction would give the family would be insurmountable. Uncle Roland was hell-bent on building the Queen's Quarter, as was I. Thus far, our situation had not been resolved. He still had not officially won the bid, and we still had failed to eliminate the #1 competitor.

To make matters worse, Uncle Roland was being heavily scrutinized in the media, due to the publicity Mo's arrest had garnered. Media pundits searched archives, consulted with their snitches ... did whatever it was they did. They put two and two together, came up with their own version of the truth.

The way they saw it, Maynard Jackson was targeted because of his business dealings. His primary business being real estate, coupled with my family's business being real estate, it wasn't hard to speculate Mo's motive. Never mind the fact that all of Mo's real estate purchases combined couldn't add up to one of Maynard Jackson's lowest purchases. Never mind the fact that Mo and Maynard had never bid on the same property. Never mind there was no way to prove a connection since the bidding for the Queen's Quarter was not public information. Also, unbeknownst to the media, even if they could draw a connection, Maynard Jackson couldn't afford to be in the conversation for the Queen's Quarter. He had suffered a recent setback, which was why he acted as a mouthpiece, instead of an actual principal in the deal (although his involvement in the process guaranteed him a share in any profits.)

The media didn't know the full backstory, so they sensationalized things. They weaved a tale to make it appear as if Mo was doing his father a favor. Made it appear like the Padmore family was the Black Mafia Family.

Unfortunately, we were about to give them a reason to think that way.

After much discussion, it was decided that we had to act first, take control of the situation. Leave it all on the field, so to speak. I vehemently disagreed. Thought the heat was too high already. So did Cadillac and Dirty. But in the end, the Don had spoken, and the decision was made.

The witness had to come with us until after trial.

How Uncle Roland discovered the witness's location, I'd never know. All that mattered was he had it, and expected action. As usual, the plan fell in my lap with a healthy assist from Cadillac and Dirty. They had no clue as to the real reason Uncle Roland was so hands-on. All they knew was their brother's life was on the line and their father had spoken.

Based on our intel, the best course of action was to storm the safe house from both entrances, grab the witness and leave out through the back. There were guards looking after him, but Uncle Roland assured us they would be nowhere in sight if we struck on the night he suggested.

When the night came for us to make our move, Dirty was acting real paranoid, pacing back and forth in the house while we waited on Cadillac to return with the hardware. Concerned, I had to confront him.

"What's up, cuz?" I asked.

"Don't know, man. Shit just don't feel right, cuz." He was wringing his hands so hard, I thought he was going to break 'em.

"Don't worry 'bout it. It's not that serious," I said, trying my best to calm him down. If he was distracted when we went in, his worst fear would probably come true, ruining life for us all. "Just like pulling a job, but instead of bringing money out, we just bringing somebody out, that's all." I reasoned.

"Shit just don't feel right," he insisted, as if I hadn't said a single word. I chalked his apprehension up to him worrying about his family and businesses, should something go wrong.

After all, we hadn't gone out on a caper in damn near a decade. A lot had changed. He stood to lose a lot if things went awry. We weren't teenagers with our whole lives ahead of us anymore. But I learned a long time ago that fear brought your worst concerns to surface. A little fear is always good, if you put the right motivation under your ass. But the fear Dirty was exhibiting was crippling, the kind that paralyzed men at the worst time. We definitely didn't need that, so while we waited on Cadillac, I continued to assuage his fears.

Thankfully, Cadillac returned before Dirty's fears could settle in any deeper.

We suited up in our black fatigues and doubled-checked our weapons. I was carrying a sawed-off shotgun with a .45 in one of my cargo pockets. Dirty carried a Heckler and Koch MP-7. Cadillac carried his trusty Desert Eagles in underarm holsters.

On the drive over, we were all quiet as we rummaged through the plan in our minds over and over, silently praying the cops didn't pull us over in our tinted-out, murder-black SUV.

Fortunately, we made it to West Charlotte without any problems and located the house in minutes. Cadillac slowly crept by, allowing us to scope things out. The house looked completely deserted. I expected to see, at least, one car in the driveway belonging to security, but there was not even one.

"You sure this it?" Dirty asked, bringing my thoughts to surface. "Don't look like nobody here."

"Supposed to look like that, jackass!" Cadillac spat. "It's a fuckin' safe house."

"I'm just saying …" Dirty replied, weakly.

"Yo! Do me a favor. Don't say shit!"

"Both of y'all chill," I advised, looking at my phone. We weren't supposed to make our move until Uncle Roland texted that things were all-clear. Cadillac found a nice little cut down the street from the house, and backed the truck up in it. The dull-black paint job and matching rims afforded us somewhat of a little cloak. Luckily, the streets were empty at this time of night, so we didn't have to worry much.

We must've waited about ten minutes before the text came through on my phone.

I clapped my hands, ready to roll. "Let's do it."

We approached the house in a straight line from the truck. Cadillac broke around to the front door, Desert in one hand, lock-pick tools in the other. Meanwhile, Dirty attacked the back door with his equipment while I stood guard with the gauge, eagerly eyeing my watch. We had prearranged a 45-second window to conquer the locks. Dirty had his done, and was waiting on my signal in 30 seconds. In 45 seconds, I tapped him on the shoulder, and he slid the door open. As we entered the house, we saw Cadillac close the front door at the other end of the hallway.

Weapons drawn, we silently cleared each room in the house. Kitchen. Bathroom. Both dens. All were empty.

We crept up on the first bedroom and slowly pushed the door open. It was empty.

We found him in the other bedroom, sleeping, butt-ass naked with a used condom still wrapped around his limp penis. We looked at each other. Even underneath our masks, we could read each other's smiles. This was going to be too easy.

Then we heard the toilet flush in the adjacent bathroom.

All barrels swung in that direction. The door opened, and a beautiful woman emerged with nothing on but the scorpion tattoo covering the red skin of her left breast. It took a second for her to grasp what was happening, but when she saw the red beam from Dirty's MP-7 paint her scorpion's tail, she screamed. Real loud.

"Bitch, shut the fuck up!" Cadillac smacked fire from her jaw, and she crumpled to the dusty floor in a heap of naked bones. Her screaming roused ole boy from his sleep. As soon as he looked at us, me and Dirty threw the steel in his direction.

I pumped the shotgun as hard as I could. The loud *click-clack* echoed throughout the small room. "You bet not move!" I ordered through clenched teeth. The scrawny Mexican's condom slowly slid off as he pissed on himself, throwing his hands up in surrender.

"*¡Yo no muerve! ¡Yo no muerve!*" His eyes bulged like he had took a blast.

"¡Silencio! ¡Ahora mismo!" Cadillac called over his shoulder to the Mexican from where he was applying zip ties to the woman's hands. Dirty whipped his zip ties out and wrenched the man's hands behind his back while I kept the shotty trained on him, just in case he felt lucky.

In just a few seconds we had regained control of the situation, and were preparing to make our exit. That's when we heard voices in the house.

"You all right in there?" someone called. Another voice laughed, said, "We told you no company after midnight. Your lady-friend gotta go, unless she really wants to get worked over."

We froze. Cadillac had the naked lady by the arm, dragging her toward the door, while me and Dirty had the Mexican hemmed up under each arm. When we heard the voices, we stopped on a dime, all eyes on the door.

Someone tapped on the door, and it seemed to swing open in slow motion. In that brief second, I could hear my heart thundering in my ears like Miami bass music. It seemed as if an eternity passed before a tall, white dude materialized in the doorway, followed by his twin, closely on his heels. The moment they saw us, they reached for their sidearms.

Too little. Too late.

Cadillac reacted first, squeezing off two rounds in the blink of an eye. Holes the size of Ping-Pong balls pierced the center of their foreheads almost simultaneously. A millisecond later, their heads exploded in a mist of crimson, before chunks of their brains escaped through the gaping holes in the back of their heads.

The woman and the Mexican both screamed in unison, prompting more savagery. Cadillac pushed the woman in front of him and put two through the back of her head. I actually saw most of her brain splatter the floor in front of my feet! I nearly hurled up my food.

Then he swung the barrel in our direction.

Best believe we got the fuck up outta the way, leaving Cadillac an open shot at our package.

He popped the witness twice in the chest before his body dropped. Then he stood over him and hit him four times in the face.

By the time he finished his reign of terror, the slide on his bird was locked back, and the barrel steamed as if it was roasting. As for our witness, he was unable to be identified; not just as the witness ... but as a human.

We stepped over the two men in the doorway, and proceeded to clear the rest of the house from potential danger, or would-be witnesses. Assured that everything was clear, we escaped to the awaiting truck, and disappeared into the night.

29

SOLDADA

I rushed to the safe house as soon as I got the call. I was not prepared for what met me upon my arrival.

Yellow tape was everywhere, cordoning off the house. Seemed like fifty million police cruisers were on the scene, their light-bars illuminating the twilight. Two medical examiner vans were backed onto the lawn, directly in front of the door. In front of one van was an anchorwoman from Fox News, broadcasting live from the scene, as well as camera crews from the TV series *First 48*. Locals were out, spying to gather info to learn about the tragedy that had befallen their small community, while Shante Harris scouted interviews from them.

I parked my Audi behind Constantine's Aston Martin and pushed my way through the phalanx of plainclothes detectives. The whole homicide division must have come out for this one. I spotted Constantine conferring with the lead investigator and hurried over. From the look on his face, I could tell he wasn't pleased with what he was hearing. I stepped closer to glean what I could.

"Sir, you don't need to see this. It's as gruesome as could be. Blood everywhere, brains scattered about, it's just ... gory."

"Look, Detective, that's my witness in there. I'll go where I damned well please!" Constantine yelled at him, stepping past the barricades. He noticed I had arrived and motioned for me to follow him inside.

The first thing I noticed was the smell. The acrid stench of blood assaulted my nostrils as soon as my foot stepped over the threshold. From the doorway, I could see people hunkered over two bodies strewn awkwardly in the doorway of a room. I followed Constantine to where the officers were. To the left were two bodies. Both white males, both with huge holes in their foreheads. Upon closer inspection, I noted the backs of their heads were missing. (To my disgust, I found the missing portion of the skull at my feet; I almost stepped on it.) The wall inside the room had been turned pink from the chunks of brain matter and blood scattered around. I nearly slipped and fell in more blood as I turned to enter the room.

Suddenly, my breath grew ragged. I placed my hand on my chest to steady myself.

"You okay?" Constantine asked. I nodded. "Sure?" I nodded again. He grabbed my arm. "Come on."

The officers parted and we entered the bedroom, the nucleus of the crime, where Michael and two major A.D.A.s awaited us. One look at what lay before me and I screamed.

A woman's naked body lay in the middle of the floor, crumpled over awkwardly, as if she was sleeping. More than half of her head was missing, making it next to impossible to identify her. Large chunks of what used to be her brain, combined with fragments of her skull, littered the room. From all the blood, we couldn't tell what belonged to her and what belonged to the body formerly known as Jorge de la Cruz. Jorge's corpse was missing its head, which lay detached a few inches up from the body. Even if it was attached, it wouldn't have mattered.

Jorge's face was caved in beyond recognition, the recipient of countless bullets.

After I screamed, I don't recall much else. All I remember was that Constantine ushered me out of the room, outside into the frigid air. "Why don't you stay out here?" he suggested. "I'll go inside and see how bad things are."

See how bad things are? I respected Constantine and all, but even Helen Keller could see things were fucked up. Not only did our safe-house resemble an Iraqi bomb blast, but without Jorge, my case was screwed.

I cupped my face in my hands in a desperate attempt to collect my thoughts. How did this happen? Then, like a lightning bolt, it hit me.

I gathered myself and stormed inside to confront the one person I felt was responsible. Apparently, great minds think alike, because I walked up on Constantine reading Michael the riot act, just outside the bedroom door over the dead bodies.

"Where were you?" Constantine inquired, narrowing his eyes.

"Yeah, where were you?" I chimed in. Constantine glanced my way disapprovingly, but he didn't rebuke me.

"I-I was home!" Michael stammered. "I left about eleven, when the guards showed up."

"Who was here?" Constantine demanded.

"The witness and the guards. That's all."

"Where'd the hooker come from?"

Michael shrugged. "She wasn't here when I left."

I listened intently as Constantine interrogated Michael, scrutinizing his answers as if he was a defendant on the witness stand. In my eyes, he was. I had no doubt he had slipped some kind of way, and allowed Netta to extract the location of the safe house from him. In my mind, she in turn, told Carlo the location of the safe house, who then sold the information to the Padmore family. Far-fetched, I know, but there had to be some kind of explanation for our star witness getting slaughtered a week before he was to testify before the grand jury. Constantine fired question after question at Michael. He shot them down like a human Patriot missile. In the end, we were right back to square one; only now, we had four new murders to add to the one we were initially prosecuting.

Suddenly, chaos erupted. Flashbulbs popped and reporters clamored toward the street. I peeked through the gathering crowd and saw a long, black Mercedes Maybach ultra-luxury sedan slide right past the wooden horses, right past the crime scene tape, sliding to a halt almost on the lawn of the house. Two burly, black men hopped out the front of the Mercedes, one hand plunged inside their sport jackets, while their free hand waved the crowd away. The crowd eased up enough to allow them to release their passenger from the back. Maynard Jackson IV.

"Oh, shit," Constantine murmured, and then ran to meet Maynard Jackson. Constantine pushed him back into the

Mercedes, then climbed in behind him, where they sat for an eternity with the two bodyguards posted up on both sides of the half-million dollar car, in plain view of the cameras. So much for the façade; after tonight, all of Charlotte would know the great Maynard Jackson IV rolled with security now. Reality had made an appearance. And Maynard Jackson was scared shitless.

30

Anthony

For the past few weeks, the Padmore name had reverberated throughout the city like the shot heard 'round the world. I couldn't turn on the television without seeing someone reporting about the tragedy in West Charlotte. They flashed the names of the guards that were killed, accompanied by their patrolman photos.

Yeah, they were former cops.

They showed photos of the young woman as well. Apparently, she was only moonlighting as a call girl. By day, she was a student at UNC-Charlotte, studying law. She was a looker, too! In the pictures her hair was wavy, and she had green eyes. She used to be a cheerleader for East Meck High School. They showed pictures of her in her cheerleader uniform. 'Course I couldn't look for too long because I didn't remember her beauty. All I remembered was her head exploding like a piñata.

All I could see was prison.

I don't know what the fuck Cadillac was thinking that night. Killing dude was not part of the plan. We were supposed to kidnap him, make it appear that he went rabbit because of the pressure to testify. Killing him only magnified the heat on us. When I called him on it, Cadillac was his usual arrogant self.

"Fuck 'em! He was a rat and the bitch was a whore. They both deserved to die. Fuck 'em both," he spat.

When we broke the news to Uncle Roland, he went stone quiet. I mean, I'd never seen him so quiet in my life! We thought he was gonna erupt like a volcano, spewing rage everywhere. But he didn't. He simply asked us two questions:

Were there any more "problems"? Did anyone see us? Cadillac told him no on both accounts, and he seemed pleased with that. Cadillac shot us an *I told you so* look. Other than that, he remained quiet.

Now Dirty, he was tripping. The whole ride home from the job, he kept moaning and whining. "Did you have to kill them? Aww ... dayum. Dayum! This is bad. Murder? Double-murder? Aww, damn!"

Finally, I grew tired of his bitching and shut him up. Shit, he hadn't even been to jail; he didn't know shit about doing time. I was the one with Damocles's sword hanging over my head. Damocles was a mythical figure I read about in the joint. From what I could remember, he was a dude who was forced to sit under a sword suspended by a single hair because he had fucked up. That was how I felt right then, like I was hanging onto my freedom by a hair. And unlike Dirty, I knew what the other side of the fence was like. So screw all that shit Dirty was screaming. Since the night of the murders, he had been avoiding us. However, he had to face us today.

Thanks to the work we'd put in, Mo was being released today, and we all were expected at the courthouse. Uncle Roland had rented a stretched limo for the occasion. We all piled in at 9:00 a.m. sharp. Me, my aunt and uncle, Cadillac, Dirty, Rose, and even Big Drew. Our message was clear and resounding: we are a family, and nothing was going to derail us.

We were expecting to encounter a circus at the courthouse, due to the media coverage the case had generated, but only one news team awaited us at the base of the courthouse steps. We deftly sidestepped them and proceeded to the room where the hearing was being held.

As we took our seats in the gallery behind the defense table, I peered around the courtroom and noted all the usual suspects were present, except Soldada and Constantine. At their table, sat a high-yellow, Braxton-looking dude I didn't remember seeing last time. He kept looking over at our family, smirking and shit, like he thought everything was funny. I stared right back at his bitch-ass.

The deputies brought Mo in, still dressed in his bright county colors. He gave us a slight smile before taking his seat beside Theron. The judge banged his gavel to bring court into session, then read off the docket number. I could tell from the expression on his face he wasn't pleased about what he was forced to do, but he had no choice.

"On the matter of the *State verses Padmore*, the charge of Murder in the First Degree ..." The judge took a deep breath and dropped his head. The words on the cusp of his tongue were interrupted by Soldada and Constantine sneaking into the courtroom. The judge raised his head at them, as if hoping for a prayer.

But God was on the side of the Padmores today.

Constantine and Soldada sat meekly behind the prosecution's table as the judge continued, "Based on the evidence before me, or lack thereof ..." He shot Constantine a contemptuous look. "I am forced to dismiss all charges against the Defendant, *with prejudice.* You are free to go, Mr. Padmore, with the court's apologies. Good luck to you, sir."

"Yes! My baby! Thank you, Jesus! Come here." That was my aunt, beckoning for Moses like she had just spit him out of her womb. Her cries of joy were echoed by all of us. Even Big Drew got in on the celebration, slapping Mo on the back repeatedly. Between the congratulations, I stole a peek at Soldada. As expected, she was staring at us like we stank, her mouth all turned up and twisted. She noticed me looking at her, and her face flushed, as her hand flew to her mouth. Fear registered in her watery eyes.

She was scared. Petrified!

I smiled, blew her a kiss. She bolted from the courtroom.

After collecting Mo, we all retreated to Cadillac's home for dinner and a party. Numerous family supporters were there to show Moses some love. Food and drink were plentiful, so it didn't take Moses long to get buzzed. Cadillac turned the heaters on inside the pool, and we moved the party outside. Cadillac had a few of the girls from the agency over to welcome Mo home properly. Two of them were new to the agency, but they were representing lovely in matching yellow thong bikinis. And they couldn't keep their hands off Mo. I just knew he was about to have the time of his life. My mind flashed back to my first night in Anguilla, and I shuddered at the pleasant memories.

Out of my peripheral, I saw Rose calling me. I followed her inside to Cadillac's home office, where Uncle Roland awaited me. Rose deposited me onto the couch and left us alone. Through the thick cigar smoke swirling around his head, Uncle Roland regarded me.

"I'm proud of you, son." He grunted. "You showed your dedication to the family. You proved yourself loyal. Showed you have what it takes to be a leader. Fuck that, you showed you are a leader."

Funny, I didn't feel like a leader. I felt stronger in some aspects, weaker in others. My conscience was beginning to bother me about the murders I'd committed. I was beginning to feel like my cousin was my secret enemy, and I felt like my heart was an icebox. Of course, I didn't reveal any of this to my uncle.

He continued, "Sure, you had help, but you were the planner. Things couldn't have been done without you. And now ... you will be rewarded."

The confusion I felt must have registered on my face, because he clarified his statement and made my day. "We won the bid," he told me. "The other guy backed out. We won the bid to build the Queen's Quarter. Whoever Maynard was bidding for must have gotten spooked and backed out."

"Are you kidding me?" I couldn't contain my glee.

"Do I look like a comedian?"

I let his news soak in. We won the bid ... we won the bid ... The Queen's Quarter. *Millions!*

"Yeeeeah!!!" I jumped over the coffee table and hugged my uncle. "Whoa! That's what I'm talking 'bout, bay-bee! When does everything start?"

"I just spoke with Rose about getting all the money in the right places. Barring any problems, we should be breaking ground in a couple of weeks."

"A couple of weeks? Word? That's what's up."

"That's what's up indeed." Uncle Roland chuckled.

Those words were music to my ears. I left that office feeling like a new man. All the previous concerns about my misdeeds evaporated like water in the Sahara. The ends justified the means. A year after coming home, I was about to become a multimillionaire.

The upcoming summer was shaping up to be beautiful. The only thing missing was someone to share it with.

Or was it?

Shaun Sinclair

31

SOLDADA

I couldn't allow what went down in the courtroom. People were dead and a huge chunk had been snatched from the case I was building, all because someone had betrayed me. I was determined to find out who! To add to matters, Constantine was questioning my ability and integrity. He told me, in no uncertain terms, that I had fucked up. I had let the Padmore slip through my fingers. *Like I was supposed to foretell a massacre!* Of course, I couldn't, but I still felt like there was more I could've done, like maybe explore my reservations prior to the slayings. See, all along, I felt something wasn't right, but I was too afraid to voice my concerns because I didn't want to be mocked. Basically, I punked out. There was nothing I could do to bring those people back, but I could bring to justice the people responsible for their demise.

That's why I was here. For justice.

I banged and banged on the door, but no one answered. Looking at my slender watch, I realized it was after eleven p.m. Not exactly late, but not exactly early either. I turned to leave and heard the door crack open at my back. I turned to see Netta peeking out. "Yes?" she asked.

"Uh, I need to talk to you. Are you busy?" I had to look away from her hypnotic gaze.

She smiled. "Come in."

A rich, exotic fragrance massaged my nostrils the moment I crossed the threshold. I followed Netta through the dark corridor into a great room illuminated by small lamps on round glass tables, framing a burgundy suede sofa. The burgundy

243

theme continued throughout the room as a plush burgundy afghan rug was spread over the center of the dark hardwood floor. Wooden sculptures were scattered about the room, standing on pedestals, like they were guarding the place. Netta even wore a deep red silk robe that stopped at the middle of her thick thighs, showing off her muscular legs.

She directed me to the plush sofa. "Have a seat."

"Thanks, but no thanks," I declined. "I don't plan to be here long."

"Girl, please, you look a hot mess. Look like you need to sit down and relax," she remarked. I self-consciously rubbed my hand over my mane, but I continued to stand. "Suit yourself. I'm getting some tea. Want some?" Not waiting to hear my answer, she disappeared, her long ponytail swatting her backside.

While she was gone, I searched the room for something that would offer a deeper glimpse into who she was, a family photo … mementos … anything. I saw nothing!

When she returned with the drinks, I was still standing in the same place I was when she left. I declined the drink, and she placed it on the table.

"So, to what do I owe this visit?" She sat on the sofa, pulled her legs underneath her body, with her right arm stroking the back of the chair. Her robe opened slightly.

I swallowed the lump in my throat. "Information. I came for information."

"About?" She sipped her tea.

"The murders."

"Murders?" Her face was poker, but just like I'd been taught, I looked for other clues. I found my proof when she looked down and to the left. Sure enough, she was hiding something. I carefully prodded on.

"You watch the news. You know."

She cocked her head to the side. "What is this, some witchhunt?"

I decided to cut right to the chase. "Way I see it. I have a dead witness. Only one person other than myself knew of his whereabouts. Well, there was another, but he's dead."

"What does any of that have to do with me?" Netta asked, coyly.

"Well ... the other person was new to town. Didn't really know much about people here, like yourself. It would be easy for you to extract information from him and sell it to someone for the right price."

"Excuse me?" she replied, all indignantly. Like I said, she was good. "What kind of bullshit are you bringing to my home at this time of night, chica?"

I tried to calm her down, clarify my position. "Listen, we have a mutual friend who has his hands in all kinds of pots. The location of my witness was very important to some people. For the right person to learn that information, it would be very valuable ..." I purposely left my words hanging, hoping she would get the point.

"You're definitely a lawyer," she mumbled.

"Look, if you come clean right now, I promise I will grant you immunity ..." I choked my words off because a bewildered look suddenly appeared on her face.

She whispered, "Are you trying to set me up?"

"Excuse me?"

"You're wearing a wire."

"What?"

She stared me down. "Take off your clothes."

"What?!"

"Take 'em off."

"Fuck you!"

She rose from the sofa, walked over to where I stood, and attempted to pat me down. I dodged her hands. "Get off me!"

"I think you're wired."

"You're wrong!"

"Let me see."

Sure, her allegations were preposterous! And I didn't want her hands anywhere near me, but if it would lead me closer to the truth ...

I allowed her hands to roam my body in search of a wire. She seemed to enjoy it too much. She rubbed her soft hands over my bare arms, up my polo shirt, and down the side of my jeans. Then she ran her hand up my stomach, underneath my shirt, and palmed my bare breasts. I cringed, but my body warmed all over. She held her hands there for a few seconds then slowly rubbed them back down my stomach to the top of my Claiborne jeans. I sucked in air and held my breath until she was done.

"Satisfied?"

"No." *No?* "Strip." *Strip?* "Take off your pants, shoes everything. I believe you're wearing a wire."

"Look, this is ridiculous," I huffed, adjusting my shirt.

"You're the one that wants information. I *may* have it for you, but it must be on my terms. Shit, I don't know why you're acting bashful. It's not like I haven't seen it all. If it'll make you feel better, I'll take mine off, but I refuse to speak another word until I know you're not wired."

I started to tell her it wasn't necessary, but she had already discarded her robe, revealing her beautiful dark body. I was at a loss for words. I was at a loss for what I came for.

Information.

I reluctantly took off my clothes, piece by piece, until I stood before Netta with all my business exposed. My pants bunched around my ankles without panties since I wasn't wearing any. She explored my body with her eyes, and mine returned the favor. She reached out, hugged my naked curves like a Porsche. Didn't feel like she was searching for a wire, felt like she was searching for a fire ... and she found it when she slipped her finger between my legs. I moaned so loud I didn't recognize my own voice. She drove her middle finger deep inside my fiery wetness and found my G-Spot like her finger had a GPS attached to it. I weakly tried to resist, but before I could muster any real will, she dropped to her knees before me, and feasted on the softest place on earth.

My inner juices slid freely down my legs, and Netta lapped every ounce up with her long tongue like a thirsty kitten. She pulled me to the floor with her, and really went to work. I felt her long tongue probing my insides. Felt like a long, hot, hard penis, except it bent in about three different places. Felt like it was transforming inside of me. I was so gone in ecstasy that when she slid her wet finger in my mouth, I gripped it with my jaws and sucked it like it like a lollipop, feasting on my own sweet juices. Soon, I was coming over and over again. Netta laid her tongue in front of my pussy, and accepted everything I offered. Then, she slowly slid my body and began kissing me gently on the mouth. It felt ... different at first, but after a few pecks of awkwardness, I couldn't tell the difference between her and a man, except her lips were a lot softer.

Between kisses, she asked, "You ever ate a woman's pussy?" I shook my head, mesmerized into silence by my orgasm.

Without warning, Netta slid her body up mine until her shaved vagina was right in my face. She hesitated briefly, and then lowered her precious, damp, flesh on my mouth. I resisted at first, kept my mouth shut like a real gangster. When I couldn't hold my breath any longer, I finally opened my mouth. Can't say it was involuntary because ever since that night she tasted me, I often wondered what it would be like to taste her. I wondered, what was the appeal of a woman licking another woman?

Now I knew.

The taste was incomparable. Yes, it was salty and sweet at the same time. Yes, it was soft and velvety. And it was definitely wet. Still, I wasn't particularly thrilled ... until I saw Netta's reaction! She was bucking on my face wildly, her gray eyes locked into the back of her head so that only the whites of her eyes gleamed. Her thick thighs were locked on the sides of my head, shaking lightly, while she unleashed a steady moan like a cat being screwed.

Between my thighs, I felt the waterfall coming. I was super aroused from giving another woman pleasure. Netta reached down and opened herself up more, inviting me to more of her velvety softness. I swirled my tongue around inside of her tightness, then came the waterfall. I wasn't so far gone that I was going to swallow another woman's cum, so I attempted to move aside and let her drench the floor. Instead, Netta clasped her thighs around my head and wouldn't let me move until I had swallowed every ounce of the essence that she poured into my mouth, marveling at the taste.

I left Netta's place about an hour after I was forced to drink from her sweet cavern, but not before she gave me some valuable information. The whole ride home, my thoughts drifted between what she'd told me and my sexuality. Was I gay? Bi? Both? Confused?

By the time I arrived home, I only wanted to crash and sleep the night away, then follow up everything tomorrow. Unfortunately, when I opened my front door, I realized that wasn't going to happen.

I gripped my Glock and braced myself.

I had company.

~

Anthony

"Give me one reason not to blow your brains out."

I heard her voice before I saw her. Smelled her before that. "Because you love me," I whispered.

I set the tone just like that. I had come for one reason and one reason only. Not because I wanted to. Not for business. None of that bullshit. I came because my heart led the way.

"Excuse me?" She shut the door behind her and stepped into the room, where I sat in the chair, facing her. Her pistol was leveled at my head, but even amid the dim room I could see her shaking.

I stood, walked right up to her until the gun rested at my forehead. I bowed my head into the barrel and spread my arms wide. "Shoot me or drop it."

I felt her grip tighten on the pistol. I felt her breath quicken. I braced myself.

But the pistol remained at my head.

"You know, no matter what I do ... I just can't shake you," I whispered. "I'm poised to sit on top of the world, and I still can't shake you ... I still feel empty without you. Why?"

"Because you don't deserve to feel whole," she whispered back. "Animals like you belong in a jungle." She pushed her pistol into my head, barrel first.

"Ahh ... an animal?"

"Yep, you and your whole lot, I know what you did!" she hissed. "You're evil! You don't deserve to live."

"Then kill me," I dropped to my knees before her. "Because without you, I'm already dead."

She exhaled, then dropped her arms to her sides. I felt her tears splash onto my head. "Why are you doing this to me?" I reached up slowly, removed the pistol from her hand, and tossed it across the room. "You know why?" I gripped her arms, trying to shake the answers into her.

"I know what you did to those people."

"What are you talking about?"

"You hired Carlo Barnes to get you the location of my witness, and then you had him and those people slaughtered. All so your cousin could be freed."

She said Cadillac's name and I froze. Then as she continued to speak, I realized she didn't have a clue. She was in the ball park, but she hadn't even left the locker room yet. She still didn't even know we were related!

"Car who? Soldada, what are you saying?" I tried to make her look like she was crazy, but she insisted she knew something. So I let her think what she wanted to think. "I didn't come here to discuss conspiracy theories." I stood and cupped her chin in my hands. "I came to discuss us."

"There is no us," she exhaled loudly.

Damn, her breath smells funny.

She broke my grip, walked into the kitchen, and turned on a light. I looked her over. Loose jeans. Polo shirt. Nike sneakers. Her hair was messy and her eyes were puffy and pink. She gulped down a glass of water, her hand still shaking. I closed the gap to keep pressure on her. My heart was aching, and I needed to deal with it.

I eased up behind her, whispered in her ear, "Tell me you don't love me, and I swear I'll leave right now."

She hesitated, and my heart skipped a beat. "An-Anthony, it doesn't matter."

"Tell me."

"It doesn't —"

"Tell me!"

She spun to face me. "I love you! Okay! Is that what you wanted to hear? I love you! Damn it!" I smiled. "Even though you are a murdering criminal ... I still love you."

"Don't you see! We're one and the same." I put my fingers to my eyes, then hers. "We are here. We just have two different agendas. Together ... together we'd be unstoppable, Soldada. I love you, and it's not going anywhere. And I know you love me. So what are we going to do about it?"

~

Soldada

Anthony was on some bullshit! I couldn't believe he'd brought this confusion to my door. He obviously was a pain freak. But like a pitbull, I couldn't shake him. No matter how hard I tried, I just couldn't shake what I felt for him. He was the only man I'd ever loved.

But it just could not be. Or could it?

No! I told myself that over and over. *No.* However, I tried to substitute Carlo for him. Didn't work. I even slept with a woman, but when I came, it was his face I saw, his penis I craved inside of me. And when Moses Padmore walked? I secretly rejoiced because I didn't want to cause Anthony any more pain.

All of this became evident as I looked back into Anthony's eyes. All of this became irrefutable and painfully obvious.

"I don't know," I told him. "I don't know what we're going to do."

"Well, let's start with this."

He scooped me into his powerful arms and carried me to my bedroom. There, he laid me on my bed gently, removed my clothes, and we slowly and meticulously made love. As he pushed in and out of me, I wondered if he could smell Netta's scent on me, wondered if he could taste her on my lips as I did, and I wondered if he felt his heart was about to explode from so much loving, as I did.

Afterward, as I lay in his arms, he told me how he was on the cusp of closing the biggest deal of his life. Told me he wanted me to share in his success, that he no longer viewed me as the enemy because I couldn't hurt him anymore. Of course, I corrected him. Told him the investigation was still open regarding him and his uncle, but he brushed it off.

"Nah, we're clean now. There's nothing to hide. Nothing you could hurt us on," he assured me confidently. "Plus I'm one-hundred percent sure that, if there was something on me, you would take care of it."

I rose up on one elbow. "What makes you so sure?"

"Because you love me," he said simply. "And you love this dick too much to be without it."

I shrieked like a school girl. Chided him on his vulgarity, but deep down inside … I knew he was right.

Shaun Sinclair

32

Anthony

For the next nine months, Soldada and I spent a considerable amount of time together. At my place, her place, and brief excursions out of town. In fact, every second I didn't spend on the Queen's Quarter was spent with Soldada. Unfortunately, as the Queen's Quarter neared completion, my free time became less and less.

Turned out, Uncle Roland ended up footing the whole bill for the Queen's Quarter. For whatever reason, his business partners were reneging on him now. After all that negotiating, when Uncle Roland finally won the bid, these mu'fuckas left him holding the bag. Ain't that some shit?! Didn't matter though, Uncle Roland was a born hustler, so he did what he did best. Hustled.

After convincing me to turn over every red cent I had in exchange for a greater percentage, he went after all the wealthy people he knew, extending them a one-time offer to *own* their units in the Quarter. I mean he was damn near giving units away at $100,000 a pop. Just to give a proper understanding, the condos were projected to start at $500,000 for a one-bedroom, two-bath. Shit was so sweet, some guys were snatching up two and three spots. A few players from the Bobcats and Panthers bought condos, as well as some banking execs. More than a few local businessmen bought units for their mistresses, and I'm sure we sold a few units to the local drug kingpins as well. When I saw how quickly units were being snatched up, I liquidated almost all of my assets to purchase a higher percentage from Uncle Roland. He agreed on one condition: I had to get off my ass and help him sell more units.

I called up old contacts, new contacts, everybody I knew. When I couldn't sell any more units, I unearthed a new opportunity. I proposed, in addition to the office space on the first few floors of the Quarter for rent, we add a unisex hair salon and spa, clothing boutiques, childcare center, and dry cleaning service. Uncle Roland thought it was a brilliant idea! Not only would it raise the profile of the Quarter, it would also generate extra income for us, especially if the businesses were ran by former members of the Ladies of Distinction because he would get a cut, as would I.

Cadillac didn't like the idea one bit. He already felt Uncle Roland was shitting on him for not allowing him to invest in the Quarter in the first place. He eventually let Dirty and Moses invest, but Cadillac? Nada.

One day I finally had the opportunity to ask Uncle Roland why. That was when he revealed to me the ultimate truth that it was he who had given Cadillac the brainchild of Ladies of Distinction. He thought of it, bankrolled it, set it up, and established the base clientele. In return, Cadillac was supposed to give Uncle Roland 50 percent of everything the business made. Things were all good, at first. Then I guess Cadillac started getting greedy and believing his own hype. He began paying the 50 percent on time in the beginning, but as the pockets grew longer, Cadillac's arms grew shorter. The initial 50 percent dwindled to 30 percent, then to 20 percent, then nothing. Unc had to resort to strong-arm tactics to even get a minimal return on investment. Finally, he decided to cut Cadillac off as a business partner, but he still wanted his money.

I recalled Mona telling me that she gave Cadillac the brainchild for L.O.D. In the interest of truth (since someone was obviously lying) I called Unc on his version of the story. I'll forever remember his reaction: "*MONA?! Ha!!!*"

Sensing I wasn't convinced, he attempted to put my curiosity to rest.

"Mona is a good girl at heart," he began. "I've known her longer than the both of you, met her fresh out of high school.

Saw a lot of potential in her, so I *arranged* for her and Carlo to meet. They hit it off like old friends, fell in love and started talking marriage. I had an idea to make some money, but I didn't want to soil my name. Since Carlo needed to find a better way to eat, but was too stubborn to take advice, I planted the seed in Mona's head, so she could take it to him for me. The rest is history.

"She actually told you it was her idea?" He sounded amazed.

"Yeah, she did."

He sighed. "Just goes to show you ..." Suddenly, he turned serious. "There's three types of woman to avoid, A.P. I don't give a damn how fine she is, how fat her ass is, or ... whatever. Stay away. I tried to tell that son of mine, but he's hardheaded."

Shit, I was wondering what type of broads these were, was wondering if I was already bitten. "Who are they?" I inquired, anxiously.

He smiled, ready to depart with the jewel. He ticked off on his fingers. "A damsel in distress, a woman scorned, and a woman who is more ambitious than you."

Instantly, I compared all three with Soldada. Damsel in distress? She was when I met her. More ambitious than me? She definitely had ambition. Scorned? Hmm ...

Was Uncle Roland insinuating Mona was one or all of the above? I had tangled with her and escaped unscathed. Or had I? See, that was why Unc stayed pissing me off! The same reasons I loved talking to him were the same reasons I hated it. He made me second-guess things I previously knew were true.

I thanked him for the advice, then dipped to call Soldada. I hadn't seen her in a couple of days and all the stress of the Quarter had me tense.

I needed to get a ball off.

~

Soldada

I had my red nightie on, eagerly anticipating my baby's arrival. I hadn't seen him in a couple of days, and my body quivered with every thought of him.

For the past nine months I had been blissfully happy. Anthony and I were giving *us* a try, and I couldn't be more pleased. I admit, that first night he came back to me I was apprehensive. I was distraught over those dead people, I was saddened about my case being taken away, and I was confused about anything Netta. Netta had confirmed that Carlo and Roland Padmore were definitely connected. She wouldn't elaborate on the specifics, or to what extent. All she told me was if I wanted to find out what happened to the witness and other victims, I definitely had to begin at Carlo.

Unfortunately, I couldn't use the information.

Constantine took me off the case. I was still assigned to his Special Cases division, but as far as anything Padmore, I was persona non grata. Constantine felt I was responsible for Moses Padmore going free. He was heated! The only time I saw him more upset was when it was announced Roland Padmore's corporation would build the Queen's Quarter, the biggest thing to happen to Charlotte since the Bobcats came to town. Everyone who was anyone was scrambling to get a piece of that real estate. I surmised this was the property Maynard Jackson almost lost his life over. If I was being totally honest, as much as it was worth, if I had the heart, I'd probably kill for it, too.

And the love of my life was at the center of the operation.

When I found out Anthony controlled a nice stake in the towers I was ecstatic! My baby had really done a one-eighty, changed his whole life around and become the embodiment of second-chance opportunities, a beacon of light for convicted felons everywhere.

Of course, any joy I had was short-lived because every day I went to work I was reminded of just what he'd done to achieve his success. I knew that he really hadn't changed his ways at all. He just found a smarter way to do his dirt, found a bigger field to play in, found a bigger pot of loot. He never admitted anything to me, of course, but I just knew.

Constantine had erected a giant triangle containing all the players in the Padmore family and their associates, and posted it up on the bulletin board in his office. Roland and Anthony were at the top. Leroy Padmore and Moses Padmore were on the bottom, along with Carlo Barnes. Guess Constantine had discovered Carlo was one of the family associates. There were numerous photos of other people I did not recognize. I memorized every facet of that board for later reference. It seemed like every day, as more and more agents filtered through the office, more people were added to the board upon their departure. Since I was no longer allowed in Constantine's office, I had to settle for stolen glances to stay abreast of the players in the investigation.

I suspected Constantine knew I was seeing Anthony Padmore because he went from being smitten with me to disgusted. He never said more than two words to me now; outside of barking orders about new cases I was assigned.

In my place was Michael. He picked up my slack and was seemingly being handed the "Golden Boy" tag. It was now Michael, on the steps of the courthouse when Constantine sent yet another unlucky person to retire in prison. It was Michael, looking into the camera swearing to bring a reign of justice to criminal circles. Michael! Michael!! Michael!!!

For the first time in my life, I knew what it felt like to fail. I didn't dare mention anything about my feelings to Anthony, didn't want to pollute our pocket of paradise with drama. However, I knew sooner or later we would have to step into the water with the sharks.

I heard a key slip into the knob and braced myself to greet my love. Seconds later, Anthony stepped into my castle looking like a king. He was wearing a black two-piece suit with a white shirt open at the collar. His long diamond chain swung to his navel, and his ears were lit up with 3-carat stones. He had recently let his beard grow out, and it blended into his sharp tempered fade seamlessly. His hands held a bouquet of bright-red roses.

"Thank you, baby." I kissed him full on the lips, while taking my roses from him.

"They weren't for you," he joked. "But after seeing you in this ..."

I blushed. "Thank you," I sang, walking to the kitchen to put the roses in a vase. I made sure he saw the G-string I was wearing. By the time I turned around he was halfway naked with his erection threatening to burst through the seams of his silk boxers.

"Whoa, let me help you with that," I chimed.

I walked over to him, released his aggression, and put it inside my mouth, sucking him gently. He rubbed his hands through my hair slowly while I praised his ample blessing. I looked up into his eyes as I drew him in and out of my mouth, desperately trying to make him feel how he made me feel. His eyes fluttered. "Sol ... Sol ..." he groaned. I knew what he liked, so I played with his balls while continuing to stroke and suck him. Wasn't long before I swallowed our children. He came so hard he was also on his knees by the time he finished pushing his semen down my throat. We both collapsed on the floor, breathing like asthmatics. However, I was not done.

I straddled him and rubbed my dampness over his penis until it grew hard enough for me to slide it inside me. I rode him like a jockey, leaning over to whisper in his ear just how much I loved him. Through moans, I begged him to never leave me. Through moans, he promised he wouldn't. I purred to him just how good he felt inside of me, filling me up. He went deeper. I slammed my wide hips down onto his manhood hard. He thrust his hips up harder. I shivered. He jerked. I wailed. He moaned. I scratched. He pulled. I squeezed with my muscles. He squeezed with his hands. He erupted inside of me. I flooded him.

As we lay on the floor, spent and barely awake, A.P. relayed to me that the Queen's Quarter would be opening in two weeks. A big party was scheduled with all the bigwigs in town expected to attend. He was hosting, and he wasn't too pleased. A.P. liked to play the background, but as vice president of operations for the Queen's Quarter, he had to play his position. I thought it would be good for business, as well as good for the city to see the face of a young, black man at the helm of one of the largest things to come to the Queen City. It could only hint at the promise available here. The ex-con thing could work either way. I explained, in detail, the way I felt. As his other half, I had an obligation to steer him in the right direction. In the end, he agreed with me, although he still found it hard to think about mingling with some of the same people who ostracized he and his family for so many years. I won him over when I told him that "success is the biggest revenge." He smiled and kissed me, long and deep.

He was also concerned about some inner-family strife. Seemed some family members were jealous of his lofty position in the Queen's Quarter. He mumbled something about his sacrifices, the things he did for the family to *eat*. How he was favored by his uncle because of his loyalty. Too much information for me, I *was* still deputized by the court. Hence, I had an inherent obligation to justice. The less I knew, the better for all of us. So I kissed him to silence his confessions.

Shaun Sinclair

33

Anthony

Tonight was my night. The culmination of a lifetime dream, teamed with a year of plotting, planning, and execution. Whatever it took to get the job done, we did it, and now it was paying off.

Today I became a man.

Today was the official opening of the Queen's Quarter. Our shit! The shining jewel in the family's crown. As soon as the doors cracked open at nine a.m., I became a millionaire. On paper, and in reality. I breathed a heavy sigh of relief and had to sit down when Rosa phoned me with the call that I had ascended into the hallowed five percentile. However, my glee was short-lived, as I had a full day ahead of me. As VP of operations for the Queen's Quarter, I was charged with overseeing the issuance of keys, security, P.R., and the media tour for the grand opening. I had delegates in place for everything else, but the media tour was my personal responsibility. So I donned a tailored pinstripe suit and purple silk tie and went to work.

As I arrived at the Quarter, I was met by people from Fox news, ABC news, and both urban radio stations in the city. After posing for a few photo ops, I led them inside, making jokes with the cameramen about scuffing my marble floors with all the wires from the equipment. I slowly paraded them through the lower floors, pointing out the unisex salon, adjacent to the upscale clothing boutique. From there, we took the glass elevator to the second floor, which housed the childcare center, kitchen/cafeteria, media room, and nursing station. Our childcare center was designed to handle fifty of the city's best children up to twelve years old. One of the reporters, whom I suspected was a new mother, was so impressed with our strict admissions procedures that she applied for admission right there on the spot (on the quiet tip, of course.)

From there, we climbed the wide stairs to the third floor. They were shocked to find that even the stairwell was marble. (I knew they would be impressed. That' was why we took the stairs.) I previewed our available office space for rent on the third floor, then stepped onto the elevator, so I could give them a tour of our luxury condominium units. I led them to one of the most lavish units we offered. It was there that I took a seat on a leopard-print sofa, crossed my legs to show off my new python-skinned dress shoes, and conducted the interview.

"Why did your company choose Charlotte to build such an ambitious tenement?"

"Charlotte is my home. It has down-south charm with northern sensibilities. We were just rated one of the Top 5 best American cities to live in."

"It appears that everything in the Queen's Quarter is top-shelf; what is the price tag on this project?"

"I don't want to get specific, but somewhere in the neighborhood of thirty."

"Thirty ..."

"Million. However, what the Queen's Quarter means to the city of Charlotte is priceless."

"Your firm is the first African-American owned firm to complete such a huge project in the history of this city. What do you think this will mean for African-American developers in the city, and moreover, in the South?"

"Well, first of all, the only color that matters in any business is green. The fact that my family happens to be black is inconsequential. Our only goal was to bring a first-rate luxury-living experience to rival any Trump building right here to Charlotte. There is a need, and more importantly, a right to have something like this here. Now, the Queen's Quarter only has sixty-four floors, but who knows? Maybe we'll double that number in the future."

"Ok, Mr. Padmore, last question. Your cousin was recently acquitted of some pretty heinous charges in court. Early

speculation is that his arrest was directly related to the acquisition of this very property. You, yourself, have served time in prison. Care to comment?"

"Absolutely. First of all, the allegations levied against my cousin were preposterous. I'm elated that the justice system worked as it should, and exonerated an innocent man. As for myself, I have served time in prison, and it was during that time that I realized the potential I possessed. I am delighted that we live in a country that allows second chances. I hope I can be an inspiration to others who find themselves in similar situations."

"Thank you, Mr. Padmore."

"The pleasure was all mine."

As soon as the interview was over, I headed straight to the dealership to pick up my gift to myself. A brand new Lamborghini Gallardo. Then it was right back to the Quarter to meet and greet the new tenants as they were issued their new keys. I felt like a bobblehead as I nodded up and down at our new tenants.

From there, I had to meet with Uncle Roland, Theron, and our other accountant for a working lunch to go over even more numbers and figures, but first I stopped by the Glass Quarter, the circular restaurant on the sixty-fourth floor of the building to check on Rose and Dirty. Rose was coordinating everything for the gala later, and, of course, Dirty was handling the menu. While I was there, I observed a huge box of shrimp with a South Carolina address stamped prominently on the side of it. I couldn't hold back my smile. Dirty was gonna be Dirty regardless of whatever. I had begun to worry about him because he had been acting strange since the night Cadillac killed that guard. Thankfully, slowly but surely, he appeared to be coming around.

On the way over to the restaurant, I had a blast dipping through traffic in my Lambo. Mine came with the standard 6-speed gated shifter, unlike Cadillac's paddle shifter in his Ferrari. My Lambo was fly-yellow, fast, and loud. It was like a lion was chasing me every time I dropped the throttle.

I arrived at the restaurant with a big shit-eating grin on my face and tossed the keys to the valet. All eyes were on me as he parked my ride right up front, so people could salivate and wonder who I was.

It felt good being the man.

I was determined not to let anything spoil my mood, but as usual, Unc had other plans. After going over figures for the better part of an hour, he dismissed everyone so just he and I could talk. (More like he grilled me while I seethed.) Of course the topic of discussion was Soldada. Apparently, he'd just found out we were *fucking* (as he put it), and he wasn't pleased at all. I tried to make light of the situation, but he was dead-ass serious.

"All the pussy in the world and you have to want *hers*? Have you forgotten she tried to put me *and* you in a box forever?" He argued. I could see his point, but I assured him things were different. "You better fuckin' hope so, boy! I don't like it one bit but ... you're a grown man. Just know where your loyalty lies."

He gulped down his martini in one whop, blew through his huge nose, and loosened his bright tie. "That damn dick of yours is a magnet for trouble, boy," he swore. "Should've been a damn eunuch."

We joked around a little more before we dispersed in opposite directions.

On my way home I received a call from Soldada. Apparently, she wouldn't be able to meet me at my place, so we could attend the party together.

"Something's come up at work, baby," she whined to me through the speakers in my Lamborghini.

"What, Soldada? What could be more important than this moment right here?"

"I don't know, baby. He's being really cryptic."

"Probably because he knows what this night means to me and he wants to fuck it up for me. Miserable bastard!"

"No, Anthony, probably not. There was a huge bust with some Mexicans a few minutes ago," she explained. "Lots of heroin, money ... just a mess. Probably has something to do with that. You know we discovered there was a mole for one of the Mexican gangs inside the CPD, so he probably doesn't want to tip his hand."

"Yeah, all right."

"Anthony, don't *be* like that, baby! Please? I apologize, but you know I'll be there. Wouldn't miss it for the world."

"Yeah, it's cool," I lied. In reality, I was feeling some kind of way, but I wasn't about to let anything spoil my mood. This was my day, and nothing was going to spoil it. Her cancellation just meant Mo got her seat in the limo.

At 8:00 p.m. sharp, I stepped outside my building suited and booted in a one-off custom creation from an up-and-coming designer from Brooklyn, New York. We had gifted him boutique space on the bottom floor of the Queen's Quarter. He, in turn, blessed me with a black-on-black double-lined satin tux with a platinum-colored bowtie to wear to the grand opening tonight. I was sure to have a real Tupac kind of night, all eyes on me. Just to be sure, I buried my ensemble beneath a black full-length mink. The coat flapped in the wind as I watched the BMW limo draw to a halt in front of me on the curb. The rear window slowly descended, and out popped Mo's shiny black face.

"What up, Shawty!" he yelled. "Let's ride."

As the Beamer stopped at the red carpet entrance to the Queen's Quarter, a flock of eagles seemed to tumble around inside my stomach. I was so anxious my palms were drenched. This was highly abnormal for me. In the past, when we pulled capers, I was always the cool one, keeping everyone else calm. They used to call me Icebox A.P. I was so cool. But something just didn't feel right tonight.

From behind the tinted glass of the limo, I peered up at my baby glimmering in the light, all glass and metal, looking like something from an episode of *The Jetsons.* The visual was almost enough to quell my nerves, the pride I felt deep enough to extinguish my jitters. I downed the snifter of cognac I had been nursing and tapped on the window. Showtime.

Big Faiz, one of our security guards for the night, snatched open the rear door of the limo. Mo exited first amid flashbulbs and boom mics. He waved to the gathering of press and well-wishers, as if this was his affair. I allowed him to bask in his moment of retribution for a moment. This was his sweet get-back to a city that counted him out, a big *fuck-you* to the authorities that tried to stick a fork in him.

Seconds later, I stepped out, pulling my heavy mink collar around my neck to combat the late February chill. I heard legions of people calling my name as I waved at the gathering. Big Faiz had to clear a path just for me to make it inside the building. Once inside, we had to make a beeline past even more people straight to the private elevator, but not before this bad redbone opened her coat and flashed her titties at me. In that quick glimpse, I noted everything on her was red. Dress. Heels. Hair. Lipstick.

And nipples.

I had to get used to this kind of treatment. Felt like a celebrity already, and this was just the beginning.

Inside the elevator, we ran into the Super Bowl MVP, a hometown legend. He attended Independence High, where he led them to four undefeated seasons, before journeying to Chapel Hill to perform even more theatrics for a season. Then, it was off to the NFL, where he won a championship with the Giants. However, Charlotte was his home, and when he was home, he had a serious fetish for a certain lady of distinction. As the elevator ascended, he congratulated me on my success, and thanked me for letting him purchase his unit for the cheap. Inside the mirror on the elevator wall, I tossed his date, Sarah, a thumbs up, and prepared to entertain.

When the doors parted open on the sixty-fourth floor, what I felt was indescribable. I stood in the entranceway, taking it all in. The place was wall-to-wall packed with some of the city's finest people. I spotted some people from the mayor's office, couldn't miss the giraffes that played for the Bobcats, or the tanks that played for the Panthers either. And Rose had the place laid! Three open bars. The Crowd Motivator spinning records. Cyrstal and glass everywhere. Classy servers, some dressed in only body paint, making the rounds with free food and drink. This was exactly what I envisioned.

I stepped off the elevator and shucked my mink. "This what I'm talking about, brother," I commented to Mo.

"Word. Ain't nothing but top notch bitches in here." Mo was two steps ahead of me, even with a limp, and headed straight to the bar. Meanwhile I scanned the room looking for either Uncle Roland or Soldada. I didn't spot either of them, but I did see Cadillac politicking with my dude, Spanky.

Spanky was this guy from the Chuck that we used to get money with back in the day when we first stepped our game up to taking off trucks. Spanky was a straight-up jackboy, started out taking off ballas, straight-up murdering them. Then he graduated to taking off check-cashing joints until he linked up with us. He hit a few jobs with us and was straight for awhile. I thought he had retired, but he was definitely doing something to get money because it seemed he was one of our tenants. I started to go speak with him, have a word for old time's sake, until I saw Cadillac eyeballing me, smirking and shit. Cadillac was on some bullshit! I could feel the hate leaping from his eyes, could smell it permeating the room. I would've thought he would be happy to see a brother come up, but not him. He wanted all the spotlight. I was about ready to lay my hands on him, just to teach him some respect.

"Feels good, doesn't it?"

I had been so focused on Cadillac, I hadn't even heard Unc creep up behind me. "Yeah, yeah, no doubt," I admitted, beaming.

Uncle Roland placed his hand on my shoulder. "I'm happy for you, son. Out of all my boys, I knew you were going to be the one," he shared. "I finally feel like I've made it. After all the years, all the things I've done, this is the best of 'em all. We've done a good thing today."

Uncle Roland was glowing, happy. I'd never seen him so relaxed. He had the look of a made man. "I feel the same way," I said. "If someone would have told me seven and a half years ago, when I went down for that truck, that it would lead to this, I would've told them they were crazy. Couldn't have imagined this in a million years, ya know?" I glanced to my left to see if Mo could hear our chat, didn't want him to get offended with the compliments. He couldn't. He was too focused on the ladies in the room. "You know I really appreciate you bringing me in on this whole deal, Unc. Really means a lot to me."

Uncle Roland raised his hand to silence me. "Don't even mention it. After the sacrifices you made, you deserve it. You could've taken the route a lot of these other guys are taking out here, and brought this family to its knees, but you didn't." He was talking about me not snitching when I caught my beef. To him, a product of the old school, that was the pinnacle of manhood. "'Course, if I would've even thought that you couldn't hold water, I would've had you taken care of." He chuckled, but not so deep down inside, I knew he was serious. Didn't matter though, I just wasn't built like that.

"Look at my son," Uncle Roland scoffed, pointing in Cadillac's direction. "My pride and joy, a fuckin' pimp. Turned him on to some real money and he got carried away."

I sized Cadillac up and Uncle Roland was right. He did look like a pimp, strutting around in a caramel-colored three-piece pinstriped suit with two of the new girls clinging to his arms. I'd already spotted Netta and a few of the other girls working the room, delivering business cards.

"I don't know what's up with him," I said.

"Yeah, well, I got my eye on him, and you should, too. He ain't right, A.P. Don't trust him as far as you can throw a mule. He ain't right."

I was listening to Unc, but my mind was on Soldada. I managed to peer through the flood of diamonds on my Rolex and saw that it was close to midnight, and she still hadn't shown up. I whipped out my iPhone to blast off a text when I felt a tap on my shoulder and heard a familiar voice.

~

SOLDADA

We stepped off the elevator into the Glass Quarter, and I could feel my face blush. We, meaning, myself, Constantine, Michael, and our security. Even though I knew I was rocking the hell out of the black satin slip dress Anthony had purchased for me, I just couldn't feel good about myself. Tremors slithered through my body as I kept reminding myself that I had come to Anthony's coming-out party with his sworn enemy in tow. But what was I to do? Constantine and Michael had ambushed my home and held my personal space hostage while I prepared for the evening. I'd even peeked out from my bedroom and caught Constantine scrolling through my phone as if he was investigating me. Don't get me wrong, I knew he was probably hip to our relationship, but he had never come at me this strong. Besides, it was technically a conflict of interest since I had been removed from Anthony's case.

Hell, who was I kidding? I was stuck between a brick wall and a hard pipe.

It appeared that my night wasn't going to ease up, for the first person I saw when we walked in was Carlo. It felt like ages since I'd last seen him! Oh, he had called me periodically, trying to weasel his way back into my thong, but I assured him he'd never get a whiff of this good gushy again. Initially, he tried to test his game, but he eventually got the point. Had to admit though, he looked good tonight. Thankfully, he hadn't spotted me, so I diverted my gaze before my energy drew his slimy ass in my direction.

Scanning the room, who did I see but Netta, slinking her sexy ass through the room like a panther on the prowl, all black beauty and curves. She was a vision to behold, and the butterflies in my stomach attested to that. She resembled a chocolate angel in her white sheer dress. She noticed us and changed her path. I hoped she was coming for Michael, because I had no words for her. She had been calling me nonstop as well. She was actually worse than Carlo, trying to sniff all up in my stuff like she was entitled to it just because I'd allowed her to taste it a time or two.

"Hello, Michael," she sang, reaching out to stroke his arm. She turned to Constantine. "And you, too, Mr. D.A. Glad you accepted the invitation."

"Wouldn't miss it for the world," Constantine replied like a whipped puppy. If Michael was still fucking Netta, he'd better watch himself, because Constantine was drooling over her like a savage, like he wanted to hike her dress up and work her out in front of everybody. While they conversed, I was wondering why Netta was doing P.R. for the Padmores. Was Carlo in on this also? Was that why he loaned his services out to the Padmores?

"And you're Soldada, right?" Netta said to me. I forced a hard smile. "Glad you could make it also, although I don't recall sending you an invitation."

I shrugged my shoulders. "You know what they say, guilty by association."

"Tell me about it," she echoed, with a veiled hint. "Well, enjoy yourselves," she said, turning to leave. "Oh, by the way, drinks are at the bar." She slid me a sly smile, and pointed to the bar. I followed her finger and saw what the joke was all about. Bitch.

Anthony was at the bar with that same high-yellow heifer from the basketball game, showing all his teeth.

~

*A*nthony

"Yeah, Mona, you're right. I have come a long way," I agreed.

Mona was looking FINE! Her cinnamon-hued hair was pulled back into a tight bun, and ice dripped everywhere from her ears to her heels. A purple dress hugged her body like a sheath on a dangerous weapon. Her hips flared out like a mermaid. And that ass?! Serena who? Beyoncé what? None of them could touch her.

"You're not looking too bad yourself," I complimented her, mentally scouting an angle to get inside those drawers again.

She patted her hair. "Thank you, Anthony." Her eyes twinkled and she grabbed my arm. "You know, I don't know what happened between us, but I do miss your company. I really miss you," she purred, seductively.

"I kinda miss you, too," I admitted.

"Kinda?" She punched me in the arm. "So you too big for the little people now?"

"Nah. Just saying …"

"What? What you saying?"

I chose my words carefully, not wanting to spoil a chance to tap that ass again, but also wanting things to remain clear between us.

"I miss the way we feel when we're together but not the drama that came along with it."

"Drama?" She recoiled indignantly. "Anthony, there was no drama. We had one little problem. Carlo."

"Yeah, but he was the deal breaker."

"Why?"

"Because we don't fuck behind each other."

She laughed like I was Bernie Mac reincarnated. A good, hard laugh that shook her body and rocked her head back. That slight little motion pushed her chest out and allowed me to see her nipples harden. For a brief second, I recalled how they felt clasped between my teeth.

"Since when?" she challenged.

"Since we knew better."

"Humph! Well, you must be a hard learner then," she mumbled.

"What was that?"

"Nothing. Let's not talk about him tonight," she suggested. "If we would've kept him out of our lives a long time ago, maybe I would be sharing in your success tonight."

Mona stroked the bottom of my chin with her forefinger. Felt so good I got caught up in the moment and closed my eyes. When I reopened them, Soldada was standing behind Mona.

"Ahem ... excuse me." Soldada tapped Mona on the shoulder. "Do you mind? That's my man that you're pawing on."

"Really?"

"Hmm-mm."

"Sorry. Hi, I'm Mona." Mona extended her hand, and Soldada just looked at it. I was silently praying shit didn't pop off and ruin my party. The look on Soldada's face could melt a glacier. Finally, much to my relief, she shook it.

"Nice to meet you, Mona. I'm Soldada." Then, as if Mona was an apparition of some sort, she breezed right through her and into my arms. "Sorry I'm late, baby, but you wouldn't believe the day I had."

As Soldada proceeded to tell me about her day, Mona beat a hasty retreat, but not before mouthing the words, *call me*. I followed the curve of her ass with my eyes as she walked away. When she was out of my line of sight, someone else caught my attention.

Constantine Annapolis!

His back was turned away from us. He was yakking with some white dude, but I knew it was him. The nerve of this bastard to show up to our shit! He might have been the shit out there, but this was our little utopia. He was not welcomed here.

I searched the crowd, looking for a contingent of security to throw Constantine out on his ass. Suddenly, I saw trouble break through the crowd and head our way gripping a bottle of Ace of Spades by the neck.

"Lil cuz, what's the bidness?" Cadillac slurred, reaching out with his free hand to hug me with Soldada squished between us. The scent of alcohol leaped from him.

"What the …"

Soldada elbowed Cadillac in the gut. Hard. "Get off me!" she bellowed.

He lurched back. "Oh, it's like that, lil mama?" He turned to me. "Cuz, I know you killing this hot little piece of ass." Just when I thought it couldn't get worse, this fool smacked Soldada on her ass and cuffed a chunk of it.

I pushed him. "Nigga, is you crazy!" I tucked Soldada behind me and got right up in his chest.

"What, lil cuz? You gonna take up for that slut? Remember, I done had the pussy. Shit, me, you, Netta, and ain't no telling who else."

CRACK!

I popped Cadillac in the jaw so hard that it echoed over the music like a gunshot. He crumbled to the floor at my feet while people scampered as if I held a pistol in my hand. He recovered quickly, wiped the blood from his mouth, and cackled like a hyena.

~

SOLDADA

"Damn, she putting it on you like that? Bet she ain't tell you she like to eat pussy, too, did she?"

I looked over Anthony's shoulder hoping he'd kick him again to silence his disrespect, but he appeared to still be in shock from striking him. Carlo struggled to his feet and addressed me.

"Tell him, bitch. Tell this pussy-whipped mu'fucka how your ass beat down Netta door all late, so you could come in and eat her pussy. *Tell* him!"

Anthony went to swing again, but his punch was interrupted by Roland Padmore's large hand. He snatched Anthony up in a half-Nelson while the big guy, who always accompanied Mr. Padmore, hemmed Carlo up from behind. All of it happened so fast, I was lost in translation, until I heard Carlo call Mr. Padmore *Dad*.

Time screeched to a halt. Amid total chaos, my world went quiet. *Nah, Dad, let the nigga go,* I thought I heard him say. I just knew my mind was playing tricks on me. *Dad? Dad?*

"Y'all are family. Don't let no woman come between y'all," I heard the big guy say.

Right then, it couldn't have been any more apparent. Carlo wasn't doing bidding for the Padmores; Carlo *is* a Padmore! It made perfect sense. He and Anthony were in Anguilla *together*, together. Carlo had warned me about Moses Padmore because that was his *BROTHER!*

"I told you to clean this shit up, didn't I?" Mr. Padmore barked at Anthony, then turned to Carlo. "And you! You trying to ruin what we've built? Both of you, right now, let's go!"

Anthony turned to me. "Are you okay?"

I slapped his hand away. "Get away from me!"

"What? What's wrong with you, Soldada?" He pulled at me with one hand, while Mr. Padmore tugged on his other arm.

"I can't believe you lied to me!" I screamed, almost in tears. All this time, they were related. All this time he knew about Carlo and I, and didn't tell me. I couldn't believe it.

"Lied? Lied about what, Soldada? What are you talking about?"

"Is there a problem over here?" Constantine asked. All of the commotion must have summoned him over. He slid an arm around my waist, while eyeing the Padmore clan with action and malice dancing in his eyes.

"Mind your business, dawg," Anthony snapped at Constantine. "Now, Soldada, what's up? Talk to me."

All I could do was look on, helpless, as my life and love capsized right before my eyes. Eventually Mr. Padmore's sway won over. He barked orders at his family again, leaving no room for refusal. I saw the hurt and confusion in Anthony's eyes as he fell in step behind his clan.

Thank God he couldn't see the hurt and anger in mine as I turned to face my boss and mentor.

"What the hell just happened here?" Constantine demanded.

"I ... don't know really," I answered honestly.

"Well, you better tell me something, because from where I stood across the room, it looked to me as if you were cavorting with the enemy."

I had no patience for this shit. Michael, looking down on me like I was dog shit. Security, ready to beat me up. Spectators zoomed in on our moment, cameras rolling and flashing.

"Excuse us a moment," Constantine told our entourage. "I need to speak with Soldada in private." When they were dismissed, Constantine gave me as much of his attention as he could in a crowded room. "I've known about you and Anthony Padmore for quite some time," he revealed.

"And?" I huffed with much attitude, ready to do battle. If it was going down, let it go down.

"And ... I knew that he and Carlo Barnes were cousins, more like brothers, actually. They were raised in the same house by Roland Padmore."

Talk about feeling foolish. I felt like the shortest person in the world; when it rained, I was the last to know.

"What I didn't know," Constantine continued, "was that you had history with Carlo also. When I did discover that fact, I thought that it was you that leaked the location of that dead witness."

"What makes you so sure I didn't?" I taunted, since he had kept so much from me.

"I know you didn't do it because I received a visit recently."

"From who?" I inquired, not even bothering to hide my frustration.

He smiled. "Carlo Barnes."

34

Anthony

"I will not tolerate fighting among this family! I never have and I never will."

We were ducked off inside an office at the back of the ballroom. Me, Cadillac, Dirty, Mo, and Uncle Roland. Four alpha males jockeying for position. But there was only one don.

"*You!*" That was me. "I told you not to let that damned girl cloud your allegiances."

"But I didn't —"

"Shut up! I'm talking now. As of right now, you choose: this family or that slut. And Carlo, you stop all the bullshit, and pay my money or you will be banished from this family."

"Banished? Man, Dad, I'm just trying to live. You need to tell Loverboy that. He the one fuckin' up." Cadillac wiped more blood from his lip while he tried to throw me under the bus. "Think he all high and mighty 'cause he seeing a little paper now. Nigga, don't forget you was in a box while I been out here getting money."

I was tired of him throwing that history in my face. The box. A box. Locked down. Blah, blah, blah. "Nigga, don't *you* forget, if it wasn't for me, *you* would've been in that box. *You* fucked up!"

"You the one that got shot! We were in the clear!"

"'Cause you didn't play your position! If you would've covered your man right, he never would've been in a position to shoot me. Ain't that right, Mo?"

"Mo ain't got no room to talk. If it wasn't for me, *he* would be in a box."

Guess the rest of us weren't there. I guess he picked the lock by himself, cleared the house by himself, did everything solo. In reality, he fucked that up, too. I told him so.

"Bullshit! Everybody was supposed to die. Survival of the fittest. We had to take them out!"

A soft knock at the door silenced our bickering. Dirty answered the door and barked at whoever had the audacity to interrupt us. Then he stepped aside and let the man enter.

Uncle Roland went to greet the ADA at the door.

"What the fuck is he doing here?!" Mo screamed, rushing toward the light-skinned guy that tried to bury him. Uncle Roland held his hand up and Mo froze on a dime. The guy whispered in Uncle Roland's ear and I saw something I never saw before register on Uncle Roland's face.

Fear.

Suddenly, all hell broke loose. Rosa stormed in the room screaming at the top of her lungs about the police ransacking our party. Through the crack in the door, I could see police stampeding the room, knocking guests over. At a glance, there appeared to be about thirty sheriff's deputies, and just as many city cops pushing their way through the room. A few feet from the door, I saw Constantine conferring with one of the deputies. Soldada was beside him, cringing.

"What? What you see?" Dirty asked, peering over my shoulder. We both saw Constantine point in our direction. "Oh shit!" we said in unison.

Cops were coming our way. Full speed. Constantine leading the charge. I craned my head over my left shoulder. Looked at Uncle Roland. He stood transfixed in place alone; the ADA had disappeared. I glanced at Cadillac. A slight smirk tugged at the corners of his mouth. Dirty appeared just as confused as we were.

"They're coming this way," I advised everyone.

"I know, son. Let them through."

"Daddy, what's going on?" Rosa cried.

"I don't know exactly," Uncle Roland admitted. "Just gather your mom, and keep her calm. She knows where all the money and anything else we may need is located."

"But, Dad?!"

"Just be cool, Rose."

The cops entered the room with their hands on their weapons, scowls on their faces. All business. A tall deputy with a blond crew cut and bulging muscles barged past me, took center stage with a stack of papers in his hand. He cleared his throat ceremoniously, and called out, "Roland Cecil Padmore?"

"Yeah!"

"Leroy Landry Padmore?"

"What!"

"Moses Padmore?"

Mo dropped his head.

"Anthony Lamont Padmore?"

"That's me, what's up?" I piped up.

"You gentlemen need to come with us, please," Crew-cut stated.

"For what?" Uncle Roland demanded.

"We have warrants for your arrest."

"For what?" Unc repeated.

Crew-cut consulted the papers in his hands. "For the murders of Jorge Rivera Luis Cruz-Rivera De Juarez, John Sanders, Jr., James Bartharlomeuw Jones, and Robin Gomensa."

"Murder? I didn't kill anyone," Uncle Roland protested, while the rest of us remained silent.

Just then, Constantine entered the room, smiling. "I know, which is why your warrant says Conspiracy to Commit Murder, Roland. See, we know you ordered the job, and your sons and nephew carried it out." He addressed the deputies. "Cuff them. Cuff them all, and let's go!"

They smashed my face into a wall, so I couldn't see behind me. But I heard things clearly. I only heard three other sets of cuffs clicking besides mine. When I was spun around and escorted from the room, I saw that Cadillac stood unharmed. He and Uncle Roland were locked in an intense stare-off.

That was when it hit me.

The first face I saw when I was led through the party was Soldada. Both hands were clasped over her mouth as tears raced down her pretty face. She mouthed the words, *I didn't know.* But it didn't matter; even if she would've known, she was powerless to stop it.

Theron bolted past me to Uncle Roland, cuffed behind me. My aunt trailed behind him, weeping inconsolably.

And everyone was snapping away with their camera phones.

We all piled onto the private elevator. A deputy apiece, along with sucka-ass Constantine. As the elevator descended, matching my mood, Constantine just couldn't resist taunting us, couldn't refrain from taking a cheap jab.

"Roland, do you know what the Mann Act is?" he asked. "Are you familiar with it?"

Uncle Roland, smooth even in presumed defeat, didn't even dignify that question with a response.

Constantine continued, "Well, your son is very familiar with it. Before this is all over, you will be, too. Know why?" he laughed (cackled really.). "Because the *Mann Act just tore your whole family apart."

T<small>HE</small> E<small>ND</small>

***Mann Act** — transporting females across state lines for immoral purposes (prostitution). A federal offense, punishable by up to ten years (each count).

ABOUT THE AUTHOR

Shaun Sinclair is a native of Atlantic Beach, South Carolina. An Army veteran, he has also worked as a law clerk for six years. He uses his experience as a law clerk to make his stories pop with authenticity. Mr. Sinclair is the founder and owner of Pen 2 Pen Publications. His company's motto, "Putting Power into the Pen" is also its mission statement, as Mr. Sinclair rediscovered his gift of penmanship while incarcerated. He strives to use his success as motivation for others to triumph over adversity, and gives back to his community through the Sinclair Literary Scholarship, which awards worthy high school students for literary achievement. He is also a contributor to Don Diva magazine. Mr. Sinclair resides in North Carolina with his family.

Q&A with Shaun Sinclair

Where did the inspiration for this novel come from?

When I was incarcerated, I used to devise plans in my head about how I was going to make money when I was released. I knew I had to think entrepreneurially because society is often very biased and discriminatory toward felons. So, after I eliminated the option of going back to the streets (illegally) to get money, I began researching all of the legal ways to make money. The escort service was one of the businesses that kept coming up. Potentially very lucrative, and legal, it was a no-brainer. I contemplated how to execute this vision down to the minutest detail. Years later, after I wrote a few books, I decided I needed a story that was fresh, edgy, and sexy. The escort service provided the perfect backdrop, so I planned to make that business the backdrop of the story, but when I began writing the story, the characters took on a life of their own. When the characters show up to show out, you have to give them room. So I just humbled myself and allowed the characters to tell their stories.

Who are the characters in *Forbidden: A Gangsterotica Tale* based on?

*Well, two of the characters, **Anthony Padmore** and **Roland Padmore** are based on my brother and my daddy. Both of them are deceased. My brother passed away from cancer when he was thirty-four years old, and my daddy was murdered when I was just eight years old. I often wonder what they would be doing if they were still alive. My brother's name is Anthony, and he had the vibe that Anthony Padmore has. Stylish, suave, debonair, and a natural hustler. Granted, he wasn't a jack boy, but he was definitely in the streets. With the drive he had, if he would have focused, he could have had the vision and success that Anthony Padmore attained, and also been burdened with the same choices and responsibilities.*

As for my daddy, his name is Roland, and he was just a real man's man. He was thirty-three years old when he was murdered, but he appeared to have the wisdom of the elders. He worked in construction by day, and dabbled in "other things" at night. He was a "street dude" as well, but his era was the seventies and eighties, so the perception of a "street dude" was different. He was a born leader, respected by everyone. If he would have had an opportunity to live and grow, I'm sure he would have been the type of guy that Roland Padmore is. Granted, I don't picture my dad being as ruthless as Roland Padmore, but his drive to succeed was definitely based on my daddy.

__Soldada Andrews__ is a mixture of a few women that I know. She is a combination of beauty, ambition, intelligence, and sex appeal. Women like that always seem to love a bad boy! Soldada is the perpetual idealist, but she is naïve to the world. I wanted to show her life unfold and her idealistic views get shattered in the process. She has it all together professionally, but her personal life is in disarray. Unfortunately for her, her personal and professional life are inextricably entwined. Add in a dose of love, and we have a potent mix of sure disaster. I enjoyed living and writing through her eyes. People often ask, how do I write from the perspective of a woman so well? The answer is simple: I am a great listener. I have had lots of interaction with women, from my aunts and sisters, to the women I chose to deal with in my life. In all of them, there are some consistencies across the board, as just being women. However, there are also some intricate parts of their nature that make them unique. That is what I love to explore when I write from a female perspective.

__Carlo "Cadillac" Barnes__ is a character that I really felt strongly about. He is a representation of the character — or lack thereof — of the guys in the street today. No loyalty, no respect for the rules of the game, no love for anyone or anything but themselves, but, boy, can they make a dollar! These guys have all the trappings of success, and are the envy of the city on the outside. Inside they are bankrupt when it comes to integrity. I wanted to create a character that is representative of all those things to show the street guys who may read this book that the game has changed. He is often the most hated character, so I think I did that justice.

__Constantine Annapolis__ is the manifestation of the "new" D.A. He is ruthless and prejudice, but hides it all behind *swarthy good looks that may make someone think twice about his intentions. This is the new face of institutional racism. All across the country, there is a war on brown and black people, and it is being carried out through the criminal justice system. People were becoming awakened to the daily injustices of institutional racism, and began to cry foul. You know, they see young brown and black boys and girls being hung out to dry by W.A.S.P. prosecutors, and they started speaking out. So in response to that, the powers that be have gotten smarter. They began putting people in place that resemble the people being prosecuted. This new person is who Constantine Annapolis is representative of. On the surface, this may be an attempt to rectify the problem; however institutional owns no color. It is a system. We must recognize it and defeat it.*

What is Gangsterotica?

Gangsterotica is a marriage of street lit and erotica. I coined that phrase to characterize some of my books because I make a conscious effort to concentrate on both of those themes in those books. I strive to inject an equal balance to satisfy both genres. The reason why I am so adamant about pushing this genre is because I take exception to other people creating limiting genres for authors. Terms like "urban" and "hip hop" are genres that limit the author. I figure if someone is going to coin a phrase for my books, then it might as well be me. Also, in my experience, a lot fans of erotica scoff at street-lit, and vice versa. I enjoy both genres, and I feel that if a story is written that blends both genres seamlessly, then more readers will gravitate toward those books.

How long did it take you to write this book?

This book was written in three months. When I'm really focused, that's all it takes to write a book because I always write them in my head first.

When is the sequel expected to be released?

The sequel should be released in early 2015.

Turn the page for an exclusive sneak peek of

FORBIDDEN 2

Coming Soon from
Pen 2 Pen Publications

1

For a week straight my dreams and nightmares merged seamlessly together, as visions of suspended paradise clashed with my gloomy reality. Dreams so vivid I could smell the warm azure waters and hear the birds chirping our own chorus, only to be interrupted, seconds later, by a huge black locomotive careening through our island shrilling doom. For a week straight, I lay in bed unable to move, afraid to answer the endless barrage of phone calls, or turn on the television. For a week straight, I wallowed in pity, bathed in pain, and mourned the loss of my heart ripped from my chest.

Each time my eyes opened I saw remnants of our love smothering my living space. Poster-sized pictures of us at Myrtle Beach. Expensive vases he purchased to fill with the colorful flower arrangements he gifted me daily, some delivered personally, others by courier. His scent, Cashmir, wafting up from the burners sprinkled around my home soothed and tortured me simultaneously. The expensive heels he showered upon me in a short period of time littered my home like remains from a mass gravesite. Deep-black. Powder-blue. Shiny-silver. All with red bottoms. My satin sheets still carried his scent, his aura, making him virtually inescapable.

I couldn't believe he was really gone, yet each time I dared turn on the television, his absence was confirmed.

For the past week, the arrest of the Padmore Family had been at the top of the news chain. It had even made national headlines. Each night on the evening news, a different angle was explored, always accompanied by the same 15-second clip of torture. The 15-second clip of Anthony, Roland, Moses, and Leroy Padmore being herded out of their multimillion dollar enterprise in handcuffs would probably be etched into my mind forever. For me, it was akin to seeing Jesus carrying a cross. And just like so many, I felt as if I was without salvation.

Ironically, it was being reported in the media that I was the catalyst to their demise. It was being alleged that my boss, Constantine Annapolis, the great district attorney for Mecklenburg County, had assigned me the case he had deemed unbreakable, and I cracked the case. Overnight, my name had been thrust into the stratosphere. Reporters bombarded my home, office, the gym I attend, and the places I once dined ... all in an attempt to secure that coveted interview from the young apprentice of Constantine Annapolis. They were demanding to know anything about me, and were offering ridiculous sums of money for a just a sound byte. I declined all the offers, but, of course, I couldn't hide forever.

Today my hiatus from life was ending. I had been summoned by the great Constantine. I was expected in his office at 9:00 a.m. sharp, presumably to discuss the remainder of my career. I dressed in my best clothes: Gray wool two-piece skirt suit, white silk blouse, black pumps with a red bottom. I combed my long, curly hair out, let it frame my face to shield my cloudy mood, and then placed oversized oval-shaped D&G sunglasses over my puffy eyes. At 8:05, I snatched my door open, ready to battle the world.

But she blocked my path.

"You're a hard woman to locate, Soldada." She snarled my name as she barged past me into my home. She was shorter than me, petite yet curvy in all the places men desired. A light sheen of makeup frosted her smooth reddish skin. Her short, wavy hair was shiny and neat. She wore a skirt suit similar to mine, except hers was blue with a red scarf. She strutted on tall heels made of python skin, the iridescent hue proclaiming their authenticity. A rich fragrance crept by and tickled my nose like only the good stuff could.

Stunned, I turned in my doorway. "Wait, and who the hell are you?" My hand inched toward the Glock pistol, nesting beneath my left armpit.

"You might want to close that door," she suggested.

"Who are you?" My fingertips caressed the handle of the Glock.

"Close the door."

"Who. Are. You?"

"Look, close the fuckin' door, and I'll tell you who I am."
She reached inside her large, python-skinned handbag. I
palmed the Glock. She walked toward me, her hands raised in
surrender. I stepped toward her, my eyes never wavering. She
reached around me and closed the door. "Soldada, we need to
talk."

I eyed my slim Cartier watch. "I'm almost late for work.
What could be so important that it would make me late for
work."

"This is worth the wait," she claimed.

"Really?" I crossed my arms. "Just what do we have to talk
about?"

She sniffed hard, coughed, then swallowed. "My family."

Shaun Sinclair

2

Anthony

As soon as I realized I was awake, I hopped from the bed, planted my feet firmly on the floor, and scanned the tiny cell for any threat. Crouched in a fighter's stance, I felt stupid when I discovered I was in the cell alone. Flashbacks from my previous bid still haunted me. Days when I had to fight or fuck to preserve your manhood. I shook off the memories and dug deep to muster enough strength to face the new day. The drab smell of jail and the cacophony of decadent sounds surrounding me attempted to thief my resolve, but I slayed those demons. Nothing could steal my joy today. Today was my bond reconsideration hearing, and I remained optimistic that I would go home. Back to my penthouse, back to my wardrobe, back to my Lambo ... back to my woman. Back to my beautiful life.

The guards rescued me from my cell just after breakfast was served. They cuffed and shackled me, then surrounded me — one in front, both sides, and behind me — as they shuffled me down to the legal section of the jail. I was surprised they didn't stuff a muzzle over my mouth the way they were handling me. They had shut the whole wing down just to move me. As soon as they sat me down at the thick Plexiglas in front of Theron, I tore into him.

"What the fuck is going on, Theron?!" I roared. "I can't hardly use the phone, they won't let me buy food, they fucking with my mail, and on top of all that, they got me in P.C. like I'm some fucking rat!" By the time I was done, I was standing, leaning on the glass. If my hands weren't cuffed, I would've had them in his face.

Theron calmly raised his palms. "Calm down, Anthony. I'm working as hard as I can. I have your uncle barking orders at me left and right, this bond hearing preparation, and I have to prepare statements for the media ... it's a lot."

"Don't tell me to calm down! I'm the one sitting in this fucking cell facing the death penalty for something I didn't do." I calmed down, just a little, and sat back in the chair. The shackles on my feet shuffled, reminding me of my predicament.

"I'm going to try real hard to get a bond for you all today. It's going to be hard on capital charges, and if I am successful, the bond may be extremely high," Theron warned.

"That's no problem. We can use the Quarter for collateral," I suggested. "It's worth millions. It should cover all our bonds." That was a stretch, I knew, but with that monster-sized carrot dangling, there wasn't a bondsman in the country that wouldn't cover our bonds.

Theron shook his head. "That's one of the assets they froze."

"What the fuck do you mean?"

"They froze your assets. Anything believed to be gained from criminal enterprise is subject to seizure," Theron explained.

"But we haven't even been convicted?!" I argued.

"It's just a lien right now," Theron clarified. "You can thank your woman for that."

I frowned. "Who? Soldada?" Theron nodded. "What does she have to do with this?"

"*Everything!* She's the head honcho on this case."

"No way. Get the fuck outta here! Soldada wouldn't do that." I shook my head vehemently.

Theron leaned forward and smacked the glass. "You better wake the fuck up, Anthony! She is your enemy. She means you no good. Who do you think is behind all this? It's all over the news, *man!* She flipped on you, brought you down, played you for a *fool.*"

No matter how hard he fed it to me, my heart wouldn't digest Soldada playing me and setting me up. "Nah man." I shook my head. "This is some mix-up. Soldada would never do that."

Theron adjusted his gold tie on his cream shirt. "And what makes you so sure?" he challenged.

I thought about all the wonderful times we shared, the declarations of love, the explosive sex, the vacations ... I thought about the happiest times of my life. I shook my head. "She just wouldn't. Trust me. All right?"

Theron raised his bushy eyebrows. "Trust you? Really? You willing to put your life on this trust? Have you spoken with her? Seen her? Have you even seen the news?" I shook my head to all of his answers. "Exactly!"

"Just get me out of here," I told him. "Get me a bond, and I'll make everything right. You have to!" I pleaded.

Theron shook his head sorrowfully. Sadness crept into his eyes as silence descended upon us. He whispered, "I'll do my best."

Made in the USA
Monee, IL
01 September 2021